WAIT FOR THE DAWN

Jess Foley

arrow books

Published by Arrow Books in 2004

3 5 7 9 10 8 6 4

First published in the United Kingdom in 2004 by Century

Arrow Books
The Random House Group Limited
20 Vauxhall Bridge Road, London, SW1V 2SA

Random House Australia (Pty) Limited
20 Alfred Street, Milsons Point, Sydney,
New South Wales 2061, Australia

Random House New Zealand Limited
18 Poland Road, Glenfield
Auckland 10, New Zealand

Random House (Pty) Limited
Endulini, 5a Jubilee Road, Parktown 2193, South Africa

The Random House Group Limited Reg. No. 954009

www.randomhouse.co.uk

A CIP catalogue record for this book
is available from the British Library

The Random House Group Limited supports The Forest Stewardship
Council (FSC®), the leading international forest certification
organisation. Our books carrying the FSC label are printed on FSC®
certified paper. FSC is the only forest certification scheme endorsed by
the leading environmental organisations, including Greenpeace. Our
paper procurement policy can be found at
www.randomhouse.co.uk/environment

MIX
Paper from
responsible sources
FSC® C016897

ISBN 0 09 946647 3

Typeset by SX Composing DTP, Rayleigh, Essex
Printed and bound in Great Britain by
CPI Cox & Wyman, Reading, RG1 8EX

Wait For The Dawn

Jess Foley was born in Wiltshire but moved to London to study at the Chelsea School of Art, then subsequently worked as a painter and actor before taking up writing. Now living in Blackheath, south-east London, Jess Foley's first novel, *So Long At The Fair*, was published in 2001, followed by *Too Close To The Sun* in 2002, and *Saddle The Wind* in 2004.

Praise for Jess Foley

'If all sagas were as convicing and exuberant as this, the world would be a better place. I loved it' Monica Dickens

'Jess has really captured the sense of a family united against great odds. The heroine is strong but flawed as all good heroines should be and as we follow her triumphs and trails we see her change from a girl to a woman in the most dramatic and satisfying of ways' Iris Gower

'A gripping saga . . . The author writes with exuberance and style, and the central characters are totally convincing. The climax of the story is superbly etched' *Northampton Chronicle & Echo*

'A magnificent, beautiful book . . . exciting, moving and riveting from start to finish' Margaret Pemberton

'A compulsive and well-paced story' *Wiltshire Times*

'An earthy tale of love, longing and tragedy' *Swindon Evening Advertiser*

Also by Jess Foley

So Long At The Fair
Too Close To The Sun
Saddle The Wind

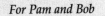

For Pam and Bob

PART ONE

Chapter One

Lydia did not need a second guess to tell that her mother wouldn't be going to church. A single glance at Mrs Halley's bruised cheek and one could be sure she wouldn't be setting foot outside the house that day.

Putting down plates on the breakfast table in the kitchen, Lydia looked at her mother, willing her to lift her gaze, but although Mrs Halley must have felt Lydia's burning glance she kept her eyes averted.

'I'll finish getting breakfast, Mother,' Lydia said. 'Why don't you sit down.'

'Sit down?' Mrs Halley said. 'Why would I sit down?'

'You look – a little tired.'

'I'm not tired. I can't afford to be tired; there's too much to do.' Mrs Halley took up the bread knife and cut two slices off the loaf on the board. That done she turned back to the range and moved the frying pan onto the heat, then moved back to the table and took up a dish of fresh eggs. Lydia wanted to say, *I know what happened; I heard you cry out*, but she kept silent. It would not do to acknowledge for one moment the abuse that had been suffered.

As Mrs Halley kept busy with the preparations for breakfast, Lydia turned away, facing the speckled looking glass above the old settle. Her reflection showed a young woman of twenty-one, above average height, with dark grey eyes and arching brows and a fine, rather narrow face. Touching at her fair hair, she looked past her own image to take in that of her mother. Mrs Halley was a small woman,

3

shorter than Lydia by three or four inches, and slight and wiry of build. She had been pretty once, it was plain to see, but the passing years had taken their toll, and nowadays she appeared a little careworn, sounded a little hollow in her infrequent laughter and looked a little threadbare in her smiles.

Suddenly a sob burst from the older woman's throat and she set down the eggs. Quickly Lydia was moving to her side, arms reaching out. 'Oh, Mother, don't. Oh, please don't cry.'

'I'm sorry, dear. Take no notice of me – I'm just being foolish.' Avoiding Lydia's arms, she lifted her apron to cover her face. 'Take no notice,' she said, her words muffled by the fabric.

As she finished speaking there came the sound of footfalls in the hall and moments later Mr Halley entered the room. He carried his jacket in his hand.

Mrs Halley spoke without looking at him. 'I'm just putting the eggs on,' she said.

He laid his jacket down on the settle and took his watch from his waistcoat pocket. 'We're in plenty of time,' he said. 'There's no rush.' Without looking at his wife he pulled out his chair at the head of the table and sat down. He was a tall man of forty-nine, with thick, springy hair that had been grey since he was in his thirties. Cleanshaven, he was handsome, with strong, regular features, and an upright carriage. His voice, rather deep and strong, was touched with a note of kindness and solicitousness as he spoke to his wife. The tone did not fool Lydia for one moment, however. It was what she would have expected after such an incident.

'Good morning, Lydia.' He flicked the merest glance at his daughter, as if afraid of catching her eye. There was no fear of this, for Lydia could not face him, could not bear the thought of meeting his gaze, of seeing any hint of an awkward smile of greeting.

4

'Good morning, Father,' she said. 'I'll pour your tea for you. It's just this minute made.'

'Oh, by the way, Lydia,' Mrs Halley murmured now as she shuffled the frying pan on the hob, 'I shan't be coming to church this morning.' Her voice was only just there. 'I've got several things I want to get done, so I thought I'd stay at home.' She was trying to sound casual, doing her best to put an offhand note into her words, but they hung in the air, coldly exposed.

'Well,' Lydia said, as she poured tea into her father's cup, 'you won't be missing anything in the sermon that you haven't heard before. And if the Reverend Hepthaw should happen to say something new we'll be sure to tell you about it.' She set the cup and saucer at her father's right elbow, and then poured for herself.

'We certainly will,' her father said, 'but he hasn't done such a thing for several years now.' He took up a spoon to stir his tea, then smiled awkwardly towards his wife. 'I doubt that you'll be missing anything, Emmie.'

Emmie he had called his wife. He usually addressed her as Emma or Mother. It was a sign that he was touched by guilt that he used the diminutive of her name. There was also the business of Mrs Halley missing the morning service, in itself unusual. At any ordinary time, on any ordinary Sunday, Mrs Halley wouldn't have dreamed of not accompanying them to church for morning service. This particular morning, though, was different, and it was no more than Lydia expected. In the past there had been tales told with averted eyes of running into doors, or tripping over steps, but they had only succeeded when the girls were very young. It had not been too long before Lydia – and her sister Ryllis after her – had put two and two together.

The eggs done, Mrs Halley added two to a plate of bacon and placed it before her husband. As she did so, Lydia

5

couldn't miss the way her father reached out and very lightly touched the side of his wife's hand with his forefinger. The briefest touch it was, but she saw it, and saw in it all the guilt of last night's act.

'I think perhaps your mother's coming down with a cold,' Mr Halley murmured. 'It'll be better if she stays at home this morning.'

'Yes, it will,' Mrs Halley said, then added, 'I'll get your breakfast for you now, Lydia.'

Taking her seat at the table, Lydia said, 'Oh, Mother, very little for me. I'm not that hungry.'

'You must eat,' Mrs Halley said, to which Mr Halley added, 'Yes, indeed, there's no telling how long Hepthaw's sermon might last.' He smiled as he spoke, as if aware of being amusing, but there was no humour in his self-conscious tone.

'There you are, dear.' Mrs Halley set down a plate of bacon and eggs in front of Lydia.

'What about you?' Lydia enquired. Her mother's place at the table was bare.

'Don't worry about me; I had something earlier. I'll just have a little tea.' With this, Mrs Halley took her seat at the table and Mr Halley glanced at the two women and then closed his eyes and clasped his hands. Lydia and her mother did likewise.

'For that which we are about to receive,' Mr Halley gravely intoned, 'O, Lord, make us truly thankful, and help us to be deserving of Thy bounteous gifts. Amen.'

'Amen,' the two women murmured, and breakfast began.

After grey days of bitter cold, the February morning was surprisingly bright and mild, and Lydia breathed in the clear air as she walked beside her father through the village streets in the direction of the church, whose spire rose up

6

beyond the intervening rooftops. She wore her grey woollen cape and her dark blue bonnet, with a little dark grey muffler around her neck.

Capinfell was a small village of some three-hundred-odd souls, situated in the county of Wiltshire, the village lying just north of the market town of Merinville, and twenty-five miles north-west of the city of Redbury. It boasted no railway station of its own, so that those hopeful of travelling by train had to walk or take a coach ride to Merinville where the nearest station was situated.

On the way to the village church of St Peter's, Lydia and her father made most of the journey with little or no conversation between them. As they walked they encountered two or three other villagers bound for the church or on errands, and Mr Halley smiled in his grave way, murmured a good morning and lifted his hat to them.

The church was a little more full than usual on this particular Sunday morning, and Mr Halley muttered to Lydia as they entered that the past harsh winter days were making the people look to their sins. The sermon delivered by the Reverend Hepthaw, was, as usual, meandering. Fortunately, however, it did not last an unconscionable time, so before too long the last hymn had been sung, the last prayer prayed, and the worshippers, to a man feeling better for the experience, made their way out into the air and thence towards their welcome Sunday dinners.

At the church doors the Reverend Hepthaw stood shaking the Sunday-clean hands of his departing flock, smiling at them, and voicing his wishes to see them in a week's time. When Lydia and her father drew level with him, the reverend's ruddy face beamed and he took their hands warmly. But where, he asked, was Mrs Halley this morning? He trusted, he said, that she was well; it wasn't often that she was missing from a Sunday morning service. Mr Halley replied that his wife had a slight cold coming on,

7

but should be better by next Sunday. They thanked the cleric and moved out of the shadow of the church walls into the weak winter sunshine. There Mr Halley glanced around to ensure that they were not likely to be overheard, then murmured into Lydia's ear, 'Reverend Hepthaw's nothing more than a silly old fool. If I couldn't do a better sermon that that I'd give up.'

As a lay preacher, and an evangelist, Mr Halley took his own sermons very seriously. He had become a devout believer in his late twenties, and his passion had not diminished in the intervening years. On two or three evenings a week he was away from the house, preaching at venues in Capinfell and the nearby villages where he had now become as familiar as the rain. For the most part he preached to the converted, rarely, to his regret, reaching those who would rather suffer their sins than give up their evenings at the local tavern. This coming week he was due to preach at the Temperance Hall in the nearby village of Pershall Dean, and also at a small community hall in Lipscott. Neither Lydia nor his wife would be accompanying him. Lydia had long ago made it clear that one morning of worship, that on a Sunday, was sufficient for her needs, and he had swiftly come to accept that she would not be persuaded otherwise. As for his wife, on his jaunts abroad she was more of a hindrance than a help, for in order to get to his various arranged venues he had to find shortcuts by traversing the fields, and she had proven irritating in her inadequate attempts to keep up.

Now, as the man and his daughter made their way through the churchyard, between the old gravestones on either side of the path, Mr Halley said to her, 'I suppose you saw the letter that came from Amaryllis yesterday?'

'Yes, Mother showed it to me,' Lydia replied. 'I heard from Ryllis myself, anyway, earlier in the week.'

8

'You'll be pleased to have her home for the weekend. Certainly your mother will be.'

'Oh, yes. I'm so looking forward to seeing her. I can't wait for Saturday. I'll stay on in Merinville after work and go and meet her from the train. This'll be her first weekend off so far this year.' Lydia raised an eyebrow. 'I'm afraid the Lucases are not very generous with their time.'

'Well, that's as may be,' her father said. He was not about to admit that the employers he had chosen would be in any way deficient. After a moment he added, 'I wish the girl would settle. She doesn't seem to get any happier.'

Amaryllis – or Ryllis as she was generally known – was sixteen years old, and had gone away into service at the age of thirteen. At present she was employed at a household in the village of Barford, situated some miles distant, and south-east of Redbury. She had not chosen her employers, Mr and Mrs Lucas; they had been chosen for her by her father who, impatient with Ryllis's perceived procrastination in finding a new post a year earlier, had taken it upon himself to find her a position. So it was that she now found herself a general maid of all work with employers who, if her letters to Lydia were anything to go by, used her with little regard to her strength and energy.

Lydia, on the other hand, had remained living at home, finding employment in the Merinville button factory, Cremson's, where her father worked as a foreman on the factory floor – though not for her the work at the finishing tables engaged in by some of the other local girls, her father had made sure of that. Through his instigation she had gained a place in the office, writing up letters and accounts and bills of trading. She did not enjoy the work; it was dull and repetitive – but for the time being she must put up with it. Still, she was glad of it, glad of the steady employment and clean work, and extremely glad, too, that she had not gone into service like her sister.

As Lydia and her father came to the church gates a young woman of near Lydia's age broke away from a small group of four people and came to their side. She was Evie Repple, a friend of Lydia's from years past. Of Lydia's height, she wore a brown straw bonnet and a pale brown cape with a darker brown ribbon threaded at the hem.

'Hello, Lyddy,' she said, smiling warmly, and then turned to Mr Halley. 'Good morning, sir.' Her smile of greeting to Lydia's father was tentative, for she had never been at ease with him.

While Lydia responded with smiling words of greeting for her friend, Mr Halley gave a nod and a cool smile. 'Evie,' he murmured. 'And how are you this morning?'

'Very well, thank you, sir.' Evie turned then to Lydia. 'Shall I see you later, Lyddy?'

'Yes,' Lydia nodded, 'I'll call round for you this afternoon, shall I?'

'Yes. If it stays fine we can go for a little walk if you like.'

They parted then, and Lydia and her father passed through the gates into the lane. As they turned their steps in the direction of home, two or three of the other villagers murmured good mornings to them. Lydia returned the words of greeting pleasantly, but when her father responded his smiles rarely reached his eyes. For the most part he held many of the other villagers in contempt, despising them for their lifestyles which he saw as loose – and even those who regularly attended church services he somehow managed to see as hypocrites. For the most part, only those who came to his own prayer meetings did he seem to regard as somehow worth saving. For the rest he had little time.

As the two of them emerged from the lane and moved to cross by the green, a dog came bounding towards them. The creature, familiar to them, was a young, good-natured cross-breed, appearing to be part Welsh border collie and part unspecified mixture, the property of one Mr Alfred Canbrook, who now came across the green in the dog's wake.

'Good morning to you, Mr Halley, Miss Halley,' Mr Canbrook said, briefly raising his hat and exposing his balding grey crown.

Returning the man's greeting, Lydia and her father halted before him. Lydia, finding that the man's eyes lingered on her own, for a moment trying to hold her gaze, immediately lowered her glance and bent to pat the dog and stroke him.

Mr Canbrook said, 'Oh, he always had a soft spot for you, Miss Halley, but don't let him become a nuisance.' Bending, vigorously patting his knees, he called the dog to him. 'Tinny! Here, boy!' Obediently the dog moved to his master's side, and at a further command sat down on the grass. 'There, that's better.' Mr Canbrook gave the dog's head a pat and straightened. He was a widower in his early fifties, in physical stature barely an inch taller than Lydia herself. He had small, rather pinched features, his noise and cheeks reddened by a little network of fine broken veins. Now his cheeks lifted as he smiled warmly at Lydia.

'So you two good people have just been to church, have you?'

'For our sins,' Mr Halley replied stiffly.

Mr Canbrook said, 'Perhaps one day I should go.' He spoke with a slight smile, as if the matter were one for levity. 'I'm sure my soul must be in need.'

'There are no souls that are not,' Mr Halley said. There was no trace of humour in his own expression.

'Ah, no doubt.' Mr Canbrook nodded. 'But not this morning. This morning I had to drive over from Merinville on a little business – and now, having done it, I thought I'd give Tinny a little run on the green before we start back.'

He looked down at the dog which, tired of sitting still, got up and looked at his master. Mr Canbrook said to him, 'All right, Tinny, we're going. You really should learn to be a little more sociable, shouldn't you?' Again his hat was lifted. 'I'll wish you both good day,' he said, smiling to the pair, then, turning, started away over the grass.

As Mr Halley and Lydia continued on their way, Mr Canbrook went off towards his pony and trap and Lydia waited for the disparaging words to be uttered about the man. They weren't long in coming. 'Conducting business,' Mr Halley said with a little snort. 'Conducting business on a Sunday. The man has no shame whatsoever. It would do him good to spend an hour in church now and again. Even a minute wouldn't come amiss. The man's naught but a self-avowed atheist.' He shook his head and clicked his tongue. 'For the life of me I can't see what your mother finds laudable in the man.'

'Well, it's just that he was once kind to her,' Lydia said. 'I suppose she speaks as she finds.'

'Yes, well, I don't find the man to my liking at all. I could never condone his heathenish ways.'

The Whitehouse, the Halley family's home, was a cottage of whitewashed Cotswold stone with a red tiled roof, situated in Cobbler's Lane on the western side of the village. The house had two bedrooms on the first floor, one shared by Mr and Mrs Halley and the other occupied by Lydia, who shared it with her sister when she was at home. The ground floor of the house comprised a front parlour and then a small entrance hall that separated it from the kitchen and a lean-to scullery. There were few signs of anything approaching luxury in the house, but its humble furnishings were homely and comfortable and clean. Little had changed in it during Lydia's lifetime that she could readily recall; everything seemed to remain the same, from the religious pictures that hung on the walls, to the antimacassars and the mantel drapery embroidered by her mother. The rear of the house looked out over the kitchen garden to fields and woodland that swept down into the vale, and this too was constant, only changing with the seasons.

It was just past noon this particular Sunday when Lydia and Mr Halley got in from church. Lydia took off her bonnet and cape, then went into the kitchen to find her mother preparing vegetables at the table. Mr Halley, after taking off his hat in the hall, had gone straight into the front parlour, where a bright fire was burning.

Lydia was glad to see that her mother looked a little better. Her face was still swollen, but she appeared not quite so downcast. As Lydia took her apron and put it on, her mother said, 'Did your father go into the front parlour?'

'Yes, he said he wants to work on his sermon.'

Mrs Halley nodded. 'How was the service?'

'The same as always. Thank heaven Mr Hepthaw's sermon didn't go on too long today. Perhaps Mrs Hepthaw has something special going into the oven and told him not to be late. I saw Evie outside the church; I'm going round to see her this afternoon.'

'Who else did you see?'

'The usual people. We met Mr Canbrook.'

'In church? Surely not.'

'No, not in church. He was out with his dog. He said he'd come to Capinfell on business.' She peered a little more closely at her mother. 'How are you, Mother? Are you feeling a little better?'

'Yes, I'm fine,' Mrs Halley said. 'I'm absolutely fine.'

Lydia looked at her and gave a nod, then glanced around her. 'Right – so what shall I do?'

'I've prepared the meat, and it mustn't be overcooked this time.' Mrs Halley straightened from the table and set down the knife with which she had been cutting up the carrots. 'How was he – while you were out?' she asked in a whisper.

'The same. He was no different.' Lydia kept her own voice very low. 'Though he had very little to say.' A pause, then she asked, 'Are you sure you're all right?'

'I shall be, dear.'

After a moment of hesitation, Lydia said, 'I heard you cry out last night. I could tell when it happened.' There – it was said; she had never before dared bring it out into the open.

Mrs Halley's eyes briefly widened with surprise at Lydia's words, then she turned her head, looking towards the hall, as if fearful of being overheard. 'It's all right,' Lydia said, 'he's busy with his sermon.' After a moment she reached out a gentle hand towards her mother's bruised face, not quite touching. 'Does it hurt much?'

'Not much now. Hardly at all.'

'Tell me,' Lydia said. 'Tell me what happened.'

'Oh, my dear, it does no good to dwell on such things. He didn't mean it.'

'But, Mother –'

'No, he didn't. And afterwards he was so – so remorseful.'

'Yes, I've no doubt of that.' A pause, then Lydia added, 'There are moments when I feel I could almost hate him.'

'Oh, no, dear, don't say such a thing. Don't think such a thing.'

'Well – I hate what he does. I can't help it. Was he always like it, since you were married?' She waited for her mother to answer. 'Was he?'

Mrs Halley was not comfortable with the theme of their conversation. Avoiding Lydia's eyes, she said, 'No. No, not at the beginning. At the beginning things were all right. At the start he was always kind and considerate. It was only later that his temper became so – so volatile.'

'What caused it?'

Mrs Halley did not answer, but just gazed wistfully off into the room.

'There must be a reason,' Lydia said.

Mrs Halley turned back to her and gave a deep sigh. 'Well – of course much of it has to do with his work. So much of it.'

'His work? What about it?'

Mrs Halley did not reply at once, but turned her head, listening for any sign of her husband coming in. Then she said, continuing in a whisper, 'Well – I'm sure you must be aware that he – he's a disappointed man. Very disappointed. He's never achieved in life what he should have.'

'But – but that happens to many people.'

'I know that, my dear, but it affects some more than others. He certainly never achieved what he was capable of – and he had all the ability. Oh, he had that all right. He had the ability, but he didn't really have the necessary chances. It's not new, the situation, of course, but it's none the less hard. He was from such a big family as you know, growing up in Hampshire – all those brothers and sisters. There was so little money, and nothing to spare to send any of them to college, no matter how bright they were, how deserving.' Mrs Halley gave a deep sigh. 'Not achieving your heart's desire when you're young is all right, for you think you have time to make up the loss, but as you get older it gets too late. It doesn't matter if opportunity comes knocking – there just isn't the time any more to take advantage of chances that might come by.'

Lydia stood in silence. Her mother had a soft voice, pleasant and low timbred. She had been born the daughter of a vicar and a governess, and her slightly more polished tones and grammar had set her a little apart from the other women in the village. They had also influenced Lydia and Ryllis in the way they spoke.

Now Mrs Halley went on, 'I'm afraid nothing's going to change for him now. He'll stay at the factory, and carry on with his preaching in his spare time, and of course, it's not enough for him. He's watched other people make it higher, and he's still where he is, with no chance of things changing. Don't be too hard on him, Lydia.' She picked up the cabbage from the table and absently picked off one of the outer leaves. 'He's a good man, at heart. Believe me, he is. He's just so – terribly strict in his way – it's how he was brought up, I'm afraid – and he has this dreadful – temper – that gets the better of him and flares up so. Afterwards he's always so sorry. I was always so glad,' she added, 'that he's never ever turned his anger on you.'

'No, he's never done that,' Lydia said, 'though he's turned it on Ryllis on occasion. There've been times when I've seen him white with anger over something she's said or done, and she's never deserved it. Why her and you and not me?'

'Oh, Lydia,' Mrs Halley put her bruised head a little on one side, 'surely you can see that where he's concerned you can hardly do wrong.' She set the cabbage down and picked up the knife. 'Come on, my dear, let's get on with dinner. Things could be a lot worse.'

Over the meal Mr Halley was kind and considerate, and continuing solicitous of his wife's feelings. Expressing his satisfaction with the food, he gave her words of praise for the lamb and the roast potatoes and vowed that no other woman in the village could make a currant pudding that was half as good. Afterwards, when the dishes were being cleared away, he said, still guiltily not meeting anyone else's eyes, 'Emmie, the other day you were speaking of needing a new nightgown. Well, why don't you get yourself a length of cotton next time you go into town? That would be nice, don't you think? Perhaps Lydia will help make it up for you. She's so good with her needle.' He turned to Lydia. 'Or when you go to meet Amaryllis from the train, you could buy it then, from Canbrook's. It'll be on your way. Which reminds me, perhaps tomorrow you could take in your mother's lamp for repair – and also get a new wick fitted while you're about it. Drop it off at Hammondson's, will you? They'll do a good job. You could go there in your dinner break.'

The lamp he spoke of was much treasured, having been a present for him and his wife on their marriage. It was a colourful thing with a china base decorated with two or three delicately painted cherubs and a spray of roses. Unfortunately Mr Halley had accidentally given it a hard knock recently, and one of the cherubs and two of the rose petals had been broken off. He had tried to mend it himself, but with no success for his efforts, and now the broken pieces lay wrapped in a twist of newspaper in one of the kitchen drawers.

Now, as he finished speaking, he leaned across from his chair, picked up the damaged lamp from the top of a small bureau and brought it to the table. As he set it down before him he said, 'Mr Hammondson's elder son is excellent at this kind of repair work. He'll do a good job – and probably not charge the earth.' He looked up at his wife. 'That'll be nice, won't it, Emmie? Get your little lamp repaired, and looking as good as new again.'

That afternoon, when the dinner dishes were washed and dried, and her father was resting in the front parlour in his favourite chair, Lydia got up from the kitchen table at which her mother sat with her mending.

'I'm going to see Evie now,' she said. 'We're going for a walk.'

'That's it, dear,' Mrs Halley said, 'Get some fresh air while the weather's dry.'

17

'You sure there's nothing you want me to do?'

'No, thank you. What time will you be back?'

'I'll only be an hour or so. It'll be too cold to stay out for too long.'

Leaving the house in Cobbler's Lane, Lydia made her way to Greenham Row, beyond the green. Reaching the third cottage along on the left-hand side she went round to the back and knocked on the door. It was opened almost immediately by Evie's mother who stood with Evie's three-year-old daughter Hennie at her side.

'There you are, Lydia,' Mrs Armstrong said. 'Evie just 'as to get her bonnet and cape and she'll be ready.'

Two minutes later Evie came out, tying up her bonnet strings, and the two young women started away.

At twenty-three, Evie was two years older than Lydia, and they had remained close friends since, as children, they had met in the local schoolhouse. Evie had been married but was now widowed. Her late husband, William, who had worked on a nearby farm, had died three-and-a-half years earlier, falling from the top of a hayrick and breaking his neck. He had been twenty-four years old. Evie's daughter, Henrietta, had been born six months later. Now, living with her mother in the cottage, Evie earned her living working in the dairy of a nearby farm, while her mother took in washing and cared for Hennie at home.

Moving off side by side along the narrow lane, Lydia and Evie walked on the hard earth. Beyond the border of the hedgerow the fields of Wiltshire stretched out to the horizon. Up above, the sky was pale blue. To Lydia it felt as if all the countryside were waiting for spring.

'It's a beautiful day for a change,' Evie said. 'It does a body good to get out for a spell.' She spoke with a slightly breathless air, in an accent somewhat broader than Lydia's. She was a pretty girl, with reddish hair and a sprinkling of freckles on her nose and upper cheeks.

'Was your mother too busy to come to church this morning?' she asked after a moment.

Lydia hesitated. 'Yes, she was. What with one thing and another.'

'What did your father think of the sermon?'

'Oh, Father would just like to be up there himself, and putting a little more passion into it. He's much happier when he's doing the preaching, rather than listening to somebody else. He doesn't really approve of Mr Hepthaw – much too lukewarm for Father's liking – but there, I think there are so many people my father doesn't approve of.'

Evie smiled as she said, 'Does he approve of your admirer?'

'My admirer? What are you talking about?'

'You know what I'm talking about. Mr Canbrook.'

Lydia laughed loudly, hooting out into the clear air. 'Mr Canbrook, my admirer! What nonsense.'

Evie laughed along with her. 'Maybe nonsense to you, but I don't think it's nonsense as far as Mr Canbrook is concerned.'

'Evie, he's older than my father. I'm sure he is.'

'Ah, but his age apart, I think there are many who reckon he'd be a good catch.'

'For who? Not for me.'

'You're too fussy by half. He's got a good business going. That nice family drapers. Whoever married him would never want for anything. It's several years now since his wife died, and I reckon he's thinking it's about time he got married again.'

'Well, we'll have to wait and see who's the lucky lady.' Lydia smiled. 'What makes you say he's after me?'

'Well, he somehow always manages to be where you are. Look at the way he is in his shop. The few times I've been in there with you, he always manages to be the one to serve you. He's just so attentive. And then there's your coming out of church and finding him there, like this morning. I mean, his coming all the way over to Capinfell. And he's done it more than once.'

'He was here on business. He said so.'

'Even so. I saw him there on the green after church, making a straight line for you. I wonder he doesn't start going to church himself so that he can sit next to you in the pew.'

'Enough, enough,' Lydia said, laughing. Although she joked about the matter, she was aware of Mr Canbrook's interest in her. The way he smiled at her, the way he caught her eyes in his glance when he could. It was not something she would wish to encourage.

Lifting her arms, she spread them out into the bright air and said, 'Oh, I do like this part of Sunday, when all the work is over.'

'Yes,' Evie said. 'To work all the other days of the week is just too much.' Then she added, slyly smiling, 'Though some people have it easier than others.'

'I work hard in the office,' Lydia said.

'Really?' Evie grinned, 'Well, if you tell me so.' She sighed. 'Sometimes I think I might have liked an office position too.'

'It was Father's idea,' Lydia said. 'It was his idea for me to go on the staff.'

'Why not your Ryllis as well? Was he content for her to go away from home, into service? I s'pose he must have been.'

'I don't know,' Lydia said. Then after a moment she added, 'Sometimes I think I could almost envy our Ryllis.'

'What? Being in service?'

'No, being away from here.'

'You mean you want a different job?'

'It isn't just Cremson's.'

'Then what? Are you talking about Capinfell?'

Lydia dismissed the notion with a wave of her hand. 'Oh, there's nothing wrong with Capinfell.'

'Then what?'

Lydia looked off into the bare branches of the trees. 'It's partly to do with Father,' she said at last.

'Is he ill?'

'Ill! He's never ill. No, it's not that.'

Evie remained silent. After a few moments Lydia said:

'He – he mistreats my mother. It happened again last night. Oh, he gets in such rages. This morning her cheek is swollen. That's why she didn't go with us to church.'

Evie said after a moment, 'And this has happened before?'

'Yes – I'm sorry to say it has.'

'Oh, Lyddy, I had no idea. How terrible.'

'Yes. Yes, it is.'

Evie was silent for a second, then she gave a little nod of realisation. 'Yes,' she breathed, 'of course. Now I see.'

'What d'you mean?'

'I remember now. I remember once I called round for you and saw your mother with her eye blacked – and it happened on another occasion too: I remember she gave some story of having had an accident. Of course I was too young to question it. I had no idea of the truth.'

'Oh, Evie,' Lydia said, 'you must never breathe a word. Promise me you won't.'

'Of course. Of course.'

'The terrible shame of it, if it should ever be known. Oh, how can my father be like that? Those folk who go to hear him preach – they've got no idea.' Feeling tears threatening, Lydia took a handkerchief from her pocket and dabbed at her eyes. 'I can't bear to see my mother suffer like this.'

'Has he ever been like that – violent – to you?'

'Never. I don't think he'd do anything to harm me. Oh, he's flown into rages with Ryllis at times, and on occasions

21

he's struck her – though nothing serious, not like with Mother.' She paused briefly then added, 'Sometimes I just feel I need to get away from it all.'

'Do you really think you might – leave?' Evie said after a moment.

Lydia nodded. 'I'd like to. I've been looking at advertisements in the papers, in the classified columns. There are interesting-looking positions all over the place, work I'm sure I could do. At Seager's in Redbury, for instance. They're often advertising. They have so many places on their staff they're always wanting someone or other. I could possibly get a position there.' She put her hands up to her face, frowning. 'I just feel the need to get away, and what is there for me in Capinfell? It's a decent enough place, but I've got nothing here. I can see no future here at all.'

'What on earth would your father do – if you left?'

'I don't know. Anyway, it's only a dream. I can't go anywhere. I can't go and leave my mother. At times I think I'm the only kind of support she has.'

Chapter Two

The next morning when she took the coach into Merinville with her father for her day's work at Cremson's, Lydia carried with her the damaged lamp, along with the broken pieces of the cherub and the rose petals. Later, during the dinner break at one o'clock, she hurried from the factory gates to the ironmonger's in the square. There she talked to the elder of the two Hammondson sons – he had a reputation for being artistic – and showed him the lamp base and the broken pieces. She was pleased to hear him say that he could make a good job of a repair. It would be ready for collection, he said, at the end of the week.

In the same row of shops alongside the square was that belonging to Mr Canbrook, where he worked behind the counter of his family draper's, helped by his assistants, and here Lydia went for the fabric for her mother's nightgown. To her great relief, she saw at once on entering the shop that Mr Canbrook was absent. She made her purchase fairly quickly, and was glad to find that her business had concluded and he had still not made an appearance. With the length of cotton wrapped up and stowed away in her basket, she left the shop to start on her short journey back to the factory.

She might have known, she said to herself seconds later, that such fortune was too good to last, for hardly had she walked thirty yards from the draper's storefront window when she heard her name called and knew at once that Mr

Canbrook had appeared and had seen her. She stopped and turned.

'Miss Halley . . .'

She stood waiting on the street corner as he came towards her, his hand raised in greeting. Tinny was trotting at his heels.

'Miss Halley . . .' A little breathless he reached her side and came to a halt, his hand now grasping his hat, briefly raising it. 'I say, Miss Lydia, this is a bit of luck, catching you just before you vanished. And it was only yesterday that I saw you in Capinfell.'

Lydia didn't think from her point of view that good luck came into it; nevertheless she smiled, and then, after a pause, for something to say, asked him how he was.

'Well, I'm feeling all the better for seeing you,' he said. 'May I ask what brings you into the square today?'

'I just stopped by to visit the ironmonger's, and then called in at your shop for some cotton.'

'Oh, I'm sorry I wasn't there myself to serve you. I trust you got what you wanted.'

'Oh, yes, indeed, thank you.'

'Is this your dinnertime from Cremson's?'

'Yes, it is.'

'And you're going back there now, are you?'

'Yes.'

'Have you had a little dinner? Some sandwiches or something? I doubt you've had time, have you?'

'That's all right. I hardly eat anything in the middle of the day.'

He frowned, shaking his head. 'My dear girl, you must eat something. You've hours of work left in front of you.' He hesitated a moment, then said, 'Look there's a decent little teashop along there.' He gestured back along the shops. 'Why don't you come in there with me and have a cup of tea and a sandwich? Get a little refreshment.'

24

'Oh, that's very kind of you, Mr Canbrook,' Lydia said, 'but I really have to get back to work. There just wouldn't be time. We only get half an hour.'

'Every time I see you,' he said, shaking his head, 'it seems you're dashing off somewhere. The next time I see you I shall insist that you stop and have some tea with me. How would that be?'

Lydia said nothing to this. She hardly knew what to say to him, but that had always been the way whenever they met. Over the years of her employment at Cremson's, she had often had reason to call in at Canbrook's draper's, and had come to be familiar with Mr Canbrook's small, efficient figure. Always he had been most pleasant and attentive towards her, whether she was on her own or in the company of one of her workmates. However, her first encounter of any significance with him had taken place some three years ago when, one summer day, she and her mother had come to the town and had been making some purchases in the shop. A bee had flown into the premises, and had alighted on her mother's bare hand when she had taken off her glove to feel the texture of some silk. The bee had stung her, and Mrs Halley had given a little yelp of shock and pain. Quickly Mr Canbrook had come to her side and urged her to a chair. To Lydia's alarm, the perspiration had broken out on her mother's brow and her hand had swelled up. Swiftly, then, Mr Canbrook had got tweezers and extracted the bee's sting, after which he had sent one of his young assistants, Mr Federo, to the nearby teashop to fetch a pot of tea. While the young man was gone Mr Canbrook had applied to the site of the sting a little bicarbonate of soda. After a while Mrs Halley had recovered sufficiently and, after thanking Mr Canbrook for his kindness and sipping a little tea, she and Lydia had gone on their way. The incident had not been forgotten, however, and from that time on Mrs Halley had always spoken of the middle-aged widower with warmth and appreciation.

It was because of the man's previous exhibition of kindness and consideration that Lydia must always now give him the benefit of the doubt; and whereas she might in some other case, with some other man, have been cool in the face of his warmth, where Mr Canbrook was concerned she could not be.

'So what do you think of that?' Mr Canbrook was saying. 'I shall look out for you the next time you're round by the shop, and if I see you I shall insist that you come and have some tea with me. That goes for your mother too, of course.'

Lydia smiled. 'Very well, then,' she said, and then added, 'I really think I'd better get on, Mr Canbrook. If you'll excuse me.'

He smiled again and touched at the brim of his hat. 'Of course. I mustn't keep you, but remember what I said. I shall be on the lookout.'

Work at the factory finished for the weekend at one o'clock on Saturday, and when the time came Lydia said goodbye to her father and set off for the market square. She would go and pick up the lamp if the repair was finished, buy some collars that her father had asked her to get for him, and then go and meet Ryllis from the train.

She went first to the ironmonger, and at the counter asked if the lamp was ready. It was the senior Mr Hammondson she spoke to, and he said at once, 'Ah, yes, that's a job concerning my son, miss,' and called back into the shop, 'Manny? Special customer here for you.'

The proprietor's son came at once and smiled at Lydia in greeting, saying without hesitation, 'Ah, yes, miss, you've come for your lamp,' and turned back into the rear. When he reappeared a few moments later he was carrying the lamp base. Carefully he set it down on the counter, gave it a wipe with a duster and turned it so that the site of the repair was facing Lydia.

'Well,' he said, 'what do you think?' He was a tall young man with fair hair and pale eyes.

'It looks perfect,' Lydia said, nodding to endorse her words. 'It's quite wonderfully done.'

The young man was justifiably proud of his craftsmanship. 'It took me a while,' he said in his heavy Wiltshire accent, 'but it was a job worth doin' and it turned out better than I'd 'oped for.' He pointed with his finger. 'Look there, where the breaks were – you can 'ardly see the joins.'

Very carefully, he wrapped the china base in a length of old cloth, and then took Lydia's basket from her. As he laid the package inside he said, 'I replaced the wick as well, Miss, so everything should be fine.'

When Lydia had paid him, and thanked him again, she went back out onto the street. Her next errand was to buy her father's collars from the draper's, a job she did not look forward to, for it meant that she would almost certainly run into Mr Canbrook again.

She walked along the side of the square until she came to the draper's and went in, but if she had thought that Mr Canbrook could be avoided she was swiftly disillusioned, for he was almost the first person she saw. He was standing on a stepladder, replacing some items on a shelf above his head. As Lydia entered he turned to her with the attention that he would give to any new customer, but then, seeing who it was, beamed broadly.

'Well,' he said, 'if it isn't Miss Halley come to see how we're getting on.' Quickly he climbed down from the steps. There were other customers in the shop, being served by the assistants, but Mr Canbrook gave his attention solely to Lydia. 'To what do I owe this pleasure?' he murmured. 'Have you just come to see me, or are you going to disappoint me by saying you only want to buy something?'

Lydia smiled uncertainly at the man. 'Hello, Mr Canbrook,' she said. 'I've come to buy some collars from you, if I may.'

'Ah, well,' he sighed, smiling, 'at least you're here, that's the important thing. Collars, is it?'

Lydia said, 'I want half a dozen for my father. He takes size fifteen and a half.'

'It shall be done.' So saying, Mr Canbrook turned to a young man, who, having just finished serving a customer, now stood behind the counter, folding linen napkins. 'Mark,' Mr Canbrook said to him, 'six standard collars, fifteen and a half, for the young lady here, if you please.'

The young man at once went to a shelf and drew from it a box. Putting it on the counter he took from it a pile of collars, located those of size fifteen and a half, and counted out six. That done he carefully wrapped them in tissue paper. He gave Lydia the price and she counted it out from her purse and put the coins into his hand.

'There you are,' said Mr Canbrook, as the young man turned back to his business with the napkins, 'you've got your father's collars. And where are you going now, may I ask? Back to Capinfell?'

'Not yet,' Lydia said. 'I'm to meet my sister from the train.'

'Where is she coming from?'

'Redbury.'

He nodded. 'What time is her train due in?'

'Two-thirty.'

'Oh, well, you've got lots of time before you need to go to the station. Have you got other errands?'

'Well – no.'

He beamed, and lowering his voice, said, 'Then you can have some tea with me, can't you? You told me you would, the next time you were in Merinville.'

'Well . . .' she said, and then after a moment's hesitation. 'I haven't got *that* long . . .'

'Oh, but the teashop's only a few doors along.'

'I don't know,' Lydia said, knowing now that she could hardly get out of it. Then, making up her mind, she nodded and smiled. 'Very well, Mr Canbrook, thank you very much. It would be very nice to have a quick cup of tea if you can spare the time from your business.'

'That's excellent,' he said. 'It's not too busy this afternoon, and I shan't be gone long.' He turned and smiled at his two young male assistants and the middle-aged female, whom Lydia had heard him refer to as Miss Angel. 'You'll be all right for ten minutes, won't you? I'll only be along at the teashop. One of you can come and get me if you need me.'

Moments later the man was leading the way out of the shop. As they stepped outside there was a little flurry of movement, and suddenly Mr Canbrook's dog was there, tail wagging enthusiastically.

'Oh dear,' said Mr Canbrook with a shake of his head. 'Sorry, Tinny old boy, but this little jaunt's not for you.' The dog looked up at him with mournful eyes. 'We're not going anywhere, old chap,' Mr Canbrook said, 'so you might as well go on back into the shop.'

'Where did he come from?' Lydia said.

'He's got a basket in the back room.'

'Can't he come with us?'

'Well, I would take him, but there are some people in the teashop who'd frown, so we'd better not.' He bent and touched the dog on the head. 'All right, Tinny, go on back into the shop, there's a good lad.'

Mr Canbrook held the shop door open, and obediently the dog turned and trotted back inside. Mr Canbrook then turned back to Lydia. 'All right, let's go and get some tea.'

The teashop was busy enough, with only a couple of tables unoccupied. 'There's a spot,' Mr Canbrook said as they entered, 'let's go and sit over there,' and they made their way to a table against the far wall. As they took their seats Lydia placed the basket on the empty chair. When the middle-aged waitress came over, Mr Canbrook said to her, 'Look, Mrs Winnow, I have a friend visiting me today from Capinfell, Miss Lydia Halley.' The woman smiled a hello at Lydia and asked what they wished for. They would have tea, Mr Canbrook said, and the woman asked, 'Would you like some cake as well?' Lydia said no, the tea alone would be fine.

The woman went away again, and in the little silence that fell between them, Lydia became aware of the chatter of the other people in the teashop. After a while, she said, 'Mr Canbrook, why do you call your dog Tinny?'

'Oh – because he was a tin ribs.' He gave a little chuckle.

'Because he was a tin ribs?'

'It's not a long story,' he said. 'One day, two or three years back, I was driving along near some spot where gypsies had had a campsite, and I saw this little wreck of a dog hanging about: no more than a puppy, just a few months old, and obviously abandoned. So I took him home with me and cleaned him up and fed him. He was so thin, I called him Tin Ribs – which is what my mother sometimes called me when I was a skinny boy. And Tin Ribs became Tinny, and now that's all he answers to.'

'He's so fond of you,' said Lydia.

'Oh, yes, he is that. And I'm very fond of him. He's became a nice little companion for me. It's been good for me – having lost my wife – to have something around that needs to be cared for.'

The waitress came then with their tray of tea, and when everything had been set out and they were left alone again,

Mr Canbrook asked Lydia if she would pour it out. She did so, and Mr Canbrook took up his cup and blew on the hot tea. His fingernails were clean and square cut; his hands were large for a small man.

'So,' he said, 'you're off to meet your sister.'

'That's right.'

'What is her name? I don't think I've heard you say it.'

'Ryllis. Amaryllis.'

He nodded. 'And what is she doing in Redbury?'

'She's in service in Barford. She's just coming back for the weekend. She'll return to Barford tomorrow.'

'Does she like her work?'

'No, not at all, I'm afraid.' Lydia sipped at her tea. 'She'd like to change it.'

'Oh, dear. That's a pity.'

'I'm afraid it is. She won't be happy until she's found a different situation.'

'And what about you, Miss Halley? How are you getting on at work? Do you enjoy it at Cremson's?'

'I can't say I enjoy it. I'm afraid there's not much variety or interest in the work at a button factory, but I have to do something to earn a living.'

He nodded. 'Indeed. We all must do that, but it helps if we can find something we enjoy doing. I don't know what I would do if I didn't have the shop. It was my father's before me, so I haven't known anything else. What will happen to it when I die I've got no idea. Still, no good talking about that.' He paused. 'I haven't asked after your mother. Is she well these days? She wasn't with you when you came out of church last Sunday.'

Quickly Lydia said, 'Oh, she's in excellent health, thank you,' then adding to the lie: 'A slight cold to overcome but nothing really. I'm sure you'll see her in the summer. She enjoys coming here to Merinville to do her shopping.'

They continued to talk of this and that, and throughout

31

the mundane chatter Lydia wished for the time to pass so that she could get up and leave.

At last, the tea had been drunk, it was five minutes past two, and it was time for her to make her leisurely way to the railway station. Emerging from the teashop, she and Mr Canbrook walked the short distance to the entrance of his shop. There he glanced in through the glass door, seeing customers standing at the counters. 'The lads and Miss Angel are busy,' he said. 'I mustn't stay out.'

Lydia thanked him for the tea, and he said what a pleasure it had been, and that he hoped he'd see her in Merinville again before too long. Lydia then took her leave of him.

Walking fairly slowly, taking her time, and pausing now and then to look in at the shop windows, she had only gone about fifty yards when she heard her name called. Turning, she saw Mr Canbrook coming towards her at a rapid pace, one hand raised to hail her. She stood and waited for him to catch up.

'Ah, I caught you, Miss Halley,' he said. 'Just in time.' He had obviously come out in a hurry, Lydia observed; he had come without his hat.

'I seem to be making a habit of this,' he said, 'running after you in the street, but I had some very quick second thoughts – and I wanted to say something to you.'

Lydia nodded, waiting.

'First of all,' he said, 'this is for you.' He was holding a small, simply wrapped brown-paper package. 'Just a little something. It's a length of lace. Nottingham lace. Very pretty, and handmade. I thought perhaps you might be able to use it on a nightgown or a blouse or something.'

Lydia took the package from him. 'This is so terribly kind of you, Mr Canbrook,' she said. 'I don't know how to thank you.' Carefully she laid it in her basket beside the lamp base.

'Your pleasure is enough thanks,' he said. He paused, as if searching for words. 'There's something I'm bound to ask you . . .'

'Oh, what's that?'

'It's just that . . .' He swallowed, sighed. 'Oh, this is very difficult for me, but – the thing is . . . Oh, listen – I wanted to ask you a question earlier, but I couldn't get up the courage . . .' He stumbled to a halt. Lydia kept silent. After the space of a couple of seconds he went on: 'What I wanted to say, is . . . Oh, Miss Lydia – I hope you don't mind me addressing you so . . . but – oh, I have to ask you: is there . . . is there some young man on your horizon? Some acquaintance of yours – some special acquaintance who is – well – someone who has a place in your heart? A special place. Oh, I know I'm a lot older than you, and for a girl like you who – well, I can't imagine you'd see me as much of a catch. But do you have someone? If you do, tell me and I'll never trouble you again. Do you?'

'Mr Canbrook,' Lydia said, 'this is such a surprising thing to . . .' Her words trailed to a halt. She stood with her basket in one hand and her other hand up to her cheek. 'I don't know what to say,' she ended lamely.

'Just tell me – is there someone special in your life – someone who means something to you?'

'Well, no, there is not,' she said. 'But on the other hand –'

Quickly he broke in, 'Oh, please don't tell me you could never look at me.' Then he fell silent, as if waiting for her to do just that. When she said nothing, he went on: 'I want to ask – if you think it would be all right if I came to see you one day. We'll start to get some nice days now. Perhaps you'll be kind enough to say we might go out for a walk or something. What do you think?' He looked at her for a moment. 'I might be making a complete fool of myself.' He sighed. 'Anyway – I must let you get on your way. You must go and meet your sister.' He started to turn, then turned back. 'Look – with your permission,' he said, 'I'll write to you.' With an awkward bobbing little motion of his balding head, he turned again and started back the way he had come.

Lydia was in plenty of time to meet Ryllis, and had a few minutes to kill on the platform before the train came. At last it drew in, the doors were opened, and there was Ryllis, stepping down on to the platform. Moments later the two sisters were embracing. They had not met in some weeks, not since Lydia had gone into Redbury to spend a few hours with Ryllis who had been sent into the city by her employers to do shopping.

Their coach for Capinfell was not due to leave for fifteen minutes, so they sat on a nearby bench to wait.

'Oh, what a relief!' Ryllis sighed, 'to be away from Barford for a while. It's wonderful to get away from that dreadful house and those awful people.'

'Ryllis,' Lydia said, 'they surely can't be that bad.'

'Oh, believe me, I've said nothing yet – but I'm not going to sit here complaining. It's too nice a day, and for the rest of today and tomorrow I don't even want to think about the Lucases.'

Whereas Lydia's voice was low in timbre, Ryllis's had a lighter tone. She had a lighter air. Whereas Lydia could be grave and serious, Ryllis hardly ever seemed so. They were unlike in their appearance also. Where Lydia was tall and slender, Ryllis was much smaller in stature, and tended a little to a soft roundness in the curves of her limbs. Where Lydia's straight hair was fair, so Ryllis's curling hair was dark. There was no doubt that for straightforward pretti-ness Ryllis's nose was a little too short and her full-lipped mouth a little too wide, but at the same time there were in her face a freshness and a radiance that were rarely to be matched. Sitting on the bench in the winter sunshine, in her brown cape, and with her face framed by the frill of her bonnet, she looked the picture of health and attractiveness.

'How is Mother?' Ryllis asked. 'And Father? I assume they're all right, otherwise I would have heard.'

'Yes, they're both fine, and looking forward to your getting home for a while.'

'Well, Mother maybe.'

'Oh, Ryllis,' Lydia frowned, 'don't say that. Father's looking forward to seeing you. He just doesn't – express things in the same way as Mother.'

'That's true enough.' Ryllis sighed. 'Well, I shall just have to try not to annoy him while I'm home. I always manage to do so in some way, it seems.' She paused. 'Though at some time I've got to have a word with him.'

'What do you mean?'

'I want to leave the Lucases. I've been there well over a year and that's long enough. I know Father isn't going to be pleased when I tell him, but it's *my life*, and if I want to leave a position I should be able to.' She tapped her bag. 'I've bought one of the local papers with advertisements for positions. I'll have a look at them when I get in.'

Ryllis asked Lydia then how she had spent her time whilst waiting for the train to come in, and Lydia told her of her meeting with Mr Canbrook and going with him for tea. Ryllis sat almost open-mouthed while Lydia related the details of the meeting, and told her also of the gift of the lace and Mr Canbrook's remark that he wished to call on her, and would write to her with a view to doing such a thing.

'Oh, well, fancy!' Ryllis exclaimed. 'I wonder what Father would have to say about that!'

'I shan't tell him,' Lydia said at once, 'and you mustn't say anything either. Nor to Mother. If she knows, she might feel duty bound to pass on the information to him.'

'Well, whether you tell him or not he's bound to find out at some time.'

'No, he's not,' Lydia said, 'because Mr Canbrook won't be calling at the house, and he won't be writing to me either.'

'How'll you stop him? He's obviously that keen.'

'I'll write to him first. I'll do it tomorrow. He'll get it Tuesday morning.'

'What will you say?'

'What *can* I say? I'll simply tell him that I respect and admire him, but that's as far as it goes. I'll just have to make it clear, as politely as I possibly can, that there's no future in his calling at the house to see me, or in sending me letters.' She gave a wry smile. 'Father'd be very curious, seeing me get a letter from Merinville.'

'And imagine what he'd say if he found out who it was from.'

Lydia frowned. 'He mustn't know. I'll stop this before it has a chance to go any further.'

'I suppose you're right,' Ryllis said. 'Mr Canbrook sounds quite a nice old man, though. And giving you that lace . . .' She gestured to Lydia's basket. 'Let's have a look at it.'

Lydia picked up the little package, partly unwrapped it and opened it up. Exposing the lace, she said, 'Oh, it's beautiful.'

'It certainly is,' Ryllis said.

'He told me it's handmade.'

'I'm sure it is. It's lovely.'

Lydia sighed. 'What d'you think I should do about it?'

'Well, you could put it on a nightdress. It would look lovely down the front, or on the yoke. There's plenty there.'

'No,' Lydia said, 'I don't mean that. What I mean is, I don't know whether I should keep it – or send it back.'

Ryllis's eyes widened. 'Of course you should keep it. He's given it to you, hasn't he?'

'I know that, but if I'm going to send him a letter telling

him not to bother writing or calling at the house, it seems hardly the thing to do to accept presents from him.'

'But it's just a piece of lace, for goodness sake. It's not a carriage and pair. You can't seriously think of sending it back.'

They said no more at this point on the matter, for the coach was seen approaching. Five minutes later they were climbing on board.

Mr Halley was not at home when they arrived – he was out arranging one of his prayer meetings – but Mrs Halley was there, waiting to welcome her daughter. Even as Ryllis threw her arms about her mother her attention was drawn to the fading bruises on her face. 'Mother, what happened to your face?' she asked.

Mrs Halley drew back a little and dismissed the question with a waved hand. 'Oh, nothing, my dear. Just a little accident – which will teach me to be a bit more careful in future.'

Nothing more was said on the subject, and the three set about making tea. As they drank it a while later, Ryllis sat at the kitchen table, opened up the newspaper she had brought from Redbury and studied the classified advertisements. There were three situations offered that she thought might be suitable, and these she circled with heavy strokes of a pencil. Lydia sat at the table watching her, as did Mrs Halley while she prepared vegetables.

'Are you going to write off for those positions?' Lydia asked.

Ryllis shrugged. 'Well, there's no harm in doing so, and if I get a new job it can't be worse than the one I've got now.'

'Oh, Ryllis,' Mrs Halley said, 'do you hate it so much where you are?'

'Yes, I do,' Ryllis replied. 'I can't wait to get away, to move on to some other place.'

37

'But if you leave you'll lose the money for the year so far,' Mrs Halley said.

'That's something I'd have to put up with,' Ryllis replied.

'Easier said than done. Your father won't be pleased. After all, he got you the post in the first place.'

'I know that,' Ryllis said, 'but I didn't ask him to. He took it upon himself. And why? Because he wasn't satisfied with the way I was going about it, that's why. He went on as if I didn't want to work, as if I didn't want to get a position.' She turned to her mother. 'Oh, I know he'll be angry if I tell him I intend to leave, but – oh, it isn't a pleasant life working for the Lucases, not by any means.'

Mrs Halley said, 'I know the work must be hard, but it usually is in service.'

'I'm not complaining about the hard work,' Ryllis said, 'though it's very hard indeed. It's other things. For one thing I don't have anywhere properly to sleep. I've told you that. The cook has her own bedroom, but I have to make do with a little shelf in the kitchen under the dresser. I have to put down a little pallet every night, which I get from the outhouse, and stretch out there. It's so hard and uncomfortable. Then there are the times when Mr Lucas decides not to go to bed at a decent time, but comes to the kitchen and sits in front of the range – it being the warmest place in the house at the time. Which means I can't go to bed. I can be as tired as anything, but I have to stay up. I have to sit on a hard chair in the cold scullery, just waiting for him to finish reading his papers and go off upstairs. Sometimes he's there until the early hours – which means I get hardly any sleep.'

'Oh, that's unfair,' Lydia said. 'You poor thing.'

'And another thing,' Ryllis said. 'My going on errands to the farm up the road, maybe to get extra cream or milk or anything else they need. I hate it, because when they're in a hurry for whatever it is I always have to take the shortcut and go through the field where the cows are grazing.'

'Cows are generally harmless creatures,' Mrs Halley said. 'I shouldn't think they'd be any danger to you.'

'It's not just the cows,' Ryllis said. 'Sometimes they let loose the old bull, and he's that protective of his herd. He's come at me a few times, and I've had the devil's own job to get away in time – and trying to run while carrying a full can of milk isn't the easiest thing, I can tell you. He doesn't like me, that old bull. Well, I don't like him either.'

'But do you have to go through the cow pasture?' Mrs Halley said. 'Can't you go around, by the road?'

'Oh, I could, but that's such a long way. It takes forever to go by the lane, and I haven't usually got the time. Mrs Lucas wants her cream or butter when she wants it. She doesn't want to wait an hour. No, there's nothing for it but to go through the cow field. Still –' she laid a hand flat on the newspaper before her, 'if I find another job soon I can say goodbye to all that.'

Chapter Three

Mr Halley came in just after six, finding Ryllis helping her mother and sister in the kitchen. As he came in, Ryllis turned to him and said, 'Hello, Father – I'm home.'

He nodded, a grave half smile touching his mouth. 'Ah, so I see, girl. And are you well?'

'Yes, quite well, thank you.'

'Good. And let's hope you enjoy your weekend at home.'

At this Mrs Halley said, 'Yes, my dear, you enjoy it. I don't doubt you've earned it well enough.'

'Well,' Mr Halley said shortly, 'I think Mr and Mrs Lucas might be the best judge of that, so that question'll have to go unanswered.' He took off his hat and sat down in his chair at the side of the range. Obviously he was not in the best of moods.

'How did you get on at Pershall Dean?' Mrs Halley asked tentatively.

'How did I get on?' He spoke through gritted teeth. 'I didn't get on at all. I've got to go back. I walked all the way over there to see that booby Winsford about the prayer meeting in the community hall on Monday night, only to find he's not there, and his wife had no notion of when he's coming back. I stayed nearly an hour for him and he didn't show. In the end I just got sick of waiting. All that time wasted, and now it means I've got to go back. Thank heaven there's a moon.' He shook his head in disgust. 'Some people are completely unreliable.' He sat there with his lips working, the anger evident in the line of his mouth.

'I'll get you something to eat,' Mrs Halley said, 'and make you some fresh tea.'

With Ryllis's help, Mrs Halley set about preparing some dishes of food. As they busied themselves, Lydia said, 'I got your collars, Father. I put them up in your room. I got the lamp too.'

'Thank you,' he said. 'So, the lamp's been repaired, has it? Might as well have a look at it, then, I suppose.'

Lydia got up from her seat and moved to her shopping basket on the side table. From it she took the lamp base and handed it to her father. Carefully he lifted off the cloth wrapping. He held the lamp in his hands, turning it around and studying the mended section.

'What do you think?' Mrs Halley said. 'It looks very good, don't you think?'

He nodded. 'Ah, it looks all right.'

'A new wick's been put in as well,' Lydia said. 'Which the young man didn't charge for.'

'How much did he charge for the repair?'

'Tenpence.'

'Tenpence,' Mr Halley said. 'I should think it ought to be good work for that money.' He set the lamp on the table, then fumbled in his trouser pocket and brought out his small leather purse. 'And how much were my collars?'

'A shilling.'

He opened his purse, shook out coins and counted them out. 'Get my debts settled,' he said, 'before anything else is done.'

Lydia held out her hand and he dropped the coins into it. As he put his purse away, Mrs Halley stepped to the table and said to him, 'May I, Father?' and reached out and took up the lamp. Carefully she set it before her, turning it so that the light caught the cherubs and the roses. 'Why, you can barely see the joins,' she said. 'That young man, Mr Hammondson's son, he's clearly a very clever young man.'

41

'Oh, he is,' Lydia said, 'and proud of his work too. Rightly so as well.'

'Yes, rightly so,' Ryllis said, leaning over. 'Look at that rose. I swear that if you didn't know it, you'd never think it had ever been broken.'

Delicately with one finger she touched the tip of one of the mended rose petals, and then at once came her father's voice saying, 'Well, don't test the break, girl. Unless you want to see it broken all over again.' He looked around. 'Where's the shade and the funnel? We might as well put it all together.'

'I'll get them.' Lydia went to the cupboard under the stairs, and brought out the lampshade and the funnel and set them on the table. She also brought a container of oil, from which she filled the reservoir. Carefully she set all in place, and soon the lamp was complete again.

A few minutes later Mrs Halley set before her husband a plate of salad and cold meat, with potato salad, cheese and pickles. Then fresh tea was made and a mug was placed at his right hand. He ate in silence for a minute or two, and then said to Lydia, 'Was it busy in the centre at Merinville today?'

'Quite busy,' Lydia said.

'There are some days when it can get unbearable. Mind you, that's usually on a Thursday, market day. Did you see Cranbrook in his shop when you got the collars?'

'Yes, he was there.'

'Did he have his dog with him?' Mrs Halley said. 'He often does.'

'Tinny, yes. He was there with him.'

'He doesn't have the dog in the shop, does he?' Mr Halley said.

Lydia said, 'Yes, he does. He has a basket there in the back.'

Mr Halley shook his head in disapproval. 'It doesn't

42

surprise me. I'll never understand the man.'

At this Mrs Halley spoke up. 'I know you don't care for him, Father,' she said, 'but he was so very kind to me that time, when I got stung by the bee.'

'Well, that's as maybe,' Mr Halley said. 'He didn't do anything that anybody else wouldn't have done.'

'I don't know about that. He was very kind, and I've always found him to be extremely pleasant.'

'Have you now?' he said. 'Well, I never liked the man. His wife neither. That busybody of a woman, and one who showed little respect at times, always ready with a sharp comment if things weren't to her liking. I do believe she used powder on her face. Sometimes I wondered how they kept their customers.'

'Oh,' Mrs Halley said, 'it's a very successful business.'

'I know it is,' said her husband. 'It's amazing how success can sometimes come to the most undeserving of men. Men who are unbelievers.' He sniffed. 'I believe he has a fine house in Merinville too.'

'He doesn't live over his shop?' Ryllis asked.

'He used to, I'm told,' Mrs Halley replied, 'but I believe that was before he was married. By what I've been told, his wife had the house left to her by her father, so after they married he moved in there.'

'I should think Mr Canbrook does very well,' Ryllis said.

'And what would you know about it?' Mr Halley asked sharply. 'Are you so knowledgeable?'

Ryllis shrugged. 'Well, it's just that he – he employs several members of staff, and they seem to be kept busy enough.'

Mr Halley swallowed a mouthful of ham and said, 'Anyway, it doesn't figure what any of you tell me about the man, because I don't like him – and right now I'm tired of hearing his name, and of the wonderful things he's done.'

'How's your tea, Father?' Mrs Halley said, eager to mend fences. 'Could you eat another slice of ham?'

He did not answer. Idly, he had picked up the copy of the newspaper that Ryllis had brought back. He was staring at one of the pages.

'What's this?' he said.

His voice drew their attention, and three pairs of eyes saw that he was holding up the paper, turning it towards them. The page put to their view showed columns of classified advertisements, some of which showed Ryllis's pencil markings.

Frowning, he pointed to one of the circled advertisements. 'Is this you?' he said to Lydia. His tone was darkened with disappointment. 'Lydia, don't tell me you're thinking of leaving Cremson's.'

No one spoke. Then Ryllis broke the silence. 'No, Father,' she said, 'it was me. I wrote on the paper. I got it when I was in Redbury today.'

He glared at her for a moment, then pushed his half-finished plate away and slapped the paper down on the table, the jolt making the shade of the lamp rattle on its newly repaired base. Then with his finger he jabbed at one of the marked entries.

'So,' he said to Ryllis, 'it would appear that you've got your sights set on moving on. Is that right?'

Ryllis did not answer.

'Well, miss,' he went on, 'when you want to start thinking of another situation, perhaps you'd have the good manners to talk to me about it first.'

'But Father,' Ryllis said bravely, 'I've wanted to talk to you about it, but I never think you want to listen.'

Now his voice rose in his growing fury. 'Don't you dare talk to me like that,' he said angrily, a little fleck of spit flying from his lower lip. The room went quiet. 'I think we should get something understood,' he added. 'You are

44

sixteen years of age, and still my responsibility, and even for a sixteen-year-old you're immature. Sometimes I think you haven't got the brains of a rabbit. That being said, you are not in a position to choose a post for yourself.'

'But Father,' Ryllis cried, tears suddenly spilling over and running down her cheeks, 'I hate it at the Lucases. I've as good as told you in my letters. You know that.'

'Oh, I do, do I? What I know is that you've got a job that many a young woman would be pleased to have. You're well fed, and they give you the occasional half a day off, and a weekend sometimes, like now. You even get clothes given to you by Mrs Lucas. I don't know what sort of position you've got in mind, but I doubt very much that you'd find another one any better.'

'What do I want with Mrs Lucas's old cast-offs,' Ryllis said passionately. 'For one thing she's almost twice my height. I can't wear her clothes. Besides, they're horrible. As you said, I'm sixteen. What do I want with some worn out old clothes of an old-fashioned woman of fifty?'

'I'll tell you what you want,' he said, his lips thinned into straight lines, 'and that is to show some respect for your elders and betters. I've met Mr and Mrs Lucas, and I've got the highest respect for them. Have they ever abused you? They never have, have they?'

'Well, no, but –'

'No, and they're not likely to. Mr Lucas is a much respected man in the law, and his wife is a good woman, I've got no doubt.'

'But, Father –' Ryllis's face was wet with her tears.

'Enough!' he cut in. 'Why can't you be more like your sister? You don't hear her complaining about every little thing, but you, you're never satisfied. I found you a very suitable position, but you've refused to settle into it or even make any attempt to be happy.' He slapped the palm of his hand down on the table. 'I don't want to hear any more.

45

And as for this –' He picked up the newspaper, folded it once and tore it across and across, then tossed the pieces down on to the table. 'That's what I think of that. Now, young lady, I suggest that you go upstairs to your room and try to get some sense into your head.' He waved a hand. 'Go on. I'm sick of the sight of you. I've got to go out in a few minutes, and I don't want to see your ungrateful face again before I go.'

Ryllis got up, her hands clasped over her mouth, and, with a sob, turned and ran out of the room. At once Mrs Halley rose to her feet, ready to go in pursuit. 'Stay where you are,' Mr Halley said, halting her. 'It won't hurt her to cry for a while. It'll do her good to have to face reality for once. She never does. She lives in a dream world and never thinks of anyone but herself.'

Mrs Halley sat back down. For a few brief moments they heard overhead the sound of Ryllis's feet, but then all was quiet again. Lydia stared down into her cup. On the mantelpiece the old clock ticked into the quiet. Mrs Halley got up and moved to the hall door. 'I must go up to her,' she said.

'I told you no.' Mr Halley got to his feet. 'I told you to leave the girl alone, and I meant it.'

'But she's so upset. I can't leave her like that. Sometimes you're so hard on her.'

'Don't speak to me like that,' he said. 'I will not be defied by you, nor by my children.' He pointed to the chair so recently vacated by his wife. 'Sit down. I tell you, sit down.'

Still Mrs Halley remained standing. The pair stood facing one another.

'I told you to sit down,' Mr Halley said, glaring at her. He was almost white with anger.

After a long moment Mrs Halley lowered her eyes and sat back down in her chair.

'Now.' Mr Halley moved to the bureau and took up his

hat. He put it on, then turned to face his wife and daughter.

'I'm going back out now,' he said, 'and I hope by the time I return there'll be a little change of attitude in this house. I'm talking specifically to you, Mrs Halley. Perhaps when you're through encouraging your younger daughter in her contrary ways we can find a little more pleasure in the house.'

He put a hand up to adjust his hat, then moved to the doorway and stepped down into the scullery and out of sight.

The echo of the sharp closing of the scullery door rang briefly and then swiftly died. In the silence Lydia and Mrs Halley sat at the kitchen table. They sat there for two or three minutes, neither looking at the other, neither making a sound. Then Mrs Halley rose from her chair, moved to the hall door, opened it and started up the stairs. After a moment Lydia could hear the murmur of voices as her mother and Ryllis spoke together. Two minutes later Mrs Halley was coming back into the room with Ryllis following at her heels.

'There,' Mrs Halley said, 'now we can all three relax. We'll get tea for ourselves and do as we want to for the evening. If he's going back to Pershall Dean he won't be home for a while.'

'There are times I could wish he'd never come back at all,' Ryllis said.

'Hush, Ryllis,' Mrs Halley said. 'Don't say such things.'

The three of them prepared a light meal for themselves, and later, as they washed the dishes in the scullery, Ryllis said, unable to let the matter drop: 'I don't know how I always manage to upset Father so much, but somehow I've always had the talent for it.'

'It's not your fault,' Mrs Halley said. 'He gets into these moods when things don't go as he expects, and then gets into his tempers. There's no reasoning with him at such times.'

'Well,' Ryllis said, 'I'm afraid he's going to get upset again, because I intend to keep my eyes open for another position.'

When the dishes had been put away, the three left the scullery, to settle back in the kitchen. Lydia lit the newly repaired lamp and it sat on the table glowing amid them as they took to their sewing and mending. Gradually their moods lightened, and eventually they were smiling as they spoke.

Ryllis was working on a nightdress for her mother, with the cotton that Lydia had earlier brought from Merinville. Leaning in a little closer to the lamp, trying to catch the best of the light, she began to tell of life at the Lucases' house, and to relate anecdotes of little incidents that had taken place there. Most of her stories, Lydia was amused to observe, were those that showed Mr or Mrs Lucas in a bad light. Clearly, in Ryllis's book there was to be no respect shown for her employers.

'And there's the time she went out to the pigsty,' Ryllis said, speaking yet again of Mrs Lucas. 'She had a friend visiting, and was showing off the place – but can you imagine, keeping a pig? A lawyer keeping a pig? You'd have thought they'd have enough money to buy a piece of bacon whenever they wanted it, rather than keeping a pig of their own with all the smells and the mess, but no, they have to have their own pig.' Ryllis shook her head in contempt, and then gave a little laugh as she thought back to the incident that had given rise to her anecdote.

'Anyway, there she is, Madam Lucas, one afternoon, with her visitor from Redbury or somewhere, and takes her down to the kitchen garden to show her the produce, and on the way back they stop by the pigsty. I was out in the yard at the time, having just got in some vegetables for

Cook, so I saw it all. Mrs Lucas had brought from the kitchen a bit of something for the pig to eat – though on normal days she never even noticed that the creature existed. But here she was, showing off her little kingdom, and stopping at the pig's pen she leans over and tosses this bit of food for it. I don't know exactly what happened then, but the next second she's yelling out, "Oh, my brooch! my brooch!" and is leaning way over the rail, stretching out her hand. I ran up to see what was wrong and just at that moment – oh, my God! – just at that moment she loses her balance.'

Ryllis gave a great hoot of laughter at the memory so fresh in her mind and put her hand to her face. 'Oh, poor woman,' Mrs Halley said, unable to stop herself smiling. 'What happened? Did she fall in? Don't say she fell in.'

'No, she didn't fall in,' Ryllis said. 'Unfortunately. I'd have loved it if she had, but you should have seen her none the less.' Her words were interspersed with her peals of laughter. 'Oh, you should have seen her. Talk about lack of dignity. There she was, trying to reach out for her brooch, which was down in the mire, but then suddenly the pig is there, snuffling up to her, all curious, and then she's having to push the creature away, and she gets sort of stranded over the rail, so that for a second you don't know whether she's going over or not.' Ryllis could barely speak now for laughing. With her arms she demonstrated how Mrs Lucas had lain across the bar, her hands swinging wildly. 'I tell you,' Ryllis shrieked, hardly able to get the words out, 'she couldn't get up. She looked like one of those beetles that land on their backs, their legs going every which way! I tell you, if you –'

Suddenly her words stopped, for her swinging left hand had caught the lamp a heavy blow, rocking it on its base, and sending the sound of an impact on the glass shade ringing out in the room. All laughter was forgotten in the space of the time it took for the inhabitants to gasp aloud, and all three of them turned their eyes to the lamp, Ryllis, clutching the cotton fabric to her cheek, giving a little cry and saying, 'It's broken!'

Lydia stood gazing at the lamp as if mesmerised. The same expression of horror was on Mrs Halley's face as she sat close to the lamp, one hand at her mouth. The lamp's shade was cracked from top to bottom, and it was a wonder to Lydia that it had remained in one piece.

Silence reigned in the room, silence touched only by the sounds of their breathing.

At last Lydia said, her voice almost a whisper, 'Perhaps Father won't notice it.'

'How could he miss it?' said Ryllis. 'Anyone'd be bound to see that.'

'We'll get another one,' Mrs Halley said.

'That's all very well,' Ryllis said, 'but tomorrow's Sunday. We can't get to a shop before Monday. What do I do in the meantime?'

Lydia and Ryllis were side by side in their bed. Neither was sleeping. Lydia, lying on her side, could feel the tension emanating from Ryllis's body just a foot away. They had barely spoken since getting into bed some twenty minutes before. As they lay there they heard the church clock strike ten and Lydia silently counted off the strokes. Both of them were listening.

Then, at last, there came the sound of footsteps on the cobbles beneath their window. Lydia tensed even more, lying almost rigid on the mattress, and though no whisper passed between them, she knew that Ryllis was doing the same. Lydia drew in her breath, listening even more intently. Their father had returned home.

Downstairs in the kitchen Mrs Halley also heard the sound of Mr Halley's boots in the yard, and applied herself once more to her sewing. The damaged lamp, its flame turned out, had been put on the side, and the room was lit by a smaller lamp that sat on a small table at her elbow. With the broken lamp not in plain view it was hoped that Mr Halley would not notice the damage. Then, on Monday, Lydia could buy a new shade when she went into Merinville – one that matched, if possible.

There came the sound of the back door opening, footsteps across the flags, and then Mr Halley came up the step from the scullery and entered the kitchen. Mrs Halley could see at once from the set of his mouth, from the way he moved his tense body, that things had not gone well for him. Nevertheless she felt bound to ask, 'How did it go, Father? Did you meet the gentleman you set out to see?'

He took off his hat as he spoke, and threw it down almost violently on to the shelf beside his chair. 'It didn't go well at all,' he said shortly, 'and as for that imbecile Winsford – he still wasn't anywhere in evidence by the time I returned. I had to wait a further half hour before he got in. Then it turns out that the hall isn't available after all on Monday.' He drew back his lips over his teeth. 'It meant the whole journey was for nothing.' He looked up towards the ceiling. 'Are the girls upstairs?'

'Yes, they are.'

He pulled out his chair at the head of the table and sat down. Then he bent and began to untie the laces of his boots. At once Mrs Halley got up and started towards him. 'Here – let me do it.'

He straightened, and she came to him and crouched and untied his boots and eased them off.

'I started a blister on my heel,' he said. 'That walking, that wasted effort.'

'Oh, dear. You want to bathe your foot?'

'No, I'll just rest it. It'll be all right.'

'It'll be no trouble. I'll put the kettle on.'

51

'I just told you, it'll be all right.'

She nodded. 'I'll get your slippers.'

A minute later his slippers were on his feet.

'Is there anything I can get you?' Mrs Halley said. 'You want some tea or something?'

'Yes, a cup of tea would be welcome. I should have thought you'd have the kettle on already.'

'It won't take but a few minutes. It's already filled.'

Standing at the range she moved the kettle on to the heat. As she did so he took off his jacket and hung it over the back of his chair. Then from the dresser drawer he took a notepad and a pencil.

'Are you going to start work?' Mrs Halley said. 'Aren't you tired?'

'As I walked I worked on my sermon,' he said shortly. 'I want to get it down while I think of it. While it's still fresh in my mind. At least something might be salvaged from this evening.' Then, frowning, he added, 'I can't see by this dratted useless lamp. Where's the other one?' Getting up from his chair he moved to the dresser and took the repaired lamp and brought it to the table. Then, removing the shade and the funnel he struck a match and lit the wick. After adjusting the wick and the flame he replaced the funnel and took up the shade.

It was as he moved the shade around in his hand to set it back on the base that he saw the crack. He held it up before him.

'What is the meaning of this?'

Shocked by the fury in his face, Mrs Halley stood motionless and speechless by the range.

'I asked you,' he said, 'what is the meaning of this?' He turned the shade to get a clearer view, and then took up the base with the funnel and held it closer to the shade, letting the light fall clean upon the break.

'Who did this?' he said, and when there was no answer,

said again, 'Who did this?' This time he almost screamed the words. 'Tell me! Answer me!' He slammed the shade down on to the table top, so hard that the glass shattered, sending splinters flying across the room. Mrs Halley flinched but did not move. 'Answer me,' he said grimly. 'Who did it? It wouldn't be Lydia, for she'd have owned up – she wouldn't have crept off to bed, afraid to face me.' He paused. 'Was it Amaryllis?'

No answer came, and after glaring at his wife for the briefest moment he turned and, still holding the lamp base, strode towards the door to the hall and the stairs.

'No, Father,' Mrs Halley said, and then as he turned to face her, added: 'I did it. I broke the shade.'

'You,' he said. 'You.' His teeth clenched, his breath coming in loud gasps, he burst out, 'Can't we keep anything intact in this God-forsaken house! Does everything that comes in have to be ruined?' Then, drawing back his hand to its limit he threw the lamp.

Hurled with all his force, it struck the corner of the table, the china and glass of the base and the funnel immediately breaking, sending up a showering spray of flaming paraffin.

Chapter Four

Lydia and Ryllis sat up as their mother's screams rang out into the night, then leapt from their bed and, still in their nightdresses, ran down the stairs and into the room.

The scene that met their eyes was like something out of a nightmare, something not even to be imagined in the darkest moments. The room was full of smoke, and their mother, shrieking, her clothes and hair all ablaze, was running from one end of the room to the other. As she ran she scattered furniture and anything that was in her way, as if somehow she could escape from the fire that was enveloping her. Their father, trying to put out the flames, was flapping at them with his hands, but at the same time not getting near enough to be effective. Seeing the girls enter the room he cried to Lydia, 'Get a blanket! Get a blanket!' and Lydia turned and dashed back up the stairs. In her bedroom she snatched blankets from the bed, rushed back downstairs and, without hesitating, dashed at her mother with the blanket outstretched in both hands and wrapped it around her. Then, as the flames were smothered, Mrs Halley fell back onto the window seat. When at last, certain that the fire was out, Lydia and her father pulled the blanket free, they saw that Mrs Halley's clothes were scorched and charred and that there was scarcely a hair left on her seared and blistered head.

'Father,' Lydia gasped hoarsely as the three of them stood looking down on the gravely injured woman, 'Ryllis must go and fetch Dr Harvey.'

'Yes,' Ryllis was already moving to the hall door, 'I'll get dressed and go at once.'

'It's all right,' Mr Halley said quickly, 'I'll go.'

'But Ryllis can run so fast,' Lydia said. 'She'll be there in no time.'

'I told you, I'll go,' he said. 'Besides, I'm already dressed.' He turned and looked to the window, beyond which the full moon shone down from a clear sky. 'And I shan't need the lantern; the moon's bright enough.' He looked back at the form of his wife as she lay there. 'Don't leave her,' he added. 'I'll bring back the doctor as soon as I can.'

Moments later he had gone from the house, and from the window Lydia and Ryllis glimpsed him walking quickly through the yard. As he disappeared from sight Ryllis turned and ran upstairs, to return moments later with a fresh blanket which they gently laid over their mother. She then moved back to the hall doorway. 'I'll go on upstairs and get dressed, Lyddy,' she said. 'Then when I come down you can do the same.'

While Ryllis went upstairs Lydia pulled up a chair, and sat and bent over her mother. She wanted to wrap her in her arms, but did not dare touch her for fear of causing her further hurt. 'Oh, Mother,' she murmured, leaning closer, the tears streaming down her cheeks, 'what a dreadful thing to happen.'

She did not expect her mother to respond, but Mrs Halley said haltingly, 'He – he didn't m-mean it.' The words struggled out through her cracked and blistered lips, while her eyes rolled in her head. She tried to sit up. 'Be-believe me. He didn't – mean it.'

'He didn't mean it?' Lydia felt herself go cold. 'I don't understand.'

'The l-lamp. He – didn't m-mean to hurt me. He – he . . .' Then Mrs Halley's words trailed off and her eyes closed as she sank back into her seat.

'Mother? Mother?' Lydia whispered the words, but although she could see her mother's chest rising and falling with her breathing, it was clear that she was unconscious. Lydia's hands were clutched to her face. She could do nothing but sit there, and pray that her father would soon return with the doctor.

She was sitting in the same position a few minutes later when Ryllis came hurrying downstairs, now wearing her day dress and pinafore.

'All right, Lyddy,' Ryllis said, 'I'll stay with Mother now while you go and get dressed.'

Upstairs in the bedroom, by the light of a candle, Lydia hurriedly took off her nightdress and changed into an old frock. Moments later, as she stood before the small glass and glanced at her pale reflection, she thought of the words her mother had spoken: *He didn't mean it.* The question came into her mind: *He didn't mean what?* She had no answer, and it did no good to dwell on it. Quickly she smoothed down the skirt of her dress, blew out the candle and started back down the stairs.

Dr Harvey lived on the far side of the village. Having settled down for the night, and not expecting any calls, he had hurriedly stirred himself and brought Mr Halley back to the little house in his carriage. By the time of their arrival Mrs Halley was conscious again. Lydia and Ryllis had brought more blankets for her, but she still felt cold, and when Dr Harvey appeared at her side she was lying shivering, her teeth chattering. Seeing her again, Mr Halley gave a little cry and rushed across the room.

Lydia and Ryllis stepped back as their father came to his wife's side. He knelt down, tears shining in his eyes, his face pale. 'Oh, Emmie,' he murmured. He groped for her hand for a moment and, taking it, said, 'I've brought Dr Harvey, Emmie. He'll soon have you right again.'

He released his wife's hand, straightened and stepped aside. At once Dr Harvey was there, taking a seat on the kitchen chair that Lydia had placed for him, and bending to the woman.

As the doctor ministered to her and took in the extent of her injuries he murmured comforting little words. Then he said softly, sympathetically, 'Oh, dear, this was an unfortunate accident, Mrs Halley, wasn't it?'

'Y-yes,' Mrs Halley stuttered. 'I was c-careless.'

The doctor gave a little nod. 'So it seems,' he said kindly. 'Lamps can be such dangerous things – all that paraffin.' Then turning to Mr Halley at his side, he added directly, 'Very unfortunate indeed, but it's so easily done.' He gave a sigh. 'It's a bad business. Dropping a lamp like that. I've had other cases. Burning paraffin – it can be truly dreadful.'

The doctor stayed some time longer at the house. At one time he spoke of Mrs Halley being moved to the cottage hospital at Hurstleigh but she would have none of it. She would remain where she was, she insisted, and rely on the care of her husband and daughters.

After he had done what he could for her, and given her a little chloral to deaden the pain and help her to sleep, the doctor said he would leave, but would return in the morning. Mr Halley saw him to the door, where he asked him quietly how he judged his wife's injuries.

The doctor looked grave. They were very serious, he said, and it would aid her greatly if she could be persuaded to go into the hospital.

When he returned just after eleven the next morning to see his patient he found that she had died less than an hour before.

It had not rained in several days, but on the morning of the funeral the clouds, which had gathered during the night, opened and let fall the threatened downpour.

Lydia and Ryllis, the tears streaming from their eyes, stood at the low-curtained window of the parlour and watched as the small funeral cortège moved away from the house, the umbrellas of the mourners opened up against the falling rain.

Even after the short procession had passed along the lane out of sight, they remained at the window. Victorian manners generally frowned on females being present at a funeral graveside, and so the sisters remained behind. Never having been to a funeral, they had to rely on magazine illustrations and paintings and verbal accounts to have any idea of what went on. Certainly they had their imaginations, and in Lydia's mind's eye she saw her father standing at the graveside along with the other mourners, and could almost hear the raindrops drumming on the black domes of their umbrellas. Would the sound drown out the words of the Reverend Hepthaw as he delivered his melancholy address over their mother's coffin? Lydia could see her father as clearly as if he were beside her, standing with straight back and head bent, the muscle in his jaw working in a steady, rhythmic movement, his eyes swimming with tears behind his steel-rimmed spectacles. What would go through his mind? Would he be focused solely on the loss of his wife or was a part of him judging and criticising the words of the Reverend Hepthaw?

Lydia could scarcely believe that it was all happening. Was it only just over a week ago that she and Ryllis and her mother had been sitting over their teacups while Ryllis had so amused them with anecdotes from her life with the Lucases? Surely it wasn't possible. Surely the whole horrific story could not be real.

When their father and the handful of mourners returned to the house after the funeral Lydia and Ryllis served them tea and sandwiches and cake. Then, when the platters were empty and the visitors had gone, the two sisters changed back into their everyday dresses and pinafores and carried the dishes into the scullery where they washed and dried them. In the meantime their father sat in the front parlour, warming himself over the remains of the fire.

'Well,' Ryllis said as she wiped her hands, 'I suppose tomorrow I'll have to set off back for Barford again.'

'I wish you didn't have to go,' Lydia said.

'Yes, I too wish that I didn't have to go, but there's nothing for it. Now that the funeral's done I've no reason for staying away. Mind you, even though it was for a funeral I'm sure the Lucases resent my absence.'

Lydia gave a sigh. 'I wish I were leaving here as well.'

'You mustn't think about that,' Ryllis said. 'You'll be needed here at home even more now. You won't be able to think about getting a job in Redbury or anyplace. Not now. Father won't be able to manage without you.'

'Maybe he'll have to.' Lydia lowered her voice with her words and looked towards the door. 'While you were upstairs changing,' she said, 'Mother said something to me.'

'When I was upstairs? What are you talking about?'

'On the night when she was so badly burned. Father went for the doctor and you and I were here with her. You went upstairs to change out of your nightdress –'

'Yes . . . what about it?'

'While you were gone Mother said something.'

'What? Said what?'

Lydia took a deep breath and looked again towards the door. Then, her voice falling to little more than a whisper, she said, 'She couldn't speak very well, but she said to me, "*He didn't mean it.*" She was talking about Father, of course.'

'But what – what did she mean by that?'

'I don't know, but it was to do with Father and the lamp.'

Ryllis put her hands to her cheeks, her blue eyes wide. 'Oh, Lyddy . . .'

Lydia stood for a moment or two in silence, then said firmly, 'But it does no good to guess at things, to conjecture. We have to put it behind us. Whatever happened, it must have been a – it must have been an accident.'

Ryllis returned to Barford the day after the funeral, and following her departure Lydia felt that she was going around in a daze. Not only was there her grief over her mother, but she also had to face her father, at which times she could not help but wonder what had been behind her mother's words.

Nothing, however, was said between them for some days, until one evening when he came into the kitchen to find her sitting silent and alone, her head bowed, the tears damp on her cheeks.

'I know how you're feeling,' he said gruffly. Then a long pause went by and he added, 'We must . . . help one another.'

She could not bring herself to speak, nor to look at him, and, gazing down at the floor, merely gave a brief nod.

'I came to find you,' he said after a moment. 'I wanted to give you this.'

She looked at him now, opening her eyes and raising her glance to him. He was standing before her, holding something. Lying on his palm she saw her mother's watch, a little gold half-hunter that she had rarely carried, but had always treasured.

'You must have it,' he said. 'She'd want you to have it.'

'Oh, Father . . .'

As she moved to take it he drew his hand back again and held the watch up before his eyes. For a moment Lydia could see it reflected in the lenses of his spectacles.

'I gave her this,' he said. 'The day after she promised to marry me. We went into Redbury together and bought it. She was so thrilled, so excited.' He carefully opened the watch, looked closely at the face for a second or two, then held it to his ear, cocking his head slightly as he listened. 'It has a whispering little tick,' he said. He held it out again at arm's length. 'Yes, take it. She would want you to have it. I too.'

He laid the watch on the open palm of her hand and then bent her fingers over it. Lydia felt the pressure of his fingers on hers for a moment, then lowered her hand. As she did so he turned away, and she saw the slump of his shoulders, the drooping of his head.

'Father,' she said, 'are you all right?'

He did not turn to her, and she could not see his face, but she heard his quick, indrawn breath, and then his words, gruff in his throat:

'*I* did it.'

'Father –'

'*I* did it,' he said again. 'I threw the lamp. She didn't drop it. I threw it.'

Lydia could feel her heart beating in her chest. She did not speak. She did not know what to say. Then he turned to face her, and she could see the glisten of tears in his eyes as he gazed into her own.

'It hit the table,' he said. 'It hit the table and – and just – just exploded. I didn't mean it.' He put his hands up to his face and bent his head. 'I was in such a temper – such a rage. It happened in a second. Like a coward I – I led the doctor to think that she'd – dropped it, the lamp, but she didn't.'

Lydia said, 'Oh, but – but it was an accident.'

'Yes,' he said hoarsely. 'It was an accident.' He lowered his hands and added, looking off towards the darkened window, 'I can see the images in my mind all the time. I can't get rid of them.'

He turned away from her then, and without another word went from the room. Lydia watched him go, the little watch clasped warm in her hand.

*

The May morning was pleasant and warm, and Ryllis had enjoyed an errand to the village post office. Not only had it given her the opportunity to be out in the spring air, but it had also taken her away from the house for a while. Now, however, she was on her way back to The Laurels, and her little time of freedom would soon be over.

A part of her way took her beside a small thicket where rooks nested in great numbers, and suddenly, as she passed beneath a tree, she was startled by something falling close to her shoulder. She jumped back a little in shock, thinking that perhaps something had been thrown at her. She looked down to see what it was, and there on the ground near the tree's roots she saw a baby bird. After looking at it for a moment, she bent, peering closer. The bird was a rook, obviously having come from one of the many nests above.

'What's wrong? Is anything the matter?'

She started at the voice, and turned to see a young man standing a couple of yards away. She had not heard his approach. He was of middle height, with brown hair and dark eyes, and looked to be around eighteen or nineteen. He wore a cap, with a tweed jacket and dark corduroy trousers.

'It's a baby rook,' she said to him, and added, 'It gave me a bit of a start. It fell down right beside me as I was walking along.'

The young man stooped, looking at the bird. It lay on its back, its half-feathered wings trembling.

'It's been chucked out of the nest,' he said.

'But why?'

'The parent birds will do this to their young – if there's something wrong with 'em.'

She had heard of such things but had never been close to it before. 'Oh,' she said, 'it seems too cruel.'

'Well, that's nature's way. What's the point of the parent

birds spending all their energy getting food for a chick if it's not going to live? So that's what they do. I guess they can tell right enough if there's something really wrong – and they get rid of it. Push it out. All the food has to go on the ones that are healthy. Makes sense, really, if you think about it.'

Ryllis nodded. 'Yes – but at the same time it does seem very cruel.'

'Like I said, it's nature's way.' He bent closer still to the bird. 'Look at it, its legs are all deformed.'

Ryllis stooped, bending closer, and now she could see clearly what the young man indicated. The chick's legs were twisted up to its body, its claws clenched in tight little knots.

'That would never survive a day,' the young man said, 'even if it got so far as getting out of the nest.'

'No – I suppose not.' She frowned. 'So there's no way of – of saving it, is there?'

'Not a chance.' He shook his head. 'For a start you wouldn't know what to feed it on. They don't eat just any old thing, you know. They have special foods at different times in their rearing. The parents know what to bring 'em, but you don't and I don't. No, you can't save this little creature. It'll die whatever you try to do for it.'

'Oh, but – can't we do anything at all? I hate to see it just lying there. Trembling like that.'

He said without hesitation, 'Best thing to do would be to put it out of its misery. Put an end to its suffering.'

'We should – kill it?' she said.

'It'd be the best thing, the kindest thing.'

She shook her head, giving a little shudder. 'I couldn't do it. Oh, I couldn't do it.'

'I'll do it, don't worry.'

She stood there then, while he stepped away, bending over the ground, and watched as he selected a large stone.

63

He came back to her side and stood over the stricken bird.

'You don't have to look,' he said.

'No.' She had already turned her face away.

She closed her eyes tightly and then heard a slight thud as the stone struck.

'It's all right,' she heard him say. 'It's done.'

Still she could not open her eyes.

'It's all right,' he said again. 'It's dead.'

May gave way to June, and the summer months came blazing in. During the days Lydia saw little of her father, for at Cremson's he was down on the factory floor while she was in the office with her two male colleagues, surrounded by ledgers, receipts and bills and other paperwork. In the evenings, however, it was a different matter. Unless she was visiting Evie, or he was out in connection with his preaching, they were thrown together.

Lydia washed and cooked for the two of them, but as they sat over the meals she prepared she could barely think of words to keep a conversation going. They had never had a lot to say to one another, and now, with the loss of her mother, Lydia became more and more aware of her restlessness and the need in her to change her scene.

It could not last, and as she sat with Evie in her little kitchen one Sunday afternoon she confided that she had taken steps to change her situation.

'I've written off to Seager's,' Lydia said. 'I posted the letter yesterday afternoon.'

'Well,' Evie said, 'you threatened to, and that was before you lost your mam.'

In their conversation the two young women were keeping their voices low, for Hennie lay curled up on the sofa, sleeping under the cover of a small rug. Evie sat beside her.

'Yes, well, now I'm even more determined to go,' Lydia

said. 'I need to get away, and now that Mother's gone there's no reason for me to stay on.'

'But why d'you have to move out of the village? Surely you could find something close by.'

'I have to move away. I just don't want to stay here.'

'Have you told your dad?'

'No, not yet.'

'When will you tell him?'

'I don't know, but he has to know soon.'

A letter came from Seager's a week later, arriving on a Friday, and was waiting for Lydia when she got in from work that evening. Her father, who was working late at the factory, knew nothing of it.

Lydia sat in the kitchen and read it through. A brief letter, it thanked her for her application and invited her for an interview.

At once she got pen and ink and paper, and sat down to write back that she would be pleased to be there at the appointed time. After that she wrote a letter to her sister:

> The Whitehouse
> 13th June 1890

My dear Ryllis,

Thank you for yours of the 9th. I'm glad to know you're continuing well. This is just a quick note – no time to write more – to tell you that I am to be in Redbury on the morning of Saturday, 21st of June. I have secured an appointment at Seager's the department store at twelve o'clock. I know that you sometimes visit Redbury on a Saturday on errands for Mrs Lucas, so I'm wondering if you might be coming into town on that day and, if so, whether we can meet and have some tea or coffee. It would be lovely to see you. If you can, then I suggest we meet in the little teashop beside Peacock's tobacconist in Regency Street. I'll make sure of being there at one-thirty, by which time my interview should be long over. Please write back at once and let me know if you can manage it. And even if you're not sure as yet whether you can get into Redbury on that day, I'll still go to the teashop in the hope of seeing you.

In your letter you hinted at having some good news for me. Well, I hope it is, and that when we meet you'll be able to tell me more.

I can say nothing further now, as I want to take this to the post. I am, as always

Your loving sister

Lyddy

Ryllis replied almost by return to say that it wasn't possible for her to plan ahead as regards going into Redbury, for Mrs Lucas never let her know more than a day before whether she would be required to go. However, she wrote, if she should be sent into the town she would do her very best to be there at the teashop at one-thirty as Lydia suggested.

On the day Ryllis's letter arrived, Mr Halley had gone straight from the Merinville coach into the village on an errand, and Lydia had reached home before him and found Ryllis's letter lying on the mat in the hall. As she sat reading it in the window seat rain began to fall. Minutes later her father came hurrying past the window and turned in at the back door.

As he came up the step from the scullery there was a flash of lightning and then the growling of thunder sounded in the distance. The rain teemed down, bouncing up off the cobbles in the yard.

'There you are.' He came into the kitchen and found Lydia still sitting at the window. 'You were lucky. You got in before the rain started.' He took off his hat, shook the water from it and laid it down on the table. The pitting of the rain sounded heavy on the window pane.

'I see you've got a letter,' he said, nodding towards the letter and envelope in Lydia's hands.

'Yes,' she said. 'It's from Ryllis.'

'Oh, yes? And how is she?'

'She's well.' A moment of hesitation, then she added, 'I'm hoping to see her in Redbury on Saturday.'

He said nothing to this for a moment, but just looked at her from where he stood beside the table. Then he said, a falsely casual tone in his voice, 'Mr McCabe mentioned to me that you're not going into work on Saturday morning. Says you've asked for the day off.'

'Yes, that's so.'

An awkward little smile touched his mouth. 'Something's come up that must be very important, I should think – for you to take time off and lose the pay.' He gave a short chuckle. 'Unless you just want a holiday and can afford to forfeit the money.'

'No,' she said, 'I can ill afford to lose the money, as you well know, but I have to have the day off work.'

She volunteered nothing further, and he stood there, waiting, as if it were only a matter of time before she explained herself. He said at last, 'So – is it something vital – or is it something to do with your sister? Is she in some kind of trouble?'

'No, it's nothing to do with Amaryllis. She's not in any trouble.'

'Well, that's something, then. That girl could exercise the patience of a saint.' He began to take off his jacket. Frowning, he said, 'Lydia, there's something up. What is it? What is it you're not telling me?'

67

'It's not a secret, Father,' she said. Then, taking a breath she plunged in. 'I'm going after another situation.'

'What?' His brow creased in puzzlement, as if he had misheard her.

'I'm going after another post. Away from Cremson's.'

'Away from Cremson's.' He repeated the words flatly; it was not a question. 'But where will you go? What else is there in Merinville?'

'I'm not thinking of Merinville.'

He frowned. 'Where, then? Hurstleigh? Go *too* far and you'll spend all your time travelling – and if you're travelling for hours every day it'll mean we'll have to get someone in to cook and clean for us, won't it? It's not going to be like Merinville and back every day, and you'll soon get tired of it, mark my words.'

'I don't plan to do that.' She had been skirting the subject all the time. Now she said, 'Father, I'm going away. To live.'

'Away? To live?' There was incredulity in his voice, and he looked at her with his mouth slightly open. 'What are you talking about? How can you go away? This is your home.'

'I've applied for a post at Seager's in Redbury.'

He looked stunned, frowning, standing there facing her while the rain lashed down behind her.

'So it's not *definite* you're going, then,' he said after a moment. 'I mean, you haven't got the job yet?'

'No, but if I don't get one at Seager's I shall go after something else.'

He was staring at her, his mouth slightly open. In a tight, stilted voice he said, 'You're going away from home. You're leaving home.'

She nodded. 'Yes.' She could hear the rain on the window. When she looked at his hands she could see that the knuckles were pale.

'I don't know what to say,' he said.

'I shall be back to see you very frequently. You can depend on that.'

'I see.' His tone was different now. 'I don't want any kindnesses from you. I don't want to have my daughter patronise me.'

'I wasn't. Oh, please, Father, I wasn't.'

Silence again, then he said gruffly, 'Why are you going? That's what I'd like to know. Are you so desperate to get away?'

She could not answer.

'It's because of your mother,' he said. 'Losing your mother like that, so suddenly. It must affect a daughter. You're not thinking straight.'

Lydia said after a moment, 'Well, whatever it is, Father, I just know I have to go.'

He nodded. 'Well, you go ahead, then. You'll soon find out that the city streets are full of failures who've gone there to better themselves, and you'll be one of them, you'll see.'

'I sincerely hope not, Father.'

'I still don't understand it,' he said. 'Why you need to go.'

'I'm twenty-one years old,' she said, 'and I know it isn't much of a change just to go to Redbury, but it's a change of sorts, and perhaps it will enable me to discover what I want to do with myself, with my life. Because at present I've got no idea at all.

'And if you don't – discover what you want to do?'

She shrugged. 'I don't know – but I've got to try.'

Chapter Five

Lydia was up early on the morning of the 21st and leaving the house to catch the coach to Merinville. She wore her grey dress, with a dark flannel mantle that she had finished making just a few days earlier. In recognition of her continuing mourning for her mother, she had put a little black crêpe on her dress and also on her black straw hat.

On the previous day she had heard from Ryllis, who still had no idea whether or not she would be required to go shopping into the town on the Saturday morning, but was still in hopes that it would happen.

Mr Halley, up very early as usual, had barely spoken to Lydia over breakfast. He knew where she was going, but he remained silent on the subject. Lydia had said to him the previous evening that she was hoping to meet Ryllis while in Redbury, and left the statement open, inviting him to say something, but he had ignored the words. She could not be sure of the reason for his silence. Was he sulking or was he just deeply hurt? She had tried several times to instigate a conversation but he would have none of it, answering her merely with monosyllables or brief sentences that closed any avenues that might have led to an opening between them. Later, when she had left the house to walk to the Rising Sun, from where she was to take the coach, he had barely responded to her brief words of goodbye.

Sitting on the coach, she tried to put all negative thoughts out of her head. He would probably come round, though there was no guarantee of it. She had observed him for enough years to know that he was totally unpredictable where some things were concerned. Still, that was something that only time would deal with, and now she must concentrate on the matter in hand, that of her forthcoming interview with Mr Donovan, the employment manager whom she was to see at twelve o'clock.

She got to Merinville just before ten, and from the station took the train to Redbury, arriving well before eleven. There in the crowded, busy town she passed a little time in a small coffee shop and then made her way to Seager's. She was still early, so she spent a while wandering through the store. She had never realised quite how vast it was. Set on three floors, it seemed to offer everything that one could possibly need in life, and she moved from department to department looking around her in continuing amazement at the variety of goods on display.

Eventually, though, the time approached for her interview, and after making enquiries she left the shop proper and made her way to the top floor, where the offices were situated. Here there were low ceilinged-rooms, and the atmosphere of the place was busy in quite a different way.

Stepping out of the lift, she came to a small office in a foyer, and was directed along a corridor with offices on either side. Some of the doors were open and inside she could see people at desks, writing with pens or at typewriting machines.

At the end of the corridor she stopped outside a closed door and knocked. It was answered almost at once by a tall young man in a grey suit.

'Miss Halley?' he said, smiling at her.

Lydia nodded, 'Yes,' and smiled nervously back at him.

'I'm terribly sorry,' he said, 'but Mr Donovan's been called away on an urgent matter. We had no way of letting you know, I'm afraid. I do apologise.'

Lydia didn't know what to say, and merely nodded again.

'Your appointment was at twelve,' the young man continued. 'Mr Donovan asks whether it's possible for you to come back at one o'clock. Or if that's not convenient perhaps you'd prefer to come back another day.'

'Oh, no. No, I don't want to leave it for another day,' Lydia said at once. 'No – I'll come back at one.'

'Mr Donovan's terribly sorry about it. Are you sure it's all right?'

'Yes, perfectly. I'll come back later.'

'If you'd prefer to stay here,' he said, 'there's a small waiting room along the corridor.' He gestured with his hand.

'No, that's all right, thank you. I'll go for a walk and come back at one.'

He thanked her, and she thanked him, and she turned and made her way along the corridor. As she rode down in the lift, she wondered what she should do about Ryllis, who might well be on her way from Barford now, and before too long she would be making her way to the teashop, expecting Lydia to join her. At that time, if all went as planned, Lydia could be just about finished with her interview. With luck, she thought, she could get to the teashop without keeping Ryllis waiting too long.

Now, with almost another hour to kill, she wandered around the store again and then had a cup of coffee that she did not want in the small coffee shop on one of the upper floors. Then, when it was time, she got the lift back to the top floor. There, after letting the young man know that she had returned, she moved along to the waiting area indicated by him and sat down with a magazine.

One o'clock came and went and still she was not called for her interview, but then at last she heard footsteps approaching, and the young man was coming towards her with an apologetic expression on his face.

'Miss Halley,' he said, 'oh, I'm so sorry. Mr Donovan was delayed longer than he'd foreseen. He's only just got back into the office. If you'd like to come along now he'll be very happy to see you.'

Lydia, much relieved, thanked him, rose, and picked up her basket and bag.

'This way, please.' He led the way, and Lydia followed him back into the corridor to the door which she had earlier knocked upon. She followed him inside and he showed her to an imposing desk behind which sat a middle-aged man with grey hair.

'This is Miss Halley,' the young man said, and the older man got to his feet, shook Lydia's hand and invited her to sit.

As the young man left the room, Mr Donovan took his chair behind the desk again. 'Miss Halley,' he said, 'I'm most dreadfully sorry to have kept you waiting. Unfortunately something came up and I was quite obliged to leave the office for a while. I do hope it hasn't inconvenienced you too much.'

Lydia assured him that it had not.

'I'm glad to hear it,' he said. 'Time is precious for everyone.' He smiled at her, and clasped his hands before him. 'And we want to get off on the right foot, don't we?'

She smiled back, and felt that she might begin to relax a little.

Stepping smartly through the streets, she headed for the little teashop where she and Ryllis had hoped to meet. It was now past two o'clock. The interview had gone on longer than she had anticipated, and she had only just been released from it. She could not believe that Ryllis would still be waiting. Surely she would have got tired and given up long before this time.

Lydia turned through the square, passed into one of the

73

side streets, and eventually came to the teashop. Moments later she was inside and looking around. As she had feared, there was no sign of Ryllis – but in any case, there was no knowing whether Ryllis had even managed to get into Redbury today in the first place. After a few seconds' hesitation Lydia approached a woman behind the counter.

'Yes, miss?' the woman said. 'What can we get for you?'

'I had arranged to meet my sister here,' Lydia said. 'She's sixteen, a little shorter than I, dark-haired, pretty . . .'

'Oh, yes, miss,' the woman nodded. 'I know who you mean. She was in a while ago. Had two cups o' tea and then left. Wearing a dark blue cape and a black straw bonnet with crêpe trimming.'

'Yes, that would be her,' Lydia said, and added, 'I don't suppose she said anything to you before she went?'

'No, miss, she just up and left.'

Lydia thanked her and went outside on to the street again, where she stood with the pedestrians moving around her. From here she was able to see the town hall clock. It was a quarter past two. She had no idea what to do, and after a minute of standing there she set off, wandering through the streets, looking around her.

During her meanderings, constantly on the lookout for any sign of Ryllis, she stopped to make a couple of purchases. The first was on seeing punnets of strawberries on sale at a stall in the square. She decided to buy some for her father, who was very fond of them. He had tried on occasions to grow them over the years, but had always lost out to the slugs and the birds. Her second purchase was at a secondhand book stall, where for twopence she bought a little book of Lord Byron's poems.

Then, after well over half an hour of wandering she came to a stop. She was getting nowhere. During her search she had even returned once to the teashop, just in case Ryllis had decided to go back there, but, as she expected, there was no sign of her, and by all accounts she had not been back in the meantime. Lydia now began to wonder whether Ryllis might have decided to return to Barford. In which case she, Lydia, might go on searching for ever.

At one side of the main square was set a little garden, like an oasis. It had within its confines a white marble drinking fountain, and a decorative archway of thatch, while a cascading laburnum tree cast shade over a couple of old wooden benches. Lydia hesitated for a moment, and then went into the garden and sat down in the cool shade of the tree, setting beside her on the bench her bag and basket. The sun was strong in a cloudless sky, and the day had become extremely warm. There was just one couple besides herself there, and she was glad of the peace and the chance to rest as she watched the pedestrians moving back and forth about the square. From here she had a good view, and should be able to see Ryllis if she happened to walk by.

The minutes passed. From a nearby tower a clock struck the hour of three. The sun shining through the laburnum threw a dappled shadow over the bench and the flags below, and Lydia continued to sit there. The elderly couple got up and moved away into the square. After a little further rest, Lydia told herself, she would take one more meander through the main streets of the town, and then, if there was still no sign of Ryllis she would give up looking.

As she sat gazing out she became aware of a shadow moving on her left and, turning, she saw the figure of a tall man carrying a briefcase moving into her line of vision. He stepped to the fountain, briefly put his hand into the stream of water, shook it, and then wiped it dry with a blue chequered handkerchief. As he put the handkerchief in his pocket he moved to the other bench close by and sat down. Lydia moved her gaze back to face the square. Another five minutes, she told herself, and she would get up and resume her search.

All at once she was distracted in her thoughts by a wasp that came hovering over the basket with the strawberries, and she flapped out at it with her hand. The unwelcome creature flew away, but unfortunately her fingers caught the handle, and the next second the basket was tipping over and falling off the bench, spilling the book and the strawberries onto the flags.

Even as she gave a little gasp of surprise, there came an exclamation from the man, and he was at once rising and stepping towards her.

'Here – let me help you.' Stooping low, he began picking up the strawberries and replacing them in the little punnet. Lydia thanked him, and between them in a few moments they had rescued the fruit. 'They'll be perfectly all right once they've been washed,' the man said. He had a light, warm voice, with no immediate discernible accent of the West country. Lydia thanked him for his kindness, and he touched his bowler hat to her and said he was glad to be of service.

He still held in his hand her little book of poems, and now he said, 'D'you mind . . .?' and glanced at its spine to read the title. 'Poems of Lord Byron,' he said. Then added, 'Or is it the *Bad* Lord Byron: mad, bad, and dangerous to know?'

'Perhaps not so bad,' Lydia said. 'My father called him a man without a soul. But how can a man who wrote such beautiful things be without a soul?'

The man opened the book, turned the pages and then read:

> *'So, we'll go no more a-roving*
> *So late into the night,*
> *Though the heart be still as loving,*
> *And the moon be still as bright . . .'*

He closed the book and handed it to her. 'Oh, I think he had a soul,' he said.

Lydia placed the book in her basket beside the strawberries, then looked back at the man. He must be in his mid-twenties, she thought. His smile was warm, showing white, even teeth. He had dark brown hair, and grey eyes that looked steadily back at her. He wore a formal looking suit of charcoal grey with a fine, pale grey pinstripe.

Suddenly conscious of his returning glance, she was aware that she was staring, and quickly she looked away and off into the throng of pedestrians moving about their business.

'Are you looking for someone?' the man asked.

'Yes,' she said. 'My sister. We'd planned to meet here in Redbury, but I was late and we missed one another. Consequently, neither of us knows now where the other one is.'

'Oh, dear. What shall you do if you can't find one another?'

'Well,' she said, 'I shall just have to give up and go on home, and so, I suppose, will Ryllis.'

'Did you come into Redbury especially to see her?'

'No. I had to come in on business, but as my sister sometimes has to come in here on a Saturday to do shopping it seemed like a good opportunity for us to meet for a cup of tea. We don't get many chances.'

'May I ask where you've come from?'

'Capinfell.'

'Ah, yes.' He nodded. 'I know of it, though I've never actually been there. Beyond Merinville, isn't it?'

'Yes.' She turned her head, once again looking about her.

'Where did you arrange to meet?' he asked.

'At a small teashop in Regency Street. The trouble is, I was so late getting there, she must have given up waiting.

She'll probably have done what I've been doing – gone walking around the place, looking. It's such a shame, for she can't always get away. Now I don't know *what* to do. She might well have started back to Barford by now.'

Neither spoke for a few moments, then he said, 'Did you get your business completed here?'

'I beg your pardon? Oh, yes, I did, thank you.' She gave another distracted sigh. 'What am I going to do? This is so foolish. Should I stay in one place or start wandering around again? I suppose I could try the teashop one last time.' She gave a little chuckle. 'I'm quite lost, it seems.'

'It's always a good idea,' he said, 'to have one special place to go to.'

'I – I'm sorry?'

'What I mean is, perhaps you don't have to be lost, but if you are lost, then it's as well to have a special place to run to.'

'Oh?' she said.

'And for a start,' he added, 'a place where a loved one would know where to look.'

She nodded, smiling. 'And what kind of place would that be?'

'It doesn't really matter. Though it'd probably be as well to choose a place where you can wait in comfort.' He looked around them. 'This place would do as well as any other – even if the weather's bad, I should think. If it rains you could always duck under the little thatch there.'

'Yes, I suppose so.'

He shook his head. 'It's a shame you've missed your sister. What did you say her name is?'

'Ryllis. Amaryllis. Oh, and I was so looking forward to seeing her today.' She looked up at the blue sky. 'It's such a beautiful day. I thought we might buy some sandwiches and tea or lemonade and have a little bite in the park or somewhere.'

'Well, it'd be a perfect day for it, but so it should be.'

'Why's that?'

'Well, today is the 21st, the longest day of the year.'

'Oh – yes. Yes, of course.'

'Don't you think that's special?' He nodded. 'I do. Only good things should happen today. And –'

He broke off, for suddenly Lydia was rising from her seat, looking out into the square.

'Ryllis!'

She took a step forward as Ryllis came hurrying towards her out of the throng.

'Oh, Lyddy!' Ryllis carried a large, full basket over her arm. 'Oh, what a relief, Lyddy,' she said. 'I thought I'd never find you.'

The two sisters embraced. 'And I'd just about given up too,' Lydia said as they drew apart. 'I thought surely you must be on your way back to Barford by now.'

'I almost was. What happened? I waited for ages in the teashop.'

'I'm afraid my interview got postponed,' Lydia said. 'Anyway . . .' She turned now to the man, who stood nearby watching the reunion. 'Thank you so much,' she said to him, and then, 'Sir, I'm afraid I don't know your name.'

'My name is Guy,' he said. 'Guy Anderson.' He smiled, taking in Ryllis. 'And quite obviously this is the missing young lady.'

Lydia said, smiling, 'Yes, this is my sister, Ryllis Halley. And I'm Lydia. Lydia Halley.'

He shook their hands, then said with a self-satisfied smile, 'Well, you see, Miss Halley, I was right, wasn't I?'

'You were right?' Lydia said. 'What about?'

'About choosing a special spot, in case you ever find yourself lost.'

Lydia said, turning to Ryllis, 'Mr Anderson says one should always have a special place, in case one ever loses

79

one's way. That way, a loved one will always know where to look. He chose this place.' She gave a little laugh as she turned to him. 'It looks like you're right, Mr Anderson. Perhaps you've got secret powers.'

He chuckled. 'Perhaps I do. It works for homing pigeons, and it worked for you two, didn't it?'

The three laughed together, then the man said, 'Well, I mustn't keep you ladies. I understand that you, Miss Ryllis, have to go to Barford.'

'Yes,' Ryllis said, 'and I haven't long before I must start back.'

'Then I shall leave you to your picnic or whatever you plan to do.' He picked up his briefcase, touched a hand to his hat. 'And I'll wish you a good day.' He gave a little smiling nod to each of them in turn, and as Lydia and Ryllis said their goodbyes, turned and stepped away.

Standing side by side the two sisters watched as he moved off among the people, as his figure diminished and vanished in the distance.

'Well,' Ryllis said, 'how did you meet *him*?' There was a definite note of approval in her voice.

'Oh – he just came by while I was sitting here catching my breath.'

'Very handsome,' Ryllis said.

Lydia heard herself say, 'D'you think so?'

'I do – and I'm sure you must do too. How could you not?'

Lydia ignored this last remark and, changing the subject, said, 'Well, what shall we do?'

'I'll have to start back by four,' Ryllis said. 'Which doesn't give us long. Even so it'll be remarked on, my being late. Still – can't be helped. If I get told off, I get told off.' She gestured across the square. 'We'll go to that teashop, shall we?'

The teashop was busy and noisy, but it was close by.

They managed to find seats inside where it was cool, and there ordered from the maid glasses of lemonade, and for Ryllis a small slice of game pie.

'Well,' Ryllis said, giving a contented sign, 'here we are at last.' Then, leaning forward across the table, she said, 'So – tell me how your interview went at Seager's.'

'Oh, it went very well,' Lydia said, a note of excitement in her voice. 'The employment manager, Mr Donovan, was extremely pleasant, and he told me a lot about the store, and the goods they sell. Oh, it's a marvellous place, Ryllis, just marvellous. I never realised it was quite so vast. Of course I've been in there occasionally over the years, but – oh, you just can't have an idea. That store sells just about everything that a person could wear or carry.'

'Yes, I know. I take it, then, that you've been offered a position.'

'I have.' Lydia gave a breathless little laugh. 'I showed Mr Donovan my reference from Cremson's and he seemed to think it was very satisfactory. He spoke of vacancies in several situations.'

'What will you be doing, then?'

'Well, I told him I'd prefer to be in one of the offices behind the scenes, rather than out serving customers in the shop proper. So – I've been offered a position in the postal order room. They have such a huge volume of orders coming in by post for the different goods, and they need a great many staff to keep up with it all. Mr Donovan says there're over fifty clerks dealing with the postal side of the business.'

'Over fifty!'

'Yes, they're that busy.'

The maid brought their order at this point, and they sipped at their drinks and Ryllis took a mouthful of her pie. Then, looking up over her glass, Ryllis said, 'When do you start, Lyddy – at Seager's?'

'Well, I have to give my fortnight's notice in at Cremson's, which I'll do on Monday.' She gave a little shrug. 'So I guess I can start in two weeks. Oh, there'll be so much to do in that time. For one thing I'll have to find myself some lodgings. Mr Donovan got one of his clerks to give me the names and addresses of a few landladies who are looking for respectable people.' She tapped her bag. 'I've got a list of them, so that's what I want to settle before I start back to Capinfell.'

Ryllis raised her eyebrows a little. 'I wonder what Father will say to all this.'

'I can't imagine. Though he knows the worst of it now, and he's barely talking to me as it is.'

'Well,' Ryllis said, 'he'll get used to the idea in time, particularly once you've gone, but it might not be easy in the meantime.'

Lydia shook her head and frowned. 'Yes, I know, but – oh, let's not talk about that. I don't want to think about it.' Then, her brow clearing, she said, 'What about you, little sister? Enough about me. What's been happening to you? How are you getting along at The Laurels?'

'Oh, about the same.' Screwing up her pink mouth, Ryllis added, 'Nothing seems to change there, more's the pity.'

'Oh, but you somehow seemed a little – happier when you wrote. In your letter to me you hinted at having something to tell me. Something good. Wasn't that so?'

And now Ryllis smiled. 'Well, yes. I *have* got something to tell you, and it *is* something good, I think.'

'Well?' Lydia waited.

Ryllis finished the last of her pie and pushed the plate aside. 'I met someone,' she said.

'Oh?'

'Yes, I was returning from the post office in Barford last month, and – I met someone.'

Lydia took a sip from her glass and waited.

Ryllis went on, 'There was a bird, fallen out of its nest. A baby rook. Well, not fallen out of the nest, but tossed out by the parents. It landed right by me as I was walking along beneath the trees. It gave me a little start; I wondered what it could be. And then . . .' she smiled again now, 'then this young man came along, just as I was looking at the bird, and he said we should take pity on it and put it out of its misery, and kill the poor thing.' She shrugged. 'So – that's what he did. He got this big stone and – and killed it.' She gave a little shudder. 'Oh, *I* couldn't have done it.' She took up her glass, found it empty and set it down again. 'Anyway, his name is Thomas Bissett.' She smiled again. 'He's eighteen, and he lives in Barford. His father's a farmer, but not some little farm – quite a big affair, with lots of land and quite a grand house, too.'

Lydia smiled. 'Well, you kept that little secret to yourself.'

Ryllis smiled. 'Yes. I don't know how. I so wanted to write to you all about it.' She frowned. 'D'you think it's all right, Lyddy?'

'What d'you mean, all right?'

'Well, you know – what with Mother having just died in March and . . . Well, I mean, there I am, finding some – well, some happiness. Perhaps it doesn't seem quite right. Coming so soon.'

'Oh, Ryllis, don't think like that.' Lydia put out her hand and pressed Ryllis's wrist. 'Mother would want you to be happy. If you really like this young man, I mean, and it seems you do.'

'Oh, yes, I do. Oh, I really do, Lyddy.'

'Tell me more about him. Is he nice looking?'

'Oh, yes, he is. He's a good bit taller than me. He's got brown hair and brown eyes – and he smiles a lot – which is very nice. He's been working in London with his uncle. London, imagine!'

'Have you had the chance to meet much?'

'Not a lot, but it's something to look forward to when we get the chance. Oh, Lyddy, I like him so much, and it makes working for the Lucases almost bearable.'

'Well, that's saying something. So do I gather that you won't be looking for a new situation just yet.'

'Not just yet.' Ryllis's smile was wide.

'One good thing,' Lydia said, the thought suddenly occurring to her, 'if I take the post offered to me at Seager's – and I see no reason I shouldn't – then it'll be so much easier for you and me to meet. I shall be living here in Redbury, and you're so close by in Barford.'

'Oh, that'll be so much better.'

Having kept a watchful eye on the old clock over the fireplace, Ryllis gave a sigh and said, 'Lyddy, I must go. It's getting late and I've got to get the coach.'

'Yes, I'd better get busy as well.' Dipping into her bag, Lydia took out the watch that had been her mother's, opened it and checked it with the clock.

'You've got Mother's watch,' Ryllis said.

'Yes. Father gave it to me. He said she'd want me to have it.' Briefly Lydia paused. 'That's all right with you, isn't it? You're not upset by that, are you?'

'Oh, of course not.' Ryllis patted Lydia's arm. 'It's right that you have it. You're the elder. It has to be yours. Good heavens, of course I'm not upset.'

Lydia gave a little nod and murmured, 'Oh, Ryllis, you're so sweet. Thank you.' Then, with hardly a pause, she went on, 'I – I wanted to talk to you about something too. Something in particular.'

'Oh? What's that?'

'Something Father said when he gave me the watch.'

'What? What did he say?'

'He – he spoke about the night Mother was burned so dreadfully.'

'Oh, Lyddy . . .' Ryllis put a hand to her mouth as the memories came flooding back. 'Go on,' she said.

'He said – he told me that he threw the lamp.'

Ryllis gasped. 'Oh, no! Not at her – oh, dear God, don't say that.'

'No, he didn't throw it *at* her,' Lydia said quickly. 'He threw it down in his anger and it hit the table, and the burning oil all splashed up and – well – we know what happened then – but it was an accident.'

Ryllis remained with her hand up to her mouth for a moment longer, then lowering her hand, she asked, 'And did you believe him?'

'Yes, I did. I do believe him. And if you'd heard him, Ryllis, you'd have believed him too.' She paused. 'I've wanted to tell you this, but I couldn't say it in a letter. It had to wait till we met again.'

'Of course. I'm so glad you told me. I'm so glad.'

'Father – he's so remorseful now. I feel sorry for him, and that makes it more difficult for me – with my intention to move away – but I've got to do it. I have to.'

'Yes,' Ryllis said, 'I know.'

The two sisters sat looking at one another for a few moments in silence, then Ryllis said with a sad little smile, 'I must go, Lyddy, or I shan't have a job to go back to.'

Leaving the teahouse, Lydia and Ryllis went back out into the sunlight and set off across the square, heading for the railway station from where the coaches departed. The coach for Barford was already pulling in when they arrived, and Ryllis quickly put her arms around Lydia and hugged her.

'Now, Lyddy, you let me know as soon as you can where you'll be living, and once you're here we shan't have to wait too long between meetings, shall we?'

'No, we shan't.'

'What'll you do now?'

'Well, I shall go and try to find myself some lodgings – and then I must go back home and break the news to Father. I'm not looking forward to that.'

People were boarding the coach, so Ryllis gave Lydia a peck on the cheek, took her fare money from her purse and turned away. Two minutes later Lydia was waving to her as the coach started off along the street.

Lydia watched the coach turn out of sight at the corner, then took from her bag the list of lodging houses given to her by Mr Donovan. She looked at the first one on the list, glanced about her to get her bearings, and set off.

Lydia felt somewhat tired as she sat on the coach taking her from Merinville to Capinfell that evening, but she was none the less quite pleased with herself, for she had the satisfaction of accomplishment. She had secured a situation with Seager's store, and had also found suitable lodgings, starting in two weeks' time when she would arrive to take up her employment.

They were situated in Little Marsh Street, some fifteen minutes' walk from the department store, which would be ideal, for she would never need to spend money on cabs or other carriages. On ringing the bell at the house she had been shown upstairs by the landlady, Mrs Obdermann, a tall, heavily set woman with grey hair in braids that were coiled into rings over her ears. She seemed friendly enough, and told Lydia that in the past she had several times let out her spare room to staff from Seager's, and that she got no tenants that were there but on the warmest recommendation. The room she showed Lydia was small and right at the top of the house, with a ceiling that sloped down to the low wall on one side. It was simply furnished, but looked very clean and tidy, and for this Lydia inwardly breathed a sigh of relief. She had heard a myriad stories of unfit lodging-house rooms, and did not want to find herself adding to the list of anecdotes. 'I have to make it clear, miss,' the landlady told her, 'I allow in the room no pets, no food and no gentleman callers,' and Lydia said that she would not be considering any of the three. So she had told Mrs Obdermann that she would take the room, and had given her a deposit, saying that she would take up occupation on Sunday, the 6th of July.

And now here she was, on the coach, and it was drawing into Capinfell.

'I bought some lovely strawberries, Father,' she said, as she walked into the kitchen from the scullery. 'I got them from a market stall in Redbury, and they were too good to resist.'

Mr Halley was sitting at the table in the kitchen, working at his papers, his notes for one of his sermons spread out in front of him. He turned to her as she came into the room and watched as she set her basket down on the table.

'I saw Ryllis,' Lydia said.

'Ah, did you now. And how is the girl?'

'She's well. A little happier, I think.'

'I'm glad to hear it, and it's not before time.'

A little silence fell. Lydia took off her cape and hat, then said, assuming a casual tone, 'We had a glass of lemonade together. Then I saw her to her coach.'

'I see.' A long pause, then he said, 'And what about you? Did you keep your appointment at Seager's?'

'Yes.'

'And?'

She hesitated for a second then said, 'I – I've been offered a position. As a clerk. In the postal order department.'

'And did you accept?'

'Yes.'

'I see.'

'I start work there on Monday, July the 7th.'

'Just two weeks away. Not long.'

'No, not long.'

'I see,' he said again. He did not look up from his notes, nor move his pencil which was poised in his hand. 'Well, I don't mind telling you, you'll be missed at Cremson's,' he added. 'You've been there five years now in that office.'

Lydia didn't know what to say. After a second she said, 'I'm sure I shall miss it too. Still . . .'

He set his pencil down now, but still did not look directly at her. 'Are you – are you bettering yourself?' he asked.

'Oh, Father, I always would like to think I'm doing that – whatever step I'm taking.'

'If it doesn't work out for you, I suppose there's a chance you might get your position back. I know Mr McCabe likes you a lot. He always speaks highly of you. But there, that remains to be seen. You can't rely on it, though.'

'I know that. I wouldn't expect to have it back.' She took a breath in the silence, and added bravely, 'I wouldn't want it back.'

His eyes widened behind his spectacles at this; a faint look of shock briefly registering.

'I don't mean to belittle the work, Father,' Lydia quickly said. 'It's just that I want to move on. To do something different, to – to widen my horizons a little.'

'And you reckon you'll do that in the postal order department of Seager's, do you?' His voice was cold.

'It's a start,' she said with energy, 'and that's all I'm looking for. The man I spoke to, Mr Donovan, he said there's plenty of opportunity to better myself, plenty of chances for promotion for the right person, he said, 'and that's all I'm looking for at this point – opportunity.'

Her father gave a deep sigh and stared down at his papers. 'Well,' he said, 'I have to be quite honest – and tell you that I shall miss you too around the factory. I was proud of having you there in the office, of seeing you going about your business, and knowing that you had the full endorsement of the management.'

She said nothing.

He lowered his head slightly, raised his eyes to her over the rims of his spectacles and gave a sigh. 'Well,' he said, 'it seems your mind is made up, and if you're going, you're going.' He paused. 'And maybe there'll be a bed for you when you return, and maybe there won't.'

Chapter Six

In the days leading up to Lydia's departure, it appeared as if her father preferred to behave as if nothing were happening, as if it were not imminent. That Sunday morning on the day of her leaving, while Lydia did not go to the service at the church, he went as usual, and came back to the house at his customary time. In his absence she tidied her room and got on with her packing. In the course of doing the latter, she carefully folded and put away the nightdress to which she had added the piece of Nottingham lace that Mr Canbrook had given her that day in Merinville, just before her mother's death. He had told her at the time that he would write and then come to call upon her in Capinfell. He had not done so. Her mother's death had put a stop to any proceedings in that direction. Lydia had received from him a letter of condolence and that had been the end of it. Like certain other things now, she told herself as she put the garment away, it was a part of the past.

Finished with her packing, she prepared Sunday dinner for herself and her father, and on his return they sat down together to eat. In the near-complete silence that reigned at the table, he ate sparingly of the main course, and then, towards the end, when she served the pudding of pears and custard, looked at the dish before him and laid down his spoon. Hearing his intake of breath, Lydia looked at him and saw that there were tears in his eyes.

'Oh – Father . . .'

He swallowed, then said gruffly, avoiding her glance, 'I'm sorry, but I'm not so hungry.'

Lydia was unable to think of anything to say.

'You could still change your mind.' He spoke without looking at her. 'Cremson's would have you back like a shot.'

Still she did not speak, but looked down at her plate. The seconds ticked by.

'But I suppose that's too much to wish for,' he said. Then, 'Have you thought about me, what's to become of me?'

'Of course I have.'

'Well, that comes as a surprise. I had the feeling I was the last to be considered.'

'You'll be all right, Father,' she said, 'with Mrs Harbutt coming in to clean up and cook for you and do your bit of washing . . .'

'What do I want with the likes of Mrs Harbutt coming round to care for me? It's not the same.'

'Father, I'll get back to see you very soon, and I'll write to you often.'

'I don't want you doing me any favours.' He pushed his bowl away, got up from his chair and went from the room. Lydia heard the door to the parlour open and close.

Rising, she took up the dishes of pears and carried them out to the larder. When she had finished washing the pots and pans and tidying the place she looked at the clock. Another hour and she must expect Mr Lindsley, the fly-driver. Moving into the hall she tapped at the parlour door, opened it and put her head round.

'I'm just going to see Evie,' she said. 'I'll be back soon.'

Her father raised his hand in acknowledgement but said nothing. He was sitting at the table working at his papers. Closing the door behind her, she let herself out from the hall into the yard and moved into the lane.

Evie had just finished eating her dinner when Lydia

called at the house. 'I just came to say a quick goodbye,' Lydia said.

'I'll come out with you for a second,' Evie said. 'Mother'll look after Hennie.'

A minute later they were standing together at the little front gate. They had not had a chance to speak in several days.

'So,' Evie said, 'you'll be off soon.'

'Yes, Mr Lindsley'll be coming for me. I'm all ready to leave.'

Evie nodded. 'How's your dad taking it?'

'Not well, I'm afraid.'

'He's gunna miss you so much.'

'No doubt he will – and I'll miss him too.'

'But you start work tomorrow – your new job.'

'Yes, I have to report at eight-thirty.'

'How d'you feel about it now? Are you nervous?'

'A little – though I haven't had much chance to feel very much at all. It's been hectic, getting ready.' She was aware of the minutes passing. 'I suppose I'd better get back,' she said. 'There's a couple of things to do before Mr Lindsley comes. This was a very quick goodbye. I'm sorry.'

'That's all right. Don't leave it too long before you come to visit.'

'I won't – and I'll write to you soon and let you know how things are going.'

Lydia put out her hand and Evie clasped it. Then the two embraced. 'Just think,' Evie said as they drew apart. 'You're starting a whole new life.'

On returning home Lydia found her father still in the parlour. Putting her apron back on, she moved about the place doing last bits of tidying and arranging, never keeping her glance far from the clock over the fireplace, until she saw it was time that the fly was due. She took off her apron again and hung it up, then lifted down her cape and hat.

Standing before the speckled glass in the kitchen she put on her cape and pinned her hat in place. Then, moving into the hall, she tapped on the parlour door and opened it. Her father still sat at the table, his papers before him. He did not turn at her entrance.

'Father – I'm ready to go, and Mr Lindsley's due any moment to take me to the coach.' Even as she spoke she heard the sound of a carriage out in the lane and, looking across to the window, saw the fly pulling to a halt. 'Here he is now,' she said.

Mr Halley said nothing.

'Father . . .?' Lydia said. A little silence, and then: 'Father, I must go.'

Still he did not speak.

They heard footfalls on the cobbles, and then the cab-driver moved past the window. The sound of the knocker on the door was sharp.

'Here's Mr Lindsley now,' Lydia said.

Her father made no acknowledgement of her words, but continued to look ahead. After a moment Lydia moved to him, stopped beside him.

'Father . . . goodbye.'

He gave the briefest nod. 'Goodbye.'

'Aren't you going to wish me good luck? Aren't you coming with me to the carriage?'

He did not answer.

'Very well,' she said after a moment. She took a step away. 'I'll write to you, and I'll be back to see you soon.'

She left him then, and moved back into the hall where her luggage was standing. Opening the front door she greeted the driver and he took up first her box and then her travelling bag and carried them out to the fly. Lydia followed in his footsteps and climbed on board. Seconds later the driver had swung up onto the seat and they were starting away.

Even as they moved along Lydia looked back in hopes of seeing a last-second appearance of her father, but the lane remained empty.

From the window of her small room on the top floor of the house in Little Marsh Street Lydia stood looking out. She could see across the paved yard below, and over the short garden to the rear of the row of terraced houses beyond. Behind her, the room held a single bed, washstand, small wardrobe and chest of drawers, a tiny writing table with an old upright chair, and a worn easy chair. The room was as neat as she had found it a few hours before, the few belongings she had brought with her in her box and travelling bag now having been packed away in the drawers or hung up in the wardrobe. Her journey from Capinfell had involved a cab, a coach, a train and then a cab from Redbury station, and with what relief had she finally got her luggage carried up the stairs and deposited in her room.

This evening, downstairs in the dining room, she had eaten a dish provided by Mrs Obdermann, a tasty mutton stew that had been most welcome. After the meal she had come back up to her room, where she had rested for a while, and then a little later, putting on her cape and hat, she had gone out into the streets of the town, to take a stroll and look around the area and get some more immediate picture of her surroundings.

Now here she was, back again, and before her was her first night in the house.

She sighed as the memory of her leave-taking from her father came back to her, but the difficulties where he was concerned would have to remain as they were for the time being. There was no chance of mending them yet. In any case, she told herself again, he would come round to the idea in time. Once he was used to the new situation he would surely be more understanding.

She closed the curtains and stepped back from the window. It was getting late, and she must be up early for her first day at the store.

As she put on her nightdress she told herself that she was sure she would never sleep. She was far too excited, far too anxious and nervous. So much that was unknown lay before her. She blew out the flame of the small lamp then got into bed and lay down. The mattress felt strange beneath her body, the pillow strange beneath her head, but she would get used to it. One good thing: the bedding was crisp and clean and smelled fresh. It was a factor that brought her relief, for she had heard numerous stories of people finding themselves caught in lodging houses that were dirty and riddled with vermin.

For a time she lay listening to the unaccustomed sounds of the night city and then she drifted off to sleep.

She entered the staff door of the emporium well before eight-thirty the next morning, and after making enquiries was shown to the postal order department. She had been told to report to a Mr Watson, the supervisor, and on her arrival found him already behind his desk, working at various papers and ledgers. He was situated at the side of a large room, a room filled with rows of long tables stretching right across it. Already dozens of men and women were arriving, relieving themselves of their coats and hats and taking their places at the tables.

Mr Watson was a man in his fifties, tall and somewhat stooping. He seemed very pleasant to Lydia, and as he spoke to her he broke off to exchange occasional greetings with the clerks. He explained to Lydia what the procedure was and what she would be expected to do. As she had learned, there were well over fifty clerks in the department, and all of them were there to facilitate the sending of items through the post. The emporium advertised widely, and customers sent in their orders from all over the west of England. The postal order department was there to deal with those orders, whether they were for a Turkish carpet, a pair of silk stockings, or a fashionable day dress.

As the other clerks were doing, Lydia was required to deal with orders that had come in that morning. Requisition documents had to be made out, along with advice notes and invoices, and these sent by messengers to the stock department. From there the goods would be forwarded to the despatch office where they would be packed and sent off to the customer. If any particular item was at present unavailable – either through being temporarily out of stock, or because the line had been discontinued – it was the job of the clerk to write to the customer to such effect.

The hours seemed to pass quickly, and Lydia had plenty of work to keep her occupied. She had to ask many questions of her experienced colleagues in the course of her learning, but that she was indeed learning she had no doubt. There was also more variety in her work than she had anticipated; she was by no means kept in the confines of the office all the time, for there were many occasions when she was required to go out into the store proper and make enquiries of some of the salesmen or saleswomen. In this way she began to learn more of the layout of the store and of the wide range of goods that were sold there.

On Tuesday evening, back in her room after getting in from finishing her working day, she sat down at the small table to write a letter to Ryllis. In it she told her a little about her work so far at the store and of how she was settling in. She then asked whether she and Ryllis could meet that coming Sunday.

On Saturdays, Lydia was required to work only until two o'clock, after which she was free until Monday morning, and it was on Saturday that she returned to Little Marsh Street to find a letter awaiting her from Ryllis. In it, Ryllis said she would come into Redbury the next day, and would meet Lydia in the small garden beside the square where they had finally found one another on their last meeting. So the next afternoon, just before two-thirty, Lydia crossed the square in Redbury towards the little garden – quite crowded on this bright, warm Sunday afternoon – and there saw Ryllis waiting for her, sitting on one of the benches in the shade of the laburnum tree. And seeing her there, she thought at once of her previous visit to the place, when she had met the stranger who had helped to gather up her strawberries.

Ryllis got to her feet as Lydia drew near, and the two embraced. Then they sat down side by side on the bench. Ryllis wore her blue dress with the grey trim, and her brown straw hat. Like Lydia on this hot day, she wore no cape.

'Oh, Lyddy, it's so warm!' Ryllis fanned herself with her hand. 'Let's go somewhere and get out of the sun. It's too hot sitting here.'

'Where d'you want to go?' Lydia asked. 'It's too early to go and have tea.'

'Can we go back to your lodgings? I'm dying to put my feet up for an hour.'

'Come on, then.'

As Lydia prepared to get up, Ryllis said, 'Just a second. There's something I have to tell you.'

'What's that?'

Ryllis paused. 'There's someone I want you to meet later on.'

'Someone?' Lydia's eyes widened. 'Are you meaning your Mr Thomas Bissett?'

Ryllis nodded. 'The same.' She smiled. 'What do you think?'

'Well, I'd love to meet him. What's the arrangement?'

'He's coming into Redbury later. He hasn't got much time, but I said we'll meet him at four o'clock in the teashop next to the bank in the High Street.'

'Excellent,' said Lydia. 'I'll look forward to it.' She looked about her. 'Well – shall we go and have a rest somewhere in the meantime?'

Mrs Obdermann was just coming out of her sitting room when the sisters entered the hall of number 15, Little Marsh Street, and she looked with curiosity at Lydia's guest. At once Lydia said to the woman, 'Mrs Obdermann, this is my sister Ryllis, come to visit me for the afternoon from Barford,' and the landlady gave a cool little smile and murmured a greeting.

Upstairs in Lydia's room, the girls took off their hats and boots. Ryllis, giving a little groan of pleasure, lay back on the bed, her hands behind her head. Lydia sat in the one small easy chair. 'So,' she said, 'what do you think of it?'

Raising her head just enough to look around, Ryllis said, 'It's nice, and it's big enough, I reckon. I wish I had such a room at the Lucases'. Where do you eat?'

'Downstairs in the dining room. I get breakfast there, and supper, served by Mrs Obdermann.'

'What's she like?' Ryllis lowered her voice to little more than a whisper. 'That was a very old-fashioned look she gave me when we came in.'

'I know,' said Lydia, her own voice very low, 'but she's all right. I think she's just rather watchful as to who comes into her house. God forbid she should ever see a strange man here. She'd have a fit.'

'Are there any other lodgers?'

'Not right now, though usually, I understand, she has a

second one. But never any men, and she allows no male guests. She's made that clear.'

'Well, there's no danger of that, is there? You wanting to invite in a male friend. Mind you, now that you're mixing with so many new people, who knows what the future might hold.'

'Oh, Ryllis,' Lydia gave a little laugh, 'I'm not here in Redbury to form an attachment.' Then, her tone serious, she added, 'I *had* to leave. Even before Mother's death I felt I wanted to go, but she needed me there. We never spoke of it, the notion of my leaving, but I know she'd have been heartbroken if I'd gone. It was bad enough for her when *you* left home – but to be left by *both* her daughters . . .'

'Yes.' Ryllis nodded.

'And what was before me, living at home with Father, now that Mother was gone? I could see the whole picture. So clearly. Me staying on there, still working at Cremson's, and in the house just looking after Father – cleaning, doing his washing; cooking and mending for him. That's how it would go on, for years and years. It's a common story, where one daughter is left in a house. You see it all the time. Look at Ursie Woodleigh in Capinfell – on her mother's death taking over the job of looking after her father and two brothers, and there she still is, well into her forties now and without a hope of ever getting a life of her own – a husband, her own children, her own home.'

'Are you sure that isn't what you're looking for – a husband, children, your own home?' Ryllis smiled, her eyes narrowed. 'It wouldn't be before time. After all, you're twenty-one.'

'I know I'm twenty-one – and I want to be free to make my own life. Father thinks I'll end up unhappy, but that's a chance I've got to take. If my life does turn out to go wrong, then that's something I'll have to deal with, but at least it will be *my* life.' She gave an ironic smile. 'I doubt anything could happen to me under Father's watchful eye, but if something *did* happen – if I *should* meet someone special . . . Oh, I've read books where people are swept away by great passions. They love, they fall in love, and it changes their whole lives; their whole reason for living is different. I don't understand it, of course, as I've never experienced it, but it seems that it must be a most – most miraculous thing.' She grinned at her sister. 'What about you, Ryllis? Have you been in love? Are you in love with your Mr Bissett?'

'Oh, Lyddy,' Ryllis said, clasping her hands before her, and sitting up. 'Tom is a wonderful man. You wait till you meet him.'

Lydia gave a little nod. 'I'm very happy for you.' She turned and gazed from the window, looking out across the small gardens of the houses. 'Sometimes I wonder what it must be like – to care for someone in such a way. I can't even try to imagine.' She fell silent for a moment, then she said, turning back to her sister, 'Oh, what nonsense I do talk at times!' Smiling, she added, 'Oh, it's so good to see you, Ryllis. It's *so* good.'

'Yes, it is,' Ryllis replied, 'but I thought you might want to go home today. You could have gone to Capinfell today and returned tomorrow evening. It would have been very easy.'

'I know,' Lydia said. 'I thought of it. I seriously considered it – but then I thought it might be better to leave Father alone for a little while. I don't wish to be cruel, but I thought it might be as well to let him get used to the situation for a bit. D'you see what I mean?'

'Oh, yes.'

'Besides, I wanted to see you.' Lydia smiled. 'And now I'm going to meet your Mr Thomas Bissett too.'

'Yes!' Ryllis gave a giddy little laugh. 'Oh, Lyddy, I do hope you like him.'

'Why shouldn't I? If he's half as nice as you make out,

and a quarter as handsome, I should think anybody would like him.' Lydia looked at Ryllis as she lay stretched out on the bed. She was so glad that Ryllis had met someone, and it was hardly any wonder, she thought, that Mr Thomas Bissett was so attracted to her; she was so pretty. Gazing at her as she lay on the bed with her heavy eyelids closed and her pink mouth relaxed, Lydia wondered how any young man could resist her.

She looked at her watch on the chest of drawers and saw that it was just on three-twenty. 'We shall have to leave in a while,' she said.

She closed the watch and set it down. There had been no response from Ryllis. She bent closer to her, and realised that she had fallen asleep. Smiling, she picked up a book and began to read.

'You shouldn't have let me sleep like that,' Ryllis said as they crossed the square. 'You should have woken me.'

'I told you, I got reading and forgot things for a few minutes. It was hardly any time at all. We'll only be a minute or so late.'

'Even so. I don't like to keep Tom waiting.'

Lydia took in the slightly anxious look on Ryllis's face and said with a smile, 'Ah, I'm sure he thinks you're worth waiting for.' Ryllis didn't reply. Lydia added after a moment: 'What are his parents like? Have you met them?'

Ryllis shook her head. 'Oh, good heavens, no. They don't know about us, that we're meeting. Tom doesn't want them to know just yet, so he's keeping quiet on the matter.'

'Why doesn't he want them to know?'

'He says the time isn't right. He says they don't want him to get – involved with anyone yet – not at his age – so he thinks it's better to leave it for a few months. Then he'll tell them.' Ryllis put up a hand and gave her hair an unneces-

101

sary little touch. 'All this rushing. I'm going to be so hot when we get there, and I wanted to look my best. I shouldn't have slept like that.'

'You were obviously tired.'

In a few seconds they were turning into the High Street, and there, a hundred yards further along, was the bank with the teashop beside it. Ten yards from the entrance Ryllis slowed and touched at her hat and smoothed down her dress. Then, with a shrug she moved on and stepped through the doorway. As they entered, she said, with relief in her voice, 'Ah, there's Tom,' and snatching at Lydia's hand, led her through the crowded room.

Thomas Bissett was sitting at a table situated near one wall and he rose and smiled at the two young women as they approached him. Ryllis said at once: 'Oh, I'm sorry to be late, Tom, but I'm afraid I fell asleep in Lyddy's room. Anyway, this is my sister Lydia. Lydia – this is Tom.'

'How d'you do,' Thomas said formally over the loud babble of voices around them, and Lydia greeted him likewise, adding, 'I'm afraid it's my fault that we're a few minutes late. You must blame me for it.'

He nodded and took out his watch from his waistcoat pocket, opened it and said, 'Almost fifteen minutes. 'And with a smile, 'I'll let you off this time, but next time it's the firing squad at dawn.' Over his patterned waistcoat he wore a light tweed jacket. His trousers were fawn twill. He looked, Lydia thought, very smart.

'Well, ladies, do sit down,' he said. 'Another reason I'm so pleased to see you is because I've had the devil's own job hanging on to these seats.'

As the girls sat down, Lydia looked around them. The place was so crowded she couldn't see an empty table, and she reflected that they were very lucky. When Thomas asked them what they wanted, they said they would have tea and a pastry, and he said he would have the same, though he had already drunk a cup of tea while he was waiting. He turned then and tried to catch the eye of the waitress, lifting his hand in the air. He certainly was handsome, Lydia thought, and proud looking too with his high, arched nose and strong brow.

'These serving girls,' he was saying irritably, 'they take their own sweet time, don't they?'

'The poor thing's so busy,' Lydia said. 'She's run off her feet.'

'Even so,' he said, 'we haven't got all day.'

Eventually the girl came over to their table, and Thomas crisply gave the order and she went away again.

'Well,' he said to Lydia after the girl's departure, 'it's so nice to meet you after all this time. I've heard so much about you.'

'And I about you,' Lydia replied.

He smiled at this. 'And now, luckily,' he said, 'you're living and working here in Redbury. That'll make it easier for you and Ryllis to meet.'

'Yes, it will.'

They had to raise their voices over the babble around them, and a couple of times Thomas looked about him, impatiently frowning at the noise. With no sign of the tea after a while, he caught the young waitress's attention, and five minutes later she brought her tray to their table and set out the tea and pastries. Lydia poured out the tea and they began to eat and drink. As they did so, Lydia said to Thomas, 'Ryllis tells me you've been living in London for a while . . .'

'Yes, I have,' he replied. 'My uncle owns a small engineering company there, in Peckham. I've been learning some of the business.'

'Have you enjoyed it – the work?'

'Oh, in some parts. And living in London! Well, it's very different from country life. Have you ever been to London?'

'No. I'd love to go one day.'

'Yes, I would too,' Ryllis said. 'I hear it's a different world.'

'Oh, it is,' he said. 'It is. You can't imagine just how different.'

'Will you stay with the engineering work, then?' Lydia asked.

'I don't know. I've come back now for these summer months to help my father out on the farm. He needs all the help he can get at such a time.'

'I'm sure he must,' Lydia said. 'And when summer is over? What then?'

'Nothing's decided, but my folks have hopes of this and that. My father wants me to go to university.'

Ryllis said, 'Go to university? Then you'd go away again.'

'Oh, nothing's settled,' he said. 'All kinds of things can happen.'

Ryllis then spoke up to say that Lydia had just finished her first week at Seager's store, and Thomas politely asked Lydia a question or two about her work there. He did not seem unduly interested, however, Lydia thought, and she soon brought the subject to a conclusion. As she did so a small child nearby started up a crying wail and Thomas leaned across the table to murmur just loud enough for Lydia and Ryllis to hear, 'God knows why people insist on bringing their squalling offspring into such places. I suppose they're so used to the noise themselves they don't notice it any more.'

The little girl ceased her crying after a while, and, pacified with a treat, was soon all smiles again. 'There,' whispered Lydia, 'it's amazing what a bit of cream cake will do.'

Five minutes later the child had left her seat and was coming to their table. 'I had some cake,' the little girl said to them. She was probably three years old. 'I had some cake.'

Indeed, there were still traces of the cream cake on her hands and about her mouth. Not that this seemed unduly to concern her parents who gazed after her in a besotted way, as do most who think their children must of course be loved by every passing stranger. 'Now, now,' the young mother beamed after her child, 'come along, Maisie. 'We can't 'ave you botherin' people.'

'Oh, she's no bother,' Ryllis said, turning to the young woman. And then to the child, 'You're no bother, are you, Maisie?'

At the soft words, which could have been taken as encouragement, the little girl began to chatter away in her limited vocabulary, and Ryllis responded. While Lydia looked on, indulgently smiling, Thomas could barely hide a scowl. Then his expression changed, for in another second the child was turning to him and saying, 'Cake, look,' and holding out to him a battered cream-smeared fragment. As she moved closer to him he shrank back a little, holding up a hand to ward off the proffered gift. 'No, thank you, miss,' he said, trying to smile. 'I've had mine.' Then the child's mother, obviously having discerned, not before time, that her child was not welcome for quite so long, said, 'Come 'ere, Miss Maisie, and stop botherin' the nice people. They don't want your cake.' Getting up from her chair she took the child under the arms and carried her away. The look of relief on Thomas's face was not quite hidden. The next moment he was saying, 'Well, I think we might as well leave, don't you?' He dug into his pocket for change and got up. 'Oh, just a minute more,' said Ryllis, still holding her cup. 'I haven't quite finished.'

She drank down the last of her tea and stood up, and after Thomas had paid at the counter the two sisters went out on to the street. He joined them almost immediately, and met Ryllis's smile with a frown, saying to her, in a gruff mutter,

'I can't imagine why you had to encourage that little brat. As if she weren't bad enough as it was.'

'Oh, Tom,' Ryllis said, 'she was a dear little thing.'

'A dear little thing?' He threw a glance back over his shoulder towards the teashop's doorway. 'All that disgusting muck over her hands. I felt sure she was going to wipe her fingers on my jacket. She would have done, given half a chance. I can't understand why parents think their children are to be loved and admired in whatever circumstances.' Then, his scowl giving way to a smile, he added, 'Anyway, we won't let that spoil a nice day, eh? What d'you say we head for the coach? I think we should. It's quarter to six.'

'Are you going already?' Lydia asked.

'We've got to,' Ryllis said. 'Tom's parents are expecting out of town visitors, and Tom's promised to be there.'

'I see. Well – I'll walk with you and see you off.'

The three of them set off through the town, heading towards the railway station, from where many of the coaches left on their various journeys.

As they skirted the square they approached a blind man on a corner who was selling boxes of matches. Ryllis immediately came to a stop and bent her head to look in her bag. 'What's up?' Thomas said. 'What are you doing?'

Keeping her voice low so that the match-seller shouldn't hear, she said, 'That poor blind man. I must buy some matches from him.'

'For goodness sake, don't be foolish,' Thomas said. 'Keep your money in your purse. He doesn't need it.'

'But Tom –'

'Half the time it's an act,' he said. 'Half the so-called blind can see as well as you or I. Like all the perfectly able cripples you see – they're only out for what they can get.'

In seconds they had passed by the blind man and were heading on towards the station.

The coach stop was busy with traffic and people coming and going constantly. On arrival, the three found there were already a number of people waiting to board the Barford-bound coach, and, doing a quick head count, Thomas said it didn't look as if there'd be room for Ryllis and himself. 'We shouldn't have left it so late,' he said.

The coach drew in and let its passengers off, and while the outgoing passengers boarded, the horses were changed. Seeing it fill up so quickly, Thomas said irritably that there was nothing for it but to wait half an hour for the next one – at least they should be guaranteed seats on that.

When the coach was fully prepared, Lydia stood watching as it moved off along the street and disappeared from view around a bend. Then at her side, Ryllis was saying to her, 'Lyddy, there's that man we met.'

Lydia turned to her sister. 'Who? What man?'

Ryllis nodded off in the direction of a carriage that had just pulled in near the entrance to the railway station. 'The man in the square the other week. The one you spoke to when you came here for your interview.'

'Ah, yes.'

Lydia's keen gaze saw him now, the familiar-looking tall man helping an elderly woman out of a trap that stood at the kerb. As she watched, the man handed the reins to a small boy who waited nearby, then escorted the woman into the station.

'Who was that?' Thomas asked, following the girls' gazes.

'A man I met the other day when I came to Seager's for my interview,' Lydia said. 'Ryllis and I had lost each other and he helped us.'

'You want to be careful who you talk to,' Thomas said. 'There's no shortage of mashers around. You'd do well to steer clear of 'em.'

'Oh, but he was very nice,' Ryllis said, 'and very well spoken.'

'Yes, and there's many a young girl has thought such a thing to her lasting regret.'

Some minutes passed and then Lydia, who had kept her eyes on the station entrance, saw the man reappear and move towards his carriage. 'Here he is again,' Ryllis said unnecessarily, and Lydia nodded, and murmured, 'I know. Don't stare,' and then a moment later the man was turning slightly, looking their way.

As his gaze fell upon her, Lydia saw his eyes widen in surprise, and saw his mouth move in a smile. The next moment he was coming towards them.

Chapter Seven

'Well, the Misses Halley! This is a surprise.' The man's smile was broad as he looked at the two young women. 'I hope you haven't been losing each other in Redbury again.'

Lydia gave a little laugh, that rang slightly too loud in her ears. 'No, not today. No one got lost today.' She hesitated briefly, then said, 'It's Mr Anderson, isn't it? Mr Guy Anderson.'

He nodded. 'It is indeed. I'm flattered that you remembered.'

She felt herself blushing slightly then, gesturing to Thomas, said, 'This is Mr Thomas Bissett, my sister's friend. Mr Bissett – Mr Guy Anderson.'

The two men shook hands, and when the introductions were completed, Mr Anderson said, 'You're obviously waiting for a coach. Are you going back to Capinfell?'

'Not today,' Lydia said. 'Mr Bissett and my sister are heading for Barford. Unfortunately they just lost the coach. It was full up.'

'So now,' Thomas said, 'we've got to wait for the next one.'

'Oh, dear.' Mr Anderson looked sympathetic. 'When is that due?'

'Not for another half hour.'

'And is that inconvenient?'

Ryllis spoke up here. 'Mr Bissett was keen to get back home to meet certain people who were visiting,' she said.

'And what about you, Miss Halley?' Mr Anderson turned back to Lydia. 'Are you not bound for Barford?'

'No, I'm staying here in Redbury,' Lydia said. 'I just came to see my sister and Mr Bissett off on the coach.'

'I see.' A moment of silence went by, then he said, 'Well, now, listen. I just drove out a short distance to bring an old friend of my mother's to the train station. My mare likes a jaunt, so what d'you say that I drive you to Barford?' Here his eyes rested on Lydia again. 'And you, Miss Halley, can come along for the ride and keep me company on the box.' Quickly he added: 'Of course, I'll bring you back to Redbury and drive you home or wherever you want to go.'

Lydia did not answer, although she was inclined to decline the offer, but at once Thomas spoke up, saying, 'Well, that's very decent of you, sir. We'd appreciate that very much, wouldn't we, Ryllis?'

'Oh, yes,' Ryllis replied. 'That would be splendid. You'll get home in good time after all, Tom.'

'Indeed,' said Mr Anderson, 'and we might make almost as good progress as the coach.'

Both Ryllis and Thomas turned their eyes to Lydia now, looking for her agreement, and she knew she could not do anything but acquiesce.

'Very well,' she said, 'that would be very nice.'

Sitting in the open carriage, they had to raise their voices over the sounds of the wheels and the horse's hooves, and against the light breeze that threatened to waft their words away. The large, strong mare between the shafts made light work of pulling the trap and its occupants. 'So,' Mr Anderson said, after they had driven a little way, half turning, speaking to Ryllis and Thomas who sat behind him, 'have you been having a few hours' relaxation in Redbury?'

'Yes, something like that,' Ryllis answered, to which Thomas added:

'If you can call it that.'

'Don't you like Redbury?' Mr Anderson said to him.

'There's not much to like, is there?' said Thomas. 'Not in my reckoning, anyway. There's certainly not much to do there.'

'I suppose it depends what you're looking for.'

Ryllis said, 'Mr Bissett's been living in London – where the high life is.'

'London, eh?' Mr Anderson said. 'Well, now, there's a place.'

'Do you know it?' Ryllis said. 'Have you ever been?'

'Yes, a few times, and it had its moments, there's no denying.' He turned to Lydia who sat beside him. 'What about you, Miss Halley? Do you enjoy travel?'

'I haven't had any real opportunity, though I like to read of exotic places.'

'Oh, Miss Halley,' Thomas said, raising his voice, 'wouldn't you like to go to Paris and see the new tower they've just finished, that Eiffel Tower everyone's talking about?'

'Perhaps one day,' Lydia said, 'but there are so many wonders closer to home that I've never set eyes on. For one thing, I have to confess I'd love to see some of the theatres and opera houses that you find in the big cities.'

'Ah, yes,' Mr Anderson said. 'That's where the big cities come into their own. Though of course there's the theatre in Redbury – and it sometimes offers touring opera productions. Have you never been to one?'

'No, I haven't,' Lydia said. She could have added that her father would have frowned at the very idea, but said nothing more.

'Perhaps you'll go one day.'

'Who knows. Perhaps I shall.'

'What about you, Mr Bissett?' Mr Anderson said. 'Do you go to the theatre in Redbury?'

'The theatre?' Thomas said scornfully. 'Hah. I've no time for that kind of nonsense. Give me something real to deal with. You know in London they've just opened a tube railway – and it goes right underneath the River Thames.'

'Yes, so I read.'

Mr Anderson asked Thomas then about his employment, and the latter replied at length, speaking of his work at his uncle's factory. Ryllis hung on his words, laughing encouragingly as he related some amusing anecdote about one of the workers. He continued to talk animatedly for most of the remainder of the journey.

At last they saw before them the village of Barford, and as soon as they reached the outskirts Thomas asked to be let down, saying that he would walk the rest of the way. Mr Anderson drew the carriage to a halt and Thomas kissed Ryllis on the cheek and jumped down onto the road. Reaching up, he shook hands with Mr Anderson, then said to Lydia, touching his hat, 'It's been a pleasure, Miss Halley, and I hope to see you again before too long.'

'I hope so too, Mr Bissett,' Lydia replied, then added, 'You'll look after our Ryllis, won't you?'

He smiled. 'Oh, indeed. Have no fear of that.'

When Thomas had moved away, Mr Anderson started off the carriage again, and at Ryllis's directions, drove through the village to the southern side, pulling up at a large redbrick Victorian house that nestled back behind tall elm trees. As the man jumped down, Ryllis said, whispering to her sister: 'Did you like Tom? Oh, I hope you did. He gets a little fraught at times, but you mustn't take any notice.'

'Oh, he was charming,' Lydia said, then went on, compounding her lie: 'I enjoyed meeting him.'

Mr Anderson helped Ryllis down, then Lydia watched as Ryllis went in at the gate, turned to give a final wave and disappeared from view. A moment later Mr Anderson had climbed back into the carriage and was calling out to the horse, 'Ready to go, then, Tess?' and they were starting off again.

They drove for a little while, the wheels eating up the distance, then Mr Anderson said to Lydia, 'So it's back to Redbury for you now, is it?'

'Yes, that's right.'

A few moments, then he asked, 'Are you in a great hurry to get back?'

'Well, no – not particularly.'

'It's just that I don't want to push Tess too hard. As I said, she likes a jaunt, and she's a strong old girl, but she's not exactly the youngest. She likes to go at her own pace.'

'No,' Lydia said, 'we can take our time. Don't press her.'

For the most part the road was clear, and they passed only a few other carriages and carts on their way. Up above them, beyond the overhanging green foliage, the sky remained a soft azure blue, broken only here and there by small drifting clouds.

'How did you enjoy your visit with your sister today?' Mr Anderson asked after they had travelled a little way in silence.

'Oh, so much!' Lydia said. 'The time went too fast.'

'I wish I had a sister or brother,' he said. 'Unfortunately I haven't. Have you got other siblings?'

'No, there's only Ryllis and me.'

He nodded. 'Do you know your sister's friend well? Mr Bissett?'

'No, I don't. This was the first time we ever met.'

'The first time, eh?' He turned, flicked a glance at her. 'I trust you approved.'

'Approved?'

'Of Mr Bissett.'

'Ah.' She nodded.

'Do I take that as a yes?' he said, smiling. 'Do you approve?'

Lydia was silent at the question, and could have wished that it had not been asked. 'Well,' she said after a few moments, 'it's not always easy to judge, is it? Not when you're dealing with first impressions, that sort of thing. On the other hand, I'm certain he must be a perfectly nice young man.' She paused, then raised a hand towards the sky. 'Look at that sky! What a perfect day this is.'

'Oh, I see,' he said, grinning. 'Well, now that we've changed the subject and have decided to dispense with your opinions on the subject of Mr Bissett, tell me a little about your sister. She's not in the least like you.'

'What do you want to know? She's sixteen years old and is working in service.'

'How does she like it?'

'Well, she doesn't like it where she is, her present situation. She talks about changing it, but we'll have to see what happens. I know she'd like to do something better, move to another place.'

'Has that sort of work ever had appeal for you? Ladies maid, governess – anything like that?' He smiled at her. 'I realise I know nothing at all about you. Only that which I learned when we met in the square, and that was precious little.' He gave a low chuckle. 'I learned quite a lot about Mr Bissett on the drive out, but nothing much about anyone else.'

Lydia smiled in spite of herself.

'But has it?' he said. 'Has domestic work ever appealed to you? It does to many girls.'

Lydia gave an ironic laugh. 'It only appeals because there's precious little else that's available. This is a man's world, Mr Anderson, and make no mistake about it. Women could do so many other jobs, but they just don't get the chance.'

'I've no doubt you're right,' he said, 'but perhaps things will change in time.'

'I think they'll have to.' She was silent for a moment, then she went on, 'But as for me, I'm happy enough working in an office. It has a lot to be said for it. For one thing, when six o'clock comes round I no longer have to answer to anyone.'

'Oh, yes, there's a lot to be said for that. What about your parents? I suppose they live in Capinfell, do they?'

'My father does. I'm afraid my mother – died some months ago.'

'Oh, dear. I'm sorry to hear that. I did notice when we first met that you were in mourning. Your sister too. I am sorry.'

'Thank you. It was all very sudden and . . .' She let her words trail away, feeling a tightening in her throat, and did not look at him but into the hedgerows as they passed.

'It must be a dreadful thing to lose a parent,' he said. 'Fortunately both mine are in fairly good health at the moment. Though they're neither of them young.'

'Do you get on with them well?'

'Oh, indeed. Though I see less of my father than my mother. Apart from his work here he has business interests in Italy, and he spends some of his time in Florence.'

'Does your mother travel with him?'

'Sometimes, though not as much as she once did. My father's in his early seventies now, and my mother only a few years younger. He keeps saying he's going to retire from his work, but it hasn't happened yet.'

Turning a bend in the road they saw before them a public house, the Rising Sun. As they approached it, Guy said, 'Would you care to stop for a while, and have a drink and give Tess a rest?'

She hesitated. She had never before in her life been inside any kind of drinking house. 'I – I have to be in by half past seven,' she said.

'Oh, so soon?'

'I'm afraid so. Mrs Obdermann, my landlady, is serving supper for me at that time. I said I'd be back. I think she'd be angry if I let her down.'

'Oh, dear. Well, we can stop for a little while, can't we?' When she did not reply, he added, 'Don't worry, I'll get you home in time.'

She found herself agreeing, and Guy guided the mare into the yard at the side of the inn, where a young lad appeared around a corner and took the horse's bridle. As Guy jumped down, he said to the boy, 'Give her some water as well, will you, lad? She's bound to be thirsty.' He helped Lydia down on to the cobbles and together they went into the saloon bar.

It was not crowded and they took a vacant seat beside a wall. 'What would you like to drink?' Guy asked as Lydia sat down and uncertainly began to peel off her gloves.

She had no idea what to reply. She wanted nothing alcoholic. 'Is it – is it possible I could just have a lemonade – or something – please?'

'Of course. Would you like anything to eat? Oh, no, you'll be going back soon for your landlady's boiled mutton, I forgot.'

He left her and moved to the bar, and Lydia watched his tall figure as he stood at the counter, waiting to give the barman the order. She sat there, nervous and unsure in these new surroundings, aware of the clamour of voices coming from the public bar next door. What would her father think to know of her being there – sitting in a public house, waiting for a man who was almost a stranger to bring her a drink?

Forcing her mind to move to other things, she thought of how good it had been to see Ryllis again, and also how interesting had been her meeting with Thomas Bissett, but here, in spite of her wish to be generous, her thoughts were

116

touched with dismay. She had not been impressed with him at all. But then she thrust the reservations aside. What did it matter what *she* thought? What mattered was Ryllis. If Ryllis was happy with him and he treated her well, that was the important thing.

She thought again of her father – as she had done so many times since her departure from Capinfell. She wondered how he was. How was he faring without her? How was he dealing with Mrs Harbutt coming in the evenings to cook his supper? She would go to see him on the coming Saturday, she decided. She would go on the Saturday after her work, and return on the Sunday afternoon.

Guy came back carrying two glasses – lemonade for Lydia and beer for himself. He set down the drinks, sat down facing her, and smiled at her across the table. 'There, that was painless,' he said. He picked up his glass of beer, and waited while Lydia took up her lemonade. Raising his glass, he said, 'Well, here's to happy days.'

'Yes,' she said uncertainly, not knowing how it was done, but raising her glass none the less: 'To happy days.'

She took a sip of her lemonade and smiled back at him, but for all the warmth of her smile she felt only uncertainty. Glancing around her she once again took in her surroundings, and wondered at her being there.

'Are you all right?' she heard Guy say. 'Is anything wrong?'

She turned back to him. 'No, nothing's wrong. It's just that – it's so new.'

'New? This particular place, you mean?'

'No, not just this place. I mean any – public house.'

'You mean –'

'I've never been inside one in my life before.'

He frowned and smiled at the same time. 'And with a strange man too. Oh, dear. I don't quite know how to react

117

to that. Should I be sorry that I brought you in here?' Then with a more serious tone he asked, 'Are you sure you want to stay? Would you rather leave?'

'Oh, no,' she said quickly, 'I don't want to leave. It's fascinating – and very nice.'

'I don't want you to feel uncomfortable,' he said. 'Don't put up with it for my sake.'

'No, it's not like that. I'm glad to be here.'

He looked a little relieved. 'Good,' he said.

She drank a little more of her lemonade, then said with an ironic note in her voice, 'I was wondering what my father would think, if he could see me now. Not only poems by the Bad Lord Byron, but drinking in a public house. Me – in a public.'

'He wouldn't approve?'

She shook her head. 'Oh, most definitely not.'

'So I doubt that he's ever been into a public either . . .'

'Oh, yes, he has – but never to drink.'

'Then what for?'

'He goes into them occasionally to hand out tracts – but he never stays for a drink, of course, or to converse. Once his tracts are given out, he's gone.'

'Is he a cleric?'

'No, he's a foreman in a factory, but in his spare time he's a lay preacher.'

'I see.'

'He's done it for as long as I can remember. He should have gone into the church, but it didn't work out for him to do so. So – he does the next best thing.'

'He has a very strong faith, then.'

'Oh, yes.'

'What about you?'

'Me?'

'Do you have a strong faith?'

She paused, avoiding his eyes, 'I – I would like to have. I

would like to believe in something so completely. To believe, totally – it must be such a comfort. I don't think I shall ever know that – that utter certainty.'

When she moved her glance back to his she saw that he was looking at her with a very serious expression on his face, a slight frown on his brow. She gave a little smile. 'Please, this is not the subject for this time.'

'No,' he said, 'perhaps you're right, but I'm interested in hearing all about you.'

A little silence between them in the murmur of voices and the clink of glass and pewter, and then he said:

'May I call you Lydia?'

She hesitated for a second, then said, 'Yes, of course.' She could think of no other response.

He lifted his glass and held it up. 'Here's to you, Lydia. And well met.' He smiled. 'Enough and more of this Miss Halley–Mr Anderson business, don't you think?'

She nodded and smiled back at him and sipped from her lemonade.

'What are you thinking?' he said.

'Only that I mustn't forget the time,' she said. 'These light evenings, these long days – it's easy to forget how the time is going.'

'We don't have to leave just yet,' he said. 'I won't let you be late.'

'Thank you.' She took another drink from her glass, then ventured, 'You know a little about me – but I still know hardly anything about you.'

'What else do you want to know?'

'Well – your work. What is it you do?'

'I work in my father's business – his *English* business, that is – as opposed to his Italian one, I mean. Here in Redbury.'

'And what is that?'

'He owns a newspaper.'

'Really.' Lydia was impressed.

'The *Wiltshire Courier*. I've been helping him on it since I got out of the army. What else can I tell you? I'm twenty-five years old, and I've just finished several years' army service. Six to be exact.'

'Was it exciting, your military service?'

'It had its moments. I was in South Africa for part of the time, the Transvaal, but then eventually I decided that enough was enough, and resigned my commission. It wasn't an easy decision to make.'

'And now you're working in the family business.'

'That's right. As my mother tells me, it's about time I learned all about it and settled down. Particularly as my father is getting on in years. Well, they both are. Oh, I was born late in my mother's life. She tells me she'd given up all hope of ever having a child, let alone a son – which she had always wanted.' He grinned. 'So I suppose in a way I was a late blessing for her.'

'Are you now living back at home with them?'

'Yes, at the family house in Redbury, and it suits me – for the time being, anyway. I've got everything I want there, every comfort.' He smiled. 'I'm spoiled, in a way.'

'Are both your parents in Redbury now?'

'My mother is. Not my father. At the moment he's in Italy with his textile business. He plans to sell it up. It's all getting rather a lot of work for him to take care of.'

'I'm not surprised – and all that travelling.'

'Oh, it's become too much. That's one reason I gave up my commission in the army. I came to the conclusion that the time had come when I was really needed at home.' He sighed. 'So here I am – and there's so much to learn.'

'What exactly are you doing in the business?'

'My father thinks I should learn everything. So I've been observing the presses at work, and helping out all the office clerks. Just about every aspect. I'm even being sent out on journalistic assignments.' He gave a little laugh. 'So any weddings you want reporting on, let me know.'

'Oh, you laugh,' she said, 'but it sounds exciting.'

'No, not *terribly* exciting, really. Though I enjoy it well enough, and it does have its moments, there's no denying.'

'You've led a very interesting life. All your travelling in the army, and now coming home to work on a newspaper. It sounds fascinating. I haven't done anything.'

'Oh, I don't believe that.'

'It's true. I haven't had an exciting time like you. I'm twenty-one years old. I was born and brought up in Capinfell, and in all my life I haven't been further than Swindon in the north and Cannonford in the south.'

'Is it a nice place, Capinfell?'

'Oh, well, it's nice enough. It's very small. Just a village. There's the smithy and a post office, and that's about it. If you want anything else you must go to Hurstleigh or Merinville.'

He shook his head. 'I don't know any of those places. They're only names to me.' He paused. 'I can only say how glad I am that you decided to come to Redbury that day, and that you and your sister missed one another.'

Lydia looked down, unable to meet his steady gaze, the faint smile that still hovered on his mouth.

'When are you going back to Capinfell?' he asked.

'Next Saturday. My father will be most disappointed if I don't go.'

'I'm sure.' He sighed. 'Ah, well.'

As he continued to look across the table at her, she said, raising her glance to meet his own, 'I shall have to go soon. I think it's time.'

'Yes, I'm afraid it is. I'll take you home.' He took up his beer, drank the last of it and set the glass back down on the table. 'Come on. Let's go.'

Outside in the yard the stable boy brought the mare and carriage to them, and Guy gave the lad a couple of coins and then helped Lydia up into the seat and climbed up after her.

As they drove back along the road, Lydia felt very conscious of his presence beside her. For the most part she kept her eyes on the way ahead, rarely turning to take in the face of the man at her side, but many times as they jogged along she could see on the periphery of her vision that he was looking at her. She sat with her hands clasped.

'Now, whereabouts are you staying?' he asked as they moved into the outlying streets of the city.

'Little Marsh Street. Number 15. It's close to the Victoria Gardens, near Somerton Walk.'

'Oh, yes, I know roughly where it is.'

They drove on, past the gasworks, the railway station, the Great Western Hotel. There was little traffic on the roads and they made their way steadily, their pace uninterrupted. When the public gardens came in view Lydia stirred in her seat. The ending of the day was looming.

As they drew alongside the gardens, Guy called out to the mare, 'All rightie, Tess. Whoah there, old girl,' and pulled her to a halt. He turned to Lydia.

'I don't want to take you back yet,' he said. 'So I'm putting it off.'

'But I have to get back,' she said. 'I told you, I shall upset Mrs Obdermann, and I can't have that.' Her heart thumped as she looked at him. This past time with him – although they had done nothing that anyone could think of as remarkable – she felt that nothing quite like it had ever happened to her before.

'Mr Anderson –' she said.

'Guy.'

'Guy.' She paused, then added, 'May we go on, please?'

Ignoring her request, he gave a smile of satisfaction. 'You know, that's the first time I've heard you say my name.'

'Please –' she began, but he broke in, interrupting:

'I'd like to see you again. May I?'

'Well . . .' She did not know how to respond. She wanted to say, *Yes, oh, yes*, but she had no knowledge of what to do. She was far from home and this was all so new to her. 'Well . . .' she said again. How foolish she must sound, she thought; how naïve she must appear in his eyes.

'Don't say *well*,' he smiled. 'Say yes.'

She remained silent, and he stayed silent also for some seconds. Then he said, 'When you're back in Capinfell I'd like to come and call on you, if I may. I know it's probably a bit of a distance, but I –'

'When I'm back in Capinfell?' Lydia said, 'What do you mean? I'm not going back to live in Capinfell. Well, at least I have no plans to – not yet, anyway.'

'But you said you'd be returning there next Saturday . . .'

'That's just for the weekend. I'll be going on Saturday and coming back on Sunday. I'm just going to visit my father, that's all.'

'Oh,' he said with a grin, 'I misunderstood. I somehow got the idea that you had come here simply for a break from the routine – for a week's holiday.'

Lydia gave a little chuckle. 'I couldn't afford to come here for a holiday.'

'Then, what are –'

'I'm *staying* here. I'm *living* here. This is the end of my first week.'

'So you've left Capinfell.'

'Well – yes. Now I'm working here in Redbury. When we met that first time I had just come in for the day to have an interview for employment.' She smiled. 'And I got the situation I was after.'

He nodded, smiling along with her. 'That's even better. I wasn't looking forward to the jaunt to Capinfell, but now it won't even be necessary. Where are you working in the town?'

'At Seager's. I've got a job in the postal order department.'

'That's good,' he said, 'to know that you won't be rushing away out of town.' He smiled at her a moment longer, then, turning, took up the reins. 'I'd better get you back to Little Marsh Street.' Clicking his tongue at the mare, he called to her, 'Come on, Tess – heyup!' and they set off again.

A few minutes later he was helping Lydia down outside number 15.

'I'll be in touch with you,' he said. 'Is that all right?'

She paused before replying: 'Yes . . .'

'Then I shall be. Depend upon it.'

As she let herself into the house she was aware of him standing at the gate, watching her. At the last moment, just as she was closing the door, she looked back out at him, and gave a little wave. When the door was closed she leaned back against it for a second, smiling.

Chapter Eight

During the following day, Monday, Lydia frequently found her thoughts returning to Guy, and as frequently found herself wondering whether she would hear from him again. The day dragged interminably, and she could not wait for the time when she could leave the office and return to her lodgings.

The first thing she saw on entering the hallway of the narrow house in Little Marsh Street was the letter waiting for her on the small table near the looking glass. It had no stamp, but was marked in the top right corner *By hand*. The handwriting that gave her name and address was unfamiliar.

Upstairs she took off her hat and jacket, sat down in the little worn armchair and opened the envelope. It was from Guy. He had written:

> Datchet House
> Lincoln Street
> Redbury
> Monday 14th July 1890

Dear Lydia,

(Or perhaps I should have been a little more formal and addressed you as Miss Halley. Whatever . . . If I am in the wrong, please excuse it and put it down to enthusiasm.)

I am writing this soon after getting into the office, and I shall see it delivered to your lodgings later today. I couldn't wait to say how much I enjoyed meeting you yesterday. Your sister too for that matter, of course, but my first thoughts are of you. Oh, Lydia, Miss Halley, what a pleasure it was, and if you received half the joy from the meeting that I received, then you are a happy young woman indeed.

Well, now I must ask it, and risk refusal: would you care to meet again? I hope you will say yes; and in the hope that you will, I will wait for you at the south entrance to the Victoria Gardens at eight o'clock on Tuesday. If you are not there, then I shall live in the hope that your absence is due to your having been prevented from being there, and not from any lack of wish on your part.

With my hopes held high, then, I shall look forward to the chance of meeting you again, and in the meantime I shall remain

Yours truly,

Guy Anderson

With her eyes closed and her lips in a faint smile, Lydia briefly pressed the letter to her breast. Then, holding it away again, she sat for long moments just looking at it. She had read it through many times before she went down to the dining room to have her supper.

After she had eaten, and was back in her room, Lydia sat down to write to Ryllis and to her father. To Ryllis she wrote that she was very pleased at their having been able to spend some time together, and added, with a lie, that she had enjoyed meeting Thomas. To her father she wrote that her work was going well, that she had spent part of the Sunday with Ryllis, and that she would be returning to Capinfell on Saturday to spend some time with him. Afterwards she went out and posted her letters.

*

The next day, at five minutes to eight, having eaten her supper some half-hour before, Lydia left the house to walk to the Victoria Gardens.

Guy was already there, she could see as she approached, standing beside the main gate, facing away from her. He turned as she drew near and saw her, and raised his hat, smiling his broad smile.

'Miss Halley,' he said, as she came to him, and then in a lower voice: 'Lydia.'

'Hello . . .' Briefly she pondered on her next word, but could not bring herself to utter his name, so ended adding nothing.

'So,' he said, 'here you are.'

'Here I am. As you can see, I got your letter. I didn't expect to hear from you so soon.'

He shrugged. 'Why wait around?' Then he added, 'I sent it with one of the messenger boys from the office.' He spread his hands beside him. 'As you notice, I came alone. Tess has already had a good run out today, so I thought she deserved a rest. Besides, it does me good to take Shanks's pony once in a while.' He turned and gestured towards the gardens. 'Shall we walk in the park?'

'Yes – that would be nice.'

'Unless there's somewhere else you'd rather go, or something else you'd rather do . . .'

'No, a walk would be very nice. I've been cooped up in an office all day, and on a warm day like this . . .' She let the rest of the sentence go unspoken.

Together they turned and made their way between the wrought iron gates and along the main pathway. Other, narrower paths branched off from the main one, and after a while they turned to the right, taking one of the lesser paths. Lydia observed to herself that the place was a popular venue; there were numerous people there of all ages – couples, and parents with their children – all out taking the warm evening air.

The gardens were spacious and seemed to Lydia to have no limits. After a time they came through a fringe of trees to a large pond, around which benches stood at intervals.

'Would you like to sit down for a minute?' Guy suggested.

Lydia nodded, yes, and together they moved to a bench just vacated by an elderly couple and sat down. After a moment, Lydia said: 'That was so kind of you yesterday – to drive Ryllis and Thomas to Barford like that.'

'Oh,' he said, 'I was glad to do it. It was a pleasure. Your sister seems a very nice young lady. Very pretty too.'

'Well – I think so.'

'Yes, indeed. How long has she been friends with Thomas?'

'Oh, not long. A matter of weeks, that's all.' She said nothing further on the matter. After a few moments Guy said: 'Have you been to this place before?'

'To these gardens? Only just inside the gates, really. I try to take a little walk most evenings after supper, and I discovered it on one of my first jaunts. It's so close to the house. I didn't come this far, though.' She looked around. 'It's a lovely spot.' She gestured towards the water before them. 'And this must be wonderful for the children in the afternoons.'

'Oh, yes, they sail their boats. So many of them. Boats of all shapes and sizes.' He waved a hand, taking in the whole area. 'And on the open ground in the windy weather, some of them fly their kites.' He paused for a moment, then added, 'Yes, it's a nice place, but I'd like to take you somewhere a little more special. Perhaps a restaurant, or –' He broke off then added, 'Would you like to go to the theatre?'

'The theatre?' She paused. 'I've never been. It – it isn't something my father would approve of.'

'Oh, yes, your father.'

She said, avoiding Guy's glance, 'My father is, as you might have gathered, a very particular man, with very strong ideas as to what is right and what is wrong.' She looked at Guy now. 'Mind you, there was hardly the temptation of the theatre and suchlike in Capinfell. As I told you, my father is a very religious man – and his beliefs are unshakeable.'

'And do you follow him in certain things?'

'I would like to lead my own life,' she said. 'Which is one reason I came Redbury. It may not seem so much to you, having been so far around the world, but to me it was quite a big step.' She studied him for a moment in silence, then added, 'Do you find it quite dull, being back in England, after all you've seen and all you've done?'

'No,' he said. 'No, not at all. I'm glad I came back. For one thing, it's meant that I've been able to meet you.'

To her annoyance she felt herself blushing at his words, and quickly she turned her face away.

An hour later, as they walked back through the gardens together, Guy said to Lydia, 'Are you busy tomorrow? If not, I'll try to get tickets for a show. I'm not sure what's on, but I've got an idea it's a music hall.' He waited. 'What do you think? Are you busy tomorrow evening?'

She hesitated before answering, then said, 'No, I'm not.'

'Then would you like to go?'

When she said nothing, he added: 'Or is it too soon after your – your loss?' He paused. 'How long is it now – since – you lost your mama?'

'Four months.'

'Four months.' He nodded and said with sympathy in his voice, 'It's not so very long, is it?' He paused. 'Well, I won't press you, but perhaps it wouldn't be wrong for you to come out and smile a little and laugh a little. What do you think?'

She thought about it for a minute then said, 'Thank you

. . . I – I think I'd find it very – interesting.' It was the wrong word, she knew, but she was at a loss as to what to say for the best.

'Good.' His smile was warm. 'I'm really pleased. I really am. Very well, then I shall try to get some tickets. Can you meet me a little earlier tomorrow?'

'Well – at what time?'

'Say seven o'clock?'

'Yes, I should think so.'

'Seven o'clock outside the theatre?'

'Yes, all right.'

'You know where it is?'

'Yes, I've been past it.'

I don't know yet what time the performance starts, but that should see us in plenty of time. Are you sure that's all right?'

'Yes.'

'What will you do about your supper – at the lodgings?'

'I don't know yet. I'll talk to my landlady. Have you any idea what time the programme will end?'

'I don't know – though it'll be after ten. I haven't been for some time – not for a couple of years, when I was home on leave.'

She nodded. 'I shall have to arrange for Mrs Obdermann to leave the bolt off. Otherwise I'll be locked out.'

Eventually they passed through the iron gates again and went back on to the street.

In Little Marsh Street, at the door of number 15, Guy put out his hand, and Lydia gave him her own. When they had shaken hands he said, 'Till tomorrow, then – at seven.'

She nodded. 'Till tomorrow.'

Inside the house, Mrs Obdermann, who always managed to keep an eye on the comings and goings at the door, came into the hall as Lydia moved to the stairs.

'Ah, Mrs Obdermann,' Lydia said, 'I was hoping to see you. The thing is, I'm going to the theatre tomorrow night with a friend and –'

'Oh, very nice,' the landlady said. 'What time are you leaving?'

'We've arranged to meet at seven.'

'Then you must eat before you go. You can't sit in the theatre with your stomach grumbling. I'll get your supper early.'

'Are you sure it's no trouble? I don't want to put you out.'

'No, no, it's all cold food, anyway, there's no cooking to be done, but you'll have to look sharp getting back from the store.'

'Oh, yes, I know that.'

'What about when the show is over? Will you be late?'

'I don't know what time it ends.'

'Well, as you know, I usually bolt the door at ten thirty. But I'll leave it for you to do tomorrow.'

'I won't forget.'

'Please don't. Otherwise we could all be murdered in our beds.'

Lydia walked briskly back from the store the next day, and up in her room washed and changed. She put on her grey wool dress, with fresh cuffs and lace collar, the latter made by her mother in years past. When she was ready she went downstairs to the dining room where Mrs Obdermann had just set out for her a plate of ham and salad. There was fruit pie to follow. It was all quite good and tasty, Lydia thought, but nevertheless she almost had to force the food down; her excitement had taken away her appetite. When she was through she fetched her jacket and hat, wished Mrs Obdermann a good evening, and left the house.

She reached the Queen's Theatre a few minutes after seven and found Guy standing waiting near the entrance.

He smiled as he saw her approach, and went to meet her, taking her hand in greeting.

'We've got plenty of time,' he said. 'The show doesn't start till half past.' He patted his breast pocket. 'I've got the tickets.'

Looking past his shoulder, Lydia could see the billboards. 'It's a music hall, like you said.'

'Yes, are you sure that's all right?'

'Yes, indeed.' With an ironic smile she added, 'Though my father would most definitely disapprove. Shakespeare he might have tolerated at a pinch, but a music hall, no.'

A little later, when the time came, they made their way inside the theatre. It was a new world to Lydia, And she felt a thrill of excitement at the unaccustomed adventure. In the foyer she took in the ornate mirrors and the burgundy carpets with awe; it all looked so grand. There too were framed posters on the walls advertising past productions, and also photographs of famous artistes who had appeared over the years. Inside the auditorium she was amazed at the scene before her. The seats that Guy had bought were in the dress circle, and Lydia sat in her velveteen-covered seat and gazed around her. The place looked absolutely vast – and so beautifully decorated, with gold cherubs set into the ceiling, and huge crimson drapes covering the stage's proscenium arch. In the orchestra pit a group of musicians had assembled and were tuning up their instruments.

'Well?' said Guy, smiling at her as she gazed about. 'What do you think?'

'I can't get over it,' she said, shaking her head. 'It's amazing – and so beautiful.'

'If you think this is beautiful you should see the theatres in London. Some of them are absolutely huge, and the lighting is astonishing. They're mostly lit by electricity now.'

Guy had secured programmes for them, and Lydia

opened hers and looked down the list of acts that were promised. They meant nothing to her, as she did not know any of the artistes, but that did not matter. She was so excited that she could feel her heart thumping in anticipation. Then, suddenly, there was no more time to try to read the playbill, for the lights were going down, the pit band had begun to play and the curtains were parting.

Towards the side of the stage stood a small table with a grey-haired man behind it, with puffed out chest and a grand manner, and wearing a bow tie and tails. Guy leaned to Lydia and whispered, 'He's the chairman; the emcee.' And Lydia nodded, though having no idea what was meant.

Then the man, in florid language, introduced the first act on the bill. This was a trio of tumblers, three small acrobatic young men who threw one another around in the most amazing ways. Time after time their injury-defying stunts had Lydia's hands pressing to her cheeks in fearful anticipation, but the men landed safe and sound. Following them came a man in a frock coat, with a cigar, who told comic stories, some of them so rude that Lydia wondered that such things could be said in a public place for everyone to hear. Nevertheless, the audience as a whole seemed to enjoy it greatly, and gave him a huge ovation. Lydia did not know whether to applaud him or not, and ended up just clapping politely, though at the same time she did not wish to show disapproval of anything. At her side she was aware of Guy clapping with a touch more enthusiasm, but she dared not turn and look at him for fear of blushing. As for what her father would have said of the act, she thought, it was better not to contemplate.

After the comedian came two young girls who danced and sang prettily, and made saucy eyes at the musicians in the pit. They were followed by a magician and his glamorous assistant. The man wore tails and his attractive young helper a costume revealing a lot of leg and back and shoulders – which drew whistles from some of the men in the audience. Swiftly the clever man held spellbound every single spectator as he produced flowers out of thin air, and then made them vanish again just as quickly, but that was as nothing compared to other things that he could do. After asking his assistant to lie down on a little mattress, he made both rise up into the air. Lydia could hardly believe she was seeing it with her own eyes, it just seemed so miraculous. Then he used a hoop to encircle the young woman's body, proving to everyone there that she was not supported by wires. When his act came to an end the magician took his bows and the curtains closed again.

As the lights came up, Lydia turned to Guy, and knew that he must be able to read the wonder in her face.

'Is it over already?' she said as many of the audience members began to get up from their seats.

'No,' Guy replied. 'This is just the interval. Would you like some refreshment of some kind?' He gestured in the direction of a young woman with a basket who stood near one of the exits, selling oranges and nuts. 'Or we could go into the bar and have something.'

Lydia thanked him, but said that she did not need anything, and after a while the members of the audience were back in their seats and the band began to play a lively tune to introduce the second half of the show. When they had finished, the chairman came back on to the stage, this time with a large glass of ale, which he drank in one go to the accompaniment of a drum roll. That feat accomplished to a round of riotous applause, he introduced the first act of the second half, which turned out to be a young man in a light check suit who sang romantic songs in a warm, soulful baritone. After him came on to the stage a tall woman with a little poodle under her left arm wearing a blue ribbon topknot. The large lady was the famed Madame Eleanor Frabizzi. While she spoke to the audience, two stagehands swiftly erected some stands and boxes, and placed some hoops and other items beside them. When the men had retreated backstage again, the lady turned and called into the wings, and on trotted two more poodles and a terrier. One of the poodles wore a yellow bow, the other pink. The terrier wore a little black bowler. For the next twenty minutes the dogs, under the woman's commands and encouragement, performed an amazing number of feats, involving jumping on and off the boxes and leaping through the hoops. The audience responded – particularly the females – with ahs and ohs, the indulgent kind often reserved for other people's babies.

After the madame, the chairman introduced the act called *Two for Tea*, the star of which was a lithe, not-so-young man who, before Lydia's eyes, assembled from items he took from a box a large doll, a rather sinister replica of a curvaceous blonde-haired young woman who, with her purple dress, red lips and black-lashed eyes, looked to be no better than she should be. He then proceeded to dance around with the doll and sing to her, and to Lydia's gaze it was the most wonderful thing, for the way the man moved the doll around it was as if she were absolutely real. The way he was able to make her arms and legs move about was no less than amazing. The act earned the man much warm applause.

After this came the final act, Arthur Beaning and the Four Beans. This was a father and his four sons, their ages ranging from nine to fourteen. The act consisted of Arthur Beaning trying to tell the audience a joke – which of course he never managed to finish until the very end, for all the time he would be interrupted by his sons. It was very entertaining, with songs and dances and lots of comical dialogue. The audience roared their approval.

And at last the final curtain came down and the show was over.

Lydia could not believe that so much time had passed by.

'So, what did you think?' Guy leaned towards her as he spoke. Around them the other spectators were moving out into the aisles and making their way to the stairs. 'Did you enjoy it?'

'Oh, it was wonderful!' Lydia breathed. 'I didn't want it to end.'

It was after ten-fifteen when they came out on to the pavement, and Guy asked her if she would care to go for a drink before she returned to her lodgings, but she said she thought she had better start to make her way back. 'Shall I call a cab?' he said, and she replied no, she would prefer to walk.

So they set out together, walking a yard apart, through the city streets, heading for Little Marsh Street and number 15.

When they reached it, Lydia took her latchkey from her bag and turned to Guy. 'Well,' she said, 'I shall wish you goodnight – and thank you again, for everything.'

'It was a pleasure.'

'Thank you. It was a most wonderful evening.'

'There can be more,' he said. 'If you want.' A moment, and then, 'I'd like there to be more.'

She hesitated and then said, 'Yes.' It was a very small sound, just a little word, but inside her breast she could feel the beating of her heart.

'I've got appointments tomorrow,' he said, 'but perhaps on Friday you'd like to come out. We can go somewhere for dinner, if you'd care to.'

'Well – yes,' she said, 'that would be very nice.'

He took her right hand then, the hand holding the key, and impulsively put it to his mouth and kissed the back of it. As he released her he said, 'I'll call for you on Friday, at seven, if that's all right?'

'Yes. I'll be ready.'

After bolting the door behind her, Lydia climbed the stairs. Her steps seemed to fall on the treads without weight. Her whole being felt light.

Later, she lay in her bed looking up towards the darkened ceiling, just visible in the faint light that crept in from the moon. She would not be seeing Guy until Friday. How could she survive till then? She thought back over the evening, seeing herself once again in the theatre, with Guy sitting at her side. She had been so conscious of his nearness, of hearing his every little laugh and chuckle at the goings-on before them.

She was still thinking of him as she fell asleep.

On returning from the store the following day she was surprised to find two letters waiting for her. One was from her father, and the other was from Ryllis. In her father's short letter he wrote that he would expect her on Saturday, and added that he was coming down with a slight cold. Ryllis's letter was a little longer. She wrote that she had received Lydia's letter, and of how nice it had been to see her on the Sunday. She went on to say that it had been a great pleasure meeting Mr Anderson, and was pleased to hear that Lydia had taken to Thomas. 'Isn't he splendid?' she said, and then added, 'I'm afraid he was a little out of sorts when you met him – due to a troublesome tooth.'

After supper that evening, Lydia did little other than sort out items of laundry and take them to a washerwoman who lived nearby. She could pick up the items, washed and ironed, on Saturday, she was told. Afterwards, she walked on to the Victoria Gardens and strolled on the pathways between the herbaceous borders. All the time she thought of Guy as he had been walking at her side.

At breakfast the next morning she told Mrs Obdermann that she would be going out for supper, and would not need any provided in the house. The landlady asked if she planned to be back late, indicating with her tone that she didn't want to make a habit of leaving her lodgers to bolt the door. No, Lydia told her, she expected to be back before half past ten.

'I don't want you to think I'm overly fussy, Miss Halley,' Mrs Obdermann said, 'but we have to have rules, and I find it hard to sleep when I know the house isn't locked up.'

'Of course. I understand perfectly.'

There came a knock at the door at five minutes to seven that evening. Mrs Obdermann, knowing that it was almost certainly Lydia's caller, did not answer it herself, but started up the stairs to fetch Lydia. Lydia, however, had heard the rapping, and was already out on the landing as Mrs Obdermann reached it.

'Your caller, I think, Miss Halley,' the landlady said, and Lydia thanked her. She moved past her on the landing and went down into the hall and opened the door.

Standing on the step in the small porch, Guy tipped his hat and said, smiling, 'Good evening. Am I too early?'

Lydia returned his smile. 'No, not at all. I'm quite ready.' She stepped back into the hall to check herself before the mirror, touching at her hat and smoothing down her jacket. Then, as satisfied as events allowed, she moved back to the foot of the stairs, where she called up to the landlady, who still hovered on the landing, 'I'll see you later this evening, Mrs Obdermann.'

'Yes, indeed,' the older woman called back down. 'I hope you enjoy yourself.'

Lydia crossed back to the front door, closing it behind her, and Guy turned and led the way up to the front gate, beyond which the familiar horse and carriage waited. He helped Lydia up and then climbed beside her and took up the reins. As the carriage started off, Guy said: 'I thought we'd drive a little into the country and find a place to eat. Get away from the town for a while. I thought it was safe to bring the trap again; it looks promising to stay fine.'

The place they eventually decided on was the Crown and Hare, an inn about a mile out of the city. Guy said he had eaten there on an earlier occasion, when he was once home on leave from his regiment.

Leaving the horse and carriage in the care of a stable boy, Guy led the way into the inn. The interior was quite crowded, and the landlord, after greeting them, asked if they would like to sit outside. 'It's such a beautiful evenin', sir,' he said, 'and you'll be away from much of the noise.'

Guy and Lydia agreed, and the landlord showed them through the room and out of a door to a courtyard where three tables were placed. Two were occupied by people who sat eating and drinking, while a third, set in a small alcove, was vacant. Led to the empty table, they sat down on tall-backed benches facing one another. Would they, the landlord asked, like something to drink while he fetched the bill of fare? After briefly consulting Lydia, Guy asked for some wine, and the man went away, saying it would be brought to them.

'He's found us a nice spot, don't you think?' Guy said, looking around.

'Oh, yes, indeed.'

Beyond the flagged area on which the table stood lay a lawn with herbaceous plots. Just a few feet from where they sat grew roses and nasturtiums and pansies, and their scent rose up in the evening air and hung there, sweet and fragrant. A small dog came to them, stopping beside Lydia, and she patted him a couple of times before he moved on in search of attention elsewhere. Lydia took off her gloves and put them in her bag on the bench. She was filled with the same sense of excitement she had known on going to the theatre. It was another new experience. In just a few days, it seemed, her whole life was taking on a different hue.

After a little while a young maid came to them with a white cloth which she spread over the table. That done she set down cutlery, and a jug of wine which she poured into glasses. When she had gone, Guy lifted his glass. 'Here's to you – Lydia.' She held up her own glass and he touched it with his. Then he drank a little of the wine and smiled at her over the glass's rim. 'Taste your wine,' he said, and watched her as she sipped at it.

'It tastes delicious,' she said. 'It tastes of fruit and summer.' She sipped again. She was unaccustomed to wine. Only on three occasions had she ever tasted it before, and that was when visiting Evie's house at Christmas time. Three stolen occasions, and not one of them known to her father – like this glass in her hand, like this whole evening.

The landlord appeared beside the table, holding a slate from which he read off the bill of fare. They chose smoked fish, followed by roast beef and vegetables. The man went away again and they were left there in their little silence, touched only by the voices from the other tables and the laughter and murmuring from inside the inn. After a while, Lydia could hear music. 'Can you hear?' she said. 'Some-one's playing a violin.' The melody was some vaguely familiar tune whose title at that moment escaped her. It didn't matter; she loved the sound. Guy, appearing content, gave a little sigh of pleasure and from his jacket pocket took a cigarette case and a box of matches. Lighting a cigarette he blew the smoke out into the soft summer air, and Lydia watched it curl and drift away.

When their food was served they ate slowly, enjoying the fine tastes and textures. The landlord came to them again when the beef was finished and from his offerings they ordered fresh strawberries and cream, and Lydia thought again of the fruit that had spilled over the flags that day, and of how Guy had helped her to gather them up. Now, as they ate, the sound of the violin drew closer, and then there the man was, suddenly at their side, the sweet sounds of the instrument floating out. He began to play *Only Come!* When he had finished playing a chorus a man at the next table took up the song and sang along to the violin's accompaniment. He was thickset and in his forties, with an unromantic appearance, but his voice was the warmest baritone and was sweetly in tune with the strings of the violin.

> *Come, when dawn first climbs the hills*
> *To light the sky;*
> *Come when the shadows on the rills*
> *Show day must die;*
> *Come, when the last faint evening chime*
> *Is hushed and dumb; hushed and dumb;*
> *Come in spring or wintertime;*
> *But only come. Only come.*

The song ended and the singer inclined his head to the violinist and sat down to a little burst of happy applause. As the violinist moved away to another table Lydia said to Guy, 'That was beautiful. The playing and the singing.'

Guy smiled. 'Perhaps just a fraction sentimental?'

'I don't care,' she said. 'I love it.'

The strawberries were eaten, Lydia drank a little more of the wine, and then coffee was served. Taking a sip from the thick cup, she tasted the coffee – a little strong – and thought, I shall never sleep after this.

141

'What are you thinking?' Guy said.

'I was just thinking,' she replied, 'that I mustn't forget the time. I mustn't be late. I told Mrs Obdermann I'd be back by half past ten.'

'What would happen if you're late?'

'Well, nothing drastic, I suppose. I've got my latchkey, so I can get in all right. She won't have bolted the door against me, but I've no doubt she'll be listening for my return. I have to bolt the door when I get in.'

'Don't worry,' he said. 'I'll get you back.' He took a drink from his coffee cup and then gave a deep, heartfelt-sounding sigh of pleasure. 'Oh, Lydia, I'm so glad you decided to come to Redbury that day – and that you and your sister missed one another.'

Unable to meet his steady gaze, Lydia lowered her glance and took refuge in taking up her wineglass and gazing down into it. She held it with both hands, and looked down into the ruby glow. It was like gazing into the heart of some precious gem. All the time she could feel Guy's eyes upon her and and then she felt her fingers enclosed as he reached across the table and wrapped his hand around hers. She almost flinched. She did not move her hands however, but remained as she was, and closed her eyes, conscious of the very sound of her breathing and the touch of his strong fingers on her own.

'Oh, Lydia,' she heard him whisper across the table, but she did not open her eyes, and still did not move her hands.

Then she felt his fingers gently remove the fingers of her right hand from around the glass, and draw her hand towards him across the table. She wanted to open her eyes and see what was happening, but she could not. She sat there and allowed her hand to be carried to him, and, as she discovered a moment later, it was carried to his mouth, for she felt a softness upon her fingers and realised that it was the softness of his lips.

She opened her eyes then and looked across the table at him. He sat leaning forward slightly, his eyes steady upon her own, his right hand holding her own right hand to his mouth. Her own mouth formed a little O, but still she did not withdraw her hand, and she watched as, still with his eyes upon her, he moved it and kissed her fingers again, pressing his lips upon her fingertips, her knuckles. She could feel her hand trembling under his touch, and was sure that he must be aware of it too. There was nothing she could do to prevent it, however, her trembling; and it was nothing to the fluttering that was going on about her heart.

'Oh, yes,' he said, raising his head, 'I'm so glad you came to Redbury that day.'

Now, after another moment, she moved to withdraw her hand, and felt him reluctantly release her. She put down her wineglass and looked vaguely around her at the summer evening scene. She heard herself say, 'I shall have to go,' and gave a little sigh.

'Right – we'll just finish our wine and coffee and we'll go.' He drank again from his cup, then said, 'Oh, I wish you weren't leaving town tomorrow. Why d'you have to decide to go to Capinfell?'

'I told you,' she said. 'I'm going to see my father.'

'Yes, I know. I'm teasing. I just wish you weren't going.'

'I must.'

'And you won't be returning until Sunday.'

'No.'

'What time are you coming back?'

'I shall try to catch the six-twenty from Merinville, which gets into Redbury just after seven.'

'That's two whole days you're going to be away.'

'Yes.'

'Is it possible we can meet when you get back on Sunday?'

143

She frowned, shaking her head. 'Oh, I don't think so. I think I shall just feel like going back to my lodgings.'

'Oh – shame.'

'Well, for one thing I'll have to get ready for Monday.'

'I suppose so.'

'Oh, I dare not be late. I'm a new girl, don't forget. I feel every eye is upon me – and will be for a while yet.'

'Is it possible, then, that we can meet on Monday evening?'

She nodded. 'Yes, that's possible – if you wish.'

'I *do* wish.' His voice was soft, but urgent. 'I do indeed. Shall I meet you outside the Victoria Gardens again?'

She paused. 'All right.'

'Say half past seven.'

She nodded. 'Half past seven.'

'What if it's raining?'

'Well – I've got an umbrella.'

'Or you could wait opposite in the doorway of the Rose and Flag.' Then he added, 'No, no, that wouldn't do. What about your reputation?'

'Then I must pray for fine weather,' she said.

She looked around. The violinist had gone back into the inn and the people from the next table were gathering their belongings and preparing to leave. 'Really,' she said, 'I have to go. I must go.'

He nodded, and at once called the serving girl who was passing, and asked for his bill. A few minutes later he and Lydia were moving into the stable yard where the boy brought them the mare and carriage. Guy gave the lad some coins and then helped Lydia up into the seat and climbed up after her. The light was just beginning to fade.

They rode for some distance without speaking of anything of importance, and Lydia was glad to keep the conversation on safe ground. For the most part she kept her eyes on the road ahead, rarely turning to take in Guy's face.

She had put her gloves back on, but she could still seem to feel the touch of his mouth upon her fingers.

At last they entered the city again, and as the Victoria Gardens came in view Lydia stirred in her seat. The end of the day was looming. Guy called out to the mare, 'All rightie, Tess. Whoah there, old girl,' and pulled her to a halt. As the carriage stopped, Lydia turned questioningly to him.

'I don't want to take you back yet,' he said with a shrug.

'But I have to get back,' she said. To her ears her voice sounded slightly breathless. Little wonder, she thought: these past hours with him – nothing like it had ever happened to her before.

They sat looking at one another, just for a few moments looking into one another's eyes, until Lydia, feeling herself flushing in the fading light, lowered her glance and turned her head away.

Above the trees of the Victoria Gardens the moon was pale and gleaming in the clear sky, a huge white disc with all its shadows clear upon its surface. Guy lifted his gaze to it as it hung over Lydia's head, and said, 'Look at the moon. It's beautiful,' and she turned and looked up into the sky. 'Yes, it is.'

He gazed at her as she sat with raised head, a little smile hovering on his mouth. 'There *is* a man in the moon,' he said. 'You can see for yourself – and he's smiling.'

Then, leaning towards her, he put his arms around her and drew her to him, and kissed her. It was not a long kiss, just a moment's pressure of his lips upon hers, but for all she knew it could have taken a lifetime. As he released her and drew back there came from a few yards away the sound of a little cheering 'Whoops!' and glancing around they saw that the sound had come from two young urchins who were passing. Now, as the boys caught the couple's eyes, they raised their thumbs in triumph and grinned.

'Cheeky little beggars,' Guy said, grinning in spite of himself, and then turning to Lydia added, 'but I must watch your reputation. Can't have you going back to Capinfell ashamed to show your face.'

She said nothing. She was still reeling from the kiss.

'Seriously,' he said, 'I shouldn't have done that. I truly should not.' He frowned, then gave a sound that was half chuckle, half sigh. 'Though I can't truly say I regret it, not for a moment, and if I could, I would do it again.' He leaned slightly towards her. 'Would you let me?'

Lydia briefly closed her eyes and put her hands to her mouth. Everything was happening so fast. 'Mr Anderson, I –'

'Guy.'

'Guy.'

She remained sitting there. She seemed to be caught in some kind of spell, a spell that even the vulgar shouts of the boys had not been able to break, but she had no experience of anything like this. 'I must go in,' she said.

'Right,' he said, lifting the reins. 'Let's get you back to Little Marsh Street.'

With a flap of the reins and a word to the mare they were on their way for the last yards of the journey.

Chapter Nine

On the way back from the store just after two o'clock on Saturday, Lydia stopped at a butcher's and bought a piece of mutton. After that she went to the washerwoman's house and picked up her clean and ironed laundry.

Back at her lodgings she packed a few things into a bag and then went in search of Mrs Obdermann.

'Just to let you know that I'm leaving now, Mrs Obdermann,' Lydia said when the landlady answered her knock on the sitting-room door. 'I'm off to get the train.'

'And you won't be back until tomorrow, is that correct?'

'That's right. Sometime in the evening. I expect to get back about seven, but it depends on how my father is. He says he's not that well, so I might take a later coach from Capinfell, but don't worry about supper for me.'

'That's not a problem,' the landlady said. 'I'll make you a cold plate and leave it in the larder. If you're late it won't matter.'

Lydia left then, and made her way to the railway station where, after a wait of some twenty minutes, she was able to get a train for Merinville. From there she travelled by coach to Capinfell. As she rode she thought again of Guy, and looked forward to their coming meeting on Monday evening. It seemed a lifetime away.

The church clock was striking six as she walked up the lane to her home, and she could feel her heart bumping slightly as she thought of seeing her father again. But there was no need for her to be anxious, she told herself. Although he had not been warm in his letter to her, at least he had not been disagreeable.

In a way that she could not have described, the sensation was a little strange as she let herself in at the back door. She had never been away from home for such a period in her life before. Two whole weeks. It was odd, she thought: everything in the house was just the same, and yet it all seemed a little different. Then she realised: it was her mother's presence that was missing. Coming home would never be quite the same again.

'Hello, Father?' she called out as she moved through the scullery. 'Are you there?'

There was no answering voice, and she thought perhaps he had gone out, but a moment later she entered the kitchen and there he was, sitting at the table, his notes and his papers spread out before him.

She stopped at the other end of the table, facing him. 'Hello, Father.' A tentative smile. 'As you see, I'm back.'

He nodded. 'So I see.'

She had not known what to expect, but she had not really expected more. After a moment's hesitation she set down her bag and went to him, bent, and kissed him lightly on the cheek. It was an awkward gesture but brief, and then she turned away and took off her hat and jacket. 'How is your cold?' she asked.

He sniffed, and briefly put a hand to his forehead. 'I've got a bit of a headache and a stuffy nose, but I'll survive. It's not enough to keep me from my work.'

From her bag Lydia took out the package of meat she had brought. 'I got us a nice little cut of mutton,' she said. 'We'll have it for dinner tomorrow.'

After putting the meat away she donned her apron and put the kettle on to boil. When the tea was made she and her father sat drinking it at the table.

'I hope Mrs Harbutt's looking after you,' Lydia said. 'Has she been coming in to get your dinner?'

'Oh, yes, she's been coming in.'

'And did you tell her that I was coming back this weekend?'

'Yes, I told her she wouldn't be needed.'

An hour later Lydia prepared a meal for the two of them, serving some cold ham that she found in the larder. It was followed with plums and cold custard, the latter having been made by Mrs Harbutt.

Later, Lydia told him about seeing Ryllis the previous weekend in Redbury, but she made no mention of Ryllis's friend Thomas Bissett. Her father asked how Ryllis was, and also asked whether she seemed any more settled in her employment with the Lucases. Lydia said she couldn't tell, but added that Ryllis had made no complaint at their meeting. Her father replied dryly that this made a change if nothing else.

'Well, Father,' Lydia said after a while, 'aren't you going to ask me how I'm getting on at the store?'

He was silent for a moment, then said, 'And how *are* you getting on?'

'I'm getting on all right,' she said. 'The work keeps me very busy, but I'm enjoying it.'

This was not exactly what he wanted to hear, she thought, and then wondered whether he might ask about the particular work she did, but he did not. The thought then crossed her mind that he might ask how she spent her evenings. What would she say? She could not tell him about Guy. She would never dare.

'There's a young man doing your job at Cremson's now,' he said. 'It didn't take them long to find a replacement. No one's irreplaceable.'

She had to ignore this, almost, and merely said, 'Oh,' and

then asked, 'What about you? What about your preaching? Have you been busy with it?'

'Of course,' he said, frowning. 'It would take a lot to stop that. People need meaning in their lives.'

A little later, as Lydia stood in the scullery washing the dishes, he came to her and said he had to be going to Hurstleigh on business. He would be back about ten, he added.

Left alone in the house, Lydia finished the washing up, then sat down to darn a couple of her father's socks. At ten o'clock she went upstairs. A while later, as she lay in bed, she heard her father's footsteps on the cobbles and not long afterwards the sound of his footfalls on the stairs as he came up to bed.

She accompanied her father to church on Sunday morning. On her arrival there as they waited for the service to begin, she looked around for Evie, but there was no sign of her. After the service, outside in the sun, Lydia said to her father, 'Father, you start on back. I'll catch you up. I just want to have a look at Mother's grave.'

'Shall I come with you?' he asked, but she was silent while she searched for a reply and he gave a nod and said, 'No, you go on your own. I'll start home.'

She left him and made her way down the little slope of the churchyard to where her mother's grave lay close to the shade of a large yew tree. There was no one else close by. Bending over the grave she said softly, 'Hello, Mother. I've come back to see you. I think about you every day.' The stone's surface was pale and gleaming in the bright morning sunlight, the crisply-cut letters read:

SACRED TO THE MEMORY OF
EMMA MARY HALLEY 1845–1890

'I'm sorry I can't come as often to see you now, Mother,' Lydia whispered, 'but I'll get here when I can, and soon I'll bring a nice flower to plant for you. Perhaps a pretty little tea rose.' She kissed the tips of her fingers and gently touched them to the top of the stone. Then, picking up her skirts, she made her way up the slope and on to the church gate.

Back at the house she put the mutton into the oven and set about preparing the rest of the dinner. When it was ready, she and her father ate in near silence, speaking only desultorily, and of mundane subjects that were safe from dissension. Afterwards, Lydia washed up the dishes and the pans and then announced that she was going to see Evie for half an hour.

When Lydia called at Evie's cottage door a short while later she found her sitting on the sofa alone, sewing a little shift for Hennie. Hennie was upstairs asleep, Evie said, and her mother was out delivering some clean washing.

'Do you want some tea?' she asked as Lydia sat down. 'I'll put the kettle on.'

Lydia thanked her, but declined. 'I shall be having some with Father as soon as I get back indoors,' she said. From her bag, she brought out a paper bag, and took from it a little storybook with bright pictures. 'I brought this for Hennie,' she said. 'I bought it in the store.'

'Ah . . .' Evie took the book into her hands. '*Hansel and Gretel*. Oh, she'll *love* it. Oh, thank you, Lyddy. I shan't get any peace once she's heard this, I can tell you.' She leafed through the book, glancing at the colourful pictures, and then put it carefully back in the bag. 'I'll give it to her as soon as she gets up,' she said.

As Evie put the book aside, Lydia said, 'I looked out for you at church this morning.'

'Oh, I decided not to go,' Evie said. 'Hennie was being especially good, and it give me a chance for a lie-in. You went with your father, did you?'

'Oh, yes. I wouldn't dare not to.'

'How did you find him? Is he well?'

'He's got a bit of a cold, but other than that he's all right.'

'I expect he was very glad to see you back.'

'I suppose so.' Lydia nodded. 'He doesn't give much away.'

A thought occurred to Evie, and she said, 'Oh, I saw your friend the other day. Your admirer.'

'My what?' Lydia said.

'Mr Canbrook. I went into Merinville and popped into his shop to get some cotton thread. He recognised me as your friend and asked me where you were. "Where's your friend today?" he asked. "Where's Miss Halley?" I told him that you'd gone to Redbury to live and work. He looked quite put out about it.' She waited a moment for Lydia's reaction, then added, on a more solemn note, 'He mentioned your mother, too. He said how sorry he had been to hear about her – her passing.'

'That was nice of him. I heard from him when Mother died. I told you that. He wrote a letter of condolence. Just a brief note, but it was nice that he took the trouble.'

A few moments went by, then Evie said, looking at Lydia judiciously, 'I suppose you find quite a few differences now you're living and working in Redbury. I don't suppose you miss Cremson's at all, do you?'

'Cremson's?' Lydia shook her head. 'No, not a bit. I haven't got time to miss it. You've never seen such a busy office as the one I work in, and the store itself . . . I know I've told you before, but – oh, there's nothing it doesn't sell. Why, they even have a lending library. I work in the department dealing with the orders that come in by post – and you should see the value of some of those orders! You would think some people had so much money it was no object.' She gave a little laugh. 'But sometimes some of the ladies change their minds, and won't accept the goods when the van tries to deliver them. They get their maids and butlers to say they're out.'

Evie laughed at this. They spoke of various matters and people known to them both, and then Evie asked after Ryllis, and Lydia told how she had seen her the previous Sunday, and that they had had tea together.

'I didn't tell you,' Lydia said, 'but she's met someone. He came into Redbury to meet us in the teashop.'

'Oh – well, how nice. I hope you approve of him.'

Lydia said after a moment's hesitation, 'Well, as a matter of fact, I just found him to be sometimes – disagreeable, and he wasn't as pleasant to Ryllis as I would have liked him to be. Too much finding fault for my liking, though Ryllis forgave him everything, it seemed.' She shook her head. 'But I mustn't say anything else against him. Ryllis said he was suffering from the toothache, so I've probably misjudged him. I won't say any more.'

'What about you?' Evie said.

'Me? What about me?'

Evie smiled. 'Have you met anyone? Now you're living in the city. What about in your office? Or in the store? There must be so many good-looking young men around.'

Lydia gave a little shrug. 'Oh, yes, I suppose there are.'

'You suppose there are?' Evie's tone and expression were arch. 'I felt sure you'd get back and tell me you've met someone. Haven't you made some friends in the store? Surely you have.'

'Oh, well, they're all friendly enough,' Lydia replied, 'but everyone seems to be too busy for much in the way of casual chatter. The supervisor's there all the time, so everyone generally gets on with the work. It's only during our tea break and dinner break that there's any chance to chat.'

'Well, that's a start. A good enough opportunity to meet some nice young fellow.'

153

'Oh, not really. The men and the women tend to keep apart at those times.'

'Oh, that's a pity,' Evie said dolefully. 'Then what about people *outside* the store?'

'What d'you mean?'

Evie gave a little groan. 'Oh, Lyddy, you're such a disappointment. I could have bet a shillin' that you'd get back and tell me you'd met someone special.'

Lydia did not answer, but feeling Evie's eyes upon her, looked away.

'Ah, so you have, have you?' Evie said, moving her head to try and peer into Lydia's face. 'So now we're getting near the truth.' She gave a nod. 'Well, I'm glad to hear it, and I'm glad you haven't wasted any time.'

'Oh, don't,' Lydia said. 'Don't say that. Not like that.'

'I'm teasing you,' Evie said, 'but tell me, please. I've got to know everything. Is he nice looking?'

'Oh, yes. Yes, he is.'

'And what's his name? How old is he?'

'His name is Guy. Guy Anderson. He's twenty-five, and he's just come out of the army after several years abroad.'

'And what does he do? What work does he do?'

Lydia gave a sigh and looked away. 'Oh, Evie – that's just the trouble. I look at his background and – well, how can I fit into it? It just doesn't seem possible.'

'What about his background?'

'His parents are well off. Very well off. I mean, for goodness' sake, they own a newspaper – and a business in Italy.'

'Oh – sounds very grand!'

'Quite,' Lydia replied. 'And look at me. I've got nothing. My father works in a factory and I'm a clerk in a department store.'

'But if he really cares for you . . .' Evie said. 'I mean – at twenty-five he's old enough to know what he wants.' She reached out and pressed Lydia's wrist. 'How does he feel about you?' she asked.

'Well, he – I've only known him a week.'

Evie nodded. 'It's not long, is it?'

'Mind you,' Lydia said, sighing, 'it's been the most wonderful week. We've met several times. I've even been to the theatre.'

'The theatre!'

'Yes! Oh, it was so exciting.' Lydia gave a breathy, nervous little laugh. 'The whole evening. I didn't want it to end.'

Evie said after a moment's silence, 'Do you – feel deeply for him, Lyddy?'

Lydia lowered her head, avoiding Evie's gaze. 'Yes, I do,' she said. 'Do you think I'm foolish?' She raised her head again, looking earnestly into her friend's eyes. 'Oh, Evie, I know it's only been a week – but I never thought it would be possible to feel this way.'

Back at home Lydia put on the kettle for tea, and when it was made she served it with some cake that Mrs Harbutt had left in the pantry.

'It's good,' she said. 'Mrs Harbutt's fruit cake – it's very nice.'

'It'll do,' he said. 'It's not like your mother's, but you've got to make the best of what you've got. She doesn't iron my shirts properly either. Not the way your mother did, nor the way you did. Nor Ryllis, for that matter.'

Lydia said nothing. There had been no change in her father in the two weeks she had been away, but somehow her brief absence allowed her to look at him more closely. She took in the cold eyes behind the spectacles' lenses, and the thin mouth, and thought how unhappy and disapproving he looked. The lowness of spirits brought on by his cold did not help. She looked at the clock on the mantelpiece and pushed aside her empty cup. 'I think it's time I was going,' she said. 'I'll wash up and then go off to get the coach.'

As she stirred in her seat, about to rise, he said: 'You don't care a fig about me, do you?' There was a sad bitterness in his voice, and Lydia was halted in her movement.

'Don't – don't care about you?' she said. 'Of course I care about you. How can you say such a thing?'

'But you're going.'

'Well – well, I have to. I've got to get back.' She paused. 'Father, please – don't,' she said. 'Don't do this.'

'I'm being foolish,' he said. 'I somehow convinced myself that you might come home for good. I had the idea that two weeks away from home, living in lodgings and eating whatever's put before you might have been enough. I thought, the girl's bound to see the light eventually, and she'll get fed up and want to come home. I know things have been difficult here – what with your mother's going . . . but things settle down and life goes on.' He looked away from her. 'I'd like you to come home,' he said gruffly. 'I wish you'd come home.'

'Father –' she began, but he cut her off, saying, 'You don't have to go back to Cremson's, you can find another job – and if you don't, what does that matter? It's not important. We don't need a lot, just the two of us. I earn decent money. Not a fortune, but enough. We could manage all right.'

She could see it before her, so clearly. A life of days moving into weeks, into months, into years. Her youth slipping away into middle age, while her father grew old. She had seen it happen. The women were never taken seriously after a time; they were regarded with varying degrees of pity as they grew older, and became more seemingly eccentric with the passing years. And what had they to show for it – those spinsters who, in the end, were always left alone?

'Supposing I asked you,' he said, briefly stifling his pride, 'Suppose I asked you to reconsider? You could go back and give in your notice. Supposing I asked you . . .?'

Now Lydia got to her feet. 'Oh, Father, I can't do it. I'm sorry if it upsets you, but I just can't. Please don't ask me.' She felt tears springing to her eyes, and quickly with her fingers she wiped them away. 'But I'll come and see you when I can,' she said, 'and Ryllis will too. You've got two of us, you know.'

'Yes, I know all about that.' He did not look at her as he spoke. After a moment he waved a dismissive hand and said, 'You'd best get off, then, or you'll miss your coach.'

A little while later, without an embrace, without a kind word of goodbye from him, she left the house.

There was an unexpected delay at the Rising Sun inn when one of the coach horses had to be changed, which meant Lydia was late getting into Merinville. Missing her intended train to Redbury, she was forced to kick her heels on the platform for a further thirty minutes, waiting for the next one. When it came she got in with relief, glad to be finally on her way again. She felt strangely alone, and the miserable scene with her father had left her depressed and unhappy. She would not be seeing Guy until after work tomorrow. The rest of Sunday evening stretched before her.

At Redbury she got out of the train and made her way along the platform to where the ticket collector stood at his post. Beyond him, on the other side of the barrier, she saw the familiar tall figure of Guy.

He came towards her as she passed through, and reached out and took her hand.

'Lydia,' he said. 'I thought you'd never come.'

'I missed my connection at Merinville.' She could scarcely believe that he was standing before her. 'I had to wait for the next train, and then –' She broke off and gave a nervous little chuckle. 'What – what are you doing here?'

'I had to see you,' he said. His voice and face had an earnestness that she had not seen before, but she was thrilled to see him, thrilled that he had come to meet her train. Smiling, she said, 'Couldn't it wait until tomorrow?'

'I can't see you tomorrow,' he said. 'Something's happened. Something's come up.'

'What? What's happened?'

'I've got the trap outside,' he said. 'Can you ride with me for a while?'

'Well – yes, if you wish.'

'Oh, yes – please.' He took her arm and led her out on to the street to where the mare and the carriage were waiting.

Chapter Ten

They were moving away from the town centre, Lydia saw at once. 'Where are we going?' she said.

'We'll drive out a little, into the country,' Guy said. 'Do you mind?'

Briefly she hesitated. 'No . . .'

'Have you got to get back in a hurry?'

She thought of Mrs Obdermann, leaving the cold plate in the larder. 'No,' she said again. She could tell that something was amiss. 'No, it's all right. I don't need to rush back.'

Guy drove looking straight ahead of him. 'I waited for you,' he said. 'I've been at the station since five. I had to see you.'

'All that time. But why? What's happened?'

'I'll tell you. Give me a minute.' Still he did not glance at her, but kept his eyes on the road before them. He wore a brown, soft felt hat, and the brim cast his eyes in shadow so that their expression could not be seen.

After a time they were leaving the town houses behind them, and the dwellings were getting fewer, the gardens and the spaces between them larger. Then they were moving out into the open country, along a road where there was little other traffic. Still she said nothing, respecting his unspoken wish for silence. She sat close beside him on the seat, so close that often his arm brushed hers as he held the reins.

There were wheatfields on either side of them as they

drove, the wheat high and golden, waiting for the harvest to come, very soon now by the appearance of the crops. The sun on the corn was bright and oblique, the sky above hazy and settling into the mellow light of the evening. The hooves of the mare rang clear on the hard road.

They were coming up to a short lay-by now, Lydia saw, and suddenly Guy adjusted the reins and called on the horse to move to the left. 'Over now, Tessie,' he called, and the horse and carriage moved off the main road, drove on for a few yards into the lay-by, and came to a halt.

Guy gave a deep sigh, as if relaxing after sudden exertion, and Lydia turned to him on the seat, looking at his strained expression. 'Guy, what is it?'

'I had to see you,' he said. He turned to face her now. 'I had to explain that I can't meet you tomorrow. I've got to go away.'

'You've got to –' She frowned, shaking her head. 'But – but what's happened? Something's happened? What is it?'

Some moments of silence went by, then he said, 'I had a wire from my mother yesterday, in Italy. She wrote to say that my father's suffered a dreadful accident and is very ill in hospital.'

'Oh, Guy,' Lydia breathed. 'I'm so sorry to hear that. So your mother's with him, is she?'

'Yes. She went out there with him. They've been gone about three weeks.' He sighed, and sat with eyes downcast. 'I've got to go. I'd never forgive myself if something worse should happen.'

'Of course you must go.'

'My mother wrote that he's too sick to travel. She's obviously very concerned – and she's not one to over-dramatise a situation.' In a brief gesture he put up his hands, covering his face. 'Oh, Lydia, I'm so worried.'

'I'm sure you are.'

'My mother will need me to help take care of things as well. She's in no condition to do it.'

'When will you go?'

'Tomorrow. I must get there as soon as I can.'

'Of course you must.' She wasn't taking it all in as she should. He was leaving, going away. 'When'll you be back?' she said.

'Well, I hope it won't be long. I just hope we can get him well enough to travel so that I can bring him back to England again with the minimum delay.'

'Did your mother say exactly what was wrong?'

'She didn't go into detail, but she said he'd had a bad fall.'

They sat there in silence for some moments, then Guy said, 'I'll write to you, of course. I hope I shan't be away for long. My father – he's a tough old fellow. He doesn't let much get him down for long, but as I say, he's not young.' He gave a nod in affirmation of his words. 'I'll see you as soon as I get back,' he added.

'Yes . . .' Lydia said, then went on, 'It was such a surprise – to find you standing there, meeting the train.'

'A nice surprise, I hope.'

'Oh, yes. Of course.'

'I couldn't wait for your train to get in. I was so anxious to see you.' He glanced about him. 'It's the most beautiful evening. Look up, there's barely a cloud.' He turned on her a grave smile. 'And you're here now. We're here now. Don't you think we should make the best of it? While we can, before I have to go away.'

She did not know what to say, and merely gave a little half nod.

'Shall we drive out a little further?' he said.

'If you like.'

'When did you last eat?'

'I had a little tea and cake with my father before I started out.'

'Well, I'm quite hungry. I've hardly had anything all day. If I might suggest . . . we could pick up something on our way and have a picnic of sorts.'

'On our way? On our way where?'

'Well, we'll decide that, shall we?' He paused, as if waiting for a reaction. When none came he smiled again, more cheerily this time. 'Shall we drive on, then?'

'Very well.'

Guy flapped the reins and clicked his tongue to the mare, and they set off again, moving back out on to the road.

They drove steadily for half a mile, when they entered the little village of Kippis Norton. There was an inn situated on a corner, the Five Elms, and Guy suggested that they stop there to buy some provisions. He drove into the stable yard and pulled up the mare.

'Shall you wait here or come in with me?' he asked Lydia, and she said she would wait.

He put the reins into her hands and jumped down on to the cobbles, and she turned on the seat and watched as he strode away, and his tall, straight figure turned the corner towards the inn's entrance.

He was gone for almost ten minutes, and when he returned he carried an old basket with fraying handles. The basket was clearly full.

'Look,' he said, holding up the loaded basket. 'Look what I got.'

He handed it up to Lydia and then swung on to the seat. Taking the basket from her he placed it on his knees. 'Look.' He lifted up a package wrapped in a teacloth. 'Sandwiches,' he said. 'Beef sandwiches, and cheese sandwiches, some slices of ham, and two pieces of game pie.' He laughed. 'We must eat with our fingers, but that's all right, yes?'

'Of course.'

'Of course,' he repeated. 'It's the best way.' He put the sandwiches back. 'And something to drink.' He lifted up a bottle of wine, its ruby colour intense in the sun. 'And glasses, look. They're not the best quality, and one's a bit chipped, but I said that that wasn't of any importance to us. I paid the landlord for them, so we don't need to take them back.'

'There's so much,' Lydia said. 'There's enough for an army.'

'A small regiment, maybe.' He grinned at her. 'Anyway, we shan't go hungry.'

After he had set the basket in the well of the carriage he turned the mare and they moved back out to the road.

'There is a place,' Guy said as they drove along, 'where I used to go as a boy. An old clay pit. Long since discarded for the production of clay, but a lovely spot. Shall we go there? It's very secluded and peaceful.'

'It sounds very nice.'

At her words he smiled and nodded, then called out to the horse, 'You hear that, Tess? Off to Willen Water.' Turning to Lydia, he added with a wider smile, 'She's pleased as well, you can tell. Well, why not? She's a creature of taste.'

Willen Water turned out to be some two miles beyond Kippis Norton, and they reached it by a winding drive leading off from the road with a cornfield on one side and a spindly copse on the other. Passing through a wide gateway at the end, the path led both left and right around a lake fringed with trees, mostly willow and silver birch. Guy took the left path, and drove the carriage around beside the water. Eventually they came to a secluded area not too far from the water's edge, and there he pulled the mare to a halt and jumped down. After he had helped Lydia on to the grass he took out the basket of provisions, and then led the mare into a shady patch nearby where he hitched her up to the branch of a hawthorn. That done, he took from the box an old travelling rug which he laid out on the grass in the shade of a birch. 'This should suit us all right, don't you think?'

Lydia nodded. 'It's a lovely spot.'

Part of their view of the lake was obscured by a rambling wild rose, and also by a lushly flowering elder. It screened them, enclosing them.

From over on the far bank they could hear the distant sounds of children playing, yelling out in glee and high spirits as they ran and leapt into the sun-warmed water. Their cries rang out over the surface of the lake.

Guy made a few adjustments to the setting of the rug, then patted it and said to Lydia, 'There – now we can sit down and relax for a while.'

She sat down on the rug, her feet out in front of her, her eyes towards the body of water. Guy stood for a few moments and then took off his hat and jacket and laid them on the grass. He was wearing a shirt with a soft collar and a blue cravat. Lydia could see the movement of the muscles of his arms and shoulders beneath the white linen. He lowered himself onto the rug. 'Wouldn't you like to take off your hat?' he said. 'It must be very warm for you.'

'Well – yes, it is a little.' She unpinned her hat, took it off and put it down on the rug. She ran fingers through her hair, relieved to feel the fresh air upon it.

'You've got beautiful hair,' Guy said. 'It's a crime to keep it hidden.'

Lydia said nothing, but the warmth rose in her cheeks. Moving the conversation on to secure ground, she said, 'So you used to come here as a boy, did you?'

'Yes, I came here a few times. My father brought me. I always loved it so. He could hardly keep me out of the water.'

'I can picture it,' she said. 'I see you as an adventurous boy.'

He gave a little laugh. 'Perhaps. Perhaps.' He turned then to the old basket containing the provisions. 'Well?' he said. 'Shall we?'

Lydia nodded, and watched as he began to unpack the basket. He laid one of the teacloths out on the rug and set the sandwiches and cold venison pie upon it.

As they began to eat he took the cork from the bottle of wine and poured some into the coarse glasses. Lydia took a sip from her glass and looked at him over the rim. He was watching her.

'Is it all right?' he asked.

'Yes, it's very nice.'

He drank from his own glass, then took a bite of a cheese sandwich. On the other side of the water the children laughed and splashed about. 'Tell me about your visit to your home,' he said.

She spoke then of her trip to Capinfell, though keeping well away from the negative side of the time spent with her father. She tried to speak only of things that were positive, and to be lighthearted. She told of going to see Evie and of taking for her child the little storybook of *Hansel and Gretel*.

'Ah, I'm sure she'll love it,' Guy said. 'It was one of my favourite tales when I was a child. I think I admired Hansel – such a plucky and enterprising young lad.' He smiled at Lydia over his sandwich, then added, 'I wish I didn't have to go away.'

Lydia wanted to say, *Oh, I wish too that you didn't have to go*, but she kept silent. He would be back again before too long, she told herself, and until that time she must be patient.

The food was simple but very good, and they ate with keen appetites. Lydia drank the whole of her glass of wine, and Guy refilled her glass. She protested a little as he did so, but he gave a laugh, saying, 'It's all right, it's all right,' and kept on pouring.

They realised after a while that the shouts and laughter of the children on the far bank could no longer be heard, and Guy peered around the screen of the foliage and looked across the water. 'It looks as though the children are gone now,' he said. He glanced out across the water in other directions. 'I can't see a sign of anyone else.'

They sat there in their own silence while the birds sang and the water was occasionally disturbed by the rising of a fish to the surface. Lydia felt very conscious of the fact that they were alone, and very conscious of Guy's nearness.

'Was it nice, seeing your father again?' he asked, and she did not know how to answer. It had not been a success, but there – had she truly expected it to be? 'It was not – not easy,' she said after a moment.

'Not easy? What do you mean? There were difficulties?'

She nodded. 'You could say so. My father – he didn't want me to leave home in the first place, and I'm afraid he's still resentful.'

Guy frowned. 'Oh, that's a shame, but – give it a little time, and no doubt he'll get over it.'

'I hope so. It's what I keep telling myself.'

'He must love you very much. Otherwise he wouldn't resent your leaving.'

'Well, yes. I – I think he does – in his own way.' She paused. 'What about you and your father? Are you close?'

He hesitated briefly, then said thoughtfully, 'Yes, I suppose we are. Though I'm afraid I haven't always been the best of sons, and that's something you become very conscious of when something like this happens – his accident.'

Much of the food had gone now, and Guy lifted his glass and drank the rest of his wine. He gestured to a pair of sandwiches that lay on the teacloth. 'Can you eat more?' he said.

Lydia pressed a hand to her breast and gave a little laugh.

'Oh, no! No, I've eaten so much already.'

'I too. So the birds will be glad of them. If not the birds, then some other creatures.' Sitting up straighter, he said, glancing over in the direction of the mare, 'We mustn't forget Tess. I brought a couple of titbits for her. I'll go and get them.'

So saying, he got up and moved to the carriage. From the box under the seat he brought out a twist of paper holding a few carrots. He went to the mare, and held a couple of them under her mouth and she took them gently and ate them. 'She's probably a little thirsty too,' Guy said. From inside the box he now took a small, rather battered pail. 'You'd like some water too, wouldn't you, old girl?' He stroked the mare's brow, then, turning, started towards the trees that grew up to the edge of the perimeter pathway.

'Where are you going?' Lydia asked from her seat on the rug, and he turned back to her and said, 'There's a stream there in the woods. I'm going to get some fresh water for Tess.'

'Oh, wait – I'll come with you,' Lydia said. 'I'd like some water too.'

She picked up her glass and moved to join him, then he led the way through the copse, finding a rough and narrow little path that wound through the trees and the shrubbery.

With the summer foliage at its height the leaves of the trees formed a canopy overhead, and cut out much of the light, but after a while they came out into a clearing where the late sun penetrated onto the soft grass. In the centre ran a fast-moving little stream, and Guy went to it and crouched down on its bank. Lydia came and stood at his side, looking down as he dipped the bucket into the clear water.

The pail full, he set it down upon the grassy bank. Then he held up his hand for Lydia's glass, dipped it into the pail and held it out to her. She took it from him and had a sip.

'Is it good?' he said.

'It's good, yes, and it's so *cold*.'

He straightened, the pail in his hand. 'Let's go and water Tess, shall we?' and started away across the grass.

Lydia, carrying the glass, moved after him. Emerging from the trees near the lakeside he took the pail to where the mare stood patiently between the carriage shafts and set it down for her. She drank thirstily while Guy stroked her neck. He turned from her then and moved back across the grass to the rug, beside which Lydia, having scattered the remains of the sandwiches for the birds, was packing the teacloths and the glasses into the basket.

Lowering himself onto the rug he smoothed it out beside him under a sweeping movement of his palm. He was not ready to leave yet. 'Here, come and sit down again for a minute,' he said, and she put down the basket and settled herself on the rug at his side.

He sat with his knees drawn up, leaning forward, gazing out at the part of the lake that was just visible past the screen of elderflowers. With one hand up to his mouth he sucked at his forefinger.

'What's the matter?' Lydia asked.

'Just a little thorn or something, from when I brushed my hand over the rug just now.'

'Let me see.'

She drew close to him and he offered her his hand. She took it and turned it over, peering. The light was mellow, fading into the long-drawn-out dusk.

'Yes, I can see it,' she said.

Holding his hand in hers, she carefully grasped the head of the thorn between her fingernails and pulled it out. 'There,' she smiled. She flicked the thorn away into the grass. 'All done.'

'And *well* done,' he said. He sucked on the relieved finger for a second or two, then added, 'I could probably have done it myself, of course, but I'd much rather you did it for me.'

'Oh, I see,' she said, smiling.

Suddenly he put out his hand and gently touched it to her cheek. 'Oh, Lydia, you look so pretty.' He gave a little shake of his head, and then leaned forward and gently kissed her on the mouth.

The touch of his lips upon hers was so brief, but nevertheless it left her almost breathless. She gave a faint little gasp and lifted fingertips to her mouth.

'Is that a shield?' he said. 'Your hand – to stop me doing it again?'

'No.'

'That's good.' He put his head on one side and studied her, a little half smile on his face. 'I so like seeing you without your hat. It's lovely.' Her hair, that waved naturally, was coiled and pinned about the crown of her head. Now Guy put out a hand to a renegade lock that had fallen in a languid curl over her brow. He twined his index finger in it and then brushed it back with his fingertips. Lydia, almost transfixed by his touch, made no move to draw away from it.

The next moment he had shifted over on the rug and, drawing even closer to her, was lifting his arms to hold her. A second after that he lowered his face to hers and pressed his mouth against her own. It all happened so fast that she had no time to protest, even if she had been moved to. Not that she was. Her heart was bumping in her breast, thudding against her ribs so powerfully that a fleeting thought went through her mind that he must surely be aware of it. And this was no brief kiss, like the first one. This one went on, and after moments of holding still and rigid, she let herself go, relaxing her stiffness within the circle of his arms, and giving herself up to the revelation of the moment. For it was a revelation, the kiss, the embrace. As a child there had been the occasional stolen games played with other village children when chaste, damp kisses had been exchanged with the boys, but that had been long ago, and the kisses had been nothing more than fun in the daring knowledge that her father would have disapproved. This was something new, beyond even the scope of her imagination.

Guy's lips were strong but soft against her own, and when at last he drew back his head from her, she felt the coolness of the evening air upon her face again, and she sat there beside him on the red plaid rug with her mouth slightly open, still held in his embrace, looking at his handsome face, now alight with passion. She felt as if she were in a dream. Could any of it be real? He kissed her again, and this time she felt the urgency of his pressure even greater than before so that her lips parted beneath his own parted lips and she felt the wetness of his tongue, so sweet, so sweet, upon her own. Without any urging on his part, she found that she was being lowered backwards onto the rug, and that he was lying above her, smothering her mouth, her face, with his kisses.

She knew enough from her life in the country to know where such things could lead, and all her life she had heard hints and warnings about such dangerous situations, but such warnings did not come to her now, or if they came they hovered only at the edge of her consciousness and then melted away, defeated. She heard Guy murmuring little sounds of endearment as he held her to him, and she wanted to say in return, *I love you, I love you*, but she kept the words within herself and let herself be swept away by the kisses that came upon her mouth, upon her face, and – even as the knowledge touched her – upon her breast. She felt intoxicated, and although a little of the sensation came from the wine she had drunk, even more, far more, she was engulfed and enraptured by the feeling of his dear nearness, the closeness of him, the touch of his skin upon her own. How long they lay there she did not know, she would never know, but the birds sang and sang, and from somewhere over to the side there came the sound of Tess snorting and pawing at the turf. Lydia's hair became unpinned and fell down, and, unbraided, swept across her naked breast and touched Guy's cheek as he bent his head to kiss her. The moments, the seconds, the minutes fled past in a whirl of little gasps and breaths and cries, and strange, unaccustomed touches and sensations. There was the urgent fumbling of fingers at her clothing, the feel of the cooling air upon her naked flesh; and now his hardness, first against the softness of her palm, her fingertips, and then against her thighs, and moving up within her; and as she gasped again, now with a fleeting, strange pain, she was pinned there by his lips, and clung to him as for dear life, and against it all the birds continued to sing out their evensong, and the wild roses and the elder blossoms drenched the air with their scent.

Afterwards, they pulled on their clothes without looking at one another. Lydia found herself moving hurriedly, while at the same time trying to affect an air of being in control. When she had dressed and done up the last button she tidied her hair after a fashion and tucked it up and pinned on her hat. As she glanced down, smoothing her skirt, she saw that there was a trace of blood on the rug; it hardly showed against the red-based plaid, but she could see it nevertheless. In the same moment as she stood looking at it, her breath almost taken by the sight, she realised that Guy had seen it too, and seeing it he raised his head and looked at her, and she thought she saw in his eyes a brief flash of regret, and a question, a wondering whether she felt regret too. She at once felt tears threaten to spill from her eyes, and she fought them back. *It's done*, she wanted to say, '*it's done,*

171

and I love you, and I have no regrets just so long as you have none, but she said nothing, only held his glance for a moment and then looked away again. After another second they heard a distant shout from across the water, one young boy yelling to another. The children were back, and suddenly Lydia became aware of the enormity of what had taken place. The step she had taken. She put her hands up to her collar, checking that it was buttoned. 'We must go,' she said. 'I must get back.'

PART TWO

Chapter Eleven

There was a pigeon walking back and forth along the windowsill, and Guy idly watched it. Beyond the bird's bobbing head the stone and brick of Florence stretched as far as he could see beneath the azure Italian sky. The walls within which he waited were all white, their monochrome relieved only by the blue and gold effigy of the crucified Christ that hung above the Sister's chair. Guy stood with his hat in his hand, and sweat on his brow. He had not long since arrived from England. It was four in the afternoon and the heat was oppressive. Most of the city was still at siesta, but he had come here to the hospital to see his father, straight from the railway station, stopping only at the apartment on the Via Rosso to leave his travel bag.

Footsteps sounded on the tiles and the blue and white clad figure of the nun came into view, descending steps and moving towards him.

'*Per favore*, signor. Please, come this way.' Her English words were heavily accented with her native Italian.

He followed her up the stone stairs to the next floor, where she led the way along a corridor. At the second door she came to a halt. 'Your father, he is in here.' She opened the door and Guy thanked her and stepped past her into the room.

As the door closed behind him he took in with a glance the scene before him: his mother rising from a chair beside his father's bed, her arms already reaching out; the room small, all white, and with nothing on the walls apart from a crucifix.

'Guy!' His mother spoke the word broken on a whimper, moving to meet him and wrap her arms about him. She kissed him on the cheek, and as she did so he saw that there were tears in her eyes. 'Thank heaven you got here,' she murmured.

'I set off first thing yesterday morning,' he said.

He released his mother and moved past her to his father who lay on his back, his legs protected by a kind of cage that kept the weight of the bedclothes off him. Guy bent low and took his father's raised hands in his own. 'Oh, Father! Father, how are you?' He was shocked at the sight of him; he looked so slight, so vulnerable lying there.

'I'm better now – seeing you here,' the old man said. His voice sounded unusually gruff, and tears shone in his eyes.

'Take this chair,' his mother said, pushing towards him the one in which she had been sitting. 'I'll take the other.' As Guy sat down she moved around the bed to a second chair that stood on the opposite side.

'Oh, it's so good you're here,' his father said. 'I've been willing the time to pass.'

'I got here as soon as I could,' Guy said. He patted his father's mottled hand as it lay on the coverlet, the bony wrist emerging from the sleeve of his nightshirt. Mr Anderson was seventy-two years old now. His hair, silver grey, seemed to be thinner than ever, and Guy thought he had never before been so aware of the lines that furrowed his brow and cheeks. What was so especially shocking, however, was the bruising. Across his nose, and across his forehead there were great yellowing bruises, where the skin was also abraded. Guy sucked in his breath at the sight of them. How frail his father appeared now that he was in this great distress, and how pathetic in this small hospital room so far away from home.

'What happened?' Guy asked, and turned to his mother. 'All you said in the wire was that there had been an accident – a fall.' He looked back to his father, who gave a deep sigh and wearily shook his head. 'Oh, son, I can't go into it right now. I haven't got the energy. Your mother will tell you everything you have to know.' He turned to his wife. 'The boy must be thirsty and hungry. Anne, dear, take him for some coffee and something to eat.'

'No, really, I –' Guy began to protest, but his father languidly raised his hand and said, 'Go with your mother, there's a good fellow.'

'But –'

'Please. I'm in no state to exert myself.' A faint smile fleetingly touched the old man's mouth. 'Don't make me try.'

'Come on, Guy,' Mrs Anderson said. 'There's a *caffè* in the square. We'll only be away a little while.'

Guy got up from the chair, gently pressed his father's hand on the coverlet and said, 'We'll be back soon, Father.' Then he turned and followed his mother from the room.

At the foot of the stairs they crossed the vestibule and went out into the piazza, oppressively hot in the afternoon sun. In a fountain in the centre water gushed from the mouths of stone dolphins and two children played, paddling in the cool water in the basin. Mrs Anderson took her son's arm and they turned to the left and walked along at the side in the shade. 'It's just along here,' she said.

The *caffè* was situated just fifty yards or so from the hospital entrance, with tired-looking shrubs in tubs beside the doorway. Guy and his mother turned and went into the shaded interior and took a table near one of the windows.

'I've been here a couple of times during the day,' Mrs Anderson said. 'When I needed some coffee or some tea. I don't like to ask the nuns; they've got so much to do. Though I'm sure they'd be only too willing.'

When the waiter came to them they ordered coffee, and Mrs Anderson said to Guy, 'Don't you want something to eat? Aren't you hungry? Come on – we've got time.'

After a moment's hesitation Guy nodded and ordered a plate of cold meats with olives, tomatoes and coarse bread. The waiter went away with the order, and Mrs Anderson watched him go, then said:

'Did you go to the apartment first with your bags?'

'Yes. The maid was there. She told me you were here and directed me.'

She nodded. 'Amelia – she's a good girl.' She paused then went on, 'Your father finds it distressing, hearing it all spoken of in front of him – his accident – and he can hardly bear to talk about it himself.'

Mrs Anderson was sixty-eight years old. She was a handsome woman, a little taller than average, and with hair, although grey, still thick and luxuriant. She wore a dove grey linen travelling suit with a pale blue blouse, and a hat of a dark grey, soft felt, decorated with small feathers. As she spoke she gazed at Guy with her affection barely hidden, an affection she had never tried to hide, that of a mother for a dearly-loved son.

'So, what happened?' Guy said.

His mother's voice was grave as she answered him. 'We were coming from the apartment,' she said. 'He wouldn't wait for the elevator. You know how impatient he can get. That lift is enough to drive anyone crazy at the best of times, but this time his patience gave out.' She paused, then added with a shrug and a little shake of the head, 'And – he fell.'

'He fell.'

'He tripped somehow, and he went from top to bottom of the stairs. I saw it all.' Suddenly the memory of it appeared too much for her to take; as she went to speak again her voice cracked and she gasped, and tears welled in her eyes and ran down her cheeks.

'Oh, Mother . . .' Guy reached across the table and put his hand on her wrist.

She patted his hand with her free hand, then took a lace-trimmed handkerchief from her bag. 'It's all right. I just can't seem to get over it. The shock.' She sat there for a moment looking down, her lips compressed, as if willing herself to stay in control. 'I'm sorry,' she said.

The waiter came to the table with the coffee and set the cups down before them. When he had gone away again, Mrs Anderson took up a spoon and stirred the coffee.

'How bad were his injuries?' Guy asked.

'Very bad. Both legs were broken, his right leg in three places.'

'Dear God.'

'They've done their best to set the bones, but they fear the right leg might be just too badly mangled to do it satisfactorily.' She put a hand up to her mouth. 'Oh, Guy, it was dreadful. The bones were sticking through the flesh. I couldn't bear to look at it. I sent a messenger for the doctor – he's a Scotsman, MacElroy; he looks after so many of the British in the city – and he came quite quickly, but it seemed to take forever for the ambulance to arrive. If your father ends up having to walk with sticks I don't know what he'll do. He's such an active man. He'll hate being slowed down in any way.' The tears were flowing freely now, and periodically she dabbed at her eyes with her handkerchief. 'He's been so brave,' she went on. 'He hasn't complained.' She allowed herself a small, rueful smile. 'Only about the hospital food. Ah, but he's such a good man, and he works so hard. The irony is, that we came out here so that he could sell up the business, and get a little more time to himself. He's got enough to do with the newspaper. He knows you won't want anything to do with it – the textile business here, I mean. Anyway, at his age he should be doing far less – and he'd just about realised and accepted that this was the situation, and then this – this terrible thing has to happen.'

The waiter came back to the table, set down a plate in front of Guy, then went away again. Guy looked at the food, the neat, round little cuts of meat, the dark olives and the large slices of tomato, and pushed the plate an inch away. He had no appetite. His mother seemed to be growing a little calmer. 'Eat something, Guy,' she murmured. 'You must eat, my dear. You won't do any good by going without.'

'I'm not that hungry, Mother.'

She gave a little shake of her head, as if it were unimportant. 'Thank God you came,' she said. 'I don't know what we'd have done if you hadn't been able to.'

'Of course I came.'

'Well, it's a great comfort to your father, your being here, and to me too, of course. Your father's been longing to see you.' She touched the side of the plate with her fingertips. 'Do eat something.'

Reluctantly Guy pulled the plate a little nearer and forced himself to eat. As he did so, his mother said, 'No, your father doesn't care for the hospital food, so I tried having some food brought in from one of the nearby restaurants, but he has no appetite, so it didn't make much difference. I tell him he has to keep his strength up.'

Guy picked at the food for a few minutes, then signalled to the waiter to bring the bill. 'We must go back,' he said to his mother.

He had managed to change some English currency at the railway station, and when the bill was brought he counted out the lire.

Back at the hospital they sat on either side of Mr Anderson's bed, and so they remained for another hour, until one of the nuns came to tell them they must leave, and that they could come back in the morning.

*

At the apartment on the Via Rosso, Guy bathed and changed his clothes. Afterwards, the cook-housekeeper, who had already unpacked his bag and put away his things, prepared a meal for them, and Guy and his mother sat picking at their food in the dining room overlooking the street.

Later, about ten o'clock, he kissed his mother on the cheek and went to bed. Lying there in the dark he thought of his father's grave condition, and felt anxious to get back to see him the next day. If his father should end up crippled it would surely have a devastating effect upon the old man, and if he should be seriously disabled there could be no doubt that so much more responsibility would fall upon Guy's shoulders.

Just before he went to sleep he thought back over the previous days, from the time of receiving his mother's wire to his arrival in the Italian city – and somewhere in all that rush of activity had been his meeting with Lydia. How far away that all seemed right now.

That week with Lydia had gone so fast, he thought. How could it have gone so swiftly? The walk in the park, the visit to the theatre, the dinner at the inn in the country, the picnic by the lake. Yes, the picnic by the lake. He had little happiness in his memories of that, particularly when thinking of what had happened at the very end. Now that he looked back on it, everything had happened *too* fast. Of course he had been so attracted to her; how could he not have been? But had it been a feeling deeper than that? So much had happened in such a short space of time, and he seemed unable to grasp the reality of his feelings. She was a beautiful, personable girl – but their very closeness at the end now left him feeling guilty and a little resentful. Resentful, perhaps, because the happening had inspired his guilt, and guilt is always difficult to suffer. He had not meant for it all to go so far, he was aware of that, and now he was touched with remorse. Had he compromised her situation? Was he getting in too deep? He recalled, too, seeing the bloodstain on the rug. If he had thought about it he would have known that she'd had no experience, but he had not allowed himself to ponder on such things. Instead, he had let himself be swept up in the delicious, captivating thrill of the moment, and now it was too late; nothing could be done. He could not go back and rewrite the tale. And so what now? Well, he had told Lydia that he would write, and so he would. He would write to her as soon as he got the chance. There would be time enough in the next few days.

In her room in Redbury, Lydia lay in her narrow bed and thought of Guy, and wondered whether he had arrived safely at his destination, and how he had found his father. With luck Mr Anderson would soon recover, and Guy would be able to return. In the meantime he would be writing to her. She prayed he would. He had said he would. She would wait to hear . . .

On Wednesday morning, as soon as visitors were permitted, Guy and his mother returned to the hospital in the piazza. There in the vestibule the senior nurse told them in her halting English that Mr Anderson had not slept well, due to the pain in his legs, particularly the right one. He had been given chloral hydrate to help deaden the pain, she said, and after a time he had managed to sleep.

'And how is he today?' Mrs Anderson asked.

The nun said, 'Dr MacElroy was here again this morning early to examine Mr Anderson. I am sorry to say that he is not pleased, but tomorrow, perhaps, it will be better. The doctor will be here again in the morning. He has asked to meet you and your son at that time.'

'Of course,' Mrs Anderson replied.

'At ten o'clock, yes?'

'Yes, we'll be here then.'

Minutes later, on entering his father's hospital room, Guy watched as his mother kissed her husband on the cheek, pressed his hand and asked how he was. He replied that he was feeling not too bad, considering everything. Guy moved to the bed then, and took his father's hand in his own, and thought how drained and exhausted he looked.

'The Sister told us you slept badly,' Guy said.

'Yes, I'm afraid it wasn't so good.' Mr Anderson nodded his head slightly on the pillow. 'The pain in my right leg was so bad, it wouldn't let me sleep. I drifted off towards morning when they gave me something to drink. A little chloral, I believe.' He pressed Guy's hand. 'Anyway, how are you, son? Have you quite recovered from your long train journey? I hope you slept well. I never could sleep on trains, no matter how comfortable they tried to make them.'

'I'm very well, Father,' Guy said. 'It's you we have to worry about.'

'Oh, I'll be all right before too long. Just as soon as this leg begins to mend.'

He began then to ask about things in Redbury, at the newspaper offices and at the house. How were the horses? How was the new groom getting on? Guy gave him answers where he could, but it was clear that his father found it difficult to concentrate. After a time, the nursing Sister came in and gave the patient a little more medicine against the ever-present pain. A little while after that he drifted off into an uneasy sleep.

All through that day when visiting hours permitted, Guy and his mother were in and out of the room. When they were hungry or thirsty they went to the small *caffè* in the piazza where they drank tea or coffee and picked at salads and sandwiches. For Mr Anderson, a little food was brought in from a nearby restaurant in the hopes of tempting him, but he had no appetite and pushed the food away.

Guy and his mother were at the hospital well before ten the following morning, and anxious for the meeting with the physician. Sitting on hard benches in the vestibule, they expected Dr MacElroy to enter from the street, but instead he came down the stone stairs towards them, his hand outstretched. After shaking Mrs Anderson's hand he was introduced to Guy. Then, the polite greetings over, he said:

'I had to see you today, Mrs Anderson. It was vital.' The man's Scottish accent was subdued; only the faintest burr revealing his origins.

Guy searched the man's face, trying to read his expression, and in it saw the gravity of the situation.

'Things have not gone well,' Dr MacElroy went on. 'In fact –' He came to a stop, as if uncertain how to go on.

Mrs Anderson said quickly, 'Please – tell me.'

'Well . . .' he shook his head, 'it's as I feared. The right leg – it's not healing as I'd hoped, and I'm most terribly sorry to have to tell you, but mortification has now set in.'

Mrs Anderson put a hand to her mouth. 'Oh, dear God.'

'Yes,' the man said, 'the situation is very grave. I'm afraid there's no cure when that happens. The only thing to be done is to – well, to cut away the gangrenous flesh. So I'm afraid it means amputation of the right leg. With luck the cut can be just below the knee, but I'm by no means certain of that. With your permission I'd like to call in another opinion.'

'Whatever is necessary.'

'I'd like to call in Signor Martinelli. Do you know of him?'

'No, but –'

'He's a much respected surgeon – and I've sent word to have him come along for a consultation later this morning. I assume you'll have no objection.'

'Of course not. We want you to do everything you can.'

He nodded. 'And of course we must act without delay. I think we should operate this afternoon, or this evening at the latest. Time is of the essence if the poison is not to spread too far.'

The doctor then said that he would be in touch later, and that in the meantime Mr Anderson was to eat nothing, and might drink only water.

When the doctor had gone, Guy turned to his mother and said: 'You go on upstairs and see Father – I'll come up in a few minutes. You need some time together.'

Mrs Anderson went up to her husband's room, and Guy gave a nod to the nun who had come to sit at her desk, and turned and went out into the square. Two minutes later he was in the *caffè*. He sat there over a cup of coffee for fifteen minutes, doing nothing but gaze idly from the window at the pedestrians and carriages moving by, then he pushed aside his half-empty cup and saucer, paid his bill and left.

In the hospital, up on the first floor, he knocked on the door of his father's room, heard his mother's 'Come in,' entered, and the moment he stepped across the threshold he became aware of a difference. There was a slight, sweetish smell in the room. He had never come across it before in his life, but he knew at once what it was. It was the smell of dying flesh. He looked at his mother as she sat on the left side of his father's bed and saw in her widened eyes that she was aware of what he was experiencing.

'Hello, Father.' Guy went to the right side of the bed, where a chair had been placed. His father lay half propped up against the pillows, the cage beneath the bedcovers making a rounded shape over his legs. 'How are you feeling today?' Guy asked. Holding his father's hand, he sat down. Seeing his father lying there so helpless, and knowing what was now ahead, it was all he could do to keep the tears from his eyes and speak over the lump in his throat.

'Well, I must confess I've been better, my son,' Mr Anderson said, 'and God willing, I shall feel better again.' He paused. 'You know what they're doing to me later on today, of course.'

His voice did not have its usual strength, and the sound of it, halting and laboured, touched Guy's heart so that for a moment he felt he could not speak. Then he said, 'Oh, Father, I'm so sorry.'

'Yes. I don't mind telling you I'm dreading it. Still,' Mr Anderson shrugged, 'there's nothing to do but put up with it.' He withdrew his hand and raised it, half turning to his wife. 'Anne . . . If you wouldn't mind – just for a few minutes.'

Mrs Anderson got to her feet. To Guy she said, 'I'm going downstairs for a little while. Your father wants to have a word with you.' Picking up her bag, she moved across the room. In the doorway she turned and added, speaking to her husband, 'Don't talk too much and tire yourself.'

Guy and his father watched as the door closed behind her, and heard her footsteps fade away on the stone floor of the corridor outside. Then Mr Anderson turned to his son.

'I wanted to talk to you, Guy, and there won't be much of an opportunity before they operate, apart from now.'

'Is it absolutely certain they're going to?' Guy asked.

'Oh, yes. There's no question of it. My sense of smell is still working all right. My leg is dying on me, it's as simple as that – and I don't think the left one is doing so well either. Anyway,' he said on a sigh, 'it won't do any good to dwell on that.'

Guy said nothing, but sat with his hands clasped.

'I want you to listen to me, Guy,' the old man said. 'I don't want to have to repeat things. Quite honestly I haven't got the strength.'

Guy nodded. 'I understand. What is it you want to tell me?'

Mr Anderson hesitated for a second, then said. 'I'm not being melodramatic here, but we have to face the possibility that I won't make it through the operation.'

'Oh, but, Father –'

'No, please, Guy, we've got to be realistic about this. With the best doctors in the world there's always the chance that things won't turn out the way you hope. This is why I need to talk to you now.' He half turned his head to where on a side table stood a glass and pitcher. 'Please,' he said, 'could I have a drink?'

Guy poured water into the glass and gave it to him.

'Thank you.' The man sipped, and held the glass out to Guy who replaced it on the table. A moment of silence passed, then Mr Anderson took a breath and went on: 'Now, then – in the event that I should – that things don't go according to plan . . .' He sighed and shook his head. 'Oh, let's not beat about the bush here. In the event that I don't survive the operation there will be certain things you'll have to do.'

Guy wanted to burst out in protest, but did not; he merely nodded, swallowed, and said, 'Yes.'

'Well, the business matters first. Get them out of the way. First of all, about the business here: *Angellini*. As you know, we came out here to sell it up, and that's what I was in the process of doing when I had the accident. It was all going so well too. The textiles business is booming right now, and I knew we wouldn't have any trouble in selling it on. That's helped enormously – the success of the company. Of course it has. We're selling a thriving one, not one that's on its last legs. Anyway –' he waved a frail-looking hand, 'the sale should all go ahead as planned. Most of the work on it is done, but it'll need a careful eye and a careful hand until everything is signed and settled. You're my heir, of course, and along with your mother you'll be running everything, but I don't want things left to her. She's not young any more and she's had enough responsibility in her life – and if I go I doubt she'll have the heart to do much in the way of work. Which is why I have to turn to you. I'm afraid most of it is going to fall on your shoulders, son, and it's a lot for a young man of only twenty-five.'

He came to a halt here, as if waiting to let his words sink in. Then after a moment he went on, 'Back home, the paper should present you with no difficulties if you use your head, and use the heads of those around you. I'm sure you're well aware that my manager, Godfrey Chemmin, is worth his weight in gold. If there's anything you want, or need to know, then he's the man to go to. He knows almost as much about the business as I do myself. Anyway, since you got out of the army you've had a bit of a taste of life on the paper, so all of that won't come as a complete surprise to you. Responsibility doesn't come easily to everyone,' he added after a moment. 'Especially someone like you, having spent most of your adult life in the army.'

'I did have certain responsibilities, sir,' Guy said.

'Yes, I know you did, but they're not the same. I don't think so, anyway. In the British army, all things being equal, you're always going to be fed and clothed and sheltered and paid, but I'm afraid that's not always the case in the world of business. It's a dog-eat-dog affair, and no mistake. You have to look after your own, for others will not.' He fell silent for a few moments then went on, 'I always asked myself why you went off to join the army in the first place. You knew how much I wanted you to stay at home. I wanted you to learn about the newspaper and the business out here in Florence, but no, you didn't want to settle. You didn't want to stay at home and knuckle down like that.' He shook his head and briefly closed his eyes, as if in a gesture of relief. 'Oh, you can't imagine how I felt when you said you were resigning your commission and coming home to work with me. Your mother, too. My God, she was so pleased. So relieved.'

'I'm glad I did,' Guy said. 'I think it was time.'

'Yes, it was time all right.' A brief, rueful smile touched at the corners of the old man's mouth. 'And perhaps just in the nick of time, too.'

Silence in the room. The sweet, sickly smell was pervasive. There was no getting accustomed to it. From the distance Guy could hear the chime of a cathedral bell.

'I don't believe you liked responsibility that much,' Mr Anderson said. 'I think you shied away from it. And commitment. Oh, yes, I think you were afraid of commitment.' The smile came again. 'You might still be, for all I know, but one day you'll learn. Perhaps you're learning now. I hope so. At your age it's time.'

'I am learning, Father,' Guy said. At that moment he felt like a child, but he had to be strong. Now it was necessary that he should be strong.

'Ah . . .' The sound from Mr Anderson's lips was long, drawn-out, almost a groan. 'Ah, dear boy,' he said, 'I have to tell you that I'm not sanguine about the outcome of this operation.'

'Father –'

'No, I'm not, and no one can make me feel differently. Oh, I wish I were fit enough to travel. I'd get you to take me home. I have very bad feelings about it all, I don't mind telling you. I haven't spoken like this in front of your mother – I can't – but I have to tell you. Tomorrow could be too late.'

The seconds ticked by. Mr Anderson lay back against the pillows, gazing out into the room. Through the open window a pale blue butterfly came. It fluttered about the room in its dancing flight, and then found its way back to the window and out once more into the air. Guy watched it as if mesmerised.

Mr Anderson had also watched the butterfly, and his head was still turned to the window after the creature had gone. 'There,' he said, his voice low, frail, 'life goes on, doesn't it? Whatever your crisis, the rest of the world keeps turning, and when you're through it will carry on turning without you.'

Shifting his glance from the window, he focused again on Guy. 'I had so hoped to see certain things before I go,' he said.

'Such as what, Father?' Guy said.

'Well, the things that most men want to see when they get past a certain age. For a start I'd like to have seen grand-children. A grandson – someone who would carry on my name, my blood, and perhaps carry on my work, too.' He sighed. 'Well, it's too late for that, I realise that now. Of course, if you hadn't decided to get a commission and gone to the ends of the earth you'd probably have been married by now . . . but that's all done with. You aren't, and that's that. Perhaps I've been hoping for too much – you came into our lives so late. We had long given up expecting a child, but then, there you were, and our lives were com-plete, fulfilled. Perhaps we should be content with that. At least we have you.' He managed a smile. 'There's no deny-ing that your mother has so longed for you to meet some nice young lady and settle down, but with your being in the army out in South Africa, we couldn't see that happening at all. She always had hopes that you'd make a match with George Fellows's daughter Clarissa. You entertained her when you were a child, and you seemed so right together, but there you are. Apparently she's still not settled – so I suppose your mother can go on entertaining her high hopes. How old would the girl be now? Twenty or twenty-one, I suppose, and she'd be a good catch. Do you remember her?'

'Yes, I remember her. I've seen her since she was a child.

She came to the house on a few occasions with her parents.'

'That's right, so she did.' He paused. 'Is there anyone in your life, Guy? Have you met anyone? I doubt it – you've only been out of the army a few weeks. You've hardly had the opportunity.'

Guy said nothing, not knowing what to say.

'What does that silence mean?' Mr Anderson said, taking in Guy with a quizzical glance. 'Do I take it that you *have* met someone?'

'Well . . .' Guy said.

'Tell me, son. It'll cheer me up.'

Still Guy kept silent.

'What's the matter?' his father said. 'Why can't you tell me? *Have* you met someone?'

'Well, I – I did meet a young woman.'

'Good. I'm glad to hear it – and not before time, if I might say so.' He paused. 'So? Where did you meet her?'

'In Redbury. She was visiting the town just for the day.'

'When was this?'

'A few weeks ago.'

'And where was she visiting from?'

'A village in the country. Capinfell. Not far from Merinville.'

'Oh, yes, Capinfell. I don't think I've ever been there, but I know of it, of course. I believe it's quite small.'

'So I believe.'

'What's her name, and how old is she?'

'She's twenty-one. Her name is Lydia Halley.'

'Halley.' Mr Anderson thought on the name for a moment, then shook his head. 'No, it doesn't ring any bells. There are the Tindall-Halleys in Hebberly . . . Is she anything to do with them?'

'I don't believe so.'

'They're a good family. You're sure?'

'Yes.'

A pause. 'Are you fond of the girl?'

'I – I met her just a few weeks ago, and I've been seeing her only this past week.'

'A very short time. You didn't answer my question. Are you fond of her?'

Guy did not answer.

'Surely you know the answer to that,' his father said. 'Who are her parents? What do they do?'

'Father,' Guy said, 'she has no background that you would recognise. She's a clerk.'

'A clerk.'

'She's a postal clerk. She works in Seager's department store.'

'A clerk.'

'Yes.'

Mr Anderson sighed. 'Oh, my dear boy, the world is full of pretty little postal clerks, and I've no doubt that you could have your pick of them, but truly, I wouldn't want you getting serious about such a girl, nice as she might be. Your mother and I – we have somewhat higher hopes for you.'

'I told you – I've known her so little time.'

'Oh, and don't think lack of time has ever prevented a man making a fool of himself.' The old man narrowed his eyes slightly, studying Guy's expression. 'You're not – serious about her, are you?'

'Serious?'

'I mean, you're not thinking you're in love with the girl?'

'Oh, Father – it's too soon for me to think of anything like that.'

'And what might that mean?'

Guy gave a little sigh of frustration. 'As I said, I've only recently met her and – and all this happening now. I feel I don't know where I am.'

'Well – you just try to keep your feet on the ground, my

lad, that's the least you can try to do. I mean, it can all seem very pleasant – you meet some young girl who's pretty and flattering – and it's easy to get carried away, but you've got to be realistic about it all. You haven't gone making foolish promises to the young woman, have you?'

'No.'

'Well, that's something. Because I tell you now, if the worst happens to me you're going to have to face a lot more responsibility every day. When the business here is disposed of, you'll still have the *Courier* to look after, and however well my manager is able to care for it, it'll still be yours, the basic responsibility will still be yours. And even if I come through it all right, I simply shan't be as able as I was. That has to be faced.' He reached out and pressed Guy's hand. 'Son, we want you to make a good match. You're not going to disappoint me over this, are you?'

'I never want to disappoint you, Father.'

'There's a good fellow. Bear in mind, son, that no matter how you might think you feel about the young woman right now, you'll get over it. Believe me, you will.'

He patted Guy's hand, and then coughed two or three times. Guy gave him the glass of water again and he drank. Afterwards he lay back against the pillows, exhausted. 'I must rest,' he said. 'We'll talk again later.'

Just before noon Dr MacElroy returned, bringing with him the consultant surgeon Signor Martinelli, and while Guy and his mother waited in the vestibule on the ground floor the two physicians visited Mr Anderson in his hospital room. Later they came down and called Guy and his mother into a small ante-room nearby.

The Italian surgeon was a tall man in his fifties with steel grey hair and a lean, clean-shaven face. As the introductions were made he shook hands with Guy and Mrs Anderson with a grave expression.

With occasional references in Italian to the surgeon, Dr MacElroy told Mrs Anderson and Guy that he and the consultant had just finished examining Mr Anderson. The situation was very serious indeed, he said, and remedial measures would have to be carried out as soon as possible.

'Signor Martinelli agrees that we must operate without delay,' the doctor went on. 'I shall assist him. The hospital is fully equipped, so the surgery can be carried out on the premises.'

'Is there nothing else to do but to operate?' Mrs Anderson said.

'No.' The doctor shook his head deliberately. 'It's the only thing to do. The gangrene is progressing at a very swift pace, so we need to operate at once. and the leg has to come off above the knee.' He half turned to the surgeon. 'Signor Martinelli will go straight now and fetch his instruments, and in the meantime I'll make sure that the operating room is prepared, and that the nurses are ready.' He took out his watch, flicked it open and said, 'With luck we'll be able to start by two-thirty, and we shall have good light.' He closed his watch and put it back in his pocket. 'Now – we must get busy.'

For the next hour Guy and his mother remained with Mr Anderson in his room, but there was little conversation, for the old man seemed exhausted by the pain and by the assault to his system. So the mother and son sat for the most part speaking only desultorily, while doing what they could to make the patient comfortable.

Then, just on a quarter to two there came a tap at the door and Sister Teresa was there, asking them to leave so that the patient could be prepared for his surgery. Mrs Anderson, forcing back the tears, kissed and embraced her husband, and Guy squeezed his hand. They would see him later, they said. Downstairs, they met Dr MacElroy who told them that they should come back in the morning at ten-thirty when visiting hours began, by which time everything would be done, and the patient would have had a good night's sleep.

After passing a restless night at the apartment, Guy and his mother returned to the hospital. Sister Teresa got up from her desk as they entered the vestibule and came towards them. While Guy tried to read her face, she said to his mother, 'Dr MacElroy, he wishes to see you, signora. He has been waiting for you. Please, come this way.'

She led them to the small ante-room they had sat in before, and on entering they found the doctor standing by the window. He turned at their approach and clasped his hands before him. Guy could see at once from the man's expression that the situation was not good.

'Please,' the doctor said to them, 'do sit down.'

Mrs Anderson sat on one of the hard wooden chairs, and said at once, 'Doctor, how is my husband?'

The doctor waited until Guy was also seated, then said, 'Madam, I'm very sorry to tell you that the situation turned out to be more serious than either one of us thought.'

Mrs Anderson reached up a hand, pressing it to her mouth. 'What are you saying?'

Dr MacElroy shook his head. 'I'm afraid the infection had travelled much further than we had anticipated. We had to amputate very high up on the thigh.' He sighed. 'And even then, we don't know yet whether we caught it all. We'll know in a very short time. I shall be back this afternoon to see how he is.'

Over the hours that followed, Guy and his mother sat with Mr Anderson whenever they could. As before, there was little in the way of conversation, and all they could hope to do for him was to ease his discomfort in whichever way might be possible, so they gave him water, soothed his hot brow with damp cloths and fetched the nurse when the pain grew too much to bear. He ate nothing.

He did not complain, but lay as before, half propped against the pillows, and the smell of rotting flesh returned and lay close under their nostrils. The nursing sister opened the window wider, but it did no good, the ghastly scent only got worse.

They knew now from the doctor – and the surgeon concurred – that there was no longer any hope. The poison had invaded his whole body. The flesh was dying on his bones.

Chapter Twelve

'*So,*' said Lydia, reading from the book, '*when Hansel looked about him there were no breadcrumbs to be seen. Somehow, they had all gone.*' She turned and looked down at Hennie who sat snuggled up against her on the sofa. Hennie's eyes were wide, and as Lydia's glance met her own the child put her hands to her mouth in a faint expression of horror, her pink lips forming a perfect little O. Distantly, from the scullery, came the sounds of chinking china as Evie washed the dinner dishes. It was Sunday, and Lydia, back in Capinfell for the weekend, had called round at the cottage to see her friend.

'So what d'you think has happened?' Lydia asked the child. 'I wonder what can have happened to Hansel's trail?'

'*I* know,' Hennie said with a nod.

'You do?'

'Yes, the birds have eaten all the breadcrumbs and now Hansel and Gretel haven't got a trail to follow.'

'Is that so?'

'Yes, and now they're lost and they can't find their way home.'

'Ah.' Lydia shook her head. 'Poor Hansel, poor Gretel.'

'But in the end they will, after they kill the old witch. Please – go on.'

Lydia smiled. 'Very well.'

Lydia continued to read from the storybook, and had just reached the point when the two children had come upon the gingerbread house when Evie came in from the scullery.

'All right,' Evie said, 'that's done. Come on, let's go out for our walk.'

'But Mammy,' Hennie protested, 'we're just getting to the good part.' She added anxiously, 'They're just about to go into the little house.'

'Are they, now? Well, I'm sure it'll keep for a while longer, dear. I'll finish reading it for you later on, when Aunt Lydia has gone off in the coach, but she hasn't got long here today, and we can't spend it all on your storybook, can we?'

She got the child's straw hat and set it on her fair curls, and put her own bonnet on and tied the strings. 'All right,' she said, 'we can go now.'

Leaving the cottage, they set out for the edge of the village and then walked out into the countryside, taking a footpath that led between fields. Beside the hedgerow the cornflowers were a bright, vivid blue, while to the right and left of them the fields of golden corn stretched out. Hennie ran skipping ahead, Evie's watchful eye upon her. They came to a five-barred gate after a while. Lydia was for opening it and passing through, but Evie said, 'Oh, let's stop here, shall we? It's such a warm day, and it'd be nice to rest.'

They found a little patch of sun-dry grass near the hedgerow, a spot now partly shaded by a hawthorn tree, and sat down.

'Did you see your Ryllis last weekend as you planned to?' Evie asked. She took off her bonnet and ran her fingers through her chestnut hair.

'Yes. She came into Redbury in the afternoon and we spent some hours together.'

'Was she well?'

'Yes, she's quite well, though still not happy in her situation.'

'How is she getting on with her young man? I've forgotten his name.'

'Thomas. She didn't say a lot, though I got the impression that she is not so happy with him as she might be.' Lydia shook her head. 'I do hope he's not going to let her down. I'd never forgive him if he made a fool of her.'

'Well, they haven't long met,' Evie said, 'so give it time.'

'Yes, you're right. Things will work out in the end.' She sighed, paused for a moment, then added, 'That's what I keep telling myself.'

'Oh? Yes?' Evie looked at her quizzically. After a moment she said, pacing her words carefully, 'Have you heard yet from your Mr Anderson?'

Lydia hesitated, then said, 'No, I haven't.'

'Nothing?'

'Not a word.'

'How long is it now since he went?'

'It's three weeks to the day since I saw him last. Since that Sunday. He told me he would be going off the next day. I assume he did.'

'Well – he'll write.'

'It's been three weeks, Evie.'

Hennie, sitting a few yards away, had taken off her hat and was filling it with blades of grass that she was carefully tearing up. 'No, Hennie, dear,' Evie called out to her, 'put your hat back on your head or you'll burn in the sun.' Hennie took no notice, and continued as before, and after watching her for a while, Evie got up and went to her. Lydia watched as Evie tipped the grass out of the hat's crown and then set the hat back upon the child's head.

'There,' Evie murmured, 'we'll see how long that lasts.' She came back to Lydia's side and sat down again. Without looking directly at her she said after a moment, 'In your letter you wrote that you had something to tell me . . .' She let the question hang in the air.

Lydia briefly closed her eyes and sighed. 'To tell you the truth, Evie,' she said, 'I'm very worried.'

Evie looked concerned. Frowning, she said, 'What about? You're not fretting about your father, are you? He's stronger than you think, I'm sure. He –'

'No,' Lydia broke in. 'I'm not worried about Father.'

Evie looked at her for a moment, then gave a nod. 'It's your gentleman friend, is it?'

Lydia nodded.

'Of course it is,' Evie said, 'but he'll be all right, and as for not hearing from him – well, you've no idea what he's having to do, have you? I mean, with his father being hurt – and it could be very badly – who's to say what his situation is. If he's as nice as you say he is, then I'm sure you'll hear from him before too long.'

Lydia said after a moment, 'It – it's not that. That's not quite it.'

'What is it, then?'

'As I told you – it – it's been three weeks.'

'Yes, so you said. Three weeks since you saw him, since he went away.'

Out in the cornfield two crows fluttered up and settled again. Lydia eyed them, unseeing. Hennie had once again taken off her hat, but this time Evie paid no heed. She looked at Lydia, frowning. 'What's the matter?' she said.

Lydia bent her head and put both hands up to her cheeks. 'Oh, God, Evie,' she breathed, 'I'm so worried.'

Evie continued to gaze at her for some seconds. Then she said, 'I see now. I think I do.' She paused. 'Are you telling me that something – happened – between you and your Mr Anderson?'

Lydia said nothing, and after a second Evie gave the barest nod.

A little silence fell between them, and in the quiet Lydia

was vaguely aware of the cheeping of birds in the hedgerow. Hennie came over to them and deposited in her mother's lap a few blossoms of cornflower. 'These are for you, Mammy,' the child said, and Evie replied, 'Thank you, dear,' in a faint, uninvolved voice, and absently touched the child's fair hair. She watched then as Hennie wandered away again and once more sat down in the grass at the edge of the golden grain. Evie turned back to Lydia.

'Would I be guessing right if I reckoned that – that you're late . . .?'

Lydia hesitated, then nodded. She could not meet Evie's eyes.

'When were you due?'

'A week ago.'

Evie sat looking at her, clearly shocked. 'Well – maybe you're just a bit late.'

'No, I'm never late. I'm that regular you could set the clock.' Lydia paused. 'I've been feeling so sick too. Yesterday morning and this morning, and yesterday when I was on the train I felt that ill. Oh, Evie, I thought I'd be sick there and then.'

Evie leaned across and briefly pressed Lydia's hands as they lay clasped in her lap. 'Lyddy – you poor thing.'

'I don't know what to do, Evie.' Now Lydia turned and looked into her friend's eyes. 'I just don't know. When I was heaving and retching this morning before church Father was very concerned. He thought it was something I'd eaten. I said it must be. I couldn't tell him what I was thinking.'

'Of course not. What are you going to do?'

'I told you, I don't know.' Lydia gave a bitter little smile. 'I really did pray in church this morning.'

'Oh, Lyddy . . .'

Lydia sat in silence, embarrassed at the situation she had revealed. 'Tell me something,' she managed to say after a few moments, 'were – were your breasts tender when you fell for Hennie?'

'What? Tender? Oh, I'll say they were.' Evie nodded. 'I see – that's happening to you, is it?'

'I'm afraid so.'

'Oh, yes, that's another sign. Definitely. I know my mam was the same – she told me.' After a few moments Evie added glumly, 'Well, I don't reckon there can be much question about it, Lyddy. I'm sorry to say it, but I think it's something you've got to face up to.'

Lydia groaned and covered her face with her hands. Her voice, muffled, with a desperate ring to it, came through her fingers: 'Oh, God, I wish I knew what to do.'

'What about your Mr Guy Anderson?' Evie said after a moment. 'He ought to be told, don't you think?'

Lydia gave a shake of her head, a gesture of helplessness, lowered her hands and held them clenched before her. 'I don't even know where he is,' she said. 'Whether he's still in Italy, or back in England.'

'Well, you'll have to find out, won't you? I mean – he has to be told. Men have got a responsibility in these things as well.'

'I know that, I know, but – oh, it's easier said than done.'

'Well – where do you think he is? D'you think it's likely he's still abroad?'

'I don't know, but – oh, no, I can't think that. I'm sure he'll have come back by now. It's been three weeks.'

'Well, you can get in touch with him, Lyddy, surely you can. For a start you know that he works for his father's newspaper. You could write to him there. They'll forward your letter.'

'Yes, I could do that, but I've got the address of his home, so that wouldn't be necessary.'

'Well, whichever way, you must write to him – wherever he is, even if he's still abroad. I mean, you don't know that he's not in Italy even now. He might not be back in Redbury. But at least if you write you'll be able to get in touch with him. Give him the chance to do the right thing.'

'But – what if he's back and – and just – doesn't want to see me?'

Evie frowned. 'You've no reason to think that, have you?'

'No, but –' Lydia gave a deep sigh and shook her head. 'Oh, sometimes I don't know what to think.'

'Well, anyway,' Evie said, 'whatever he feels about you you'll – you'll find out in time, but you can't afford to put it off. You must do it at once.'

'I know. I know. I *have* been putting it off. Just hoping against hope, I suppose, that things weren't – the way they are – that all my fears have been – for nothing.'

Hennie's voice came then, calling to her mother, 'Mammy, look, these are so pretty.' She had picked three or four more cornflowers and was trying to stuff them into the pocket of her pinafore.

'Yes, Hennie,' Evie said. 'Very pretty, but don't pick any more, there's a good girl.'

'I'm picking them for *you*,' Hennie said, coming to her mother's side.

'Thank you, dear, but that'll be enough.'

Lydia said suddenly into the peaceful little exchange, almost crying out, 'Evie, it can't be true!' And at the sound Hennie looked round at her with a faint expression of alarm on her face. Evie quickly put an arm around the child. 'It's all right, Hennie,' she said to her. 'It's all right.'

Lydia watched as Hennie squirmed out of her mother's embrace and moved away again across the grass, then said in a voice that was little more than a whisper, 'It can't be true, Evie – that I'm to – to have a baby. What was I thinking of? What could I have been thinking of?'

'Well,' Evie said, 'at such times we don't think at all, that's the trouble.'

'It wasn't meant to be like this. I thought one day I'd meet someone and get married, the way people do, and then later children would come along. It wasn't meant to be this way.'

They sat there without speaking for some moments, then Lydia brushed a few bits of grass from her skirt and said dully, 'I should reckon the time's getting on. I ought to get back home and get ready to leave. I must at least have a cup of tea with Father before I go. He'll expect it.'

Evie put on her bonnet, and called out, 'Come on, Hennie, let's put on your hat.' Then to Lydia: 'When'll you be down again?'

'I don't know. I'll let you know.'

Evie nodded, the concern written in her face, 'Oh, Lyddy, I wish there were something I could say. Something I could do to help you – to make things better – but – but there's nothing.'

'It's all right.' Lydia briefly closed her eyes in her anguish. 'I must think of what to do. The best thing. But you're right – before anything else I've got to write that letter.'

On the coach heading back from Capinfell to Merinville there was, apart from Lydia and an elderly grey-haired gentleman, a boisterous family of father, mother, and two young and spirited sons. The boys, and the parents who remonstrated with them, kept up a loud, noisy chatter continuously as the vehicle made its way along the road that wound between the meadows and cornfields, only slightly lessening their volume at intervals with the consumption of sandwiches and slices of cake. Although Lydia vaguely noticed that the old gentleman appeared at times to be somewhat put out by the disturbance, she herself was not. Keeping tight in her corner of the coach, she let it all go over her head; her mind was occupied with more immediate things than the non-stop chatter of the boys and their parents.

As the coach jogged along, she thought back over her meeting with Evie, and she knew now, after their talk, that it was no good to keep on hoping. Her worst fears had been realised. She was going to have a baby, and that was the fact of the matter.

And of course, as Evie had said, she must write to Guy. She must put out of her mind the fact that he had not sent her one single word since his departure, and write and tell him of the situation. It was the only thing to do. He had to know. He had a right to know. He had to know – whether he wanted the information or not.

How would he react? She could not guess. She was sure of her feelings for him, but of his feelings for her she could not speak; she could only hope.

Mrs Obdermann met Lydia in the hall when she returned to Little Marsh Street, and asked her how her weekend had gone. Lydia replied that it had been very pleasant and that she had found her father in good health apart from his lingering cold. The landlady then said that supper would be ready soon, for which Lydia thanked her, though she had no appetite.

When the time came, Lydia sat in the dining room and tried to force the food into her mouth. Cold tongue it was, with potatoes in mayonnaise and a green salad. To follow came apple pie with custard. Lydia did what she could to make an impression on it all, but felt that she was less than successful. When she had finished, Mrs Obdermann looked with slight dismay at the amount left on the plates and said Oh, dear, she hoped that Miss Halley wasn't sickening for something. Lydia apologised for not eating very much, and made the excuse that she had eaten dinner with her father, and also that the hot weather took her appetite away.

Soon afterwards, upstairs in her little room, she drew the chair up to the small table and pulled in front of her a writing pad and pen and ink.

With the lamp lit, and her pen poised over the paper she sat trying to decide what to write.

Eventually, after several aborted efforts, she set down:

> 15 Little Marsh Street
> Redbury
> Wiltshire
> Sunday, 10th August 1890

Dear Guy,

I hope you are well. Today marks three weeks to the day since we last met. The following day you were travelling to Europe to see your father, and I have wondered so often how you are, and indeed, after the state of your father's health. For I know you were desperately concerned about him, and could not wait to be with him and your mother, and give what support and comfort you could.

I am a little reluctant to write as I fear that you might have so many responsibilities and so much work to do that a letter would be a mere nuisance. I'm afraid I have no idea whether you are still in Italy or back in Redbury, but if you are still abroad I hope this letter will be forwarded to you. In any case, wherever you are when you receive this, I would like to ask you if you would drop me a line. Of course, ideally, I would love to see you. I will not go into it in a letter, but there is a matter of some urgency – some great urgency, in fact – that I must speak to you about. So please, do write me a line, and help to put at ease the mind of

Your friend

Lydia Halley

Lydia read through the letter, and then again. It was so poor, she thought, and did not really begin to convey her thoughts or her fears, but as for the latter, they were better left unrevealed for the time being.

She read the page through one more time, then wrote out an envelope and sealed the letter inside. Tomorrow in her dinner break from the store she would go out to the post office and send it off.

The following day, as planned, she posted the letter to Guy, and for the time being it was as much as she could do. She did briefly consider getting in touch with the newspaper office where he worked, and trying to find out whether he was back there, but she decided against it. He might object, she thought, to such prying, and she would not wish to cause him any embarrassment. He would surely respond to her letter soon, and then they could arrange to meet. She could tell him then of her situation.

A response to her letter came on Thursday. The envelope bore a Redbury postmark, but the writing on it made it clear it was not from the hand of Guy. Lydia had his previous letter still, and nothing could have made her mistake his hand for the one on the envelope. Who else could be writing to her?

She tore open the envelope and took out the letter. A single sheet of pale cream vellum, it said:

> Datchet House
> Renshaw Way
> Redbury
> 12th August 1890

Dear Miss Halley,

Your letter addressed to my son arrived this morning. It is not my custom to open his post, but the situation we are in at present is a somewhat unusual one, and unusual situations sometimes call for unusual measures. I have to tell you that my son is out of the country, in Italy, and is not expected back for some time.

However, after having read your letter, I would like to ask if you would do me the kindness of coming round to see me. Would this Saturday at four o'clock be convenient? I shall expect you at that time unless you let me know to the contrary. In the meantime I am

Yours faithfully,

Anne Anderson
(Mrs Jarvis Anderson)

Lydia read the letter over several times. At least one of her prime questions, that of Guy's whereabouts, had been answered. Mrs Anderson had returned to England, but Guy had remained in Italy. Now, however, other questions were raised in Lydia's mind: apart from her feeling that it was somewhat surprising that Mrs Anderson should open and read her son's private correspondence, she could only wonder at the purpose of the proposed meeting on the coming Saturday. Was it possible that Mrs Anderson somehow intuited the reason behind Lydia's letter? What construction had she put upon Lydia's words concerning that 'matter of some urgency'? She had no answer, and she was afraid to dwell upon it. One thing she was sure of, however – her letter to Guy would not be forwarded to him.

Saturday came, and nothing had changed. Her morning sickness was continuing, and she was also touched with it whilst at work on a couple of occasions. At those times she had gritted her teeth and clenched her hands, and waited for the moments of nausea to pass. When she finished work on Saturday at two o'clock she left the store and made her way to her lodgings.

Back in her room she sat in her little easy chair and tried to read a novel that Mrs Obdermann or the previous occupant had left in the room, but even the sensational talents of Mary Elizabeth Braddon's *Only a Woman* could not hold her interest and she gave it up after ten minutes as a lost cause; she was quite unable to concentrate and was taking nothing in. She had not written back to Mrs Anderson to say that she would not be at Datchet House at four o'clock, though at the same time she was still not sure that she would be keeping the appointment.

The time dragged on, and then all of a sudden she stirred herself. After washing, she dressed as neatly as she could and left the house at just after a quarter past three.

Outside the Victoria Gardens she caught an omnibus which took her through the town and deposited her at the library. From there she was able to take a cab the rest of the way. It turned out to be quite a long distance, and she was glad that she had not attempted to get there by walking. Alighting from the carriage, she took her watch from her bag and saw that it was ten minutes to four.

The street known as Renshaw Way was one of the most attractive that Lydia had seen in Redbury. It was situated on the northern-most edge of the town, and there were only a few houses in the whole street, not more than six or seven altogether. Nearly all of them were large, with spacious front gardens and carriage drives, and wide areas between one dwelling and the next.

As Lydia stood there on the corner she became aware that the light had changed, and looking up she saw that the sun had gone in behind gathering clouds. It looked as if rain might come before too long. *But not yet*, Lydia silently prayed, for she had brought no umbrella. She set off along the street.

Datchet House was the second house along on the left, separated from its first neighbour by a paddock where a pair of brown horses roamed. Coming to the entrance gates, which were open, she stood where the sweeping crescent drive began and looked across the wide expanse of immaculate lawn. The house was a tall Victorian building of sandy-coloured brick, with a white stucco façade. A white portico with pillars sheltered wide steps that led to the front door. Lydia stepped onto the gravel drive and moved to the steps and stopped, wondering briefly whether she should perhaps go round to the side entrance. No. She was here. Her heart starting to thump, she climbed the steps and pulled at the bell ring.

The door was opened after a short while by a tall, slim maid in a white cap and apron. She smiled at Lydia, and said, 'Yes, miss?' and Lydia told her that she had come to see Mrs Anderson.

'You'd be Miss Halley, miss, is that right?' the girl asked.

'Yes.'

'Right, miss. If you'd please to come in, I'll tell the missis that you're here.'

Lydia wiped the soles of her boots on the doormat and stepped across the threshold. She found herself in a spacious hall, with a staircase leading up from the left. The walls were hung with paintings in oils and water colours, while one huge mirror with a gold baroque frame sporting cherubs and vine leaves reflected the luxury and made the space seem enormous. She could feel the soft depth of the carpet under her feet.

'I'm to show you into the drawing room, miss,' the maid said, and walked straight ahead to a panelled door leading off. She opened it and stood aside. 'If you'd please care to go in, miss . . .?'

Lydia murmured a thank you and nervously walked past the maid into the room. The maid followed her and said, indicating the sofa, 'Would you like to sit down, miss, and I'll go and tell Mrs Anderson . . .'

'Thank you.' Lydia moved forward and sat down on the green velvet sofa. The maid nodded, saying, 'Right, miss,' and then, 'Excuse me . . .' and turned and left the room, leaving the door open.

Left alone, Lydia set her bag down beside her on the sofa and looked about. The ceiling was very high, with a deep chandelier hanging from its centre. The room was very spacious, with a grand, imposing fireplace at one end, and an open grand piano at the other. A large oriental carpet covered most of the floor, the remainder showing gleaming parquet tiles. There was another sofa, apart from the one she sat upon, and easy chairs and elegant tables on which stood bowls of flowers and china ornaments. Three tall French windows reached from floor to ceiling, leading out on to a walkway with steps leading down to a formal garden of lawns and herbaceous plots. Lydia had never in her life been in a room like it, and the sight of it alone was enough to illustrate for her the width of the gulf that separated Guy's lifestyle from her own.

She was still trying to take it all in when she heard a sound, and the next moment Mrs Anderson was entering the room and closing the door behind her.

Lydia tensed as the woman came across the carpet and, her heart thumping more strongly than ever, apprehensively got to her feet.

'Good afternoon, Miss Halley,' the older woman said, and held out her hand to Lydia. Lydia shook it weakly and murmured a 'Good afternoon, ma'am,' in reply. Before her, she saw an elderly woman dressed all in black.

'Please – do sit down.' Mrs Anderson gestured back to the sofa and, when Lydia was seated again, took a brocaded easy chair beside the fireplace. 'First of all,' she said, 'I must thank you for your kindness in coming here today.' Her voice was low, and for all its softness had the sound of strength. From a pocket in her skirt she took a pair of spectacles and put them on her nose. For a moment she studied Lydia as she sat before her, then lifted a slim hand and absently touched at the little black lace cap that lay on her grey hair. 'Yes, I'm very grateful for that. Although I could perhaps have met you at a more convenient spot in the town – convenient for you, that is – we could not have had a private conversation. A public place would not have been appropriate.' She paused. 'I hope it was no trouble for you – coming here today?'

'No, ma'am,' Lydia murmured, and then, almost as an afterthought: 'It was no trouble at all.'

'Thank you; I'm glad to hear you say that. Do you know this part of the city?'

Lydia shook her head. 'No, ma'am. I don't know a lot of Redbury yet. I haven't been here very long.'

'Oh, no, you come from some small village to the north, don't you?'

'Yes, ma'am. Capinfell.'

'Capinfell. No, I don't know it, I'm afraid.' Then, as if she regretted the momentary lapse into something that might have approached a conversation, the woman added quickly, 'Anyway, that isn't what we're here to talk about.' She pursed her lips and looked at Lydia as if studying her again. 'I had to see you, Miss Halley,' she said. 'As I told you, your letter arrived for my son – and I opened it.'

She paused here as if waiting for Lydia to say something. Lydia remained silent. After a moment Mrs Anderson went on:

'I think I said in my letter to you that I don't make a habit of opening my son's correspondence, but there are times in life when, of necessity, rules are broken. I did tell you, anyway, that my son is not here at the moment. He's still in Florence.' She fell silent, lowered her gaze from Lydia and looked out towards the nearest French window at the darkening sky. Then, still with her glance averted, she said, 'I'm very sorry to say that my husband, Guy's father, died in Italy soon after my son's arrival there.'

'Oh, ma'am,' Lydia murmured, 'I – I'm very sorry to hear that.'

'Yes, quite. Thank you.' The older woman's voice was suddenly almost brisk, as if Lydia's tone of sympathy were somehow inappropriate. 'I'm sure you'll appreciate,' she went on, 'that my husband's death has given us a great deal to do.'

'Oh, yes, ma'am.'

'Indeed it has. I myself have only recently returned from Europe. I only arrived back on Monday. After my husband's burial there I came back alone, leaving my son to continue in the management of the family's affairs. That's what he's doing now. Anyway,' she smoothed down the skirt of her black dress, 'just after I got back, your letter came for him, and I read it. When I left him there in Florence I agreed with him that I wouldn't bother him unnecessarily – he had enough on his plate as it was – so I opened your letter, as I've been doing with the other few items of post that have come for him.' She looked at Lydia and added almost sharply, 'I don't apologise for this, you understand.'

Lydia could think of nothing to say, but nodded and looked down at her hands. When she looked up again after a few moments she saw that Mrs Anderson was taking from her pocket a piece of paper. A second later she realised, to her dismay, that it was her own letter that she had written to Guy.

'I have your letter here,' Mrs Anderson said, and Lydia felt her heart thudding in her chest. She watched as Mrs Anderson pushed her spectacles up on the bridge of her nose, straightened the letter and then ran her eyes down the page. Lydia dreaded that she might read aloud from its text, but the woman did not. Her eyes moved over the letter again, then she lowered it and said to Lydia:

'Well, you were certainly right when you say you fear that my son might have so many responsibilities and so much work that a letter would be a nuisance. You're quite right – and that's what I'm here for – to save him from such. I don't wish to appear cruel, but that's the truth of it.' She raised the letter again, glancing over its contents. 'You point out to him that he hasn't written to you – and of course you know the reason for that now – and go on to tell him that on a matter of some "great urgency" you would like to see him and speak to him.'

As Lydia's heart thumped in her breast, Mrs Anderson gave a deep sigh and looked off towards the windows again. 'This is not an easy task I have before me, Miss Halley,' she said after a moment, and turned back to look directly at Lydia, 'and I possibly run the risk of appearing somewhat cruel and heartless, but you must understand that I am first and foremost a mother. My son is twenty-five years old, and he has most of his life before him. I want what is the best for him. I want him to make the most of his life. I'm like any other mother in this respect.' She reached up and took off her spectacles, studied them as she folded them, and went on, 'Guy is my only son, and I bore him late in my life. We had always wanted a child, a son, Mr Anderson and I, and after a long time it happened. Guy came to us when we had just about given up all hope of ever having a child. We had the son we wanted, and, as you can imagine, he meant all the world to us.' She set the spectacles down on a small table at her side. 'And now that my husband is gone, Guy is all I have. He is the most important thing in my life, and I cannot jeopardise any part of his future. It is everything to me, Miss Halley. I'm sure you understand that.'

Lydia felt herself nod, heard herself say, 'Yes.'

'Indeed,' Mrs Anderson said. 'He went away from us for years, joining the army and going abroad, and we lived in dread that something might happen to him out there in the Transvaal. However, he came back to us safely, only so recently, and resigned his commission, and I don't mind telling you that we were so relieved – even more so when he declared his intention of settling down and working in the family business. It was what we had always wanted.' She gave a slow nod. 'Always. Now, with my husband's death, he's been thrown into the deep end, so to speak, and he's coping remarkably well. He's had to grow up, you might say, in a matter of days, and I've no doubt that it will prove the making of him. I'm very proud of him, Miss Halley, and my husband was proud of him too.'

A little silence in the room, while from beyond the windows came the faint sound of birds singing. On first receiving Mrs Anderson's letter Lydia had wondered why she had been summoned, but she had had her thoughts – thoughts which had in turn bred her fears. Now, the more Mrs Anderson said, the more Lydia felt her fears being realised. The sensation filled her with dread.

Mrs Anderson seemed to look closely at Lydia again, as if considering the form of her words whilst studying her. Then she said at last, 'I did know about you, Miss Halley. I knew about you before your letter came for my son.'

Now Lydia found a voice, of sorts. 'Did – did Guy speak of me, ma'am?' she asked, with a little, sudden rush of gladness. If Guy had actually spoken to his mother of her, then . . .

But the next moment that little glimmer of burgeoning hope was vanquished.

'No, he did not,' Mrs Anderson said. 'In that he didn't *volunteer* anything, I mean. His father found out about you when he was lying very ill in the hospital, and asked a few questions to gain more information, and then a little later spoke to me on the matter. Naturally. He was quite exercised by it. After my husband's death I spoke of it to Guy. My husband had been deeply concerned about it all, and so was I. So – that's how I heard about you, and I learned enough to know the sort of thing that had happened – how the two of you had met in the first place, and then how you met the second time, and of your subsequent meetings over the week before he set off for Florence.' In silence for a moment she studied Lydia. 'You're a very attractive young woman,' she said, 'very pretty, and you're very presentable too. No one could deny that. I can see any young man, not least my son, being attracted to you, but it goes deeper than that. Good relationships, good – associations are not founded merely on pretty looks. I'm sure you're aware of that yourself.' She paused for a second, then continued, 'The fact of it is, I don't want my son distracted, Miss Halley. It really is as simple as that. He has too much promise in his life for me to allow that to happen. My husband and I had hopes for him, and I still maintain those hopes on my own. It is what my husband would wish. We want the best for him, the very best. Nothing less than that will do.' She paused again. 'Do you understand that?'

Things were becoming clearer now by the moment. Lydia managed to say, 'Yes, ma'am,' and fell silent again.

'It's nothing against you personally, you must understand. I would be saying this to any young woman whom he had chanced to meet and had known for only a week or so. Oh, my dear,' she frowned with a faint expression of sympathy, 'a week is nothing. I can make a guess that you grew to be rather – close in those few days, but all said and done it's no time at all, and it certainly shouldn't be seen as a basis to build a life upon.'

Lydia thought, *But I love him. I knew it in less than a week*, but she could say nothing. And how did Guy feel? He had spoken warm words to her as they lay beside the water, but they had been spoken in the heat of the moment and such words at such times could be notoriously treacherous, each one the betrayal of truth and happiness.

Mrs Anderson held up the letter briefly before her again. Without attempting to read it, she touched it with her other hand and said, 'You wrote in your letter of a matter of some urgency on which you wished to see my son.' She lowered her gaze now, as if suddenly finding the direct eye contact a little discomfiting. 'Now I'm not going to ask you what that matter of urgency was, or is, if it still exists,' she said. 'You didn't go into it in your letter, and I've no intention of doing so either.' She compressed her lips, then said, slightly defiantly, raising her eyes to Lydia's, 'It's your business, and I don't want to make it mine.' And she added firmly, 'Or my son's.'

She knows, Lydia thought. *I don't need to tell her. She knows.* She felt a terrible deep shame sweep over her, and wanted to get up and run from the room. Inside her gloves her palms felt damp.

'My son is a handsome young man,' Mrs Anderson said after a moment, 'and I'm well aware of that. Anyone would be. Also, he's from a good background with a family history that goes back a long way. One day – probably while he's still relatively young – he'll inherit everything. To put it crudely, Miss Halley, he's a good catch. I must be honest with you even further, and say that when I first heard about you I formed an opinion about you, and that opinion was not the most flattering.'

At this Lydia lifted her hands to her mouth, giving a little gasp. At once Mrs Anderson reached out to her a staying hand.

'Let me finish,' the woman said. 'As I say, the opinion I formed was not the most flattering. I had a picture of a girl that was not you. I saw a young woman who was little more than an opportunist. In short, someone who, in the parlance, was on the lookout for the main chance. I was determined to deal harshly with you.' She laid the letter down on the table beside the spectacles. 'But I think perhaps I was wrong. Oh, I have no doubt that you see everything on the credit side where my son is concerned – any girl would be blind not to – but at the same time I don't see you as a schemer. I might be wrong, but I don't. I see you as a girl who might have made a mistake, but perhaps nothing more than that.' She clasped her hands before her. 'Some day, my son will meet the right young woman and settle down – but my dear, this is not you. You are not the one for him, and he is not the one for you. I don't want to sound cruel; I said this to you before, but we have to be honest or we'll get nowhere. My son liked you, and was attracted to you, but he does not love you, and you must not entertain for one moment the idea that he does. Believe me, I know what I'm speaking of. He has certain duties now, and he's aware of them. He's aware of the course his life is to take. As I said to you just now, my husband and I had hopes for our son, and I continue to entertain, most jealously, those hopes. I hope in time he will make a good marriage, but it's too early for him to think about that. That is for the future. In the meantime he has other important things to occupy his mind and his time.' She gave a slight, sympathetic shake of her head. 'And you have no part in his plans, I'm afraid.' She paused. 'You mean well, I'm sure, but you are not the girl for my son.'

She got up and started across the room. Lydia watched as she sat down at a small writing table, at the same time putting her spectacles on her nose again. Then, turning back to Lydia, the woman went on, 'If you have made a mistake, my dear, then you will have to find some way of dealing with it.'

She knew, Lydia thought. The woman, Mrs Anderson,

had divined the true situation. However, she had no more time to think on the matter, for the older woman had gone on, saying:

'Believe me, Miss Halley, in time you will meet the right young man for you. You will, indeed. I'm sure of it. Perhaps he's there now, one of the clerks at the department store; perhaps he's some young man in your home village; but make no mistake, he is out there somewhere, and as I said, you're a very attractive young woman, and you will find someone, someone dear to you. The right one.'

Lydia listened to it all and knew that her hopes had all gone for nothing. She felt tears stinging at her eyes, and a tightening in her throat. Had Guy told his parents that he did not love her? He must have done. Obviously he had not been serious about the relationship – but what was that relationship anyway? It had lasted for no more than a week. It had been a wonderful week, but it had been only a week none the less. She realised now in that moment that it had probably meant very little to Guy – regardless of his passion and his warm words, and she was probably never going to see him again. Taking a breath she blurted out, making one last attempt:

'Mrs Anderson, one reason I wanted to see Guy is –'

'No, Miss Halley.' Mrs Anderson's hand came up, palm out, halting any possible outpouring of whatever Lydia might have to say. 'I don't want to know. I told you before, it's not my business, and I don't want to make it my business. Please, say no more.'

The words, the gesture, had stopped Lydia in her tracks, and she closed her mouth and looked down at her hands. She sat there for a moment longer, then picked up her bag and got to her feet. 'I'm sorry,' she managed to say, her voice breaking slightly, 'I must go.'

'Wait a moment.'

Raising her glance, Lydia saw that Mrs Anderson was

writing something at the table. She watched as the woman finished writing, blotted the paper, then rose from her chair and came towards her.

'Here . . . Take this. Put it in your bag.'

Lydia took the paper from her and dumbly looked at it. It was a cheque made out in the sum of a hundred pounds.

Lydia looked at the woman in bewilderment. 'What – what is this for?'

'I want you to have it,' Mrs Anderson said. 'If it comes in useful, then that is well and good, and if you have no immediate use for it, then save it for when you do.'

'But –' Lydia began to speak but could not go on. What was happening? She did not understand.

'Please, take it.'

With her words the woman moved to the fireplace and gave a tug on the bell pull. Moments later the maid was there.

'Florrie,' Mrs Anderson said, 'Miss Halley is just leaving, if you'd kindly show her out.' She turned then to Lydia. 'Thank you, Miss Halley. Thank you for coming to see me today.'

Her mind spinning, Lydia gave a nod. The next moment the maid was turning in the doorway, prompting Lydia to move. Seconds later Lydia was in the hall and the maid was opening the front door to usher her out.

Chapter Thirteen

The rain held off until just after Lydia got back to the house on Little Marsh Street. Then it came, falling heavily, and she sat in her room watching as it drenched the leaves of the cherry tree in the back yard and bounced up off the windowsill. Overhead the clouds were low and smoky grey, their ragged edges drifting as they rode the sky. When it was time she went downstairs to the dining room to eat her supper. To her relief – for she did not feel like conversation – Mrs Obdermann made only two brief appearances. She was busy at her sewing machine, she said to Lydia, and did not have the time to linger. Lydia did not find the food particularly appetising, added to which she had little inclination to eat. Nevertheless, to forestall any comment from Mrs Obdermann, she ate as much as she could.

Afterwards, she went back up to her room and there sat and tried to read. She would have liked to go for a walk, but, although the rain had stopped, the skies still looking threatening, and she was loath to take the chance. Putting her book aside, she pulled her bag towards her and brought out the cheque that Mrs Anderson had given her. She sat back, looking at it and feeling her heart pounding, partly because of the memory of the visit to the woman that afternoon, and partly because of the horror that the piece of paper induced in her.

How could Mrs Anderson have done such a thing? Did she think that Lydia's affection could be bought off like that? Is that what the money was for – to recompense her for her hurt, and to assuage any feelings of betrayal? If so, it was a waste, and only made things worse. How, Lydia asked herself, could she have accepted the cheque? How could she have taken it from Mrs Anderson and, as she was bidden, put it into her bag?

But Mrs Anderson had known. Surely she had divined the situation – Lydia's condition. It had not been spoken of – indeed, Mrs Anderson had made it clear that she did not *want* to know of it – but Lydia was sure she knew of it, nevertheless. In which case, could the gift of the money have to do with that? There was no doubt that babies cost money to bring up, so perhaps the cheque had been for the purpose of easing the coming financial burden. *If it comes in useful, then that is well and good, and if you have no immediate use for it, then save it for when you do.*

She looked at Mrs Anderson's signature, the clear, though slightly crabbed cursive text in the writing of Lydia's name, and the amount to be paid, one hundred pounds.

After a while she got up and put the cheque in the top drawer of the little white-painted chest that stood beneath the window. She must decide what to do with it – whether to tear it up or to send it back – for she would not use it, that much she knew.

With the daylight fading, she lit the gas lamps and lay back on the bed, but she was unable to rest. The room was full of ghosts tonight. After a time, she tried, for diversion, to read, and took her book up again, but for all its passions and promises it failed to touch any chord within her, and in the end she put it aside.

She closed her eyes. Tomorrow Ryllis would be coming to Redbury and they would meet for tea. Ryllis had written asking if they could meet on the Sunday afternoon. Lydia had written back saying that she would meet the coach from Barford at three o'clock, and that they could have some tea and spend some time together. It would be so good to see her again, she thought. In her mind she planned that, if she had the courage, she would tell Ryllis of her predicament.

The next morning, soon after rising, she felt sick again. She knelt on the floor, retching over her chamber pot, and trying her best to keep the sounds within her body, dreading that Mrs Obdermann, busy down below, might hear and guess at the reason.

Later, over a light breakfast, Mrs Obdermann attended and sat down with a cup of tea to keep Lydia company before going off to morning service, chatting to her about different matters: the new incumbent at the church, the weather, the government and the rising prices of just about everything. She asked if Lydia would like to accompany her, but Lydia made an excuse of having things to do before she went off to meet her sister.

Soon after two o'clock Lydia changed her clothes and then set out for the station. The day was fine. The rain of the day before had cleared the air, and the August sky was bright. She got there in plenty of time, and had a wait of some ten minutes before the coach from Barford came trundling in. Soon after the vehicle had drawn to a halt Ryllis was stepping down, and Lydia saw with relief that she was alone. She had feared that Tom might accompany her.

After the sisters had embraced, Lydia said, 'Oh, Ryllis, I've been so looking forward to seeing you. I thought we could go and have a cup of tea, and then go back to my lodgings. We can have a rest there and a good chat until it's time for you to go back on the coach.

Ryllis said in reply, 'Oh, Lyddy, I'm afraid I can't. I've got to get back to Barford. I can only stay a little while. I've got to catch the next coach back at quarter-to-four.'

'But you only just got here.'

'I know, I know.' Ryllis looked around her as the travellers milled about. 'Can we go and sit down somewhere for a while. I want to talk to you.'

There was a teashop close to the railway station entrance, and together they made their way there and found a vacant table near a window. A young maid came over to them and they ordered cups of tea. When the girl had gone away, Ryllis gave a sigh and said, 'Oh, Lyddy, I'm sorry to do this to you, making a dashing visit like this, but something's happened, and I haven't got any choice.'

'What's happened? Something with your work, with Mr and Mrs Lucas?'

'No, not them. Nothing changes there, I'm sorry to say. No . . .' She drew a breath, compressed her lips for a moment, then added, 'It's Tom.'

There was such melancholy in Ryllis's tone and expression. 'Oh, dear,' Lydia said, and then: 'What's the matter? He's not ill, is he?'

'No, he's not ill. He's very well, as a matter of fact.' Ryllis paused, put her hands up, fingers to her chin, then said, 'Oh, Lyddy, I'm so unhappy.'

'Tell me,' Lydia said. 'What has he done?'

'I was supposed to meet him last week,' Ryllis replied, 'but – he didn't turn up. I waited and waited for him by the old barn on the Kippis Road, but he never appeared.' Tears welled and she took out a handkerchief and dabbed at her eyes and cheeks. 'Oh, I don't mind telling you I was in a real old state that evening. I couldn't think what had happened to him. I imagined all kinds of things.' She sniffed and dabbed at her nose. 'Anyway, I wrote to him, telling him that I'd waited for almost two hours, and asked whether he was ill or something. I told him I was really worried, and I asked him to tell me if we could meet. I heard back from him just yesterday. He wrote saying he would meet me this

224

evening at six. So, Lyddy, I've got to go. I haven't got any choice.'

'Of course you must go,' Lydia said.

'I knew you'd understand. I got his letter too late to let you know, so I couldn't write and cancel our meeting here today.'

'No, I understand that. Well – I just hope everything goes all right for you this evening.'

'Thank you.' Ryllis gave a deep sigh. 'But there was bad news in his letter.' Shaking her head, she added, 'He said he's going up to London for a while, and won't be back for a few weeks.'

'Oh, dear.'

'He said he's going off to work with his uncle again for a while. Nice for Tom, I suppose – but not so nice for me.'

At this moment the maid came over with her tray and placed before them tea in thick china cups. Ryllis waited till she had gone, then went on:

'His folks want to see him do well for himself, of course, every parent would – and they'll be glad also to get him away from me.'

'Oh, they know about you now, do they?'

'Yes. It couldn't be kept long from them. It was bound to come out sooner or later.' Ryllis clasped her hands in front of her. 'I'm not good enough for him. I mean – look at me – a general maid. They want the best for him.'

How sadly ironic, Lydia thought. Ryllis's story was almost the same as her own – and it was true, every mother in the world wanted the best for her son, and here were she and Ryllis, both falling short of what was required. How cruel the world could be. 'I don't know what to say,' she said.

'No.' Sadly Ryllis shook her head. 'There's not much you *can* say, and you can't really blame his parents, can you? If it were my son I think I'd feel the same. They want him to have the best future possible.' She looked down at her tea, absently stirred it and then took a sip. As she replaced the cup in the saucer she said, 'Anyway, we'll have to wait and see what happens. I'm just afraid that he might never come back.' She gave a little groan. 'Oh, Lyddy, I don't know what I'd do if I lost him.'

'Well – let's hope it won't come to that,' Lydia said. 'You're really fond of him, aren't you?'

'Oh, I am. I'm that fond. I love him, Lyddy. I love him.'

As the words rang softly in Lydia's ears she could again hear herself saying almost the same thing about Guy. When she had spoken of him to Evie in Capinfell, so recently, she had used almost the same words.

As Ryllis raised her head, Lydia could see that the tears were back in her eyes. 'Try not to let it upset you too much,' she said. 'Everything might be all right. Wait and see.'

'Yes, you're right. I must try to look on the bright side.' Ryllis wiped at her eyes again and then, obviously making an effort to change the subject, asked, 'Have you heard from Father?'

'I saw him last weekend. Have you heard from him?'

'I had a letter a couple of weeks back. A very short letter, though. He never has much to say. Was he well when you saw him?'

'Yes, he's fine. Still not happy with Mrs Harbutt, of course, but there, we never expected that he would be.'

'When you write to him, you won't mention my – my trouble to him, will you?'

'Good heavens, of course I won't.'

'He wouldn't understand.'

'No, I doubt that he would.' Neither, Lydia said to herself, would he understand anything about her own situation.

Ryllis leaned across the table a little and said in a very

low murmur to Lydia, 'I'm having other difficulties, you know, with Tom . . .'

'Oh . . .?'

'Yes, well . . .' Ryllis lowered her gaze, avoiding Lydia's eyes. 'Just lately he – he wants to go further.'

'Go further . . .?'

Ryllis shook her head, almost impatiently. 'Oh, for goodness' sake, Lyddy, you know what I'm talking about. I don't need to explain.'

'Oh, I see. Yes.' Lydia gave a deep sigh. 'Oh, dear. What can I say? I just – just want you to be all right.'

'Yes, I'm sure, but I don't know what to do.'

Lydia wanted to say, *Well, of course you must say no*, but who was she to lay down rules? With the position she was in, she was the last person who should be giving advice.

'I haven't,' Ryllis said. 'I haven't given in to him. Although he wants me to, and sometimes I want to. I don't mind telling you, it's very difficult at times. I think to myself, *If I don't give way he'll get bored with me and throw me over for someone else.* So what do I do? Because at the same time I'm afraid. I'm afraid that if I do – give in to him – he'll have no more respect for me. Men don't, do they? That's what I'm told, and I can see it happening. Though maybe it wouldn't be that way with Tom.'

Ryllis's words had caused a little stab of pain in Lydia's heart. Could it be that Guy thought that way? Had she been too easy for him? Could he truly admire any girl who let herself go in that way?

'I mustn't forget the time,' Ryllis was saying. 'I mustn't miss my coach.'

'No, of course not.' Lydia dipped into her bag and brought out her watch. 'It's time we went,' she said.

When Lydia had paid the bill they went back out into the sunshine, and walked across to the coach stop where a woman and a child were already waiting. Five minutes later the coach came in.

As the coach emptied, Ryllis said, 'I'm sorry to go like this, Lyddy.'

'It's all right. I understand.'

Lydia watched as Ryllis boarded the coach, and then stood at the roadside while the vehicle was driven away.

As she turned to set off back towards her lodgings she thought once again of the irony in the situation, and a further irony came with the fact that for all her intentions to speak of her own situation to Ryllis, she had not uttered one single word on the matter.

When she got back to Little Marsh Street, Lydia went up to her room and wrote to Evie.

Sunday, 17th August

Dear Evie,

I need to talk to you at the first possible opportunity. I have to say that I have met Guy's mother, and matters have taken an unexpected turn. Are you going to be in Capinfell this weekend? If so, could we meet somewhere? I don't particularly want to go home; I don't think I can face Father just at the moment. Not with me continually being sick the way I am, and being so anxious all the time.

I'll look forward to hearing from you. Please write back as soon as you can.

Lyddy

She would post the letter on the way to the store the next day.

She received a reply to her letter on Thursday. Evie wrote:

Dear Lyddy,

Thank you for your letter. I'm surprised to hear about your seeing Guy's mother, and am curious as to how it could have happened. Anyway, with regard to the weekend, I've planned to visit Bill's mother in Merinville on Sunday. I'm taking Hennie to see her. Why don't we meet there, in Merinville? Let's say that I'll see you in the market square at four o'clock. I'll wait on one of the benches outside the corn exchange. I'll wait for half an hour. You can give me all the news then.

Evie

Lydia wrote back at once saying that she would be there.

When Sunday came, Lydia set out to catch the train to Merinville. Once there, she headed for the old corn exchange, a huge old building that jutted out into the square, with benches along two of its sides. Glancing up at the clock on the tower of the building, she saw that it was just ten minutes to four. She sat down on one of the benches on a side that was hidden from Mr Canbrook's shop which was just a few yards away. It being Sunday, the shop was closed, but on the odd chance that he might decide to call at the premises, she would be hidden from his sight.

Lydia had to wait for only a few minutes and then there was Evie's voice coming to her: 'Lyddy – there you are,' and Evie was moving towards her across the cobbles. She sat down on the bench at Lydia's side. She was alone.

'I thought you'd have Hennie with you,' Lydia said. 'Weren't you taking her to visit your mother-in-law?'

'I intended to,' Evie said, 'but Hennie's not so well today. She got up a little peevish and snively, so I decided to leave her at home with Mam.' She shrugged. 'Perhaps she's coming down with a summer cold. Anyway, it gives you and me a better chance to talk together.' She paused and asked tentatively, 'I assume nothing has changed in your – situation?'

'No – except now that I'm absolutely certain.'

'You are?'

'Yes. There is a baby.' Lydia could hardly bear to utter the words, the acknowledgement of the fact. 'There's no question of it.'

Evie nodded. 'Are you still being sick?'

'Every morning. I don't bring anything up. Which is not surprising, because usually it's so long since I've eaten, but, oh, I get the most awful sicky feeling, and I kneel there, retching and feeling absolutely dreadful.'

'I know what it's like.'

'I just hope Mrs Obdermann doesn't hear me,' Lydia said on a sigh. 'Though I don't think she will. Her bedroom is on the next floor down, and in any case, she rises a good deal earlier than I do, so I suppose she's downstairs in the kitchen when I'm getting up. I can only hope it stays that way for a while.'

They sat there in silence for a few moments, then Evie said, 'How was it that you – I'm curious to know – how did you come to meet Guy's mother?'

'Oh – yes . . .' Lydia remained quiet for two or three seconds, framing her words, and then went on to tell how she had written to Guy, and of how, to her great surprise, she had received a response from his mother. When Lydia had finished relating the details of the meeting, Evie shook her head in wonder.

'She opened and read your letter to him.'

'Yes.'

'Well – there's a mother for you.'

'I know. I was – shocked.'

'I should think so.' Evie nodded, then said, 'And she gave you a cheque – for a hundred pounds.'

'Yes.'

'My God – so much money. What will you do with it?'

'Nothing.'

'Nothing?'

'No. It's in a drawer in my room.'

There were few people about, just the odd carriage passing, the occasional couple strolling by. After some moments Evie said, 'So – what will you do now?'

'I don't know. Mrs Anderson made it clear that I have no future with her son. She made it *very* clear.'

'And what about Guy? Where is he? Is there any chance of seeing him?'

'No, he's still out of the country. Still in Italy.'

'But – but he should know about it.'

'Yes, but how can I get in touch? There's no point in my writing to him at his home or at the business. His mother would only intercede again.'

'But he's got to know.'

Lydia said nothing, but sat there with her eyes gazing off along the street.

'What are you going to do?' Evie said. 'Have the baby without telling him?'

Lydia put her hands to her face, briefly covering her eyes. When she lowered them she said brokenly, 'How can I have a baby? How could I support a child, and raise it without a husband? Oh, I know *you* have, and are doing so, and Hennie's a credit to you, but it's not the same for you. You were married. There was no shame attached to Hennie's birth. Also, it's not only that, the – the look of the thing – it's the support, the finances. It's – bringing it into the world and caring for it. Where would I live? I couldn't raise a child on my own. And I've got no mother to care for it while I work for the necessary money – not like you.'

'No, maybe not,' Evie said. Her tone was sympathetic. 'But what do girls do in such circumstances? There's not a lot that can be done, is there, except the child can be fostered, or farmed out. That happens so much. You could find some nice woman to care for your babe, and pay a little each week for its upkeep. Girls do it all the time.'

Lydia frowned. 'How awful,' she said, 'to have a child and have hardly a hand in its upbringing. To have it see someone else as its mother – I couldn't bear it, I know I couldn't.'

'I know it's not ideal – but there are not many options.'

'In any case,' Lydia said, 'there's still the shame it would bring, not only on me but on my father. He would never recover, I know it.' In her mind's eye she could see the desperate scenario. 'No,' she added, 'he'd never get over it – and he would never forgive me for it either.'

'He would forgive you, in time. Your father would forgive you anything.'

Lydia sighed. 'Don't be so sure.'

The silence fell again. Back and forth, before their eyes, the occasional townspeople went by. Lydia was not aware of them. At last she turned and said to Evie, 'What *am* I going to do?'

Evie hesitated then said, 'There is another way, of course.'

'Tell me.'

'Well – you haven't *got to have* the baby.'

Lydia frowned. 'I know what you are thinking.'

'There are ways, there are means – of course there are.' Evie was looking closely at her, searching her expression. Lydia said nothing.

After a moment Evie went on, 'There's a woman right here in Merinville. I know that for a fact. And you've got money. You've got the money from Guy's mother.'

'I wouldn't use that,' Lydia said at once. 'I'd never use that.'

'Well, whatever . . . I'm just telling you that there's a way out. You're not that far along, so it probably wouldn't be so bad. I don't doubt you'd soon recover.'

'Do you – know anyone who's had it done?'

'No, I don't but . . .'

Lydia gave a little shudder. 'Oh, what a dreadful thought.'

'I don't know whether much pain is involved,' Lydia said, 'but girls have it done all the time. We all know that.'

Lydia said, 'It's not the – the pain, the discomfort. It's also the fact that it's – well – it's getting rid of a life.'

'Yes,' said Evie. 'I never said the decision was easy.'

Lydia thought, in her silence: *How can this be – this conversation? We're sitting here in the afternoon sunshine, talking about ending a life that is only just beginning, putting out a flame that is hardly more than a spark.*

Evie studied Lydia's face for a moment or two, then said, 'I'm not suggesting you do it, you understand. I'm just telling you that it's something that can be done. You have got a choice. Of sorts.' With her last words she reached out and briefly pressed Lydia's hand.

Grateful for the touch, Lydia gave a little nod, then said, 'Yes. Yes, I know.'

Two pigeons flew down and began to strut about the ground, pecking amongst the cobbles. Lydia watched them for a few seconds then drawing up her breath, said:

'This woman you said you know of . . . You say she's here in Merinville.'

'That's right. I don't know her address, but I can get it.'

'And – can you get it soon?'

'As soon as I get back home. My mother will know it.'

'Do you know how much the woman charges?'

'No, I don't.'

'I haven't got all that much,' Lydia said. She paused, then added, 'So you'll get it for me, will you? The woman's name and address?'

233

'I'll write to you with it straight away.'

'Your mother – she won't mention it to anyone else, will she?'

'No, of course not!'

'If it should get out, and get back to my father . . .'

'Don't worry, Lyddy. Don't worry.'

Lydia nodded, relieved. They remained there on the bench, neither one speaking. There seemed to be nothing left to say. After a time, Lydia said dully, looking at the ground, 'What time is your coach?'

'I promised Hennie I'd be on the five o'clock. She and Mam are going to meet me at the Rising Sun.'

'You'd best be off, then.'

'I s'pose I had.'

'You don't want to miss it.'

'No.'

And still Evie sat there, as if loath to leave her friend in her unhappiness. The moments ticked by. Lydia gave a sigh as if it were drawn up from her soul. 'Go on home, Evie,' she said. 'Go on back to Hennie. I won't come with you to the coach if you don't mind.'

'No, of course not.'

'I'll sit here for a minute, and then I'll go and get my train.'

Lydia nodded, moved close to Evie on the bench and put her arms around her. 'You're a good friend,' she said.

Evie pressed her closer in response. 'I'll try to write to you tonight,' she said.

She gave Lydia's hand a last squeeze and got up, the movement sending the pigeons flying up. The two young women wished one another goodbye, and then Evie left, stepping away over the cobbles.

After Evie had disappeared from her sight, Lydia turned on the bench and looked up above her at the clock on the little tower of the old corn exchange. A quarter to five. Her train was not due to leave for another forty-five minutes. She lowered her glance and leaned forward, head bowed, closing her eyes, her hands clasped on her knees. If Evie was true to her word, then she would write at once with the details of the woman who could help. The thought of it, that 'help', brought the sweat breaking out on her palms. There had been so many wretched stories of girls who had found themselves in unfortunate situations and who had sought such assistance from women who made their living operating in the cities' back streets, girls who had suffered most dreadfully, and not rarely, from death by blood-poisoning. Lydia dreaded the thought of the ordeal before her, dreaded the thought of joining those legions of desperate young women, but what choice did she have?

Suddenly, with no warning at all, something touched at her clenched hands, making her start. She opened her eyes and saw before her the black, wet nose of a dog. With a start of alarm she drew back and saw the animal looking up at her with an eager, expectant gaze. Then, almost in the same moment, she realised the identity of the creature.

'Tinny!' She breathed the word, and the dog enthusiastically wagged its tail. 'Tinny, what are you doing here?' Reaching out, she patted the dog's head, stroked its back, the soft hair, and heard a voice as its owner rounded the corner of the building.

'So there you are, Tinny.' And then, in a tone of greater surprise, 'Miss Halley? Is that you, Miss Halley?'

She looked up at the man as he came towards her, and straightened, forcing a smile she was far from feeling.

'Mr Canbrook, hello.'

'Well, hello to you, Miss Halley! What a pleasant surprise!' He looked at the dog and shook his head in a little gesture of wonder. 'Tinny must have picked up your scent,' he said, grinning. 'He's a clever little tyke, that one, he is indeed. I couldn't think where he was going to, trotting off like that, and look where he was heading – for *you*.' He stood before Lydia, looking down at her. 'So, what brings you to Merinville on a Sunday afternoon?' he asked.

'I came to meet a friend of mine who was coming in from Capinfell.'

'Ah, yes. You're not living in Capinfell any more, are you?'

'No. No, I'm not.'

'No.' He nodded. 'I saw your friend from Capinfell the other day when she came into the shop. The young woman. I asked after you and she said you'd moved off, to live and work in Redbury. I couldn't understand it. That's the way of it, is it?'

'Yes,' she said, 'I'm living in Redbury now.' As she spoke the dog remained at her side, and absently she stroked and patted him.

'Where are you working in Redbury?' Mr Canbrook asked.

'At Seager's department store.'

'Oh, you're a sales lady, are you? I'm sure you're very successful.'

'No, I'm not on the shop floor; I work in the office, in the postal order department.'

'Ah.' He nodded. 'And d'you enjoy it?'

'At times. It's a living.'

He said with a smile, 'If it's just a living you wanted, I'm sure we could have found something for you here in my shop. Canbrook's doesn't have quite the floor space of Seager's, but still we do our best to be of service.' When she did not respond to this, other than with a half-hearted smile, he said, 'Are you going back to Redbury this evening?'

'Yes. My train leaves at half past five.'

He hesitated for a moment. 'I've just come in to get

something from the shop,' he said. 'Why don't you come in? I'll make you some tea before you get your train.' He looked up at the sky. 'It's going to rain, anyway, and any second now. You can't stay out here.'

As he finished speaking the first drops came down, and Lydia felt them on her forehead, on her bare wrist. She had brought no umbrella.

'Come on,' he said. 'Come inside. I'm not going to bite you.'

As she hesitated more drops fell, and more strongly, the spots darkening the dust on the cobbles around her feet. 'Yes, very well,' she said. 'Thank you.' He was a kind man, she thought; he had always appeared so, and the falling rain left no time for hesitating.

In seconds the rain was falling harder. She got to her feet, and he waited as she stepped to his side, then turned and started off smartly around the corn exchange. Tinny walked beside them. On reaching the shop's entrance the man had his keys out ready, and in seconds he had turned one in the lock and pushed open the door. He stood aside and urged Lydia to enter.

'Please . . .'

She stepped into the shop, the dog following. Mr Canbrook closed the door behind them, and turned to her. 'We'll go on through into the back. This way.'

She had been inside the shop numerous times in her life, but she had never seen it as it was behind locked doors. How strange it appeared. Everything was covered, the reels of cotton, the pins, the needles, the laces and the ribbons, the rolls of silk and linen, everything lay under coarse cotton covers, waiting for the morning when all would be revealed again for the day's shoppers.

Mr Canbrook led the way through the shop into a smallish room, with a worn sofa along one wall, and a table and several old chairs of unmatching designs. The window looked out on to a paved yard on which the rain appeared to be falling a little more heavily.

He stood and briefly held out his arms. 'And so welcome to the inner sanctum! The part that no customer ever sees.' He gave a little laugh. 'Oh, truly welcome, Miss Halley. Sit down, make yourself at home.'

Lydia looked around her and then took a seat on the sofa. It was old, of faded green velveteen. 'Yes, the sofa will do,' Mr Canbrook said. 'It's seen better days, mind you, but that goes for me as well.' He bent to the dog which stood wagging its tail. 'Ain't that so, Tinny?'

Mr Canbrook turned to Lydia again. 'I'd like to offer you some tea,' he said, 'but there wouldn't be time to get the stove going if you've got to go and catch your train.'

'No, please,' Lydia said. 'You mustn't go to any trouble on my account.'

He smiled at her. 'My dear, nothing done on your account would be too much trouble.' He turned and took a step across the room. 'I tell you what, I'll do what we often do during the day when we're rushed – nip along to the teashop and get some tea. How would that be?'

'No, really,' Lydia said. 'It's quite all right. Besides, you'll get so wet.'

'That's all right,' he said. 'I'll dodge between the spots.' He moved across the room and took up from the table a small, round tin tray and two mugs. 'And you,' he said, speaking to the dog, 'you stay here and keep our guest company.' He turned back to Lydia. 'Tea with milk, yes?'

'Yes, but –'

'Right, tea with milk it is. I'll only be a minute.'

And he was gone.

Lydia sat there, waiting, and Tinny came to her and rested his head in her lap. 'Yes,' she murmured as she stroked him, 'it's easy to make some creatures happy.'

There was no sound in the room but the ticking of a clock

on the mantelpiece and the increasing sound of the rain on the window pane. Lydia looked across and saw how the rain lashed down. She thought of Mr Canbrook, dashing along beside the square to the teashop. Then, after what seemed only a short time, there came the sound of the main door opening and closing and then footsteps as he came back through the shop and into the room.

'Here we are!'

He came in holding before him the tray bearing the two mugs, now full. 'Hardly anybody in there,' he murmured. 'Business is always slower for them on a Sunday.' The shoulders of his jacket had been darkened by the rain.

'But you're so wet,' Lydia said. 'You shouldn't have gone.'

'No, no, I'm all right.' As he set the tray down on the table he shook his head. 'A bit of rain never hurt anybody.' He took off his hat, shook the moisture from it, and hung it on a hook beside the door.

'Now . . .' He stepped back to the table and picked up one of the mugs of tea, 'Would you like sugar in it? We've got some somewhere. At least I can offer you that.' He snapped two fingers and shook his head again. 'Darn it,' he said, 'I should have asked you if you'd like a pastry or a slice of cake. They keep a nice selection there most of the time. Would you like something to eat? It'll only take me a minute to pop back.'

'No, really, thank you,' Lydia said, 'the tea will be fine, and it's very welcome.'

'Well, if you're sure . . .' He looked down at the dog which sat looking beseechingly up at him. 'No, I'm sorry, Tinny,' he said, 'but I didn't get anything for you. You'll have to wait till you get home.'

The spindly-legged table stood next to one end of the sofa, its surface marked with rings left there by excessive moisture and heat. Mr Canbrook put down the mug. 'Here you are,' he said, 'though I'm sorry it's not the best china. Still, it'll do.' Gesturing towards the table top, he added, 'It can't hurt it. It was ruined years ago.' His own mug he took up and sipped from, then set it back down on the tray. Then he pulled up one of the upright chairs and sat down.

'Well, here we are,' he said, smiling at Lydia. 'Who would have thought it?'

Lydia, unable to meet his eyes with equanimity, did not know what to say, and sat there feeling awkward and self-conscious. The only sounds were the clock and the rain. 'Listen to it,' Mr Canbrook said. 'It's a good job you're not out in that now. You'd be wet through.'

'Yes, I should be,' Lydia admitted.

'I can't tell you,' Mr Canbrook said after a few moments, 'how pleased I am that you're here.' He gave a wondering little chuckle. 'Honestly, it's like some dealing of fate. I've wanted to talk to you for weeks, and now here you are, sitting in our little back room.' The dog moved to him and lay down at his feet. 'What about that, Tinny, eh? That's a wonder, isn't it?'

Lydia smiled, and the dog thumped his tail on the floor.

'And I'm serious, Miss Halley,' the man said. 'I truly have – wanted to talk to you.' He paused, then said, 'Would you mind if I call you by your first name?'

'No,' Lydia said, 'not at all.'

He smiled gravely. 'Thank you – and I'd be glad if you'd call me Alfred.'

She smiled, but didn't know how she ever could, though she nodded as if it were no problem.

The rain pattered on the pane, now, it seemed, driven by the wind. For some moments neither one spoke, then Mr Canbrook said:

'I want to talk to you – Miss Halley – Lydia – in a very serious way.' He halted, as if waiting for her to speak. When she said nothing, only gave a vague nod, he went on,

'I hope you won't be offended at anything I have to say. I can only tell you that I have the utmost respect for you, and that whatever you think of what I'm about to say, no offence is intended. D'you understand?'

'Yes, I understand.' She was puzzled by his words, and was now curious as to what he would say.

'Good.' He nodded, paused for some moments, as if seeking out the most appropriate words, then said, 'May I speak freely?'

'Yes, of course.'

'Thank you.' He smiled. 'I'm glad I haven't frightened you away by now.' He leaned forward slightly, his hands on his knees. His expression was earnest. 'You might well wonder,' he said after a moment, 'why I've chosen to speak out at a time like this. Well . . .' He came to a halt here, as if uncertain how to continue. Then after a second or two he said, 'I asked you, some months ago, when I met you here at the shop one day, if you were engaged in anyone's affections. Do you recall?'

'Yes.' Lydia frowned slightly. 'Yes, I remember.'

'Yes, and I was pleased when you assured me that you were not. So I said then that I would write to you. I didn't do so, of course, for very soon afterwards I heard of the tragic death of your poor mother. It would have been very indelicate for me to have written to you at such a time as that.' He shook his head sympathetically. 'Oh, dear, that must have been a terrible blow for you – her passing. I was so sorry to hear the sad news.'

Lydia gave the slightest nod, and murmured, 'Thank you.'

'And I hope I'm not speaking out of turn now,' he said. A moment's pause, then he added, 'I'm not a young man. I don't need to point that out to you. I'm fifty-three years old, and it's partly due to this – circumstance – that I'm talking to you now as I am.' His voice was low, earnest. 'I was twenty-two when I met Louie, the girl who was to be my wife,' he continued. 'Louise was her name. She was three years older than I, a strong, independent young woman, and very attractive.' He smiled at the memory. 'I had to have her, although she'd hardly look at me at first. So – I played something of a waiting game. I was smart enough to do that, and at twenty-two I had time. So – I courted her. I wrote to her. I called round at her house and asked her out walking. I brought her little presents: fruit and chocolate and little things. For heaven's sake, I even composed verses for her – and pretty terrible they must have been, I'm sure!' He gave a little chuckle here. 'But I suppose they seemed all right at the time. At the start I could barely get her to acknowledge me, it seemed. She was very hard to get to know, to get close to.'

He took up his mug and sipped from it. A gust of wind threw the rain at the window, and he looked over at the sound. 'Listen to that,' he said. 'It's coming down like billy-o, but we need the rain, there's no doubt about it.' The fabric of his waistcoat looked a little stretched across his belly.

He set the mug back down on the tray and then said, 'Yes, Louie was very hard to get close to. Well, there you are, I wasn't the most prepossessing, I suppose. I mean, she was an inch taller than me for a start, and I wasn't the most handsome of the young men hanging around, but –' and here he gave a little smile, 'I suppose you could say I was the most persistent. In the end – I suppose I wore down her resistance, and I won. Yes, I won.' Another little laugh here. Then he continued, 'I like to think that she saw past the negative things and saw the real me. Or maybe I've been fooling myself all these years. Anyway, I guess when it came to it she thought she should take a chance on me – and she did. I don't think she ever regretted it. We worked in the shop together, and a capital partnership, it was, believe me.' He paused, then added, 'That was until almost seven years ago, when she died.'

He sipped from his mug again, seeming for a moment lost in his own thoughts. Lydia, wondering where all this was leading, and conscious of the time passing, sneaked a look at the clock on the shelf. She wanted to say, *It's time I left if I'm to get my train,* but she did not want to appear rude, did not want to appear dismissive of his seriousness. Besides, the rain was still falling heavily. He it was, though, who focused briefly on the hour. Looking at the clock himself, he said, 'It isn't long before your train is due, is it?'

'No – I'm afraid not.'

'But you can't go out in this,' he added, glancing towards the rain-lashed window. 'What time is the *next* train – the one after?'

'It's about half an hour later, at just after six.'

'Would it get you in too late if you took that one?'

She hesitated, but hesitated too long, and he said, 'Well, take that one, will you? The rain should have passed over by then. In any case, I've got an umbrella, and I intend to walk with you to the station. Or I'll go and get you a cab – whichever you're happiest with. Yes, I think you'd be better off in a cab, and avoid all the puddles.' He paused. 'Can you take the later train? Please?'

She nodded. 'Yes.' She had no reason to rush back to Redbury; there was nothing for her there but sitting in her room and waiting for the time to pass – to bring her ordeal closer.

He smiled his gratitude. 'Thank you.' He looked at her mug on the side table. 'You're not drinking your tea.'

'I was letting it cool a little,' she said, and picked up the mug and drank.

'Is it all right?' he said.

'Yes, thank you.'

'Not too strong?'

'No, it's fine.'

He nodded and leaned forward again in his chair. 'I was telling you about my wife, about marrying her, wasn't I?'

Lydia gave a little nod. 'Yes,' she said politely.

'Yes,' he echoed. 'Well – we were happy, all things considered. Not everything worked out as we'd hoped, but – but we made the best of things, and we were happy in our way. Then, as I said to you just now, she died seven years ago, and I've been alone since then.' At his feet Tinny lifted his head and laid it down again. Absently, Mr Canbrook bent and gave the dog a pat, and then remained as he was, leaning down with one hand on the dog's shoulder. After a while he straightened again, and looked directly at Lydia.

'I'm going to ask you something now,' he said, 'but I must first ask you not to give an answer right away. Is that all right?'

Lydia frowned, at a loss as to what to say. 'Well, yes . . .'

'I'm assuming that your situation is about the same. In that you've got no plans with anyone else? That you've got no plans to marry?'

'No.'

He nodded. 'I'm not being impertinent, truly; I just have to know if someone has come into your life. Someone special.'

She hesitated for a moment, while Guy's face came before her, then gave a little shake of her head. 'No.'

He smiled, relieved. 'Good. I told you just now,' he said, 'how I courted my wife, and how in the end she accepted me, but I haven't got time for that again. I can't wait for years this time. Oh, believe me, if I were younger I'd do it the right way. I'd send you little presents and take my time so that you could get to know me, but there isn't time. Time isn't on my side – not at my age.'

He came to a stop again, then said, his words coming out in something of a rush:

'Miss Halley – I want so to marry you.'

Having spoken he sat looking directly at her, eyes slightly wide and anxious, waiting to see how she would react.

Lydia sat without moving. She could scarcely believe what she had heard. He had given out enough hints in his preceding speech, so she should have been ready for his announcement, but her remaining preoccupation with her own thoughts had left her unprepared for his surprising words. It did not seem real. In fact nothing of the whole scene seemed to be real. She could still hardly banish from her mind her conversation with Evie, when she had asked for the woman's name and address; while another part of her mind was still struggling to know which was up and which was down; and yet here she was sitting with this man – whom she had never taken seriously in her life – and right out of the blue he was telling her that he wished to marry her.

She looked towards the window and saw to her relief that the rain had eased, had almost stopped. The skies above were clearing, changing the light.

'Oh, yes, I want to marry you,' Mr Canbrook breathed. His hands were clasped tightly before him. He was frowning in his earnestness. 'I love you,' he said. 'Oh, Miss Halley – Miss Halley – Lydia – I've loved you for years.' He hesitated for a moment as if to allow a response, but Lydia still kept silent. 'Yes, for years,' he said. 'Since the day you came here into the shop with your mother and she had the bee-sting – do you remember? Of course you do. I watched you that day, how solicitous you were, how sweet you were.' He put a hand up to his mouth, very briefly, as if he would stop his words, then added, 'And how beautiful.'

Lydia, her tea forgotten, sat looking at him, this little man with the rather fussy manner, the misshapen nose and the slightly crooked smile – a smile that he could not help but turn upon her. Her father had spoken of him as ridiculous. She could think of not a single word to say.

'I mean every word of it,' he said. 'I love you. Which is why I've gone to Capinfell in the hope of seeing you some Sunday mornings. Which is why I've asked your friend for news of you.' He shook his head and gave a little sigh of wonder. 'And I still can hardly believe it: here I've been thinking of you so much, and I find you sitting on my own doorstep.'

He fell silent, looking at Lydia as if waiting for her to speak, but still she did not, and hearing nothing from her he took encouragement from her silence and said:

'I know all the things I'm not,' he said. 'I'm not tall, I'm not handsome, I'm not young, and for all I know I might be coming over as a complete fool. Well, fool or not, I've energy to work, and I can promise you that you would not want. You'd never have to work again if you did not wish to, though I would love it if your inclination was to work alongside me in the business. The shop is very successful, and it will go on being successful after I'm gone. You'd have a good home. My house is quite large, and you would have help in the running of it.' He paused. 'Will you please think about my offer? You would do me the greatest honour if you could bring yourself to say yes.'

Lydia said nothing. She could still hardly believe the words that he had spoken.

'Will you think about it?' he said again.

Now she gave a nod and found herself murmuring, 'Yes.'

'Ah,' he said. 'Thank you. Though as I told you, I don't want your answer yet. If you give it to me too soon I'm pretty sure I know what it'll be. No, please be kind and give it to me after you've had a little while to think about it.' He smiled ruefully. 'And in the meantime I'll try to work up some courage in case the news is bad.'

'Mr Canbrook,' she said, 'I've got to go.' She started to

rise from her seat. 'I must go for my train while the rain's holding off. I think if I go now I might still make the earlier one.' Now she could not wait to leave.

He got up also. 'I've offended you,' he said, frowning.

'What? No. No, you haven't.'

'Are you sure?'

'Quite sure. Truly.'

'And – and you will – think about it?'

'Well, I –'

'Please, Miss Halley.'

'Yes,' she said. 'I will.'

He gave a little smile of satisfaction. 'I'll get my umbrella,' he said, 'and we'll go out and find a cab.'

Chapter Fourteen

Monday morning. A wave of nausea hit Lydia just as she was finishing dressing, and she knelt, retching repeatedly until eventually the spasm passed and she could straighten up, her head pounding and the sweat beading on her forehead. She had brought nothing up but a little bile, but there, she had not eaten anything in many hours.

After sitting on the edge of the bed, her breast heaving while she slowly got her breath back, she rose and finished dressing. When she was done she went out onto the landing and down the stairs to the dining room. There she forced herself to utter a cheery 'Good morning' to Mrs Obdermann, struggled to eat what she could of the breakfast of fried eggs and buttered bread, and then went off to work.

The same story was repeated on the Tuesday, except this time she seemed to retch even more violently. One thing was certain, she could not face another fried breakfast, and down in the dining room she picked at the food and moved it around on her plate, until she could find the courage to thank Mrs Obdermann and get up from the table. She would be able to eat something at dinnertime at the store, she told herself; she would feel more like it then.

'You don't seem to have much appetite lately, Miss Halley,' Mrs Obdermann said with a little sniff as Lydia turned to go from the room.

'No, I haven't, I'm sorry to say,' Lydia replied. She gave a smile that she was far from feeling. 'But it'll come back in a day or two.'

'Let's hope so,' Mrs Obdermann said, 'or you'll be wasting away to nothing.'

Lydia did manage to eat something at the store in the midday dinner break, but dismayingly a little nauseous feeling came back to plague her again during the afternoon. She fought it off, however, and hoped no one had noticed. The day dragged, as all the days seemed to drag just now, and she waited for the end of the working day to come. Perhaps, she told herself with a mixture of hope and fear, Evie would have written with the woman's name and address.

Evie had. On returning to the house in Little Marsh Street Lydia let herself in with her latchkey and saw the letter waiting for her on the hall table. She took it up and went to her room. Inside, behind the closed door, she tore open the envelope. Evie had written:

Dear Lyddy,

As soon as I got back home I set about finding the information you wanted. I'm not allowed to tell you where it comes from, but I can tell you the name and address of the woman you need to see in Merinville. She is Mrs Hoggins, and she lives at 34 Gilham Street. She's a midwife. I'm told the street is near the paint works. I don't know exactly how much she charges. I think it's in the region of ten shillings, but this was a while back. Anyway, obviously you must be prepared. Also, I'm advised that you'd best not eat before you go.

I hope this is a help to you. I wish I could do something else. Please let me know how you are, whatever you decide to do.

Evie

Lydia read the letter over again, then pulled her boots off and lay back on the bed. The letter made it all so much more real. It was time now for commitment. She had made up her mind; she would go and see the woman. She would go tomorrow, tomorrow morning. She could not waste time. Every day that passed made her situation more difficult.

She was glad that the supper served by Mrs Obdermann that night was a simple one. She ate what she could of it, thankful that for the moment at least the nausea was not present. Bearing in mind what Evie had said to her about not eating before going to see the woman in Merinville, it was on the tip of her tongue to tell Mrs Obdermann that she would require no breakfast, but somehow she could not bring herself to do so, and in the end said nothing.

The next morning when she was dressed and ready, she went down to the dining room, where she found the table already laid. As she sat down, Mrs Obdermann came into the room carrying a tray bearing a teapot and milk jug. Lydia wished her a good morning, and the landlady returned the greeting and asked her what she would like to eat: oatmeal, or pancakes, or some eggs? Lydia thanked her, but said she wanted nothing except a cup of tea.

'You only want tea?' Mrs Obdermann set down the teapot and jug and stood there beside the table. 'That's all? Just tea?'

'Yes, that's all, thank you. 'I'm not – I'm not hungry.'

Mrs Obdermann gazed at her for a moment in silence. 'Aren't you feeling well, Miss Halley?'

Lydia felt her cheeks burning under the other woman's gaze. 'Yes, I'm fine,' she said.

'Well, you're not eating properly, and I heard you being sick again this morning.'

Lydia did not know where to look, but forced herself to

hold the landlady's glance. 'I'm a little – out of sorts,' she said, 'but it will pass.'

'A little out of sorts. Well, let's hope it's nothing more serious than that. Anyway, drink your tea.' The woman looked steadily at Lydia for another moment, then started towards the door. She did not leave, however. She got as far as the doorway, stood in silence with her lips pursed, then turned back into the room, coming to a stop a yard from the table at which Lydia sat.

'Miss Halley,' she said, 'I may as well say what's on my mind now. There's no point in putting it off.' She was still holding the tray in her hands and now she set it down on the tablecloth. Her mouth was such a tight, thin little line that all trace of her lips had vanished.

'I've watched you pick at your food in the mornings for days now,' she said, 'and I'm tired of throwing good food away. We don't keep a pig, like some people do, so all food not eaten gets wasted. And why? Because you've got no appetite, you tell me. Yes, very likely.' She took in a deep breath. 'You tell me you're a little out of sorts. Well, if anyone asked my opinion, I'd say it appears to me to be a little more than that.' She spoke sharply, rapidly. Her face had gone pale; she was almost white around her mouth. 'I've heard you for days now, up in your room, heaving away as if you might bring up your very heart, and you're telling me that that's just being a little out of sorts, and it'll pass. Yes, I think it could well pass, but it might take nine months to do so.' Her pale blue eyes were wide with anger and horrified disapproval. She stood with her arms folded across her ample bosom. After a few moments she said, pushing her head forward a little: 'Well, have you anything to say, miss?'

Lydia sat as if paralysed. Hearing Mrs Obdermann's dreadful words, and seeing her standing before her, her face thrust forward so belligerently, she could think of not a single word to say. She sat there, her hands tightly clenched, raised half way up to her chin.

'Well, I see you're not denying anything,' Mrs Obdermann said, 'and that's answer enough for me.' She drew her receding chin back into her neck so that it all but disappeared. 'And I have to tell you something else, miss, and that is, that this is a respectable house. I've always kept a respectable house, and I intend to continue doing so. Oh, yes, I must confess I did at times wonder where you were when you were rushing out all those evenings the other week, but it was no business of mine, I told myself. But then there comes a time when it *is* my business. This is *my house*, and I'm not having it made a laughing stock, or the cause of sneers and disrespect. My neighbours have got eyes as well as I have, and it won't be too long before your apron is hanging high. What will they think then? What kind of house will they think I'm keeping? Well, my dear young lady, they're not getting the chance to ask the question, I can tell you that.'

She remained standing there, her arms folded. She was breathing heavily, her wide eyes glaring down at Lydia, who still sat in silence, unable to say a word, the tears stinging her eyes.

Mrs Obdermann was not moved by the sight of the tears shining in Lydia's eyes.

'I'm a fair woman,' she said abruptly. 'No one can ever accuse me of not being fair, and I'm going to be fair with you. And I'm going to be generous with you. Other landladies would have thrown you out days ago, but I'm not like that. Perhaps I'm foolish not to be like it, but that's the way it is, the way I am. So I'm telling you now, I'm giving you a chance to find somewhere else to live. I don't know who'd take you in for long in your condition, but that's your problem. All I want to say to you is that you've got two weeks, and at the end of two weeks I

252

want you out. You must find somewhere else to live. Wherever you take your problem, and what you do about it is up to you, but I want it to be no longer any concern of mine.'

She stood there for a moment or two longer, lips tightly compressed, breath coming loudly, and then turned about and left the room.

Lydia remained sitting there, her hands still clenched before her, gazing down unseeing at the white tablecloth. It was as if she could not move. A little sob escaped her, and she raised her hands and pressed them over her lips.

After a few seconds she lowered her hands, took a deep breath and got up from the table. Now, more than ever, she knew what she must do.

Up in her room she sat on the side of the bed for what seemed ages. Yes, she knew. She no longer had any choice. It was quite obvious to her now that she was not likely to hear from Guy, and also it was beyond consideration that Mrs Anderson might have changed her mind and forwarded the letter on to him. At last she got up and put on her jacket and her bonnet and gathered her reticule to her. In it she put Evie's letter and the little money she had; she just hoped it would be enough. From the drawer of her chest she took out the cheque that Mrs Anderson had given here, and for a few moments stood with it in her hand. Perhaps a situation such as this was what Mrs Anderson had had in mind, she thought. But no. She would make her own way in whatever she was going to do. After a moment she carefully tore the cheque across and across, and dropped the pieces into the waste basket. She was ready to go.

Mrs Obdermann was nowhere in sight as Lydia went down, but she could hear her at work in the kitchen. As Lydia passed through the hall the small clock on the bureau gave the time of five past ten. Outside the house she set off for the railway station.

It was well after eleven by the time she reached Merinville, and after asking directions of the ticket collector she eventually found herself in Gilham Street. It was situated towards the edge of the town, two facing rows of mean-looking, narrow terraced houses, at the end of which reared up the high grey walls of the paint factory. Number 34 was halfway along on the left. Most of the street was unmade, the footways on either side being laid with cinders.

In front of the house, as with all the houses in the street, was a small yard, roughly paved for the most part, with a few tired-looking flowers growing in the centre and along the sides. It would have been going too far to call it a garden. The gate was almost off its hinges and hung drunkenly, one edge of it scraping the ground. Lydia stood outside and looked along the short path to the front door. Her heart was pumping against her ribs and she could feel her palms damp. Taking a deep breath, she drew herself up, pushed the gate open the rest of the way and stepped through.

She was aware of each pace she took along the path, each one moving her forward to the brown-painted front door and the single step at its foot. She lifted the knocker and rapped on the door. It was opened in a few seconds by a short, slightly-built woman of about fifty years of age. She had dark, greying hair pulled back into a bun at the nape of her neck, and spectacles. She wore a stained apron over a faded blue dress.

'Mrs Hoggins?'

'Yes?' the woman said, frowning, peering at the stranger's face.

'I – I was given your name,' Lydia said. 'I asked –'

She got no further, for the woman suddenly leaned

forward, grasped Lydia's left wrist and pulled at her, urging her over the threshold and into the narrow hallway.

'That's it, dear.' The woman closed the door. 'We don't want all the neighbours knowing our business, do we? Now, then . . .' She squinted up at Lydia's face, and then looked her up and down. 'Do I take it dear that you're 'ere looking for a little 'elp?'

Lydia hesitated then gave a nod. She was vaguely aware of the drab, scuffed paper on the walls, the worn linoleum under her feet, the stale smell of fried bacon.

'Yes, indeed,' Mrs Hoggins said, 'and I'll wager that someone you know 'as got herself into a bit of a pickle, is that it?' She gave a little laugh. 'Someone not too far from where I'm standin', I'd reckon. Yes?'

Lydia did not know how to answer, and the woman put her head on one side almost coyly, and said, 'You don't need to be shy with me, dear, and you don't need to be nervous neither. There's nothin' to be shy nor nervous about. If you've come to Minnie Hoggins you've come to the right person.' She smiled suddenly, revealing overly pink gums and long, brown-stained teeth. 'Can I ask who sent you, dear?'

'Well,' Lydia said, 'it – it came in a roundabout way, and I don't know who it really came from – your name and address. I was just – just told that you could – could help me.'

'And indeed I can 'elp you, my dear. That's what I'm 'ere for.' She paused. 'And I s'pose you wanted it today, did you?'

'Well . . .' Lydia gave a nod. 'Y-yes.'

'Yes, these problems don't do with 'angin' about, do they? It's not a thing you can put off, is it? Though I 'ave to tell you it's not really convenient right at the moment.'

Lydia gave a little groan. She couldn't be asked to go away and come another day. 'Please,' she said.

'Well, all right, dear. Though you've caught me at a bad time, I 'ave to say. Still, we'll manage. Now, I tell you what.' She smiled suddenly again, stretching her lips back over her long teeth. 'You go and make yourself scarce for a bit, will you? I've got to go out and call on one of my expectant mothers, but it's not very far, and I shall be back in an hour. Can you wait until then, dearie?'

'Yes.' Lydia nodded.

'That's fine.' The woman gestured with her thumb, jabbing towards the right. 'There's the park, up the road a bit and to the left, then turn left at the ironmonger's and you'll see it in front of you. You could sit in there for a while, in the park, if you wouldn't mind. It's only five minutes' walk. Or there's the public on the corner. Same direction. The Running Hind. You could get a cup of tea there – but don't 'ave any milk with it, and don't 'ave anything to eat, all right?'

'Yes.'

'Then come back in an hour and we'll see what we can do for you.' The woman stepped to the door, opened it and stood aside as Lydia went through and onto the path. 'All right, dear,' Mrs Hoggins said, 'I'll see you in an hour.'

With the front door closed behind her, Lydia walked up the path and onto the cinder footway. Turning right, she walked along the street until she saw an ironmonger's shop on one corner, and on the opposite corner the public house that Mrs Hoggins had spoken of. Ahead of her, when she turned to the left, she saw the entrance to a park, with its greensward stretching away behind iron railings. She would have liked to go into the inn and have some tea – she had drunk nothing all day – but she could not bring herself to go alone into such a place.

She went through the gateway into the park and walked along the gravel path. Eventually she came to a vacant bench beside it and here she stopped and sat down. From her bag she took her watch and looked at the time, judging the hour when she must return to Mrs Hoggins's house. She settled herself to wait.

There were very few people about. A young mother came by with two small children, one of whom was throwing up a ball. An elderly man and woman strolled past, an old terrier walking along at their heels. A young man came riding a bicycle. She watched them all, briefly thinking of the lives they were living. If they only knew, she thought, of what was going through her own mind; of what was to happen to her body in a very short time.

She dreaded returning to see Mrs Hoggins, but she felt she had no choice if she was to get on with her life. Besides, she had made her decision and she would stick to it. That was the purpose of her being there. Now that she was so close, so close to the thing being done, she could think ahead to what she would do once the ordeal was over. She was in a position to make plans. One thing was certain, she could no longer stay with Mrs Obdermann, even though she would cease to be in her present delicate situation. In fact she did not know how she could ever face the woman again, even during the short time she was to remain at the house. Yes, she must find new lodgings as soon as possible.

Perhaps, she thought, it would be better to move back to Capinfell, give up her job at Seager's and get right away from Redbury. She thought how pleased her father would be, were she to return to live in the family home. How lonely he must be, she thought: in the space of just a few weeks he had lost his wife, and his remaining daughter living at home had gone to seek her future elsewhere. He would not necessarily show it, but he would surely be very happy if she should return to live with him.

Which she could do, of course, and possibly she could find work at Cremson's again – or if not Cremson's there was bound to be something else available to her. She had no fears of forced unemployment. There were other factories, and no end of shops and other establishments needing employees.

She suddenly had a picture of Mr Canbrook's draper's shop. She saw it bustling and busy on a market day, and then as she had seen it last Sunday, when it was closed to customers, with the shutters up, the covers over the goods and the rain lashing down against the window. She thought again of Mr Canbrook's proposal. How unreal it was, how strange, and how impossible too.

The minutes passed by. Dragged by. When she thought of going back to Mrs Hoggins's house the sweat broke out under her arms and on her palms, and she clenched her fists and waited for the moments of panic to subside. What was she about to do? Apart from the dread of the operation that was to take place – and she had heard something of what happened in such instances – there was also the thought that she was destroying a life. But what choice did she have?

At last the hour passed, and she got up from the bench and set off back the way she had come.

It did not take her long to reach the house and, her mind in a kind of daze, she walked up the path to the front door and rapped with the knocker. Mrs Hoggins answered it almost immediately and quickly drew Lydia inside.

'Well, here you are, dear,' the woman beamed as she closed the front door. 'I'm sorry about having to abandon you for a while, but you understand, I'm sure. My lady down the road is near her time, and nature doesn't wait around. Anyway, come on through.'

She led the way along the passage, past a rising flight of

stairs, and to a door at the end that opened into a scullery.

'Here we are. We shall be all right 'ere.'

Lydia followed her into the untidy room. Unwashed dishes were stacked up on a draining board and on shelves. The table in the centre of the room was bare of everything except a sheet of oil cloth.

'Did you go to the public?' the woman asked conversationally.

'No. I sat in the park.'

'Well, that's nice. The weather's particularly nice right now.' She smiled. 'Now, I'm not going to ask you your name, dear. It's none of my business, in any case. So no names, no pack drill, eh?'

She moved then and closed the door, and a moment after she did so there came from some other room the distant yell of a child, followed by a long, squalling wail. Mrs Hoggins cocked her head and clicked her tongue. 'Oh, take no notice of that,' she said. 'My two grandchildren are staying with me right now, but they won't come in 'ere.' Her tone turned brisk as she added, 'Well, would you like to take off your jacket and bonnet dear? You might as well be comfortable. Not that you'll be 'ere that long.'

Lydia put her bag down on a chair, then took off her bonnet and jacket.

'Now,' Mrs Hoggins said, 'before we go any further, dear, we must settle up the matter of the payment. You've brought money with you, have you?'

'Yes.' The word was barely more than whispered.

'That's good. I'd like to help out young ladies for nothing, but I'm afraid it's just not possible. How much did you bring, dear?'

Lydia reached for her bag. 'I've got eleven shillings . . .'

Mrs Hoggins's face was a picture. 'Eleven shillings, I'm afraid that's not going to get us far, is it? The cost is eighteen shillin', dear.'

'But – that's all I've got, and I was told that that was your – your charge. Eleven shillings or so. Or in the region of that.'

'Oh, no, I 'aven't charged as little as that in years. I'm afraid times don't get easier, dear; they gets 'arder. I'll wager you've noticed that yourself. And I don't notice prices goin' down in the shops, do you? Oh, no, dear, I'm very sorry, but I don't think we're going to be able to do any business today. You'll 'ave to try somebody else. My charge is eighteen shillin', and not a penny less.'

'But – oh, I don't know anyone else and – this is all the money I've got. I've only been in my new job a few weeks. I just haven't got any more.'

Mrs Hoggins's eyes were wide, and untouched by sympathy. 'Well, that's a shame, isn't it? But I'm afraid there's nothing we can do for you, dear.'

'But – but I've come all the way from Redbury and –'

'Yes, dear, we know all about that. We've all got our sad tales to tell, and you're no different from the others who come 'ere.'

Mrs Hoggins folded her arms and stood there in silence, lips pressed together. Lydia realised that the next move was up to her. 'Could I – could I send you the rest when I get my wages?' she said tentatively.

'No, I'm sorry, miss.' Mrs Hoggins's tone was a little more businesslike. 'That's not the way we do things, I'm afraid. Sad to say but that kind of thing never works. I tried it in the past, but somehow the young ladies forget, and I end up doing it all for next to nothing. No, no, it 'as to be money on the spot or there's no business.' She paused. 'Have you got something besides your bit of money? Some jewellery, perhaps.'

Lydia raised her hand to touch a little cameo brooch she wore at her throat. 'Well, I've got this,' she said, and unclipped it and handed it to the woman.

Mrs Hoggins squinted over it and sniffed. 'I'm afraid that won't get you far, dear, bit of tin like that.' She handed the brooch back to Lydia who sadly pinned it back to her blouse.

'You've got nothing else?' the woman said.

'Well . . .' Lydia took a deeper breath and said, 'Well, I've got a watch. A gold half-hunter. It was my mother's.'

Almost before Lydia had finished speaking Mrs Hoggins put out her hand, open palm up. 'You got it with you now, 'ave you? Let's see it, then.'

Lydia found herself moving to her bag again, looking into it and bringing out her mother's watch. She held it in her hand, her hand close to her breast, still unsure what to do, but Mrs Hoggins was in no such doubt, and she reached out and took it and held it close to her face. She opened it, studied it for a moment or two, then closed it again. Looking up at Lydia she said: 'And you've got eleven shillings as well, 'ave you?'

'Oh, yes, but – but surely not my money and the watch as well. I was only –'

Mrs Hoggins cut in, 'Look, it's entirely up to you, dear. The work I do is very – very sensitive, and it's work that not many women can do, I can tell you that. I can do it because of all my training, but such work don't come cheap. Like I said, if you want to look around for somebody who'll do it cheaper, then that's up to you, but you'll 'ave an 'ard job, I'll tell you that for nothin'. So what's it to be, dear. I'm afraid you'll 'ave to make up your mind as I'm a busy woman and I 'aven't got time to waste. I've got other things to do.' She paused briefly, then added, her head cocked a little, as in a gesture of sympathy and understanding, 'I'll tell you what, dear. I'd like to be kind to you, so I'll tell you what we'll do. I won't take all your money – though others would, you can be sure – but not me. I'll take just six shillin' and the watch and we'll call it quits, all right?'

Lydia gazed at her for a moment and then, biting her lip, gave an almost imperceptible nod. There was nothing for it but to go ahead. She could not stop now. She dipped back into her bag and this time brought out her purse. From it she took out three florins and laid them in Mrs Hoggins's outstretched palm.

The money and the watch Mrs Hoggins then deposited in a drawer which she pulled out from the end of the table. 'Well, that's settled, eh?' she said, and now she beamed at Lydia again. 'Money matters are never the most pleasant to discuss, are they? But it's essential that they be got out of the way first of all. I'm sure you agree.' She looked at Lydia judiciously. 'You missed your monthly, did you?'

'Yes.'

'Are you being sick in the mornings?'

'Yes. I don't bring anything up except bile, though.'

'That's neither 'ere nor there. And your titties . . .' Here the woman reached out and squeezed Lydia's left breast. As Lydia winced, the woman said, 'Tender, eh? Yes, I shouldn't think there's any possible doubt about it. You're in the family way, my dear, you can depend on it.' Without warning she lifted Lydia's skirt and laid her right hand on her belly. Through the fabric of Lydia's underclothing she briefly prodded and kneaded the flesh. 'How far along are you, dear?' she asked.

'Just – just over five weeks.'

'Mm-hm.' Mrs Hoggins nodded and lowered her hand and dropped Lydia's skirt. 'Why don't you take your gloves off, dear,' she said.

Lydia did so, and dropped them into the crown of her bonnet. Mrs Hoggins, watching her, said, 'I see you're not married. You're not wearing a wedding ring. So what 'appened? You don't look like the kind of girl who plays fast and loose, nor the kind you see 'angin' about the pub door on a Saturday. Did you have a young man who left you in the lurch?'

Lydia did not answer, but frowned in her distress. She only wanted the whole business to be over with.

Ignoring Lydia's silence the woman said, 'Oh, some men can be absolute monsters, dear, I know. Half of 'em have only got one thing on their minds, and once they've got it they're off into the blue yonder, never to be seen again.' Then, seeing the stricken look on Lydia's face, she added quickly, 'Mind you, not all of 'em are like that. Well, whatever is the truth, we can all make mistakes, can't we, and all I can tell you is that it's a good thing you come to me. We'll get you sorted out, dear, and then you can go on 'ome and get on with your life again.'

The woman went to a cupboard, opened it, and took out a wooden box, which she brought to the table. All the time as she moved she talked. 'You say you live in Redbury, dear?'

'Yes.'

'Well, I've 'elped out ladies from Redbury before, and I don't doubt I'll do so again.' She turned back to the box, lifted the hinged lid and took out a long instrument that looked like a piece of straight wire. She took a none-too-clean-looking towel from a rail and laid this down on the table, then set the instrument on it. 'Where will you be going when you leave 'ere, miss?' she asked.

'Where? Why – why, back to Redbury.'

'I'd wager nobody knows you've come 'ere today, is that so?'

'That's right.'

'And you mustn't mention it, dear, not to nobody.'

'No – no, of course not.'

'That's it, dearie. When you get back you'll need to go and lie down for a while – and you go straight 'ome, all

263

right? Don't you go walking about the town at all until this is all past, you understand?'

'Yes.'

'There's going to be some blood, so I suggest you get some towels ready, as soon as you gets in, all right? It'll be a very bright red, the blood, but don't be alarmed, you'll be all right.'

Lydia could feel her temples throbbing, while her heart hammered in her breast. She felt very hot.

'Now, dear,' Mrs Hoggins said, 'you slip off your drawers and get up on the table, all right? And pull your skirt up round your waist.'

Lydia just stood there. Mrs Hoggins looked at her with a little expression of impatience flitting across her narrow features. 'Come on, dear. We 'aven't got all day.'

Lydia began to lift her skirt, and in that same moment the door burst open and a child of about four came into the room. A little boy, he was quite naked except for a stained shirt that came down to just above his waist. Seeing Mrs Hoggins, he stretched out his filthy hands to her and gave a wail. Mrs Hoggins cursed under her breath and went to him. 'I won't be a second, miss,' she said over her shoulder to Lydia, and snatched the child up in her arms. 'You come along o' me, young master,' she said sharply, irritably, and marched through the door. A second later Lydia heard the sound of her feet on the stairs.

Lydia stood there while panic and fear swept over her in a great wave, and she suddenly knew that she could not go through with it. Whatever the outcome, she could not suffer this violation to her body, and she could not allow this dreadful creature to kill the little life that was in her.

In seconds she had picked the gloves out of her bonnet and stuffed them into her bag. In a few more her jacket was back on, and her bonnet was on her head. She could not wait another moment. She rushed to the open door, and dashed through it into the passage beyond. As she got to the front door and flung it open, she heard from behind her Mrs Hoggins's voice, calling out in puzzled outrage, 'Where are you goin' to, miss?' But Lydia was through the door and hurrying away down the path. She did not look back.

Chapter Fifteen

Back at the house in Little Marsh Street Lydia let herself into the hall. To her relief there was no sight or sound of Mrs Obdermann, and she quickly went up the stairs to her room. Later, at six-thirty, she crept back down to the dining room and saw that the landlady had left out on the table a plate of cold meat, potatoes and pickles. Lydia managed to eat a little of it – it was the first she had eaten all day – and then went back up to her room. There, lying on her bed, she once again thought over her situation.

She had taken a step by running from the woman in Merinville, and that running had left her precisely back where she started. She did, of course, have the option of going back and having the operation carried out, but she knew that that would not happen. She had committed herself now, and she would not turn back. What, then, was she going to do?

One thing for certain was that if she remained in Redbury she would have to find new lodgings – but that would not work either, for her condition could not remain a secret for long. In two or three months it would start to show, and soon after there would be no means whatever of hiding the fact.

What if she went to Capinfell? Her father would be pleased to have her back in the family home, but what would happen when he became aware of her condition?

And what about her child? When the baby was born she

wanted the best for it. What should she do? The questions turned over in her mind.

By the time she fell asleep, late that night, she was no nearer finding any answers.

Arriving at the store at her usual time the next morning she went first to see Mr Watson, the superintendent of the postal order department and apologised for missing the previous day's work, and said that she had been indisposed. He responded by saying that he thought she had been looking a little pale just lately and hoped that she was feeling better. She thanked him and went to her work-table. It would not be long before she was leaving the company altogether.

The interminable day dragged on while she arranged various sales and wrote to customers about their orders, but eventually five-thirty came round and it was time to leave. She put on her hat and jacket, took up her bag and joined the other clerks making their way from the staff entrance.

As she stepped out onto the pavement, a figure came forward from her right, moving into her path.

'Mr Canbrook.' She came to a halt, facing him.

'Hello, Miss Halley . . . Lydia.' He was holding a small bunch of miniature roses, and a little self-consciously offered them to her. 'I brought you these,' he said.

'Well . . . thank you.' She took the flowers from him. 'How nice of you.'

The other office workers were streaming around them, and Lydia stepped over towards the wall of the building, out of their way. Mr Canbrook moved with her.

'What are you doing in Redbury?' she asked.

'I had a little business here, and I thought I'd take advantage of the situation and call on you. I didn't have your address, but you told me where you were working.'

Lydia smiled. 'Well – it's quite a surprise, seeing you here.'

He hesitated then said, 'Are you in a hurry to go somewhere?'

Where could she be going? She had nowhere to go. She had no plans. 'No,' she said. 'I'm just going back to my lodgings.'

'Are they far away?'

'Not too far. Sometimes I walk, sometimes I take the omnibus.'

'If you're walking I'd like to walk with you, if that's all right.'

She nodded. 'Yes, of course.' He would be pursuing the answer to his proposal, she thought. There was, of course, only one answer that she could give.

He looked up at the sky. 'It looks a little grey, but I don't think there's any rain coming.'

They set off along the pavement together.

'We can walk through the Gardens,' Lydia said. 'That's the route I usually take.'

'Fine. You lead on.'

At the end of Queen Street they turned left on to Patton Crescent and from there made their way through the entrance into the park. Mr Canbrook looked about him as they entered and gave a nod of pleasure. 'Ah, this is very nice.'

'Yes – it is.' Lydia could suddenly see herself and Guy walking in these same gardens. She thrust the image away.

There were numerous other people on the paths, either taking late afternoon strolls or using the ways as short cuts from one part of the city to another. As Lydia walked at Mr Canbrook's side she waited for him to raise again the matter of his marriage proposal. He said nothing of it, however, but spoke of other things, the weather, the

268

harvest, his draper's shop. Lydia knew, though, that it was only a matter of time and she would have to give him her answer.

The wide oval pond was ahead of them, and at its rim three or four small boys crouched, managing little boats, their parents or nursemaids standing nearby or sitting on the benches. Mr Canbrook gestured towards a couple of vacant seats further on around the rim of the pond and said, 'What do you think? Can we sit down for a minute?'

'Yes, if you wish.'

They walked round to a part where there were no people, and sat down on a bench facing out over the water.

Silence between them. Lydia, not knowing what to say, waited for him to speak. After a while she raised the flowers to her nose. 'They're lovely,' she said; 'they're so pretty,' and then laid them down beside her. At last Mr Canbrook spoke.

'I lied to you, I'm afraid.'

'You – you lied? I – I don't understand.'

'I told you back there that I had business here in the town.' He shook his head ruefully. 'I haven't got business here. I came just to see you. That was my only purpose.'

'I see.'

He gave a sad little smile, and added a sigh. 'I have a feeling that it's a bit too early, is it? Too early to ask you for an answer, I mean.'

'Oh, Mr Canbrook –' Lydia turned to face him. 'I don't need to have time to think about it. I could have told you when you asked me on Sunday. My answer then would be the same as it is now. I'm very sorry. Really I am.'

'Ah . . .' he said, 'so you're turning me down, are you?'

'I don't have any choice, sir. I respect you enormously, and I do thank you so much for your offer. I don't dismiss it lightly. It's just that – oh, it wouldn't work – for all kinds of reasons.'

He did not speak for a moment, then he said, 'What are they, those reasons?'

'Oh – really – is it wise to go into them?' She wished now that she had given him her answer at their meeting on Sunday. It would have saved this embarrassment now, and any discomfiture. 'Can't you just – just – accept it?'

'I did tell you I was persistent,' he said.

'Yes, you did.'

'So, please. I would like to know,' he said. 'Tell me, please.'

'It sounds so cruel,' she said, 'to just say it bluntly like this – but – but I don't love you. Surely you realise that.'

'Oh, I do. I knew that. I never expected that you'd say you do. I can live with that.'

'Can you?'

'Of course. What are your other reasons?'

'Don't you think it's important – that it's vital – to have love in a marriage?'

'There would be love in it,' he said. 'I can love enough for both of us.'

'Oh, Mr Canbrook . . .'

She turned away from him, avoiding his steady gaze. She should not be sitting discussing this matter with him. It did no good to either of them. It was no help to her to spin it out like this, and also it did no good to him, to protract the matter. Better she should just say no, and end it for good and all.

Suddenly a wave of nausea came over her and she leaned forward, her gloved hands up to her face.

'What is it?' he asked. 'What's wrong?'

She pressed her hands to her stomach and drew in the air in gulps, at the same time closing her eyes. After a few moments the sick feeling began to fade. Another minute and it had almost passed and she straightened again.

'You don't look well,' he said. 'You look so pale around your mouth. What's the matter?'

'I – I'm all right.' She continued to breathe deeply.

'You don't look all right to me. Tell me what's the matter.'

'It – it's not important. I'm all right, really I am.'

'Well . . .' he said doubtfully, 'if you say so.' A little moment of silence between them, then he added, his words accompanied by a rather rueful smile, 'I have to say – the look on your face when you saw me waiting outside the shop back there. It wasn't the most encouraging.'

'I'm sorry,' she said. She felt as if she were in a fog. Her mind was spinning. Here was this man, this perfectly nice and pleasant man, totally engaged by his own pre-occupations, and she could not become involved in them at all. She could not get past the miseries in her own heart and mind. Her brain was full of questions and doubts and desperation, a desperation that threatened at any moment to flood to the surface and bring her down.

After a second she took a deep breath and said, 'Mr Canbrook, I've got to go.'

'Oh, please . . .' As she moved to rise from the bench he reached out towards her. 'Please, don't go. Not yet.'

'Oh, but . . .' For a second or two she hovered, half risen from the seat, then allowed herself to be urged back down. Sitting on the bench, she leaned forward, eyes tight shut, her mouth opening in anguish.

'Oh, Miss Halley!' he breathed. 'What is it?'

She did not answer. She could not answer. Suddenly great gasping sobs burst from her throat and she pressed her clenched fists to her mouth in a vain attempt to stifle them.

'Don't,' he cried. 'Oh, my dear girl, don't! I beg you, don't. I can't bear to see you cry.'

She sobbed again, the sound repeated over and over, her whole body shaking as she bent low. 'Mr Canbrook,' she cried through her tears, 'please go. Please leave me.'

'No,' he said. 'Not like this. I'm not leaving you like this. Tell me what's the matter.'

She turned to him now, her face full of pain and anguish, the tears streaming. 'I don't know what to do,' she said with a little moan. 'I don't know what to do.'

'Why, what is it? Tell me, please.'

Through her tears she gave a sudden, bitter little laugh, the sound utterly sad in the late afternoon air. 'I'm like Hansel,' she said.

'Hansel?'

'Yes. Hansel in the forest. The birds have eaten all my crumbs and I don't know which way to turn.'

Then, the sobs racking her body, she got up, and flinging herself from her seat on the bench, turned and headed away.

Hurrying with no idea of direction, she moved from the pond into a little grove of trees that grew nearby, and here she came to a halt and stood there panting, the tears coursing down her cheeks. Canbrook was at her side in seconds.

'Tell me,' he said. 'What is it? What's the matter?'

She shook her head and turned from him, looking off through her tears into the shadows of the little grove.

'I can't bear to see you like this,' he said. He paused. 'Is it me?'

'You?' She turned to him now. 'No, it isn't you. It's only me. It has nothing to do with you.'

'Come. Come and sit down. Come and tell me about it.' He reached out to take her hand, but the moment he touched her she drew away. He let his hand fall back to his side. 'Please,' he said, 'tell me – you're in some sort of trouble, some awful trouble. What is it?'

She did not answer.

'Tell me what it is,' he said.

She turned her face away from him again. 'I can't.'

'Yes, you can. Of course you can. I don't understand what can be so dreadful that it can affect you like this.'

'No,' she said quietly, 'you can't understand. You wouldn't believe it either.'

'I'll believe anything you tell me. I told you, I love you.'

'You can't love me,' she said. 'You don't know me.'

'I know you. I've known you for years.'

'No.' She hesitated briefly, then added, 'I'm not the girl you think I am.'

He thought about this for a moment, then said, 'I don't think there's anything you can tell me that would put me off. My feelings for you are – so strong.'

'Your feelings, you say.' There was bitterness in her voice. 'They won't withstand everything.'

He frowned. 'What is this dreadful thing you're hinting at?'

'Oh, if I told you it would finish your feeling for me for ever.'

'I think I should be the judge of that.'

Still she faced away from him, and still he waited. Then after a little silence she said, almost whispering, 'I'm to have a baby.' When she heard no response from him she lifted her head and turned to face him, looking for the horror in his gaze. There was no trace of it. 'Well?' she said. The tears were drying on her cheeks. 'Aren't you going to say anything? Or are you too shocked?'

He did not speak for some seconds, then he said, 'Such things happen all the time. It doesn't change you in any way.'

'You think not?'

'Of course.'

'Unfortunately not everyone will see it like that.'

'More fool they.' He gave a little shake of his head. 'Did you think I would be so horrified that I would turn from you?'

'Why shouldn't you?' She thought of Mrs Obdermann. 'You wouldn't be the first.'

'Those people – they can't know you.'

'But you don't know me either.'

'I know enough.' He waited a moment then said, 'Can I ask you a question?'

She replied with doubt in her voice, 'Yes.'

'The child's father . . . how does he feel about this?'

She hesitated. 'He doesn't know.' And to forestall a further question: 'I have no intention of telling him.'

Mr Canbrook opened his mouth to speak again, then halted before he had begun. After considering his words, he said, 'Well, it's not for me to ask the whys and wherefores of that. You've got your reasons.'

She nodded. 'Anyway, now you know.' She moved to step past him. 'I must go. I'll get my flowers and I must go.'

He followed her to the bench where her posy lay forlornly on the seat. As she picked it up he stepped forward and said: 'Don't go yet. I still need to talk to you.'

She remained standing.

'Sit down – please.'

She sat, and he sat down beside her. He regarded her for a second or two.

'You said just now that you didn't know what to do.'

'I don't,' she murmured. 'I can't see any way out.'

'What about your father? He'd help you, surely.'

'I wouldn't know how to tell him. I dread telling him.' The tears threatened again, and she swallowed and was silent while she gathered her strength. 'Yesterday I was given notice to get out of my lodgings. The landlady guessed at my – my condition – and made her feelings clear.' She looked away from him, over the water. 'So in a week or so I shan't even have a place to live. I'll have no choice but to go back to Capinfell, and I shall have to – have to put up with the shame. As will my father.' She turned to him now, smiling at him although the corners of her mouth were pulling down. 'Go on back to Merinville, Mr Canbrook,' she said. 'Go on back and forget all about me.'

'Oh,' he said, 'I don't think I could ever do that. You're that set in my mind.'

'No,' she said. 'As you see, I'm not the woman for you.'

'You are.'

She frowned. 'Not now.'

'You are,' he said. 'My feelings for you haven't changed.'

On the rim of the pond before them two young boys came, one of them pulling along a little wooden boat, drawn by a string. They chattered excitedly as they moved, concentrating on their task, seemingly without a care in the world. Dully, Lydia watched them go past, then said softly:

'I – I almost did something dreadful yesterday . . .'

'Oh?' Mr Canbrook gazed at her, watching her profile against the green of the sward.

'I – I was so desperate . . . not knowing what to do.' She shook her head distractedly, still facing out across the pond. 'I can hardly say it – but I went to see a woman – a particular woman – in Merinville.'

Canbrook was at a loss. 'Who? What for?'

'It doesn't matter who she is. It's what – it's what she does.'

'I don't understand . . .'

'She – she's a midwife, but she doesn't only deal with – with births.' She hung her head. 'I'm ashamed to tell you this.'

After some moments he gave a slow nod, followed by a little groan. 'Oh, God – I think – I think I understand what you're saying.'

'I didn't go through with it,' she said, whispering so

faintly that he could barely hear her. 'At the last moment I found I couldn't.'

'Thank God for that,' he said. 'I've heard of such women. And I've heard of what other women go through – the ones who seek their help.' He reached out and briefly laid his hand on her wrist. 'Dear God – going to see a woman like that – you could have died.'

She nodded. 'Yes, I know.' She looked round at him now, and the shine of tears came into her eyes again. 'I gave her my mother's watch,' she said, her voice breaking, and now the tears welled and overflowed and ran down her cheeks again. 'I treasured it. I treasured it so, and I gave it away.'

Suddenly she turned and leaned towards him, and his arms came up awkwardly and held her. His touch was tentative at first, but then as she lay more closely against him he held her tightly. She cried brokenly against his shoulder, 'I've made such a mess! I've made such a mess of my life.'

He continued to hold her, and gradually her sobbing eased and stilled, apart from a little catching of her breath. She leaned with her head against his left shoulder and his right hand lay gently on her back. After a while, when she had grown calmer, he said softly:

'I would have loved it if we could have had a baby – my wife and I. It's what we wanted, what we prayed for. We'd have given anything. It was the only thing in the way of our complete happiness. But it never happened. Though we tried everything we could think of.'

The two little boys came back, dragging their small boat through the water at the margin of the pond. Mr Canbrook waited until they had gone past, then said, almost whispering the words, a little urgency in his tone:

'Marry me, Lydia. I want you – you and your baby. Marry me.'

She was silent, unmoving as the words sank in, then she lifted her head from the shoulder of his tweed jacket.

'Are you serious?' She could hardly take in his words. 'Do you mean it?'

'Oh, I mean it. I've never been more serious in my life.'

'But – but the baby, my baby –'

'It will be *ours*. *Our* baby. I told you – I always wanted a child.'

'You would do that? Marry me and take the child as yours? Give it your name?'

'Oh, I would,' he said with a note of passion in his voice. 'I would love you both, and care for you both. To have you – and a child to call my own – it would make my life complete.'

Chapter Sixteen

The Canbrooks' house in Merinville was named Ranleigh. It stood back a little from the road behind a green lawn with a crescent-shaped carriage drive. The house was of three storeys and though not huge, was relatively spacious, comprising some ten rooms. It had a white façade, the rest of the walls being in yellow brick. On this autumn afternoon it was in the drawing room on the ground floor where Lydia sat, writing at the little table that had, since the start of her residency, become her own. Near her feet lay Tinny, her almost constant companion when he was not accompanying Alfred on his short journeys to the shop. Lydia's south-facing view as she sat, looked through a tall window on to green lawns and herbaceous plots. Out of her sight, beyond the formal design, the kitchen gardens stretched away to an orchard which ended on the banks of the river Merin. The only flowers visible on this early October day were a few late blooming roses. She had been married now for just over five weeks.

She sighed and put down her pen and looked around her. Sometimes it hardly seemed possible that she was here. Could it be? Was it really so? Oftentimes such questions rattled through her mind and she was almost required to take stock of her surroundings and her situation and tell herself yes, indeed, it was true. Following Alfred's proposal they had been married a week to the day later, the ceremony performed at the register office in Redbury. Once the matter had been decided, there had been no point in delaying matters; indeed, it was essential that they move quickly, and so they had. During the week leading up to the wedding, Lydia had worked her final day at Seager's and had moved her few things from Mrs Obdermann's and gone into a small hotel in Merinville. Ironically, her morning sickness had eased during that week and eventually had faded altogether. After the wedding she and her new husband had gone to London for three days, three days during which they ate in restaurants and went to the theatre and the opera and the Aquarium, and visited the British Museum. Although Alfred had visited London twice in his life before, it was to Lydia a completely new experience and she had been in awe and wonder at the sights and sounds around her, though she could not help but also be very much aware of the grime and soot. It was not a place to live in, that much she was sure of. This place, on the other hand, was ideal, this spot on the northern edge of Merinville, with the quiet river drifting by, and the meadows beyond where the sheep and cattle grazed. If she could be happy anywhere, she thought, then surely she could be happy here.

After a moment more she took up her pen again. She was writing to Ryllis, having that morning received a letter from her. Sadly, her sister seemed no happier in her situation. If anything she was even more unhappy. She had written to say that Thomas was still working in London, and could not say how long he would continue so. He had returned home to Barford only once since his departure in mid-August, and that had been for a very brief visit, during which he had seen Ryllis for not more than an hour. As for his letters, he rarely wrote at all, Ryllis said. He had never been one for letter-writing, but even so she had expected more than the three or four she had received.

When Lydia had finished she addressed the envelope and sealed the letter inside. She had been able to offer no comfort, and did not see how she could do so. She had never had positive thoughts where Ryllis and Mr Thomas Bissett were concerned, and could not see things changing for the good in the near future. She could only say to Ryllis that she hoped things would work out, and exhort her not to be too low in her spirits. She could not tell her that as far as she could see, the writing was on the wall, and there would be no joy in the outcome.

Pushing the letter to Ryllis aside, she took up her pen and began to write again, this time to her father.

How difficult it was to know what to say. Although Ryllis had managed to be at the wedding in Redbury, her father had refused to attend. In fact, he had not spoken to Lydia, nor written her a word, since she had told him of her intention to marry.

'You're going to be what?' he had said.

'I'm going to be married. This coming week.'

She had gone to Capinfell to see him and give him her news, though dreading the moment that she would do so. She had not been surprised at his reaction. He had stared at her, frowning, his mouth open.

'*When* did you say? *This coming week*? But you haven't known anyone long enough to think about taking such a step.'

She had kept silent at this, trying to think of words to say, words that would not heap more fuel upon the flames.

'Is it someone you've met in Redbury?' he had said. 'It must be. There's no one here in Capinfell I could think of in a hundred years.'

Then it was that she had told him that her bridegroom was to be Alfred Canbrook. He had been stunned, and continued disbelieving. 'How can it be? The man is as old as I am. Has he been calling on you in Redbury? Is that the picture?' He had spoken in a low voice, but the flesh around his mouth was bloodless with anger. 'I expected better from you, Lydia,' he had gone on to say. 'For you to go and ally yourself with a heathen – I'm bitterly disappointed in you – but you always were one to go your own way.' He was hurt too – that Lydia should have taken such a step without even consulting him. 'Which church are you to be married at?' he asked. Her reply that she was to be married not in a church but at the register office in Redbury had been the last straw. He had turned his back upon her, refusing to say another word.

And this was how the situation with her father had remained. She believed that he would come round in time, but at the moment his silence was painful and she wanted it ended as soon as possible.

Now, in her letter to her father she wrote that she was well, and hoped that he was also. She went on to say that she wished he would visit them soon, and assured him that he would always be welcome. Also, she said, she and Alfred would like to visit him in Capinfell when it was convenient.

When the short letter was finished and sealed in its envelope she got up from her seat. As she did so the dog lifted his head, looking at her expectantly.

'Yes,' she said to him, 'I'm going out to the post box. Are you coming along for the stroll?'

Tinny rose at once, tail wagging, and then followed Lydia to the door. Moments later, her hat on her head, and her cape around her shoulders, she and the dog left the house.

She posted the letters in the box in the churchyard wall and then, with a word to the dog: 'Shall we go and see your master? See if he needs a hand in the shop?' continued on. It was after six now and the late afternoon was fading. For a short while they walked beside the slow-flowing river. The water was as clear as glass, and the long tendrils of water weeds waved languidly in the current. On the bank the elderberries were rich upon the stems.

Some little distance on they left the river footpath and branched off to take the short road that led into the town. It took just fifteen minutes to reach the market square and the shop.

The eyes of Alfred and his assistants looked up as she went in, her entrance causing the bell to ring, and Alfred smiled at her over the shoulder of the woman he was serving. When the customer had gone, Lydia told him that she had come out to post letters and had decided to take a longer stroll.

With Tinny in the back room out of the way, Lydia took off her hat and coat and set herself to help in serving. The shop would not close until eight o'clock, and business was fairly brisk. Lydia had got into the habit over the last two weeks of coming to the shop and helping out where she could, and as she learned, so she was becoming more efficient.

At last eight o'clock came round, the *Closed* sign went up on the door, and the counters and other displays were covered with their cotton drapes to keep out the dust. The assistants wished Lydia and Alfred a good evening and left for the day. Not long afterwards Alfred himself was ready to leave, and soon he was locking the door behind them and they were starting through the square.

'What did you do with yourself today?' he asked as they walked side by side, Tinny trotting two paces ahead.

Lydia replied that she had worked on some sewing and mending, and in the afternoon had written letters to her father and Ryllis.

'Still no word from your father?' Alfred asked.

'No, nothing.'

'You'll hear,' he said. 'You'll hear before too long.'

'But it upsets me, this estrangement.'

'I know it does, but he'll come round. Give it time.'

When Samuel Halley returned home from work early on Saturday afternoon he found Lydia's letter waiting for him. Of course he recognised her handwriting at once. After reading it through he put it up behind the clock on the mantelshelf. She had written to him several times over the past weeks. He had not answered any of her letters.

Guy Anderson caught the train from Redbury that Saturday afternoon. He got off at Merinville and went outside the station to where the local fly-driver waited with his cab. After ascertaining that the cab was available, Guy said he wanted to go to Capinfell and, further, that he wished to go to the house of the Halley family. The driver replied as he unhitched his horse that he was not familiar with the names of the residents of Capinfell, and added, 'But it's a small place, sir, and I don't doubt you'll find your party without too much trouble.'

Guy climbed aboard and they set off. He had never been to Capinfell before, and the road leading to it was also unfamiliar to him. They drove between fields stripped bare by the harvest, and through some areas where the stubble had been burned. He took in little of the scenery they passed by, however; he was preoccupied with his own thoughts. Lydia had been on his mind so much lately, increasingly, to the point where she had haunted him in the days and had tapped into his dreams at night.

He had not written to her as he had told her he would, and his guilt and regret had grown with the passing time. Over all those weeks in Italy he had kept close to him his late father's exhortations – and those of his mother – and had tried to put Lydia out of his mind. For part of the time such action had not been too difficult. For one thing, he had been frantically busy. First, following the death of his father, there had been the funeral to arrange, and after that had come the far from easy task of disposing of the textile business. What should have been a comparatively simple matter had proved problematic and had dragged on and on before its eventual resolution.

At last, though, everything had been settled, and Guy had left Florence to return to Redbury, there to take up the directorial reins of the newspaper that had been his father's great love. Apart from the business that had required his attention, his mother too had needed him. After Mr Anderson's burial in Florence his widow had returned alone to Redbury, and there had settled into a depression that Guy, on his later return, had almost despaired of banishing.

And always, since his return, at the back of his mind was Lydia.

He spent his days in his office at the newspaper, continuing to learn in his new role. So much responsibility had come to him in just a few short weeks, and he would go to bed at night with his brain teeming with the things he had to do, and lessons to be learned. There had been no word of Lydia, and no word from her either. It was as if she were some spirit that had briefly illuminated his life and then fled again, leaving only the faint shadow of where her presence had once been.

He could not live with the situation continuing as it was, however. He was not content to accept her having gone out of his life. Before long he had called at the house in Little Marsh Street, and there he had seen Mrs Obdermann. On enquiring for Lydia she had told him that the young lady was no longer lodging there, and that she had no idea where she might be. He could, she suggested, make enquiries at Seager's department store, where Miss Halley had been working, and might be working still for all she knew.

So he had gone to Seager's, and eventually had spoken with someone in the employment office, who told him that Miss Halley had left the company some weeks before. No, the clerk added, they could not say where she had gone.

And so it had come down to his trip to Capinfell, and he had come here this Saturday afternoon to find her and, if possible, put his mind at rest.

Soon after entering the village of Capinfell, the cab-driver pulled his horse to a halt outside the premises of the local fly-driver. 'This is the man who'll know, sir,' he said to Guy. 'If 'e don't I don't reckon nobody will.'

After Guy had thanked him and paid him off he looked into the stable yard of the fly-proprietor's house. There was no sign of anyone there, so he knocked on the door. It was opened after half a minute by a middle-aged woman wiping her hands on her apron. She looked at him questioningly. 'Yes, sir?'

He was sorry to trouble her, he said, but did she know of a family named Halley residing in the village? She nodded at once, saying, 'Oh yes, indeed, sir,' and went on to describe the house and give him the address. Stepping into the entrance to the stable yard she stood and pointed off across the green. 'I don't know who as you'm wanting, sir,' she added, 'but I think it's only Mr Halley 'isself biding there now. I think both 'is daughters have gone off.'

His heart sank a little at her last words, but he thanked her and set off across the green.

It took a very short time to get to the house, a humble-looking cottage at the end of a lane. The front door was reached via the side yard, and he stepped across the cobbles and rapped with the knocker.

At first there was no answer, and he began to fear that his journey had been for nothing, but then the door opened to reveal a man in his fifties with thick grey hair and steel-rimmed spectacles. He looked at Guy from top to toe and then said merely, 'Sir?' holding the door only half open, as if keeping it ready to close again at short notice.

'I'm very sorry to disturb you, sir,' Guy said, touching at his hat, 'but would you be Mr Halley?'

'And who wants to know, may I enquire?' the other said.

'My name is Anderson, Guy Anderson,' Guy said. 'I've come from Redbury this afternoon –'

'Yes? And you wanted to see me?' Mr Halley now opened the door a little wider.

'Well, sir, in actual fact I've come in the hope of seeing Miss Lydia Halley. Your daughter, I believe, sir.'

A little pause. 'That's correct.'

'I enquired for her at her past lodgings in Redbury, and also at Seager's store where she used to work – but I was unlucky in finding her. So, I've come to Capinfell –'

'And may I ask the nature of your business with my daughter?'

'Well . . . I'm a friend . . .'

Halley nodded. 'And what did you say your name is?'

'Guy Anderson.'

'Well, Mr Anderson, I'm afraid I've got to disappoint you. My daughter no longer lives at home. Neither of my daughters lives at home.'

Guy had been prepared for this by the woman at the fly station. 'But – Miss Lydia,' he said, 'can you tell me where I can get in touch with her?'

'She's living in Merinville now,' the answer came. 'She's married.'

Guy could scarcely believe he was hearing right. 'Married . . .?'

286

'She's been married over a month now.'

Still Guy could hardly take it in. 'Your daughter Lydia,' he said. 'You say she's married?'

'I told you, over a month.' The door moved an inch under the man's hand as he drew the interview to a close.

With a faint look of bewilderment on his face, Guy took a step back. 'Thank you,' he said. 'I'm sorry to have disturbed you.' He turned and went back through the yard. Before he had gone two paces he heard the sound of the door closing behind him.

The days passed into the deeper days of autumn. It had been several weeks now since Lydia had last spoken to her father, in spite of the fact that she had written to him again. The estrangement from him preyed on her mind. She was well aware of his faults, his shortcomings as a parent, but she wanted something better than this – this silence between them that seemed to have no promise of an ending. Eventually she told Alfred that she would go and see him. She would go on a Saturday, she said, to Cremson's, and wait for him at the factory gate, to meet him when he got out of work.

When the day came she arrived at the factory with ten minutes to spare. She did not stand in full view outside, for she did not want to be waylaid by encounters with well-meaning former workmates. So she stood off to the side, hidden from the gates behind the wall of a house. There she waited, her heart beating a little fast.

At last she heard the whistle issuing from the factory building that signalled one o'clock, when work ceased for the weekend. She moved forward to take in the open factory gate, and saw the first of the employees emerging. Eventually her father would have to pass this way as he went to catch the coach that would take him back to Capinfell. She stepped back again into the grey shadow of the wall. The late October sun was pale and the breeze was unusually chill for the time of year. She drew the collar of her coat a little closer about her throat.

She watched the men and women streaming past her, their backs to her now from her vantage point, recognising several of those who had previously been her work-fellows. And then, after two or three minutes, her father walked past.

'Father . . .?

As she called to him she stepped out into the street. He came to a halt some yards away and turned to the sound of her voice. She saw his mouth open as he almost framed her name, and then saw it close again, clamped shut, as if he could not bring himself to form a word.

'Father . . .' She moved towards him and came to a stop before him.

He spoke then. 'What do you want?' Frowning, no warmth, no affection in his face. Dressed all in black and grey, he wore his work-clothes, his trousers shabby, jacket a little frayed at the cuffs. Over his shoulder hung the old canvas and leather bag, scuffed and discoloured, that he had carried ever since she could remember. 'What do you want?' he said again.

'Oh, Father – we – can we go somewhere and talk?'

'Talk? Why? What for?'

'Oh, please. I want to talk to you.'

'I don't know that there's anything to talk about.' He lifted a hand as if he would wave further words aside. 'I've got to go and catch the coach.'

She moved a step closer to him. 'Father, I need to talk to you.' Still the factory workers moved past them, some calling out goodbyes to Mr Halley, and some also with words of greeting for Lydia herself. She acknowledged them briefly, with vague smiles and distracted hellos, and kept her eyes for the most part on her father's face.

'I've only got a minute,' her father said. 'What do you want?'

'There's something I have to tell you.'

'Oh?'

She shook her head, and gave a little groan. 'Oh, Father, not like this.' She realised with dismay that they had never been able to talk properly. She had longed for it on many occasions, but it was not his way. Whether meaning to or not, he had never allowed his daughters to get too close. 'Can't we take a little walk?' she said.

'The coach won't wait all day,' he said. 'I've got to get back. I've got things to do.'

'Father,' she said, a little note of passion in her voice, 'don't turn me away like this. I've come to tell you that – that I'm going to have a baby.' She forced a smile that felt alien upon her mouth, reached out to him and grasped his upper arm. 'You're going to be a grandfather.'

He said nothing for a moment, and in the silence she thought for a split second that she could see the sudden glint of tears in his eyes, but then he was blinking and the shine was gone. Perhaps she had just imagined it. He shook his arm, only slightly, but it was enough to loosen her fragile hold, and she let her hand fall away. He hitched his bag more securely onto his shoulder. 'Is that what you came to tell me?' he said.

'Aren't you – aren't you pleased? Aren't you happy for me?'

Still he remained there, and she thought for a moment, *He'll stay, he wants to hear what I've got to say*, but then he gave a shrug and took half a step away.

'You should honour thy father,' he said, and turned from her.

'But – but, Father . . .'

He turned back to face her, just briefly, just long enough

to say, 'I've got to go. I'll miss the coach.' Then he had swung about and was striding down the street.

She stood watching as he walked away and turned a corner out of sight.

After a little while she herself moved, and headed back through the outskirts of the town towards the market square. On another day she would have gone into the shop to see Alfred and talk with him for a while, customers permitting, and probably would have stayed on to help serve. Today, though, she wanted to be alone.

That evening when Alfred came home from the shop he found her sitting in the glow of the gas lamp with her sewing in her lap. He bent and kissed her cheek. Tinny, having greeted him enthusiastically, continued to wag his tail. Lydia set her sewing aside on the small table at her elbow and said as Alfred straightened, 'I saw him. I saw my father.' Alfred waited for her to go on. 'I went to Cremson's and waited outside the gates. I caught him as he came out.'

'Oh? What happened?'

'I told him – about the baby.' She gave a deep sigh. 'He didn't want to know. He didn't even want to talk to me. I was only with him for a minute, and then he was off again.'

'Oh, dear.' Alfred joined Lydia's sigh with his own. 'He's still hurt that he didn't know sooner about the wedding.'

'It was a surprise for everybody, you and me included.' Then, her rueful smile fading, she murmured, 'Oh, but it does upset me so – this not talking. As I said, I was only with him for a minute, and then he was dashing off, to catch his ride to Capinfell. I thought, when I told him about the baby, that he'd come round, but no.'

'He will. In time. Give it time.'

'But it's been weeks now – and he hasn't answered any of my letters. Ryllis has heard from him, so it isn't that he's been incapacitated in any way.'

'He won't stay angry with you for ever,' Alfred said. 'What is his way? Is it to sulk? To hold a grudge?'

'Not usually, no. He's quick to anger – oh, more than you can imagine – and then usually it's over.'

'Well,' Alfred said consolingly, 'this time it's taking a little longer, but things'll be all right, you'll see.' Changing the subject he clapped his hands lightly – making Tinny look round in surprise and expectation – and said, 'Anyway, what else have you done today?'

She began to tidy up her threads and needles as she answered. 'I did a little crochet,' she said, 'and also I helped Mrs Starling in the kitchen.' Mrs Starling was the resident cook/housekeeper – an ageing widow, faithful and conscientious, employed at Ranleigh House since the death of the first Mrs Canbrook. There was also a young daily maid, Alice, who came in from her home nearby. Lydia, since arriving at the house, had divided her time between helping in the management and cleaning of the place, and assisting Alfred in the shop, which business she was swiftly learning as the days went by. She could have taken over the running of the house herself, but after a brief discussion with Alfred the notion was scotched for the time being. There would come a time soon, Alfred insisted, with the arrival of the baby, when they would be even more glad of Mrs Starling's services. So matters remained as they were, and Mrs Starling was left content to pursue her usual employment.

The marriage between Lydia and Alfred had of course been a great surprise to everyone who knew Alfred Canbrook, for many had believed that his widower status would continue. For one thing, they said among themselves, they had not even known that he and the young woman from Capinfell were walking out. A quiet man, he had given nothing away until he was ready for others to know, and then he had told Mrs Starling and his assistants at the shop. Everything had happened so quickly, and he and Lydia had been wed. The swiftness of the move had been a subject for talk, and the gossip would not be over yet, for as soon as the baby was born, both Lydia and Alfred were well aware, the chatterers would start counting backwards.

'Were you busy at the shop today?' Lydia said after a moment.

'Yes, very, and the new linens came in from Derby, so there was that to deal with as well. It still isn't finished.'

'I could have come along to help out,' she said. 'I could easily have done that after seeing Father.'

'Oh, we managed all right,' he said. 'Besides, I want you to take things easy for now.'

'But *you* don't take things easy,' she said. 'Sometimes I think you work much too hard.'

'I do what I have to do. It won't get done otherwise. Besides, I'm not having a baby.'

As he spoke she reflected, not for the first time, on the long hours he worked, and how he drove himself. He would be up at five-thirty each morning, and before breakfast would take Tinny for a ten-minute stroll beside the river. Then, back at the house he would have his breakfast and, before leaving for the shop, would take Lydia tea in bed. Then, unless she decided to go into the shop during the day, she would not see him until after eight in the evening when he got back.

'You could at least take Sundays off,' she said. 'Though I suppose you're already thinking of going into the shop tomorrow.'

'Well, as I said, the linens ain't been sorted, so I might drop in to get that done. You can achieve so much when the shop's quiet and nothing's going on.' He smiled. 'You don't need to worry about me. I'm fine. You don't need to fuss.'

*

Sunday, and the early November morning had been cold and damp with fog hazing the trees on the near horizon. Because of the chill weather Lydia had not gone to church that morning, as she sometimes did in the company of Mrs Starling. Alfred never went. At the start of their marriage, when asked by Lydia if he would care to accompany her, he had told her that she would have to get used to going without him. He had no need for communion with God, he said, and if there ever came a time for it, then he was going to ask God a few questions, questions that no one on earth seemed to have been able to answer. Questions such as what? Lydia had asked. Well, he had replied, Why, for one thing did He allow wars? Why, if He was so caring, did He allow good people and innocent children to suffer, while so many rascals got off scot-free and enjoyed life? 'These questions bother me,' he had said. So, he would spend his Sunday morning in his own pursuits, walking the dog and then going into the shop, to do a little work. Today he had returned to the house for midday dinner with Lydia, and then, after reading the Sunday paper for an hour, had returned to the shop again, taking Tinny with him.

Lydia was now alone, sitting by the window that looked out over the rear garden. She had helped wash up the dinner china and pots and pans, and tidy the dining room, and was now working at her knitting, making a pair of baby's bootees. As she lifted her head from her work, and gazed out, it came to her how much the scene before her was changing. The cherry trees had altered so over the past few days. One of them was now quite bare, while the other two were swiftly losing their leaves, which lay now in a yellow and brown carpet over the lawn, where a blackbird methodically tossed them aside in his search for food. The few leaves that were left on the trees trembled in the cool wind. How changed was her life, Lydia thought, how changed in such a short time. Just a few months ago she could never have dreamed that her life would turn in such a way. Here she was, married to a kind, respectable man, living in a fine house and wanting for no material thing. More than that, she was expecting a child. With this thought, Guy came suddenly surging into her consciousness and she saw him again beside the lake, and felt his touch, and breathed in the smell of him with the scent of the roses and the elderflowers. She was a little shocked at the immediacy of the visions and the sensations, and she thrust the images and the imagined feelings away. Guy was gone now, gone out of her life, and she did not expect to see him or hear from him ever again.

The room was quiet but for the ticking of the clock, and after a time she found some relief in the peace and solitude as she worked with her needles. A bright fire burned in the grate. It was just after three. Alice did not come in on a Sunday, and Lydia expected no visitors.

When she heard the knocking, faintly as it sounded through the hall, she wondered who it could possibly be. Moments passed, and then Mrs Starling was tapping on the door, entering and saying that Miss Ryllis was here, and even as the woman finished speaking, Ryllis was coming into the room. As Mrs Starling withdrew, closing the door behind her, Lydia looked at her sister with concern. She could see anguish written clearly in Ryllis's face.

'Ryllis, my dear! What is it? What's the matter?'

'Oh, Lyddy!' Ryllis stepped forward and threw herself into Lydia's arms and burst into tears.

Lydia held her for some moments, and then held her at arms' length.

'Now tell me what it is,' Lydia said. 'Come on, take off your cape and your hat and sit down and tell me. Would you like some tea? I'll get you some tea.'

'No. No, not now. Perhaps later. Is – is Mr Canbrook

here?' Ryllis's tears had ceased now, and she sounded a
little calmer.

'He's at the shop. Why? No one's going to disturb us.'

She helped Ryllis off with her cape, took her hat from her,
and then led her to the sofa. There she sat and drew Ryllis
down beside her. Taking her hands in her own, she said,
'What is it now? Tell me.'

Ryllis took a deep breath, then said, 'I – I've just come
from home.'

'You've been to Capinfell?'

'Yes, I've just come from there. I went to see Father.'

'And . . .?'

'Oh, Lyddy – he's so unapproachable.'

'Well, yes – I know he can be.'

'I just couldn't get near him. So in the end I just left, and
came on to see you.' At this she leaned forward and the
tears started again and ran down her cheeks. 'Tom's given
me up, Lyddy,' she said. 'He's forsaken me.'

'Oh, Ryllis . . .'

Ryllis leaned forward against Lydia's breast and stayed
there sobbing, her slim body heaving against Lydia's own.
Lydia could do nothing but hold her.

At last, after some minutes, Ryllis drew back and sat up,
drawing in her breath. Groping in her pocket she drew out
a handkerchief and dabbed at her reddened eyes.

'I told you,' she said at last, 'Tom hardly wrote since he
went up to London to work with his uncle, and when he did
it was only the shortest little note. Since the time he went
he's hardly been back to Barford, and then only for very
short periods. Altogether I've seen him twice in all that time
– and the second time was the last.' She dabbed at her eyes
again, and then crumpled the handkerchief into a ball in her
fist. 'Sometimes I think he only wanted one thing,' she said.

Lydia wanted to ask, *Did you – ? Oh, Ryllis, did you?* but
held back. She dared not ask such a question.

She had no need to, for Ryllis's next words came telling all. 'Just the one thing,' she repeated with a little nod of her head. 'I've been such a fool. I can see it now. I – I held back for such a long time – but I couldn't say no for ever. Oh, Lyddy, you can't know what it was like, how difficult some things can be. When you love someone you want to give them everything, and if it's in your power you never want to say no.'

Lydia said nothing, but sat with her hands in her lap.

'I loved Tom,' Ryllis said. 'I loved him. Oh, I know he could be difficult at times. He was critical of me in so many ways. He found fault with me so often – for only minor things, but they hurt – but then he'd turn round and be the sweetest person. You never knew him, Lyddy. You only met him the once.'

Yes, Lydia thought, she had only met him the once, but that once had been enough to convince her that he was not the right man for her sister.

'He's so clever, and so good looking,' Ryllis said. 'Sometimes I wondered what he could see in me.'

'What do you mean?' Lydia said. 'I should think any man would be glad to have you for a sweetheart.'

Ryllis shrugged. 'Well, whatever the truth of that, I'm still just a general maid. A maid-of-all-work. I've got none of the manners and graces his folks are looking for. It's no wonder that in the end I didn't come up to scratch. I'm not good enough for him, Lyddy, I know that's what they all think.'

Lydia waited for some moments, then said, 'How – how do you know it's over? Did he tell you?'

'Yes.' And now Ryllis clutched at herself, holding her upper arms, as if steadying herself, as if trying to prevent herself from bursting into tears again. She drew a breath, then, more in control, went on, 'Yesterday, Saturday, it happened. I'd had a letter from him in the week from London, saying that he was coming down to Barford this weekend, and would see me – that's just the way he put it: he would see me. Not that he *wanted* to, or would *like* to, just that he *would* – and he gave me time and place. I was to meet him by the old barn out on the Kippis Road. He knew the time I got off work. So, I went to meet him, and he came, and he told me. It was over between us, he said. I think he's met someone else.'

'Is that what he told you?'

'Not in so many words, but you could read between the lines. He said his life has changed so much since he went up to London. Well, of course it has. I don't doubt that it has for one moment, and it's changed *him*. When I saw him I could hardly credit the difference. His clothes, the way he wears his hair. It's all so – fashionable. You certainly wouldn't get that look in the lanes around Barford. Oh, Lyddy, I felt such a country mouse next to him. There am I making a best dress last I-don't-know-how-long, and he's already seen it dozens of times. All the young ladies he meets in London, they must be a very different kettle of fish. I tell you, I felt really shabby.'

A little silence fell between them. Past Ryllis's shoulder Lydia looked out on to the garden. The persistent blackbird was still busy overturning the dead leaves. Into the quiet Ryllis said with a sigh:

'He told me he had something to say to me, and somehow I knew what was coming, I could tell. Then he told me that he thought it would be better if we didn't meet again. Could we just be friends, he said. I said to him, "Is it over, Tom?" and he just sort of nodded, and whispered "Yes". I suppose I should be grateful that he told me to my face and didn't just send me a cruel little note, and end it that way.' She paused. 'After a time he said he had to get back home. We parted at the crossroads. I went back to the house, and he went back home. I cried so much that night. I haven't seen him since.'

'I'm afraid it sounds rather – final, doesn't it?'

'It is. Just before we left he asked me not to – not to try to get in touch with him. Oh, yes, it was final all right.'

She began to weep again, but softly now, with a little, heartbreaking keening sound. 'I did love him so,' she cried into her hands. 'I still do. Though I know it won't do me any good. I've lost him for ever now.'

A little later Lydia made tea for the two of them, and Ryllis was persuaded to drink some of it. She had wept so much, and Lydia had felt helpless to give her anything other than sympathy and understanding. Now, though, Ryllis's crying had ceased and her tears had dried. Sitting there on the sofa, she looked out unseeingly across the room.

'I told you I went to see Father,' she said.

'Yes . . .'

'He wouldn't help me.'

Lydia frowned. 'What d'you mean?'

'I got the train this morning. I arrived there just after he'd got back from church.'

'Was he surprised to see you? I expect he was.'

'Oh, of course he was. "What are you doing home here?" he said to me. I told him that I wanted to leave the Lucases' and stay at home with him and look after him. He said, "When? When your agreement is up?" and I said no, now. From today. I thought maybe he'd be pleased, and would welcome it. After all, he moans so much about Mrs Harbutt.' She shook her head. 'But he said no. He said I had to go on back. He said a contract was a contract. He said if I didn't go back of my own accord he'd take me back himself. So what else can I do? Oh, but Lyddy, I don't want to go back there. The only reason I stayed on like I did was because of Tom. Had it not been for him I'd have left ages ago, references or no references.' She gave a deep sigh. 'I did think of asking you if I could stay here with you and Mr

Canbrook for a while, just till I get settled in another post, but then I thought, no, I can't do that. I can't put my troubles on you.'

'Oh, but Ryllis, I'm sure Alfred wouldn't mind. He likes you well enough, and I'm sure he'd like to see you happy in another post, particularly after all the heartache you've been through.'

'No. No.' Ryllis shook her head. 'No, I did think I might ask, but I realise now I can't. No, I've got to go back – and after all, it's only till Christmas, and then if I feel like it I can go back to Father's and look after him. I'm sure he'd agree to it then.'

'You might feel differently come Christmas.'

'Yes, I might – and Father might also, come to that – but whatever happens, I shan't stay with the Lucases. If it don't suit Father for me to go back to Capinfell, I'll go somewhere else.'

Less than an hour later Ryllis prepared to leave.

'I must get back,' she said.

'Won't you stay a while?' Lydia asked her. 'If you wait till Alfred comes in I'm sure he'll get out the carriage and drive you to the station. I don't think he'll be long now.'

'No, it's all right, thank you. I don't want to wait.'

Lydia helped her with her cape. 'I'll walk with you to the station,' she said.

'No, really,' Ryllis said. 'I'll hurry along on my own. If I go now, maybe I'll be back before dark.'

Lydia held her and kissed her and walked with her into the hall. Then, in the open doorway she stood and mournfully watched Ryllis's sad figure walk down the drive to the street. As Ryllis moved out of sight behind the tall privet hedge, Lydia realised that she had said nothing to her about the coming baby.

Chapter Seventeen

Ryllis had awakened fifteen minutes late this Monday morning and so was behind in her chores. Mrs Claxon, the cook, who was usually so pleasant to her, was irritable because of it, and Ryllis was doing all she could to mollify her. She had overslept as she had lain awake so long last night. She had kept thinking about Tom, and then her visit to her father, and then to Lyddy. Lyddy, of course, had been completely sympathetic, but that had not helped. Her offer, to have Ryllis stay with her and Mr Canbrook until she was settled with a new position, had been tempting for a moment or two, but it would not have been right. With Lyddy only a few weeks married, the last thing she and her husband required in their home was a needy relation. No, she, Ryllis, must stand on her own feet. She would start looking for a new post at once, and when the time came she would hand in her month's notice to her employers.

'Ryllis? Ryllis?'

It was Mrs Claxon's voice that came interrupting her thoughts, and Ryllis turned to her from her seat near the range where she sat polishing a pair of Mr Lucas's boots. The cook was coming into the room as Ryllis looked up. 'Yes, Mrs Claxon.'

'The milk's gone over,' the cook said. She was a grey-haired woman in her fifties, her usually pleasant expression now distorted by anger and irritation. 'That dratted cat. The whole lot spilt. You'll have to run over to the farm and get some more.'

'Have I got to go *now*?' Ryllis asked, though she knew the answer.

'Of course now. The master'll be up demanding his breakfast at any time, and it won't be ready.'

'Right. I'll finish the boots when I get back.'

Mrs Claxon nodded. 'And you'd best go by the field – it's late already.'

Ryllis hated to go via the meadow, and she said at once, 'Oh, Mrs Claxon, can't I go by the road?'

'It'll take you an age – at least twenty minutes longer,' the woman said, 'and I need that milk.'

Ryllis put the boots and brushes down and prepared to go to the neighbouring farm. There was a sharp nip in the air this morning and she tucked in her scarf under the collar of her cape. When she had tied on her bonnet she took the enamel milkcan and left by the back door.

She set off on the far side of the wall that separated the kitchen garden from the formal lawns and herbaceous plots. Her path led her down through the orchard and then to the fence, beyond which was the pasture where farmer Heffinson's cattle habitually grazed. She was relieved to see that there was none there this morning; obviously they had not yet been driven back from the milking shed.

At the far end of the orchard there was a loose stake in the fence, and she pulled it aside and slipped through the gap into the field. Beyond that was a thorny hedge, and she stepped through it by a narrow little space and started off across the grass. She was moving towards the farmhouse which she could see in the distance, beyond a second field that she must also cross. Her boots were wet already, and she had only gone a dozen yards. As she walked she kept looking over to her left, at the same time keeping close to the hedge. If the bull should appear she would get behind the hedge, as she had done on two occasions in the past. They had been frightening times and had greatly swelled her reluctance to take the shortcut. Today, though, she was in a hurry.

She reached the edge of the first field, and as she did so she looked over to the far left and saw Mr Heffinson's herd of cows come streaming through the gate back into the meadow. Then she went on, into the next field, and towards the farmhouse at the foot of the hill.

She approached from the rear, walking up past the byre and the big red barn, to the dairy where she stopped and looked in at the door. Seeing no one inside she moved on to the rambling house and put her head around the scullery door. There was a young fair-haired milkmaid inside, busy at a sink, and she looked up and smiled.

'Mornin', Ryllis.'

'Mornin', Phemie. We had an accident with the milk,' Ryllis said, '– or the cat did.' She sighed as she held up the milkcan.

'So you need some more, do you?'

'Please.'

Ryllis stepped into the scullery and held the two-gallon can up to the younger girl. Phemie took it and led the way back across the yard to the dairy, went inside and came out again a minute later with the can full. Ryllis thanked her, took it by the handle and started back across the yard towards the meadows.

The first field was deserted, and as she crossed the wet grass she found her thoughts returning to her last meeting with Tom. How could he have said those things to her? It was too cruel. But he had seemed so awkward, standing there facing her at the side of the road, as if not knowing what to say, or how to say it. Perhaps she should write to him – though she was not by any means sure how he would react to receiving a letter from her. Not with any great pleasure, she thought.

She moved to the gate connecting the two fields, opened

it, passed through, and closed and fastened the gate behind her.

It was as she was part way across the field that the bull came charging.

She had been only vaguely aware of the cows now grazing in this second field, so caught up was she in her thoughts of Tom, but then in a great rush came the sound of a bellowing roar followed by the thudding of the bull's hooves on the grass. She whirled and saw the creature pounding towards her.

She could feel her heart leap in her breast in terror as the animal came bearing down. She tried to scream, her voice coming out in a little strangled squeak, and snatched at her skirts and ran. The full milkcan was cumbersome and heavy and her speed was hampered, but she dared not let it go. She could feel the flesh of her cheeks bouncing as she fled over the grass, her breath hoarse in her throat, the can swinging heavily, the milk slopping out between the lid and the rim.

She realised with terror that she would never get to the gap in the hedge in time. She whirled to face the way she had come. Perhaps she could get back to the gate. The milk fell from her hand and she slipped, the soles of her boots squeaking as she skidded on the wet grass. The only sounds she could hear now were her gasping breaths. Regaining her balance, she dashed back across the grass, and, wonder of wonders she reached the gate. There was no time to open it, however; she could only fling herself forward in an attempt to climb up and over. She was almost there, almost there.

The bull violently bellowed, its nostrils flaring as it flailed on the slippery grass, but its hooves caught firmly in the rutted entrance at the gate, and gripped, and in a second it was back in control, turning its huge bulk and lunging to gore her.

Its sharp left horn caught Ryllis's boot, the point hooking into the leather, piercing it. Then, as the enraged creature threw back its powerful head, Ryllis screamed again, her terror-stricken voice ringing out into the crisp morning air, but there was no one to hear her. Her foot, caught by the horn, was torn from its step on the crossbar of the gate. The bull tossed its head and plunged forward again. This time, as her hands slipped from their hold on the top bar, the bull's left horn caught her just below the waist, snagged deeply in her skirt and ripped her from the gate as if she had been no heavier than a little bag of hay.

With a toss of its head, snorting loudly, the bull threw her up, then dipped its head and caught her again as she fell. It tossed her again, and without a cry she was thrown like a rag doll, spinning round in a complete circle on the creature's horns. Her skirts billowed out, her legs and arms moving as if multi-jointed. Again the animal threw her into the air and caught her on its horns, and again, and again, and then let her fall heavily to the ground. It backed away, snorting, and Ryllis moved once on the grass, and gave a little moan through slack jaws from which blood and saliva flowed. It was enough to spur on the bull again, and it pawed the ground once with one of its forehooves and charged. The horns scooped Ryllis up, piercing deep, and tossed her so that she turned in the air like a child doing a cartwheel. Again it caught her, and as her blood sprayed out over its powerful shoulders, tossed her back into the wet grass.

This time when Ryllis fell she made no sound and was still. The bull approached her, and bent its head, nudging her with its horns. When she did not move the bull stepped back and stood there panting, its sides heaving. It pawed the ground a couple of times, and then turned and moved away across the grass.

*

A young housewife had asked for three yards of unbleached linen, and Lydia measured out the material and cut it. She had come along to the shop that afternoon, arriving shortly after three, and had spent an hour or so helping out when things got busy. She enjoyed the employment, and Alfred and his assistants were glad to see her. Now, carefully, she folded the fabric, wrapped it up, gave change for the money tendered and wished the woman a good day. As the customer turned in the doorway to step out into the square Lydia saw another figure shadow the entrance. A split second later, as the man entered the shop, she saw that it was her father.

He moved directly to her, coming to a stop facing her at the counter.

'Father!' she said in a whisper, frowning, for this was the most unexpected thing. As she spoke she was aware of Alfred looking at the two of them, and of the assistant, Mr Federo, momentarily forgetting the customer he was serving and turning towards them in curiosity. Her father had taken off his hat. He was, she saw at once, wearing his work-clothes.

Mr Halley looked at no one but Lydia. When he spoke he did not speak her name, but said shortly, 'I've got to talk to you. Can we go somewhere?'

'Why – why, yes.' She turned and looked at Alfred, an unspoken question on her lips, and he said at once, 'Take your father into the back room.'

Lydia moved along the counter and lifted the flap. 'Father – come this way, please.'

He moved through behind the counter and Lydia stepped ahead of him and opened the door. 'Please . . .' She held it as he passed through, and followed him in, closing the door, behind her.

She came to a stop before him as he stood beside the table. 'Oh, Father – I'm so glad to see you,' she said. She began a smile that, seeing his own unsmiling visage, quickly died, and then added, gesturing to a chair, 'Would you like to sit down?'

He ignored her words. 'I haven't got long,' he said. 'I've only got a minute. I'm off to Redbury.'

'Redbury?'

'This is what I've come about,' he said. 'It's Amaryllis.'

'Ryllis?' Seeing his expression, which was not quite like any she had seen on him before, and hearing the unusual tone of his voice, she felt a sudden coldness in her breast. 'Is she all right?'

'No, she's not. They just sent for me, at the factory. A young man came from the farm next door to the Lucases in Barford. The girl's been injured. I've got to get to the hospital.' It was all said on a single breath.

The chill around Lydia's heart blossomed, expanding to clutch at her, and she felt her whole chest in a turmoil of panic and fear. Her mouth was suddenly dry.

'Let me get my hat and cape . . .' The garments were close at hand, and she quickly took them down. 'I'm ready,' she said as she fastened her cape. 'We'll go now.'

He turned abruptly and made for the door, opened it and passed through. She followed. As her father stepped through the gap in the counter into the shop proper Lydia moved to Alfred's side. He was serving a customer and looked around at Lydia from the lace he was displaying.

'Excuse me,' she said to the customer, an elderly woman, and then, to her husband, added, 'Something's happened to Ryllis. I'm going with Father to the hospital in Redbury.'

He looked a little startled, but then nodded. 'Right,' he said, and then: 'But wait a minute. Let me go and get you a cab to take you to the station.'

'No, it's all right. It's not far to walk. We'll be in time for the next train.'

Her father was standing at the doorway, holding the door open.

'I'll be back as soon as I can,' Lydia said.

She moved from Alfred's side and in another second or two she and her father were out in the air.

They strode across the market square, along Upper Street and on towards the railway station. At one point, soon after starting out, Lydia asked, 'What is it, Father? What's the matter with Ryllis?' Without looking at her he merely shook his head and said, 'Wait till we get to the station. Wait till we can get a breath.' And she had to be content with that. At last they reached the station, and there they bought their tickets and moved onto the platform. There would be a wait of some fifteen minutes before the next train for Redbury came in.

'Tell me, Father,' Lydia said as they stood together on the platform. 'What has happened?' A cold wind came sweeping up the length of track and flicked at the hem of her cape. At the same time her father touched at his hat, as if to stop it flying away.

'I can only tell you what I know,' he said. 'I was at work when word came for me that there was an emergency and that someone wanted to see me. There at the factory, I mean. I went out and saw this young man waiting for me in the outer office. I had no idea who he was; I'd never seen him afore. His name was McGibbon, he said. Turned out he's a stockman for a farmer neighbour of the Lucases in Barford. He asked me if I was Mr Halley, and then said he'd been sent by Mrs Lucas. I knew right away, of course, that something was up.' He seemed to snatch at his words in the cold air. 'They don't start sendin' for you for nothing. I knew it had to be something serious. Then he told me, the young man, he said she'd been attacked by a bull.'

'Oh, my God.' Lydia clutched at herself, one hand

pressing at her chest, the other flying to her mouth. 'How is she? Is she going to be all right?'

'The young man couldn't say. He told me as much as he knew in the minute or so he was there with me. Apparently he was the one who found her. A message had gone round to the farm to see where she was, as she'd gone off to fetch some milk and hadn't returned. He went out into the field and saw her lying there. He got help, he said, and some-body dealt with the bull while he went and got hold of her. He said –' Here he seemed to choke slightly on his words, and took a breath and began again: 'He said . . . she was covered in blood and – and quite senseless. He said she was in a terrible state. He says he thought at first she – she was dead, but then he saw that she was still alive.'

He broke off here and swallowed, and looked down at the ground. Then after a few moments he raised his head and went on, his voice faltering:

'He said – he said he carried her into the Lucases' house and they took one look at her and said they must send for the doctor.' He sighed, paused again. 'The young man, McGibbon, said he was back at the farm a couple of hours later when he was sent for. The odd-job boy from Mr Lucas had come to say that Amaryllis was being taken by ambulance to St Margaret's hospital in Redbury, and that he – the young man from the farm, McGibbon, that is – should come and let me know at Cremson's.' He nodded, lips compressed. 'He came to get me right away, as soon as he could – all that way from Barford. I'm very thankful for that.' He gave a little groan and shook his head. 'Oh, dear Lord, it's a terrible business. As soon as the young man had gone I went to the boss and told him I had to leave, that my daughter was bad. He said of course I must go at once. I came to you straight away. I didn't waste any time.'

The train arrived and they climbed on board, and in the carriage found seats facing one another. The rest were

308

taken up by other travellers. Lydia and her father hardly spoke as they sat there; Lydia was anxiously looking out from the window while her father sat looking straight ahead of him, his gaze directed at some point just over her shoulder, his mouth pulled into a straight, thin line, his eyes dull behind their steel-rimmed lenses. His expression was unreadable, Lydia thought – which was nothing new – but she seemed to see a difference in the general appearance of him. He looked so much older. One lingering glance at him and she could not help but take in the deeply seamed cheeks, the shadows beneath his eyes. His whole body seemed strangely diminished in stature.

When at last they arrived at Redbury they went out of the station and Mr Halley hailed a cab to take them to St Margaret's hospital. At any usual time he would have eschewed such a luxury, but this was not a usual time.

After a while they were set down at the entrance to a huge sprawling building not far from the city's centre. Mr Halley paid off the driver, and they went inside. There, after making enquiries, they were directed along lengthy corridors until they came to Mason Ward where, they were told, Ryllis could be found.

From the corridor they stepped into a small foyer and Mr Halley knocked on an open door on the right beyond which a woman sat at a desk. She looked at Mr Halley and Lydia and got to her feet. She wore a voluminous white cap on her head and a blue uniform with white collar and cuffs, a white apron and a black patent leather belt. She gave them a grave smile as she came to them and said, 'Yes? How can I help you?'

Mr Halley, taking off his hat, said he was the father of Amaryllis Halley and that he and his other daughter had been summoned there to see her.

As soon as Ryllis's name was spoken a shadow of concern touched the nursing sister's eyes and she gave a little sigh. 'Oh, yes, poor Miss Halley,' she said. She lifted a gesturing hand. 'We didn't put her in the general women's ward, but in a small separate room at the end. Her injuries are so bad. Truly dreadful. You know that it was a bull, I suppose . . . ?'

'Yes.' Mr Halley nodded. 'So I've been told.'

'A dreadful business, poor girl. Her injuries are appalling – I've got to be quite honest. Her wounds have been cleaned and stitched as well as they could be, but I have to tell you that she's got internal injuries, and only time will determine how she'll recover from them. We plan to move her into the main ward when she starts to improve. The next hours will be crucial.'

In the silence that followed Lydia heard her father say: 'What is the – What is going to become of her?'

'We can't be sure, I'm afraid, but she's a young woman, and she's strong, so her chances should be better than most. Although, as I say, her injuries are very bad.' She hesitated, then gestured ahead. 'Come with me and I'll take you to her.'

She moved past them into the corridor. As she did so she added, 'It isn't visiting time yet, and normally you'd have to wait till six-thirty, but it's a different matter with your daughter. Please – come with me.' She said no more but led them on through double doors into a corridor, and at the end stopped outside a door on the right, where she turned to them. 'You must prepare yourself,' she said. 'She's looking very poorly.' She paused. 'I don't think she's spoken since she came in.'

She opened the door and went ahead of them into the room.

In the second that they were standing together on the threshold Lydia felt her heart leaping and pounding in her chest, and turning to her father she could tell that he was feeling the same. His hat was clutched in his left hand and his eyes were tight shut. She could see his chest rising and falling as he gulped in the air. Then he opened his eyes and reached out with his free hand and sought Lydia's own, and clasped and pressed it. It only took a moment, and then he was releasing her, and they were following the nurse into the room.

It was not large, and there was only the one bed. Ryllis lay still upon it, and the nurse moved forward, bent over her and took her wrist, checking her pulse with the watch that was pinned to the breast of her apron. Gently, she laid Ryllis's small hand back on the blanket, then turned and gestured to Lydia and her father. 'Come and see her,' she whispered. 'She appears to be stable at the moment, but I must tell you that if her condition worsens I shall have to ask you to leave. I'm sure you understand.'

Mr Halley nodded. 'Yes, of course.'

There was a straight-backed chair drawn up to the bedside, and the nurse touched the back of it and said to Mr Halley, 'Sir – come and sit down. And you, miss – why don't you pull up that stool there?'

Lydia did as she was bidden. Her father sat on the chair beside her, and laid his hat on the foot of the bed. The nurse hovered, checking on Ryllis's breathing, and then looked at some of her dressings. Ryllis lay beneath a blanket, but it did not cover all the bandages that wrapped parts of her body. They were evident about her shoulders, her right arm and her head. Her face was scratched, swollen and dreadfully bruised, her left eye puffed up and discoloured. Beneath the bandage that swathed her head, hardly any trace of her hair was visible.

The nursing sister saw Mr Halley's eyes rest on Ryllis's bandaged head and said, 'We had to cut a lot of her hair off, I'm afraid. A part of her scalp was torn away and a good deal of stitching was needed.' She let this sink in, then added in a whisper, 'I'll leave you for a few minutes. If there's any cause for alarm do come and get me, or call one of the nurses.'

Left alone while the nurse's footsteps faded outside, Lydia and her father sat looking at the small figure before them.

There was a gas lamp burning on the wall above the bed, and its light cast Ryllis's face into deep shadows, making hollows of her eye sockets. She lay with her eyes closed. Her breathing was steady but shallow. Lydia looked at her without speaking, her throat tight, tears running down her cheeks. She heard a little moan from her right, from her father, and turning slightly saw that his head was bowed, his eyes closed tight, his lips drawn back over his teeth. She watched as his hands clenched before him and his lips began to move in an almost silent murmur, and realised that he was praying.

They sat without moving for some minutes, and all the while Lydia did not take her eyes off Ryllis as she lay before them. Then suddenly she leaned forward a little. Ryllis's eyes had opened.

'Ryllis,' Lydia breathed. 'Oh, Ryllis . . .

At Lydia's side her father's light murmuring ceased.

'Amaryllis . . . ?' He leaned forward as Lydia was doing. 'Can you hear me?' he said. 'We've come to see you – Lydia and your father. Can you hear me?'

No sound came from Ryllis other than that of her breathing. She did not move. Her small, unscathed hand lay on the blanket like some pale, lost creature. Her eyes moved neither to left nor right, remaining fixed straight ahead of her, but there was a faint shine there, a sign of life. Then her fingers twitched once or twice, and Lydia saw the movement and whispered to her father, 'Look, Father. Her hand.'

He reached out and touched Ryllis's hand. 'Come on, my girl,' he whispered. 'Come on. Get better so as I can take you home.'

He began to stroke Ryllis's hand then, in a gentle, rhythmic little movement while Lydia sat unmoving again and silent.

After a time Mr Halley withdrew his hand from Ryllis's and began to pray out loud, his clasped hands resting on the side of the bed: 'Oh, Lord, spare this child . . .' Lydia looked at Ryllis's naked hand and saw that the fingers were still. There came a sound from behind them of the door opening, and softly the nurse came into the room. She moved past them on her soft-soled shoes and moved round to the far side of the bed. There she took up Ryllis's hand and put fingertips to her wrist. Lydia watched the expression on her face, saw her frown. The nurse then put her fingers to Ryllis's throat, seeking out a pulse. She shook her head and looked at Lydia and her father, and both of them saw, in that instant, that there was nothing more to be done.

PART THREE

Chapter Eighteen

The winter of 1895 had lingered, and the early April day was unusually cold for the time of year. Before setting out that afternoon Lydia had seen that Davie was well wrapped up against the chill. She had put a coat over his sailor suit, and a scarf around his neck, his fair curls being partly hidden by a little woollen cap that came down over his ears and was fastened under his chin. Now, though, in the warmth of the coffee house, his cap and scarf were off and the buttons of his coat were undone.

The coffee house was called The Blue Anchor, and catered for residents and factory workers thereabouts. It boasted solid and simple fare, and on display could be seen such things as beef pies, pigeon pies, pickled herrings and thick slices of lardy-cake and cream-decked pastries. The husband of the proprietor had once been a merchant seaman, and evidence of his interests and loves were all around the place, from the ship-in-a-bottle that rested on the mantelshelf to the wallpaper with the anchor motif that lined the walls. The place was situated just a few minutes' walk from the factory gates of Cremson's, so was handy for Mr Halley when leaving his work.

Now, the boy and his mother sat at a table together. Lydia had before her a cup of tea, which she had poured from the pot that had just been brought, while Davie had a cup of hot chocolate and a small cream-topped cake, of which so far he had only taken a couple of bites. It had been a day of excitement for him, excitement which at times had curbed his appetite.

As Davie sipped at his chocolate he took another look around him. There were so many interesting items in the room, though his favourite was a stuffed swordfish that was resplendent in a glass case over the door. He was fascinated by it. He sat there for some moments with his head back, gazing up at the object, then at last lowered his head and spoke to his mother. 'Mammy,' he said, a little anxiously, 'what's the time now?'

Lydia replied, 'Two minutes ago it was twenty minutes to three and now it's eighteen minutes to three.'

'And what time is Grandpa coming?'

'I told you – as soon as he can. He's working later today. He leaves work at half past two and he said he'll come straight here.'

Carefully the boy set down his cup. 'And d'you think he'll bring me a present?'

She put out a hand and gently touched the tip of his nose. 'Why on earth should he bring you a present? D'you think you deserve one?'

'Oh, yes, I do! You know I do.'

'But why should he bring you one, in any case?'

'You know why. Because it's my birthday.'

'Oh, is it?'

'Oh, you know very well it is, and I'm sure Grandpa knows it too.' He paused, screwing up his face. 'If Grandpa asks if I've been good, what will you tell him? Will you tell him yes?'

She smiled. 'I shall tell him the truth.'

'Then you'll tell him yes, won't you?'

'Shall I? Yes, I suppose I shall. I'd have to, wouldn't I?'

'Yes, you would, you would!'

He had raised his voice with his words and Lydia put

318

a finger to her lips. 'Not so loud – you'll disturb the ladies.'

He put a hand over his mouth, and looked around him, while the proprietor, a large, jolly-looking woman in her forties, glanced over and smiled at him indulgently. There were only four other patrons there, all middle-aged women; the place was far from busy, which suited Lydia. She chose it partly for that reason but mainly for its convenience for her father, coming from work. He had come to see his small grandson on several occasions over the past couple of years in the coffee house; it was a handy meeting place for the three of them.

Now, lowering his hand and turning in his seat, Davie was rewarded as he saw a familiar figure walking past the window towards the door. 'It's Grandpa, Mammy!' he cried out. 'He's here.'

Seconds later Lydia's father was pushing open the door and entering. As he sat down on the third chair he reached out and touched his daughter's hand in greeting. There was no kiss, but Lydia would not have expected such; it was not the way they were. He did, however, kiss his grandson, leaning over, brushing back the fair hair and planting a kiss on his forehead. He was holding a brown paper-wrapped package, which he now put down on the vacant chair at his side. His hat he set down on top.

'So,' he said to the child, 'and how is our birthday boy?'

'Grandpa, you remembered,' Davie said, beaming. 'You didn't forget it's my birthday.'

Mr Halley nodded, his smile wide. 'Of course I didn't forget. How could I?' He tipped his head on one side. 'And how old are you today?'

'You know how old I am.'

'Well, perhaps I do, and perhaps I don't. You tell me.'

'I'm four. Did you know that I'm four? And next year I shall be five.'

'Indeed you will, but four is plenty to be going on with.'
Mr Halley smiled at Lydia. 'What it must be like to be four.'

Lydia, smiling back at her father across the table, picked
up the teapot and began to pour another cup. 'Indeed,' she
said, and then added: 'While you have a chance, do have
some tea. It's just been brought.'

'Thank you, I could do with a cup.'

She finished pouring, then added milk and passed the
cup over to him. He took a swallow.

Lydia said, 'Davie's nurse has got part of the afternoon
off. So she'll be doing her shopping. I thought this would be
a good opportunity to see you.'

'Yes, very good,' Mr Halley said.

'Have you had a good day at the factory?'

It was a usual question. 'Oh, as it normally is,' he said,
and added, 'Everyone glad it's Saturday and no work till
Monday.' He put a hand into his pocket and brought out a
little brown-paper packet. He set it down on the table and
pushed it across to her.

'What is this?' she said as she took it up and pulled the
wrapping aside.

'It's nothing special,' he said, but got pleasure from
watching as she poured into her hand a little swarm of jet
buttons.

'Oh, Father, they're lovely,' she said. The surface of each
one was embossed with the head of a rose.

He nodded. 'They're a new line we're doing. I thought
you might like them.'

'Oh, I do.'

How different things were now, she reflected. At first he
had been unforgiving of Lydia in her marriage to Alfred,
but the death of Ryllis had changed all that. He had turned
back to Lydia then. She could well remember how he had
been at the time. The day after the funeral she had gone
with him to the grave where Ryllis lay buried beside her

mother. She had never seen him so shaken, not even when Mrs Halley had died. 'I wasn't fair to the girl,' he had said so many times. 'I wasn't fair.'

For a while he had ceased his preaching, and on two or three occasions over those first weeks after Ryllis's death, Lydia had gone to Capinfell and found him sitting alone in the house. He had, it transpired, only stirred from it in order to go to work.

One thing to come from Ryllis's sad end was that nothing further that was negative had been spoken about Lydia's marriage. Her father had come to accept her actions. Where Alfred was concerned Mr Halley had not exactly offered the hand of warmest friendship, but at least there was no animosity between them and they got on politely and reasonably well, and that relationship had improved greatly with the birth of Davie. Mr Halley doted on his grandson and was enormously proud of him.

While Lydia carefully put the buttons away in her bag, Davie said to his grandfather, 'Grandpa, would you show me the fish, please.' The boy slid off his chair and moved towards his grandfather, leaning against his knee.

'You want to see the fish?'

'Please. Lift me up, will you, please?'

Mr Halley rose from his seat and took Davie under the arms and lifted him up before the stuffed swordfish. 'There – can you see better now?'

Davie gazed at the fish in awe and silence, and then after a few moments Mr Halley lowered him again to the floor. 'You get so much heavier every time,' he said.

Davie sat back on his chair and took a swallow from his cup of chocolate. Then, his eyes moving to the wrapped package beneath his grandfather's hat, he said, 'What have you got there, Grandpa?'

Mr Halley nodded. 'Oh, you noticed that, did you?'

'Yes. What is it?'

'Well – perhaps that's meant to be a surprise.'

Davie grinned. 'A surprise? A surprise for me?'

'For you, you cunning little monkey? What makes you think that might be the case?'

'Because it's my birthday. You know that.'

'Yes, I do.' Mr Halley turned to his daughter. 'What do you think, Mamma? Should we let him have his birthday present?'

'Oh, I think so,' Lydia said. 'He's held out long enough.'

Mr Halley lifted his hat from the package and nodded at the child. 'Go on, then, young man, see what it is.'

Davie took up the parcel from the chair and picked at the string that tied it. When it would not give, Mr Halley took it from him and untied the knot. In seconds Davie had pulled aside the paper and pulled out a soldier with a little drum. After gazing at it for some moments he set it before him on the table. 'Oh, Grandpa, it's excellent!' The soldier was made of tin, brightly painted, and stood some eight or nine inches high, held up by a spindle that was set into a round base with small wheels. He had a tall-crowned cap of black with a yellow plume at the front, and gold epaulettes on his square shoulders.

'You like him?' Mr Halley said.

'Oh, yes! Grandpa, thank you!'

'Look –' Mr Halley pointed to the key in the small of the soldier's back. 'When you wind him up his legs kick out and it appears that he marches. I think he'll bang his drum, too.'

'Oh, let's do it, Grandpa. Let's wind him up!'

'Shall we?'

'Oh, yes!'

'All right. Shall I, or shall you?'

'Oh, I'll do it, shall I?'

'Of course.'

The child did so, holding the soldier and carefully

turning the key. At once the soldier began to swing his legs. At the same time his arms moved and his sticks beat the little drum.

'Look,' Davie breathed, and then, 'Oh, let's see him march.' Mr Halley cleared a little space on the table, and the soldier was carefully placed down on it. They all three watched then as the soldier moved across the cloth, his legs swinging out, and his arms moving, the drumsticks beating out a rat-tat-tat-tat-tat. Davie was thrilled. 'Oh, Grandpa,' he said, 'he's wonderful.'

Lydia and her father watched, pleased. 'A capital choice, Father,' Lydia said.

'I got him yesterday, in my dinner-time.'

Two weeks had passed since they had last met, and on that occasion, on a Sunday after midday dinner, Lydia had taken Davie with her to Capinfell. Not only had the pair spent time with Mr Halley, but also they had seen Evie, and the two young women had had a chance to talk together.

Now, sitting at the table, Mr Halley took a swallow from his teacup, watched Davie playing engrossed with his new toy, then said, 'And how is your husband?'

'He's well, thank you – aside from a touch of the gout, which does bother him, I have to say. Lately he's taken to driving the trap into work, instead of walking – which he usually loves to do.' She gave a little sigh. 'But other than that he's well, and working hard.'

Mr Halley nodded. 'I don't doubt that he works hard. I hear the place is always busy.'

'Oh, he runs a good business.'

Mr Halley gave a little nod in the direction of Davie. 'And will one day have a good helper, I shouldn't wonder.'

'Oh, yes. I'm sure he's got that in mind.' She paused. 'But sometimes I think Alfred works too hard. I tell him so, but it does nothing to slow him up. He seems as tireless as ever.'

'Are you not working there this afternoon?'

'Oh, yes, I shall be going there straight from here – and I mustn't be late. Mr Federo, one of Alfred's assistants, has to go off this afternoon for an appointment, so I must go in. Saturday is a very busy time for the shop.'

'I'm sure it must be. And you're taking Davie with you?'

'Yes, for a while. Ellen, is to come by and collect him later on, and take him home again. That'll leave me free to help out for a bit longer.'

'You enjoy it, don't you? Serving the customers?'

'Yes, I do. I like to be busy.'

Not long after the birth of Davie, at Alfred's suggestion, they had hired a nurse for the boy – a young woman by the name of Ellen Hockin, who lived nearby and came in on a daily basis – an arrangement that had enabled Lydia to get back to helping out at the shop again. First she had spent only a limited time there, assisting on the busier days and at other necessary times, but as Davie had grown so she had gone there for longer hours, until lately she was there almost full time.

Now she added, speaking to her father, 'It keeps me well occupied. I don't get enough to do at home, what with Mrs Starling and Alice doing most of the work in the house and kitchen, and of course Davie has Ellen, who's always ready to help out too. It doesn't leave me a lot to do, and I can't sit sewing the livelong day. Mind you, since I've had this little person I'm kept a deal busier than I was.'

'I'm sure of it.'

She looked at Davie as he sat examining his toy soldier. 'And soon Davie will have to go to school.' She addressed her next words to the boy. 'Isn't that so, Davie?'

'Yes.' He looked up from the toy. 'Did you know that, Grandpa? I'm starting to learn reading, and how to sum.'

'Well done, young man.'

'I teach him when I can,' Lydia said, 'but he needs tuition full time now.'

A young maid came over to their table and asked if they needed anything else. Lydia told her that they had all they wanted, and the girl went away again. Lydia said, turning to her father:

'Father, you must come out to the house and visit us again. You've only been the once.'

'Yes, well, maybe I will,' he said.

'You could come from work on a Saturday and have dinner with us.'

'Ah, well, maybe . . .'

'The garden is looking very nice at the moment. We have so many daffodils still out around the lawn, and the primroses are beautiful. We walked here today, and I see so many flowers are out. Cowslips were all over the meadow, and dandelions. Our cherry trees are all in full flower. Oh, Father, you should come and see us, at home, soon. Our garden's a picture.'

'Well, yes, as I said, maybe I will. You sound as if you're fond of your garden.'

'Oh, I am. That's something else I do, in the summer evenings, help out Mr Clifford – that's our gardener who comes in three or four times a week, and believe me, he's needed in the spring and summer when everything grows apace. And the house is looking so nice now that we've had the painters in.'

Davie piped up at this, looking up from his chocolate. 'My room has been newly papered, Grandpa. It's got butterflies and birds all over it.'

'Has it, now? Well, that sounds very nice.' Mr Halley smiled at the boy and then turned back to Lydia. 'You're happy there, aren't you?'

She hesitated for just the merest second. 'I've got so much to make me happy,' she said. 'I've got a fine home, and a loving husband – and he's a good husband too – and I have a son.' She put up a hand and touched Davie's cheek. 'Haven't I, my dear?'

'You mean me?' Davie said.

Lydia gave a little chuckle. 'Of course I mean you. Who else.'

'And you like Merinville,' Mr Halley said.

'Yes, I do,' she nodded, 'but I always did like it, right from when we used to visit it to come shopping – Mother and Ryllis and I.'

'You don't miss Redbury?'

'No, I don't miss Redbury.'

'Nor your friends there.'

'I didn't have any friends there. I wasn't there long enough to make any.'

'What about Mr – ?' He came to a halt, unable to think of the name that had stayed in his mind for so long. 'I can't remember his name,' he said.

'Who? Who are you talking about?'

'I meant to tell you,' he said. 'I meant to tell you ages ago, but it slipped my mind with Ryllis and everything. You've just reminded me of it now.'

'Of what?'

'It was just after you married. I was at home one day when a young man called. It must have been a weekend. He was looking for you. He said he was a friend of yours – from Redbury. A tall young man, in his mid twenties, I'd say. Dark haired. Handsome fellow.'

And Lydia knew at once who he meant. He could only have been talking of one person. Her breath caught in her throat for a split second, and then she said, 'He gave you his name?'

'Yes, he did, but I've forgotten it. Maybe it'll come to me. I would have told you sooner, but like I said, I forgot.' He gave a little shrug. 'I told him that you were no longer

326

living at home, and that you were married and living in Merinville.'

'Did he – say anything to that?'

'Not that I recall. I think he just thanked me and went on his way. Ah, yes!' He touched the side of his forehead with the heel of his hand. 'That's it. Anderson his name was. It just came to me.'

Lydia nodded, keeping silent. Her father looked a little more closely at her.

'Are you all right?' he said.

'Yes, I'm fine.'

'Are you sure? Have I said something that's upset you?'

'What? No. No, not at all.' She turned to her son. 'That's a wonderful soldier you've got there, isn't it?'

Davie nodded happily, and moved the soldier across the table again.

'Did I have the name right?' Mr Halley said. 'It's been well over four years.' He took a sip of his tea then added, 'Mr Anderson – do you remember him?'

'Oh, yes. Yes, I do.'

Could she ever forget him? It was an impossibility. He was in her mind every day. There was no day that passed that some memory of him did not return. How could she forget him? She had only to look at her son, and there was his father. She needed only to look into the face of her boy, look at his eyes with the thick lashes, and Guy was there, looking out at her. She could see him in the curve of Davie's lip, in the cut of his square shoulder. Sometimes the awareness shocked her. She would be totally unprepared for the strike of memory, when Davie would turn in a particular way, or smile in a particular way, or look back at her in a particular way, and there Guy would be, and she could see him again, and it would take her breath away. Once again it would all come back. She would think of him in a hundred visions, in the garden beside the square in

327

Redbury where they had first met; seeing him in the carriage as they drove to Barford; facing her across the table while the man sang; sitting on the bank of the lake where they had made love. There was no escaping from her memories.

'I do remember him,' she added. 'Yes, he was – a friend.'

'Perhaps I should have told him more,' he said. 'Like where he could find you – but I didn't.'

'It's all right.'

'Mammy, watch!'

Lydia's attention was taken again by Davie who once more demonstrated how his soldier could move and bang his drum, and she smiled and said, 'Ah, it's excellent, darling. I'm sure you're very pleased.'

'Are you going to celebrate your birthday?' Mr Halley said, turning to his grandson.

'I'm having a party,' Davie said, grinning happily, 'but tomorrow, when there's more time. Tomorrow afternoon.'

'Three little children who live nearby,' Lydia said. 'They're coming round for jelly and cakes.'

'Well, that sounds as if it's going to be exciting,' Mr Halley said.

'It will be,' said Davie, 'and we shan't only have jelly and cakes. We shall have sandwiches too, and a birthday cake as well, with candles on it. Isn't that right, Mammy? A birthday cake with four candles?'

'Yes, dear.'

'And we shall play games. We shall play Hunt the Thimble and Blind Man's Buff and there might even be a lucky dip. Oh, it's going to be splendid. It's going to be lots of fun.'

Lydia only half heard her son's happy prattle. She could not get out of her mind what her father had told her. Guy had called at the house in Capinfell, asking for her. So he had not forgotten. All these years she had had to keep in her head the belief that she had gone completely out of his awareness, but it was not true. He had not forgotten her.

Lydia still thought of her father's words as they walked through the town in the direction of the market square. She had said goodbye to her father, and Davie had kissed his cheek, and then, while Mr Halley had made for the coach that would take him back to Capinfell, she and Davie had set off for the shop. As they went, Davie walked at her side holding her hand, his other mittened hand grasping his tin soldier.

A sharp, biting wind sliced through the square as they turned into it, and Lydia pressed Davie's hand and held it to her skirts. 'It'll be good to get in the warm again,' she said. Up above, the sky was a yellowish grey. There was snow there, she thought. Then at last the shop front was before them, and they hurried towards it, pushed open the door, and went in.

The shop was busy, with Alfred and his assistants dealing with customers, while one or two others waited to be served. Lydia went straight through, getting a smiling nod from Alfred, and took Davie into the room at the back.

'Now,' she said to the boy, 'I've got to help out in the shop for a while, for Mr Federo has to go out into the town, and Papa and Miss Angel won't be able to manage on their own. D'you understand?'

'Yes.'

'There's a good boy. You'll have to stay in here and amuse yourself, can you do that?'

'Yes.'

'Good. I'll pop in now and again to see if you're all right.'

He was already taking his soldier out of its brown paper wrapping, in preparation to having him walk about the stained table top. 'What does Mr Federo have to go out for?' he asked.

'He's got a toothache, poor man. He's going to the barber's to have his tooth pulled.'

Davie frowned. 'Will that hurt?'

'Just a little perhaps – but it's nothing to the pain he's in with his tooth aching so.' She stepped to him and bent before him. 'Now let me take off your coat and cap – otherwise you'll miss them when you go out.'

The boy stood still as Lydia took off his cap and overcoat and scarf and mittens. 'Now,' she said, 'I should think you'll be warm enough.' There was a fire burning in the stove and she put out her hand towards it. 'Here, dear, sit by the stove if you start to get cold.'

'All right.'

'That's my good boy.' She looked into his face. 'I should think you might be tired pretty soon, so I think it would be a good idea if you have a little nap, don't you, until Ellen gets here?'

He said in surprise, 'I'm not tired,' as if it were the furthest possibility, but she said, 'Still, you might become so.' There was a woollen rug hanging over the back of the sofa, and she took it down and laid it on the cushions. 'If you get tired will you lie down here, darling?'

'All right, but I shan't be tired.'

'Well, we'll see.'

As she took off her hat and cape Alfred came in. At once he saw the soldier that Davie was holding. 'Oh, well, look there,' he said. 'That's something I haven't seen before. Did you get that today?'

'Yes, I did,' Davie said. 'I got it from Grandpa.'

'Well, that's very nice of Grandpa to do that. I hope you thanked him properly, did you?'

'Yes, I did.'

'Well done.' He turned to Lydia who was just hanging up her cape on the hook beside the door. 'I'm glad you got here,' he said. 'Peter's ready to go now. Poor man is in such discomfort. The sooner he gets it done the better. We seem to be very busy this afternoon.' He turned to Davie. 'Will you be all right in here for a while, son?'

'Yes, Pappy.'

'Good boy.' He turned and started out and Lydia, after gently touching her son's head with her hand, followed after him.

Young Mr Federo was serving an elderly man at that moment, but as soon as the transaction was complete he got the nod from Alfred and, thankfully smiling, went through into the back room to get his coat and hat. A minute later he came out wearing them and pulling on his gloves.

'Right,' Alfred said to him, 'you go on, m'boy, and I'll see you on Monday. I hope you don't suffer too much.'

The young man thanked him, wished him a good day and a good weekend, and then said the same to Lydia. In moments he was out of the shop and had disappeared from their sight.

The time passed swiftly. It was always the same on a Saturday. As on a Thursday, the general market day, many people came in from out of town to do their shopping, and they were very busy. Frequently, between customers, Lydia went into the back room to see how Davie was getting on. On the second occasion, she found that he had put his soldier aside and was lying sound asleep on the sofa. The rug was only partly over him, and gently she adjusted it so that he was covered. He kept on sleeping.

She stood there looking down at him, taking in the flush on his rounded cheek, the pink curve of his upper lip, the colour of his light blond hair. He was all that she could have wished for. She thought back to the time of his birth. There must have been a certain amount of gossip surrounding the circumstance, she was sure; a baby born eight months after marriage would always be bound to set tongues wagging, but she didn't care, and neither did Alfred, she knew.

She touched a light kiss to his smooth forehead and moved out of the room again, back into the shop proper, leaving the door ajar, and found that more customers had arrived: a woman with her three young daughters, wanting to see silk fabrics, particular designs of lace, and grosgrain ribbons. Lydia set to work at once to serve them, and with herself busy, as well as Alfred and Miss Angel, the room was filled with conversation. Another half-hour passed with the time fleeting as the assistants dealt with the customers who came in.

Freed momentarily as a customer left the shop with her packages under her arm, Lydia looked up at the clock on the wall. Nearly five. Not long to go now, then Ellen would be there to take Davie home, leaving Lydia to continue working alongside Alfred for another two or three hours. Later she and Alfred would return home, at which time she could see Davie in the nursery, and tuck him in if he was still awake.

Now she stood for a moment in her own silence while the work went on around her, and a little buzz of voices hovered in the air. She looked from one to the other in the room. Miss Angel, a grey-haired maiden lady in her fifties, and Alfred's longest-serving employee, was serving a customer with a length of blue holland, while Alfred, in spite of his gout, was up on a short ladder, checking some items of stock on the upper shelves. Taking advantage of the momentary quiet, Lydia turned from the counter and went again into the back room where she found Davie sitting up on the sofa, rubbing his eyes.

'Did you have a good sleep, darling?'

He nodded, still drowsy.

'You'll be going home in a little while, then you can have your tea. Ellen will be here for you soon.'

'Can't I stay here with you and Pappy?'

'Now, you know you can't, darling. You'll be better off at

home, and you've got a big day tomorrow with your party, haven't you?'

'Yes.'

'Will you be all right here for a while still? Till Ellen comes?'

'Can I come out in the shop with you and Pappy? I won't make a noise or be a nuisance.'

She hesitated, then said, 'I'm sure you won't. All right, then. Come out when you're ready.'

She left him then, and went back into the shop. Alfred, she found, had gone into the stockroom. She turned to the low shelf behind the counter and bent to tidy up some lengths of ribbon that she had earlier been unwrapping. As she did so she heard the sound of the bell over the door, announcing that another customer was coming in. She put the ribbons down, stood up straight, and found herself face to face with Guy.

Chapter Nineteen

She stood there looking at him, while the business of the shop went on to her right as Miss Angel and her customer murmured over their business. For all Lydia's outer stillness her heart was thumping in her chest. A part of her mind protested that it could not be true, that Guy's presence there must be some strange manifestation of her thought; her father had been speaking of him just a short time ago, that very afternoon, and here Guy was, standing before her, wearing a chesterfield coat with an astrakhan collar, his bowler hat briefly lifted in one hand, his briefcase and a paper-wrapped package in the other. He was standing just feet away from her on the other side of the counter. If she stretched out her hand she could touch him.

They stood in silence facing one another. It had been four years and nine months since they had last met, and she could see the passage of the years in his face. There was a maturity about him; she could detect faint lines about his mouth, about the corners of his eyes and marking his forehead. Little lines of care. Other than that he looked the same.

At last he spoke, frowning a little at the wonder of the unexpected meeting, but his mouth lifting slightly.

'Well,' he said, and then, giving a nod, 'Well,' again, and then, 'Good afternoon.'

A moment of silence and 'Good afternoon,' Lydia replied. She could hear her voice sounding foolish and overbright in her ears. Then she added, 'This is a –

surprise.' She wanted to smile at him, but her mouth would not obey, and she stood with lips compressed, her hands on the counter before her.

Swiftly taking off his gloves, he reached out and took Lydia's hand in his. As he briefly shook it he murmured her name: 'Lydia.' He barely breathed the word. 'I can hardly believe it. Is it you? Is it really you?'

'How are you?' she said, withdrawing her hand. 'Have you been well?'

'Yes, thank you.'

'I'm glad to hear it.' The prosaic words came from her lips and she heard them as if spoken by another. She could think of nothing to say. It was as if she were acting in a dream. Over to her right Miss Angel and her customer were talking about an incident at the market.

'I've wondered about you,' Guy said. 'How you've been getting on.'

'I – I've been very well,' Lydia said. 'Very well indeed.' A pause, then she added, 'I suppose you've been busy . . .'

'Oh, yes.' He gave a firm nod. 'I'm running the newspaper now. For better or worse.' He paused. 'My father – I'm afraid he died from his accident, while I was in Italy. He passed away shortly after my arrival there.'

Lydia recalled Mrs Anderson telling her of this when she had been at the house that day. 'I'm sorry,' she said. 'That must have been a great blow for you.'

'It was worse for my mother. She missed him terribly at his death. She died too, a year ago.'

'Oh, dear . . . I'm so sorry.'

'Thank you.' He paused, gave an awkward little shrug and added, 'I just dropped in to buy some handkerchiefs. I came to Merinville on business, and found I'd come out without one.' He gestured with a nod of his head. 'I'm just on my way to the railway station.'

'Handkerchiefs, yes,' she said. 'Did you want cotton,

linen or silk?' How stilted their conversation was, she said to herself. Anyone observing them would think they were nothing more than the merest slight acquaintances.

'Oh, linen, I think. I only want a couple, if that's all right.'

'Yes, of course. Plain, monogrammed or edged?'

'Plain, thank you.'

She was about to bend to take a box of handkerchiefs from below the counter when she heard her son's voice calling to her.

'Mammy?'

Davie was coming from behind her as he emerged from the back room. She turned at his voice and smiled at him.

'Hello, darling – so you're properly awake now, are you?'

'Yes,' the boy murmured and looked up curiously at Guy on the other side of the counter.

Guy was gazing at the child. 'This is your son?' he said.

Lydia put her hand on Davie's shoulder. 'Yes, this is my boy.' There was pride in her voice. 'This is David. Though we always call him Davie.'

Guy stepped up closer to the counter, leant his tall body over and reached out his hand. 'How d'you do, Davie?'

Davie flicked a questioning glance at his mother, then at the tall man, then put up his small hand and allowed Guy to take it.

'That's it,' Lydia said, and prompted him: *'How do you do?'*

'How do you do,' Davie said.

Guy let go of the boy's hand and straightened, his eyes still on the child. At the other end of the counter Miss Angel's customer was now looking at some samples of nankeen. The door at the far end opened, and Alfred emerged from the stockroom, carrying a number of boxes. He came along behind the counter, past Miss Angel and her customer, and took in the trio of Lydia, Davie and Guy. As

336

he approached them, Lydia said to Guy, 'Here's my husband now,' and turned, including Alfred in her smile and saying, 'My husband, Mr Alfred Canbrook.' And to Alfred: 'Alfred – this is Mr Guy Anderson. Mr Anderson is an old friend of mine – from several years back.'

Alfred put the boxes down on the counter and the two men shook hands. Lydia said, aware of the irrelevance of her words, 'Mr Anderson came in for some hand-kerchiefs . . .' As she spoke she took the box of linen handkerchiefs and set it on the counter. 'You wanted just two?' she said, and Guy replied, 'Please – if I may,' and she took out two and laid them on the counter before him. He nodded his satisfaction, and she was about to wrap them in paper when he added quickly, 'No, leave them as they are, thank you.' He paid her with some coppers from his purse, then precisely folded one handkerchief and put it into the breast pocket of his jacket. The other he put into his trousers pocket. Then into the scene came Davie's voice as he said, 'Look, it's snowing.' Lydia looked out past Guy's shoulder, and through the door glass saw flakes whirling past.

'It's snowing – on my birthday!' Davie said.

'It's your birthday today?' Guy asked.

'Yes, I'm four – and tomorrow I'm having a party.'

Alfred stooped and picked Davie up in his arms. 'Yes, he is,' he said, 'and look at him, he's getting to be the biggest boy.'

'Oh, Pappy, let me down,' Davie said, and Alfred, chuckling, set him back upon his feet. 'You don't like to be treated like a baby, do you?'

Davie said, wide-eyed, 'Well, I'm not.'

'No, of course you're not.' Alfred ruffled the boy's hair, then moved his hand to tap the top box of the small stack he had set down. 'These are the men's stockings that have just come in,' he said. 'I've checked them; they're all fine. I'm putting them up here.'

337

He stacked the boxes onto a shelf at the back, then turned to Guy and gave a little nod and a smile and said, 'It's very nice to meet you, Mr Anderson. If you'll excuse me . . .' The two men wished one another a good afternoon, and Alfred went back towards the stockroom door. Lydia watched him go, then turned back to Guy. As she did so, Davie piped up again.

'Mammy, are you coming home with me?'

'No, dear, you know I'm not. Ellen will be here for you soon.'

'I mustn't keep you,' Guy said. 'You've got things to do.' He buttoned his coat and pulled his gloves on.

Lydia nodded, trying to smile. 'Well – it's been very nice to see you.' She put out her hand and he took it again in his.

'You too,' he said.

There seemed to be nothing more to say.

'Well . . . goodbye.'

Lydia gave the briefest nod. 'Goodbye.'

Guy smiled at Davie. 'And goodbye to you, Master Davie.'

Davie smiled up at him and said, 'I got a soldier from my grandpa. D'you want to see it?'

Lydia said, 'Another day, dear. Mr Anderson has to go.'

She smiled at Guy and he smiled back. There was nothing to keep him now. He turned and moved to the door, and Lydia watched as he passed through into the cold square. The snow had stopped as quickly as it had begun. Soon all traces of it would be gone. April snow, it never lasted.

Lydia stood at the counter, looking across the shop to the doorway which Guy's shape had just filled. She could scarcely believe that she had seen him again, after all this time. He had walked back into her life, and what a quiet, undramatic little event it had been. There had been no roll of drums such as one got at the circus when some major

338

event was about to take place; there had been no fanfare to make you sit up. It had just happened. One minute he might have been a thousand miles away, and the next he had been there before her, speaking her name, touching her hand.

She came out of her reverie to hear Miss Angel's customer saying, 'Oh, look, someone's left their parcel, it seems. Must have been your last customer . . .' And looking round, Lydia saw Guy's brown paper-wrapped parcel lying on the counter next to the wall.

'Oh, dear . . .' She picked it up and looked foolishly from Miss Angel to her customer, as if expecting directions of some kind, then said hurriedly, 'I must go after him.' She turned to Davie. 'I'll just be a moment, darling.'

She was tempted to run out as she was, but thought better of it, hurried into the room at the rear and, still wearing her apron, quickly put on her cloak. Then she was out of the room again, had snatched up the package and was starting towards the door. As she did so Miss Angel called out to her, 'Mrs Canbrook, it's freezing out there. You'll need your muffler.' But she hurried on and a moment later the door was closing behind her and she was outside in the chill air.

Guy had moved to the left, she had seen, and she recalled that he had said he was on his way to the station. She turned in the same direction and felt the cold wind smack at her face. She could see Guy ahead of her, a good distance away, walking along the side of the square. Picking up her skirts, she hurried after him, the heels of her boots ringing on the snow-dusted cobbles.

She watched as up ahead he turned to the left. She ran on, gaining ground all the time, and then they were out of the square and he was walking along Greengage Street. Eventually she was close enough to be heard, and gathering her breath, she called out, 'Mr Anderson . . . Guy . . .'

He stopped at the sound of his name, turned on the spot, saw her running towards him, and once he saw the package he knew the reason for her pursuit of him. He clapped a hand to his forehead and groaned, 'Oh, my shoes!' As she came to a halt before him he said, 'Lord, how forgetful. Oh, thank you so much! Of course, I'd have remembered them when I got home.'

He took the package from her. As he did so his hand touched hers and he said, 'You shouldn't have come out in this – and without gloves or scarf or a hat. You'll catch pneumonia.'

'I'm all right,' she said. 'It's only just for a minute.'

They stood in silence, facing one another, and the cold wind blasted around the corner and snatched at the hem of Lydia's cloak.

'I – I must go,' she said. She did not move, but stayed there, only barely aware of the icy blast that buffeted her.

Guy said, 'I called at your home in Capinfell, you know, looking for you – after I got back from Italy.'

'Yes, I know,' she said, 'my father told me just today. Only today he told me.'

'Today? Just *today*?' His eyes were wide in surprise.

'Yes.'

'He told me you'd married and moved away.' He smiled, a smile touched with sadness. 'When he told me – well, I decided to leave it at that. There was no sense in pursuing you any further. I felt, in fact, rather foolish.'

'Foolish?'

'For going that far. To find you, I mean. I'd enquired at your lodgings in Redbury, and also at Seager's, but I got no success. So finally I went to Capinfell – and there I traced you to your father's home.' He paused. 'I wasn't prepared for such surprises.'

'Surprises?'

'For you to marry so quickly after I'd gone to Italy. I'd

340

had no idea that there was someone else in the picture. Was he waiting in the background all the time? Or was he new on the scene?'

She did not know what to say. 'You – you don't understand,' she said after a moment. 'It – it wasn't like that . . .' She came to a halt. She could not go further and give him the full reason.

'Well, no matter,' he said. 'I suppose it's of no consequence now.' He paused. 'Is it?'

Oh, yes, she wanted to say. *It is of consequence. It's still of the greatest consequence,* but she said nothing. She was aware that snow had once again begun to fall, bringing icy little touches on her cheek.

Guy said, 'I should have written to you, from Florence – but – I don't know – so much got in the way, and I had so much to do, what with my father's death, and then there was the disposal of his business to deal with. And I'd heard nothing from you.'

She wanted to say, *But I wrote to you – and your mother withheld the letter,* for clearly he did not know anything of it. But she could not. It was all in the past now, and there was no point in dragging up such unhappy moments. So many things now were better left unsaid. Only harm could come from raking everything over. Best to let some things remain hidden.

A few moments went by, then Guy said abruptly, 'Look, I mustn't keep you out here in the cold – though there's so much I want to talk to you about.'

Her cue was there for her to say goodbye again, but she did not. She just waited, and then into the quiet between them, he said:

'Lydia, I have to see you. I need to talk to you.'

'What – what about?'

'Oh, please – not here.'

She said nothing, and wondered briefly at the fact that

she was still standing there. Just by remaining she was getting in too deep.

'Can we meet?' he said.

'But – but what for?'

'Don't say no,' he said. 'Tell me we can meet. I don't care where, but sometime soon. Will you meet me?'

'But why?' she said. 'Guy – I'm married now. I've got a child. Things are not the same.'

'I know things are not the same,' he said, and there was regret and bitterness in his tone. 'Will you meet me?' he said again.

She did not answer.

'Please,' he said.

And she remained standing there, and by doing so knew that she was consenting.

'Do you work every day?' he said after a moment.

'Well, I'm not in the shop on Wednesday afternoons. The shop's closed then, but I have errands to run.'

'So – could we meet?'

'Well . . .'

'Where shall you be going? What are your errands?'

'I'm going to Pershall Dean – to collect some work from a couple of Alfred's seamstresses. Sometimes Alfred goes, but his gout is bad just lately.'

'Will you be alone?'

'Yes. Occasionally I take Davie with me – but not when the weather is so changeable.'

'How will you get there? By train?'

'Yes. It's only two stops on from Merinville.'

'I know it. What time are you going?'

'It has to be in the afternoon. We close at half-past two, so I shall set off from the shop about three.'

'I'll meet you,' he said. 'I'll be at Pershall Dean station – at three-thirty.'

'Oh, well, I – I don't know if I can get there by then.' She could hear the rising panic in her voice. She was getting in deeper still.

'It doesn't matter; I'll wait,' he said. 'I don't care how long, but you will be there?'

She nodded. 'Yes.'

A sudden blast of wind swept around the corner, sending the snowflakes swirling, and flattening her collar against her throat.

'Go back,' he said, 'before you freeze. I'll see you on Wednesday.' He paused. 'You will be there . . .'

'I will,' she said.

When Lydia got back to the shop Alfred looked at her in surprise. 'How could you go out in that, without your hat and scarf?' he said, frowning.

'I had to catch Mr Anderson – he'd left his parcel.'

'So I understood from Miss Angel. For goodness sake, come on in and warm yourself by the stove.'

'I'm all right,' Lydia said. 'Is Davie in the back?'

'Yes, Ellen's just arrived. He's showing her his soldier.'

As she went to move past him to go into the back room, he said, 'You never mentioned Mr Anderson before.'

'Didn't I?'

'Is he from Capinfell?'

'Mr Anderson? No, no, not Capinfell. He's from Redbury.'

'From Redbury – oh.'

She could not face him, no matter how much she wanted to, and in another moment she was moving on behind the counter, and pushing open the door to the rear room.

Ellen was in the back room, helping Davie into his coat. She was a smallish young woman of eighteen, stockily built, with a round, good-natured face. As she fastened the boy's cap, he said to his mother, 'You went out, Mammy.'

'Yes, dear,' Lydia said, 'I had to.'

'Miss Angel said you went after the man with his parcel.'

'That's right.'

'Is he a nice man?'

'Yes, he's a nice man.'

Alfred made no further mention of Guy's appearance in the shop, and Lydia was greatly relieved, for she did not know how she would have handled whatever questions came her way.

Guy had never been far from her mind before, and now, following their encounter, he was there almost constantly. She found she could scarcely wait till Wednesday came and she would see him again. But for what purpose? she asked herself. Nothing could come of it. If once they had had a chance at happiness together, that chance had long ago been spent and their lives now had taken different paths. Although Davie was Guy's son, Guy had no part in his life. Nor in Lydia's. Her life now was with Alfred, and that was that.

On the Tuesday night she lay awake in bed. Alfred was sleeping at her side, peaceful for the most part, except for the odd occasions when he would kick out a little in his sleep, his leg plagued by demon nerves that sometimes afflicted him. She listened to his breathing, generally even and quiet. No, she said to herself, she must do nothing that affected their lives together. She had not only herself to think of now. It went without saying that Davie must command the best of her caring and loving, but she owed so much to Alfred as well, for all he had given her over the years. Nothing could take that away. He had been the best of husbands in so many ways. He was considerate, kind, loving – though he was strong-minded, too, and never lagging behind when convinced that he was in the right. He doted on Davie, and Davie was, in every way other than blood, his son. And never had Alfred pressed her about the child's true father. Early on in their marriage he had asked her a question: 'Did you love the man . . .?' But Lydia had been reluctant to answer, and after a moment he had waved a hand, brushing the matter aside. The subject had never been referred to again. Lydia recalled now, with some pleasure, how, at Davie's birth, the squalling babe had been placed in Alfred's arms by the midwife, who had said to him, 'Your son, sir,' and he had raised his face and laughed with joy.

She stirred in the bed, restless, thinking of the coming day. Alfred's gout was still giving him great discomfort, so there was no question of his going to Pershall Dean. She would of course go. And she would see Guy. Her heart beat faster at the thought of it.

As was his wont of late, Alfred took the trap into the town centre as soon as he was ready after breakfast, leaving Lydia to finish her own breakfast and spend a little time with Davie before leaving him with Ellen. It was about an hour after Alfred's departure that Lydia started out for the shop, setting out to walk, as she usually did when the weather was dry. It was a pleasant way, for the most part beside the river.

She arrived to find Alfred and his assistants busy with customers, and she quickly put on her apron and joined them. The four of them worked steadily until half past two, at which time Miss Angel and Mr Federo said their goodbyes and left the premises. When the shop was closed, Lydia went into the back room and there ate a small sandwich that she had brought from home, and drank some tea that she had made for Alfred and herself. Alfred was still working; first he would be doing the books and after that he intended to check the work of one of the seamstresses who that morning had brought in a number of pairs of stockings that she had embroidered, and two little

345

jackets of Norfolk silk. Most of the goods sold in the shop came from factories, of course, but there were some things the factories couldn't do, and for the very fine bespoke work Alfred would turn to his assortment of seamstresses who lived in the vicinity and who were glad of the income. Almost without exception, the seamstresses brought the work they did for him into the shop, and rarely was it necessary for him to travel to pick it up. However, a few of them were unable to make the journey, including a widow woman and her invalid daughter who lived in Pershall Dean. It was there that Lydia was to go when her sandwich and tea were finished.

When the time came, she left Alfred still working in the back room, his mug of cooling tea at his side, and set off for the station with a light step and a nervous heart. She was aiming to catch the five past three, which should get her into Pershall Dean a few minutes before three-thirty. The day had remained dry, though there was no warmth in the pale sun that filtered through the clouds, and she was glad of her muffler and warm gloves. She had also brought her umbrella and carried with her a large burlap bag. This contained a quantity of plain stockings, table napkins and pillow cases, all to be embroidered, and would serve to bring back the finished work that the seamstresses, Mrs Castle and her daughter, were to provide.

The train was on time at Merinville station, and twenty-two minutes after boarding she was alighting at Pershall Dean. As she stepped onto the platform she saw Guy standing some yards down, then saw him turn and start towards her.

'Well,' he said, 'here you are.'

'Here I am.' She was unaware of the other travellers moving past them. She felt a strange kind of weakness as she stood there, and wondered at it, that almost five years had passed and he could still have this effect upon her.

'Have you been waiting long?' she asked.

'Ten minutes or so.' He gestured to the bag. 'What have you got there?'

'Some things that have to be sewn. I'm taking them to two of Alfred's workers, and I've also got to pick up some work from them.' She gestured off. 'They live in the village here, close to the green.'

'Let me carry it for you,' he said, reaching out for the bag.

'It's not heavy.'

'Still, let me have it.'

She handed the bag over.

'What time have you to be there?' he asked.

'I usually get there about four.'

'Do you go regularly, then?'

'Every fortnight. Mrs Castle can't make the journey to the shop, and her daughter is an invalid.'

They turned and together started off along the platform. While Lydia had been on the train, the sun had gone behind clouds, and a sharp and biting wind had sprung up, unrelentingly chill. From the station the two of them walked along the main street of the village. As they went Lydia said, 'Was it easy for you to get away from your work today?' She was speaking to fill in the silence between them. 'I can imagine how busy you must be.'

'I had to rearrange a few things,' he said, 'but it wasn't too difficult.' After a second he added, 'It wouldn't have mattered, though, however difficult it might have been; I had to see you.'

The green was up ahead, and they skirted it on its left side. Coming to the entrance to a narrow lane, Lydia said, 'I'll have to ask you to wait for me, will you?' She waved a hand, gesturing along the lane. 'The lady and her daughter live just along there.'

As she took the bag from him he looked around and said, 'I don't want to stand here. I'll feel conspicuous – not to

347

mention that I shall get very cold in this wind.' He gestured along the street. 'I'll stroll along the road a little way and then come back. How long shall you be?'

'Not too long. Something up to half an hour. They're bound to offer me tea. They always do, and I'll have to stay for a cup, but I'll get away as soon as I can. It won't be too long.'

He smiled. 'I'll try to be patient.'

She left him then and set off along the lane. The cottage gardens on either side were masses of colour with so many different flowers, while on the verge, vivid against the lush green grass, clumps of primroses looked like creamy-yellow buttons. Birds were busy, she noticed, gathering material for nesting. The cherry trees were heavy with blossom.

The two Castle women lived in the third thatched cottage along, and Lydia turned in at the small gate and went up the path. On either side in the borders grew jonquils, grape hyacinths and polyanthus. Reaching the door she gave a knock and then heard a voice calling to her to enter, and she lifted the latch and went in.

Mrs Castle was a woman in her sixties and her daughter, Mary, was in her late thirties. The latter had difficulty getting about on account of a lame right leg. She and her mother were a jolly pair, however, and made Lydia welcome to their humble but clean and tidy home. Lydia was offered tea – the kettle was already boiling – and in between sips, and nibbles at a little oatcake, she carefully folded and packed into the bag the work that the two women had completed, comprising a linen and lace tablecloth with poppies and wheat ears embroidered about the hem, two dozen heavy linen table napkins embroidered with lovebirds, and six pairs of stockings embroidered with silver clocks. Also there were two nightdresses with the ruffles hand-stitched. There were still some of Alfred's customers who wanted their clothes and other items hand-sewn as far as possible.

Lydia and the two women chatted about this and that, and at last she put down her empty cup and rose to make her departure. As she put on her cloak she thanked the two women and said she would see herself out. She knew that as soon as she had gone they would make a start on the work to be done.

Closing the door behind her, she made her way back out onto the lane and turned up towards the green once more. As she reached it she saw the tall figure of Guy coming towards her from the direction of the main street.

He smiled as they drew closer to one another. 'That was well timed,' he said as he came to a stop before her. 'Is it all done?'

'Yes, all done.'

They stood facing one another, conscious of their nearness, momentarily at a loss as to what to say.

'I've done the whole main street and back,' Guy said. 'And very slowly.' Then he added, 'How much time have you got? Do you have to rush home?'

'Well – I've a little time. Not too much, but . . .' Her words trailed off.

He jabbed back over his shoulder with his thumb. 'I passed a little inn back there and looked in. It has a nice little saloon bar. It was very quiet. We could go there and sit down and have a drink for a while.'

Lydia said, 'Yes, all right. Though I can't say I'm thirsty. I've just had some tea.'

'That's all right, you don't have to have anything, but at least we can get out of this wind. It's too keen for my liking.'

She murmured a word of assent, and he reached out and took the bag from her as they turned and set off together along the road.

The public house that Guy had spoken of was at the end

of the main street. On the wall at the front hung its sign showing a hare leaping over a crescent moon. Guy and Lydia passed under it and through the door. Within a little foyer there were two more doors, one leading to the public bar, and the other marked for the saloon bar. Guy opened the latter and he and Lydia went in.

It was a small room, with just four tables, two on either side of the fireplace, and padded benches. A bright fire burned in the grate, and the walls were decorated in a theme of cricket, showing photographs of batsmen and teams soberly posed and unsmiling. There were no other patrons in the room, but the landlord appeared at once and smiled a welcome. Guy led Lydia to the table furthest from the door and, after consulting her, gave the barman their order: a small glass of sarsaparilla for Lydia and a glass of ale for himself. Two or three minutes later Guy was sitting on the bench next to Lydia, their drinks beside them on the table. With the landlord having gone back to the public bar, they were alone in the room. Lydia had taken off her gloves, but left her unfastened cloak around her shoulders. Guy had taken off his coat and hat and laid them on the bench beside him, next to Lydia's umbrella and burlap bag.

From the direction of the other bar came the sounds of voices murmuring and the occasional chuckle. Guy took a swallow from his glass, then looked at Lydia over the rim. He gave a little shake of his head as he put the glass down on the table. 'I seem always to be bringing you to inns,' he said, 'and plying you with drinks.' He smiled. 'It's not the way I'd usually go on, but we can't stand around outside, not in weather like this.'

'Yes,' Lydia replied, 'at least it's warm and comfortable in here.'

Guy just looked at her for a moment or two, then he said, 'I can hardly believe we're here, you know. I couldn't wait for today. I was willing the time to go by.'

She thought, *These are not the words he should be using*, but at the same time they echoed what was in her own mind.

'I wasn't even sure,' he said, 'that you'd be here.'

'I told you I would be.'

'Yes, I know, but . . .' He sighed. 'Things happen. You might have had second thoughts.'

'Oh, I had those all right,' she said. 'And third, and fourth.' She paused briefly, then shook her head. 'I don't know what I'm doing here. Really I don't. There's nothing to be gained. I must be mad.'

'Oh, no – Lydia, don't say that.'

'It's true.

'Anyway –' He reached out, his hand hovering briefly just an inch above her own, and then withdrew it. 'Anyway, you are here,' he said. 'I'm so happy to see.' Gesturing to her glass, he said, 'Is your drink all right?'

'I haven't tried it,' she said.

'Would you like something else?'

'No, I asked for it just to have – something.' She shook her head. Another moment and she repeated, 'I don't know what I'm doing here.'

'Please – don't keep saying that.'

'But it's true. What good can come of this?'

'Can't we just – talk? For old time's sake?'

She nodded, but uneasily. Still that small voice kept repeating in her head that she should never have agreed to this meeting. Too much time had gone by, so much had happened. Things were not the same, their lives were not the same.

After a few moments of silence between them, he said, 'I've thought about you so often, Lydia. Wondered how you were, what you were doing.'

She wanted to say, *And I've thought about you, too*, but such words were fraught with danger, and instead she said, trying to sound almost casual: 'Tell me about yourself. Tell me what's been happening. Obviously you've been running the paper, but what about your own life? Your life when you're not at work?'

'Oh, I go on, from day to day,' he said. 'Some are full of excitement on the paper, others are quite dull.'

'What about your – your personal life? I'm assuming you're not – married.'

'No, I'm not married. I've felt no need to be. I did have – a relationship for a time, but I'm afraid it didn't amount to anything. She wanted marriage but – I wasn't ready, I suppose, and you can't keep a person hanging on for ever. She deserved better.'

They fell silent again, and into the quiet came a sudden eruption of laughter from the public bar, as if someone had told a good joke. When the sound had died away to a general murmur once more, Guy said:

'I don't mind telling you, it was the most terrific shock, to find that *you* were. Married, I mean.'

'Yes . . . it probably was.'

'Well, put yourself in my place. It was the last thing I expected.' He frowned. 'And now, seeing him, your husband – that's come as something of a surprise. He's not at all the way I imagined him.'

'You mean his being much older than I?'

'Well . . .'

'He is – older. Considerably older.'

The murmur from the public bar rose and fell. Lydia and Guy were untouched by it, aware only of themselves.

Guy said, smiling, breaking into Lydia's thoughts of doubt, 'Tell me, what of your sweet little sister, Ryllis? How is she getting along? Is she still with her young man, or has she moved on?'

Lydia put a hand to her mouth. He could not know. Of course he could not know. 'She – she's gone,' she said. 'I'm afraid she – she died.'

His face darkened with his frown of concern. 'Oh, Lydia, no. She was so – so full of life.'

'I know.' Lydia had to be careful or the tears would spill. 'She was caught in a field, by a bull. She didn't have a chance.' She lowered her head, casting her solemn face in shadow. 'I'd rather not talk about it . . . D'you mind?'

He said nothing. A minute went by, then, raising her head, she said, 'Why did you want to see me today? You said you had to see me, to talk to me.'

'Oh, yes – I had to.' He leaned slightly towards her. 'Once I'd gone into the shop and found you standing behind the counter – and then with you coming running after me in the snow – oh, I had to talk to you. All these years I've thought about you – and there you were – just when I was least expecting it.'

'Why didn't you write to me from Italy? I waited for a letter from you. It never came.'

'I know,' he said. 'I said I'd write, and I didn't.' He gave a deep sigh and said hesitantly, 'The truth is – I tried to put you out of my mind. I wasn't ready to settle – to commit myself. Even at my age. Which is why I had previously joined the army, I suppose – I wanted to travel and see the world and – and not have responsibilities. I just wasn't ready for commitment. And when my father lay so sick in his hospital bed in Florence I made a sort of promise to him. You see, he and my mother had great hopes for me – as regards marriage and other things. I – I won't go into it but – oh, I let myself be swayed. Then of course, he died, and I had so much to do, to occupy my time. I was in Italy for weeks, settling up the business, and when I came back I was learning so much, taking on so much in the way of responsibility – which was all new to me. There was my mother, too – who needed me so desperately following the death of my father. I did think of you, Lydia. Oh, please believe that – I thought of you so many times – but by the

353

time I came to look for you you'd gone. Then I found that you had married, and of course then it was too late.'

She found herself studying him as he sat beside her, one forearm along the table edge. She took in the line of his chin, his cheek, the almost thin, curving upper lip. How like him Davie was, she thought. The recognition, going through her mind, suddenly brought her back to the present and her situation. She must indeed be mad, she said to herself. What was she doing, sitting there in a public place talking to someone with whom she had had a love affair, a man who was the father of her child, a man who had come out of the past and back into her life? Only misery could come of it, and there had been enough of that already.

She could bear it no longer, and suddenly she was fumbling at the fastening of her cloak, taking up her gloves and pulling them on, her movements desperate and flurried. Guy looked at her with his eyes wide in surprise and consternation. 'You're not going, are you?'

'I must.' She touched at her hat. 'I must go for my train.'

'But –' he broke in, but got no further. She was rising from the bench and picking up the bag and umbrella and turning towards the door. She could not stay another moment. How could she put at risk all that she had gained? For that was what she was doing. 'Goodbye, Guy.' She threw the words over her shoulder, adding, 'I'm sorry. So sorry . . .' Then she was at the door, opening it and passing through.

In seconds Guy was putting on his hat and snatching up his coat. He followed her out and caught up with her just yards along the street.

'Lydia, please.' He reached out, one hand on her arm. 'Wait – we *must* talk.'

She gave a little shake, and his grip fell away. 'I shouldn't have agreed to meet you here today,' she said. 'I wish I hadn't.'

354

She went on, with Guy at her side getting into his coat as they went, first down the main street and eventually turning onto the road that led to the station.

'Lydia, don't do this,' Guy said. 'Please.'

'I've got to get back,' she replied. 'Alfred and Davie will be wondering where I am.'

'But Lydia –'

'There's nothing to talk about. Not now. It's too late. There's nothing we can say to one another that can make any difference.'

'But I care for you. You must know that.'

'Don't. Please. You'll only make matters worse.'

They had reached the station and together they walked onto the platform for the down line – and Lydia realised that of course Guy must take the same train, for the train that took her to Merinville would take him on to Redbury.

There were only three other travellers waiting on the platform, a solitary man and an elderly couple. Looking along the track, with relief Lydia saw the smoke rising that signalled the approach of the train. She could not wait to get back to Merinville and Alfred and her child.

The train was slowing, coming to a halt, steam belching out. Lydia stepped forward, snatching at the door handle of the nearest compartment. Then, as she pulled, Guy took the door and held it open. It was as he followed her inside and slammed the door behind him that she realised they were alone. Less than two minutes later the train was starting off again.

Lydia sat facing the front of the train, Guy opposite her. The next stop would be Lipscott, after which came Merinville. There was no corridor, so for the moment they were ensconced together, unable to be seen or heard by anyone else.

As the train rattled away and picked up speed, Guy

leaned forward a little and said, 'What is it? – fifteen minutes or so to Merinville?'

She nodded. 'Yes, about that.'

'I had something to say to you,' he said, 'but I didn't want to do it like this, fighting against time.'

She wanted to hear nothing. She turned away and looked at the trees and hedges rushing past, and willed the time to go by.

Then into the quiet between them he said simply, 'I *know*.'

She continued to gaze from the window, while in her breast her heart began, foolishly, to beat as if a little afraid.

'I know,' he said again, then a brief pause, and he added: 'I know about Davie.'

Her eyes flashed to him at this. 'Davie?' she said. 'You know what?'

'He is mine.'

Her heart seemed to thud against her ribs. Her hands were fists in her lap.

'Of course I know,' he said, and he leaned closer to her now, and reached out and took her hands and held them together between his own. For a moment she put up a little resistance as if she would pull away, but she did not, and remained poised, ready to move, like a bird set for flight.

'There's no mistaking whose son he is,' Guy said with a little wondering shake of his head. He gave a brief laugh, of happiness. 'Oh, God, no! He's my son, all right. I can see myself in him as a child. There's a photograph at home of me, but you could almost think it was Davie. It isn't only that, though.' He pressed Lydia's hands. 'He told me it was his birthday, his fourth birthday, and as I was walking back through the streets – just after you ran to me with my shoes – it suddenly came to me. Ever since seeing him there in the shop it was as if it was lodged somewhere in my mind, and

I worked out the time, the dates, and realised that it was so – that he had to be mine.'

Lydia sat there, and the seconds ticked by; she realised that he was waiting for her to respond, and she knew also that she had waited too long, and that she had given him the answer he expected.

'Yes.' She withdrew her hands from his touch, and lowered her eyes, unable to meet his glance so directly. She turned again towards the window, seeing nothing of the scenery that moved past. 'Yes, he is your son,' she said after a moment. 'I wanted to tell you that it was – was happening – that I was – expecting a child, but I couldn't. I tried, but you were abroad and although I wrote to you, you didn't receive my letter.'

He gave a deep frown. 'No, I didn't. I had no idea you'd written. When was this – that you wrote?'

'Oh – not long after you left for Italy. Three weeks.'

'I swear to you, I didn't receive it.'

'I know that.'

'How do you know?'

She hesitated before answering, then said, 'I saw your mother.'

'What? You saw my mother?'

'After I wrote to you at your home in Redbury I received a letter from her, asking me to go to see her.'

His eyes were wide in surprise. 'You went to the house?'

'Yes.'

'What – what happened?'

'Your mother told me that she and your father had hopes and plans for you – and those hopes and plans didn't include a liaison with an impecunious sales clerk.'

He frowned again. 'Well, I'm sure those might have been her sentiments, but she didn't say such a thing, surely.'

'Not in so many words, but that was her meaning.'

'Oh, Lydia –' He drew in his breath over his teeth. 'I don't know what to say.'

'She gave me money, too. At the time I wasn't sure why, and I still prefer not to think about that. I didn't cash the cheque; I tore it up.'

He sat back, wiping a hand across his forehead. 'Dear God . . .'

The light from the window reflected in his eyes, and she could see in them the shadow of his pain. The sight wrought an echo within herself, bringing a lump to her throat. Of course he had had no knowledge of what had gone on.

'Now,' she said, 'having a son of my own, I wonder how far I would go to protect him, to keep him in the life that I think he should have. Believe me, I think I have a better understanding of your mother now than I did at the time.'

'I'm sorry,' he said. 'I'm truly sorry. I had no idea.'

'Well – it's over. It's all in the past, I have my boy, and I wouldn't change that for anything in the world.'

The train was slowing; they were pulling into Lipscott. The thought came into Lydia's mind that other passengers might get into the compartment. If that happened there would be no further opportunity for conversation. The train's rhythm changed as the train slowed even more and eventually came to a halt. At once Guy got up from his seat, opened the window and leaned out as if looking for someone along the platform. To Lydia he said, murmuring over his shoulder, 'I don't want anyone else to get in.' His action worked, for the few travellers who came forward were put off by his presence there, and went on past to the next carriage door.

Soon the guard's whistle was blowing and the train was starting off again. Guy sat down and faced her once more.

'I understand so much more now,' he said. 'For instance why you married as you did.'

358

'Yes,' she said. She looked away from him again, out through the window. 'I was the most fortunate of women. To find Alfred was like a gift from God. He was there just when I needed him, and he asked no questions of me, made no demands. I don't mind telling you, I was desperate. I didn't know which way to turn. There seemed to be no way out.'

'It doesn't bear thinking of,' Guy said, 'your going through all that.'

She gave a little shrug of her shoulders. 'Yes – well, it's over with now.'

Taking in the view from the window she recognised familiar landmarks. She pulled her umbrella and the burlap bag closer to her on the seat. 'We'll soon be getting into Merinville. Any minute now. The distance between Merinville and Lipscott is very short.'

'Oh,' he said, giving a little gasp. 'I don't want you to go.'

'I haven't any choice.'

'Lydia,' he said, 'I must see you again.'

She hesitated. 'Why? What for?'

'Don't say that,' he said passionately. 'How can you ask that?'

'I must,' she said, and asked the question again: 'Why?'

'Because – because I have to. I knew nothing about any of this – these things you've told me.'

She leaned forward slightly, her eyes narrowing in earnestness. 'Guy, I know there are things you want to say, things you want to know, but it's too late for all that.'

'No – don't say that.'

'It has to be.' They were moving through the outskirts of Merinville; they were slowing. She touched at the collar of her cape, twitched at her bag. 'Here we are.'

'You can't leave like this,' he said. 'I'm getting off with you.'

359

'No!' Her voice was sharp in protest. 'Whatever you have to say to me, Merinville is not the place for it.'

'But, Lydia –'

The train was drawing in beside the platform now. Lydia picked up the bag and umbrella and got to her feet. She could not look at him, though she could see on the periphery of her vision that he was gazing up at her.

'Lydia,' he said again, 'you can't go like this.'

The train came to a complete stop, immediately followed by the sound of carriage doors being flung open. Guy stood up beside Lydia as she reached for the door handle. She said quickly, 'Don't get off, Guy. I beg you, don't.' The door opened under the pressure of her hand and she turned and flashed him a look of pleading. 'Good bye.'

The next moment she was stepping down onto the platform and pushing the door closed again. She flicked one final glance at his face, then turned and started away.

Chapter Twenty

Lydia arrived home to find that Alfred had got there before her, and was sitting with Davie in the conservatory, reading a storybook. It was the sound of Davie's laughter that drew her to them and she went through the drawing room to find them sitting together on the old bamboo couch, the book open on Alfred's knee. Tinny lay on the rug at Davie's feet. Alfred looked up as she entered and smiled at her over Davie's head.

'Everything all right?' he asked. 'Did you get everything?'

'Yes. I put the bag in your study. Mrs Castle and her daughter sent you their best wishes, and hope you'll be better soon.'

'Thank you.'

Davie said, 'Pappy and I are reading *Jack and the Beanstalk*. Pappy's reading a bit and then I'm reading a bit, but Pappy doesn't read it properly.' He turned to Alfred. 'You don't, do you, Pappy?'

Alfred put on an expression of shocked bewilderment. 'Me? I can't think what you're talking about. Of course I'm reading it properly.' Then he gave his attention to the book again, and resumed his reading – or supposed reading – from it, but with a swooping, exaggerated Welsh accent, and with little regard to the printed word:

'And Jack's mother cried, "Och! indeed to goodness, look you, Jack bach, you've brought no money for the cow but a handful of beans, look you, look you, boy-oh!"'

Davie shrieked with laughter, and then groaned. 'Pappy, that's not *right*! She doesn't say "look you"! You make her sound like Mr Williams, the baker.' This last was hardly surprising, since the said Mr Williams came from Swansea, and his heavy Welsh accent had hardly been affected by all his years in Wiltshire.

'Oh, no!' Alfred said, 'not like Mr Williams the baker!'

'Yes, like Mr Williams, the baker.'

'Oooohhhh, nooooo, Davie-wavie.'

'Oooohhhh, ye-e-es, Pappy-wappy.'

'You two,' Lydia said.

She watched them. Sometimes, she thought, they were like children of the same age, getting up silly voices and silly actions, like children having fun and at the same time trying to outdo one another. They appeared to her, frequently, and with no little surprise, as friends as well as father and son. She thought what a relatively happy life Davie led, secure in the love with which he was surrounded.

'Mammy,' Davie said now, 'Pappy says that in the summer we can go to Weston-super-Mare, and we can watch Punch and Judy on the sands.'

'Well, that will be wonderful, dear,' she said, nodding, and vaguely smiling, though only half her mind was on what the child was saying.

Alfred looked across at her, sensing some preoccupation. 'Are you all right?' he asked.

'All right?' She focused on him as if coming out of a dream. 'Yes, yes, I'm all right.' She smiled at him now, but the smile looked tentative. 'I'm surprised to find you at home so soon. I thought you'd still be at the shop. It's not like you to leave so early.'

'I didn't feel like working late today,' he said. 'I thought I'd rather come back, have some tea and see my boy.' He reached up and ran a hand through Davie's hair.

Tinny got up at this point, stretched and moved to Lydia, his tail wagging.

'Look at him,' Alfred said. 'He's looking for comfort.'

'Why should he be looking for comfort?' Lydia said.

Davie said, 'Because he's in disgrace.'

'Oh? What for?'

'Because he ran away, and didn't come back for ages.'

'Well,' Lydia said, 'he looks to be all right.' She half turned in the doorway. 'I think I'll go and make myself a cup of tea.' To Alfred she said, 'Would you like another?'

'No, thank you.'

As she started away, Alfred said, 'There's a letter for you, in the hall.'

'Oh, I must have walked past it.'

'I think it's from Evie.'

'Oh – she'll be writing about Sunday. I've asked her and Hennie if they'd like to come over.'

In the hall Lydia took up the letter, opened it and read Evie's words, pleased to learn that her friend would be coming to visit.

As she replaced the letter in its envelope she heard from the drawing room Davie's voice as he said, 'Pappy, I think I'd better read the book. You're not getting it right,' and the sound of Alfred's laughter rang out in the room.

There was a full moon that night. It shone through a crack in the nursery curtains, making a little shaft of light across Davie's bed. Lydia bent over and looked down at him in the soft glow made up of the moonlight and the little nightlight that burned on the bureau, out of his reach. How peaceful he looked. There was a chair by the bed and silently she drew it nearer and sat down.

Davie's face was a pale blur as she studied him, but she could still make out the shape of it, the set of his features. How like Guy he was. It was something she had come to accept; nevertheless there were times when it struck her anew, and she became aware of it as if she were learning new news.

She got up, leaned down and kissed him lightly on the forehead. 'Goodnight, my son.'

Turning, she moved to the window, lifted back the curtain another inch or two and peered out. The sky was of the deepest blue, and fine trails of cloud, like ribbons of smoke, drifted across the moon's white face, She thought again of Guy, and the moon they had watched together that night. This same moon. This same sky. She thought of Lord Byron's poem that Guy had read aloud in the little garden next to the square in Redbury that day. She had read it many times since.

She sighed, let the curtain fall back in place and turned away.

At Davie's bed she leaned down once again and looked at him in the dim light. Then, breathing his name, she straightened and left the room.

From the nursery she went downstairs to the first floor. There, next to the master bedroom was situated her little sewing room. She hesitated for a second at the door, then opened it and went inside. The moonlight filled the room and she could easily see her way to the lamp that stood next to her sewing basket on a small table. Taking a match from its box she struck it and set the flame to the lamp's wick, and then by the lamp's light turned to the shelves of books behind the small table. Her hand located the volume at once, and she drew it out and laid it down on the table beside the lamp. She opened it to the page and read the poem there:

So, we'll go no more a-roving
So late into the night,
Though the heart be still as loving,
And the moon be still as bright.

For the sword outwears its sheath,
And the soul wears out the breast,
And the heart must pause to breathe,
And love itself have rest.

Though the night was made for loving,
And the day returns too soon,
Yet we'll go no more a-roving
By the light of the moon.

As she read the familiar words, the tears stung at her eyes and ran silently down her cheeks.

Evie and Hennie arrived from Capinfell on Sunday soon after twelve, and Evie at once set to work, helping Lydia prepare the dinner. Mrs Starling and Alice and Ellen did not come in now on Sundays, so all the domestic work fell to Lydia on this day. When dinner was finished and the dishes and pots were washed, the women and the children and the dog set out for a leisurely walk. Alfred had declined the invitation to join them. Replete after his meal, and also experiencing a little discomfort from his gouty foot, he had declared himself ready to stretch out on the sofa while they were gone. 'You enjoy your stroll,' he had said. 'I'd rather be like those people on the Continent and take a siesta.' So they had left him and set out together.

It had been several weeks since Lydia and Evie had last met, and they were happy to have one another's company again. Evie had remarried a year ago, her new husband one Jack Hasper, a farmhand, like her first. Now she was expecting a child, her belly just beginning to swell the waist of her grey cotton skirt.

It was a beautiful day for a walk, with the sun shining down out of a sky that was almost clear, while a light breeze stirred the leaves of the silver birches at the side of the lane. On the common a group of boys were playing football, and Davie came to a stop and looked longingly at them, as if he would like to join in their fun. When the inflated pig's bladder came sailing through the air and landed near Davie's feet, he looked round at Lydia and then at the boys who came in pursuit, as if seeking their approval. 'Come on, then,' one of them yelled, smiling. 'Lob it 'ere.' Davie took a run at it and kicked out, and the bladder sailed into the air a few feet, prompting a small cheer from the boys. The ball was taken by a tall, freckled-faced lad who said, 'Thanks,' and gave Davie a thumbs-up. Davie was proud, and turned and grinned at Lydia, who nodded and smiled back. 'Well done,' she said.

A man came along on horseback, and Lydia recognised him as Mr Whittier, a neighbouring farmer. He also recognised Lydia, and raised his hat as he drew nearer. As he came level he pulled up his horse and turned to her in the saddle.

'Afternoon, missis.'

'Good afternoon,' Lydia responded, while Evie returned his nod with a murmured greeting of her own.

'Lovely afternoon, yes?' the man said.

Lydia agreed that it was, and Whittier jerked a thumb back over his shoulder, and said, 'I only want to ask you to keep away from my big field today. Specially with your dog 'ere. Only, me sheep are lambin' and I don't want 'em worried.'

'Oh, of course not,' Lydia said at once. 'I understand perfectly.' She looked over at Tinny, who stood a few feet away. 'We won't go near the field, depend on it. In any case,

Tinny wouldn't misbehave – would you, Tinny?' At the sound of his name the dog pricked up his ears.

'And I should warn you,' Whittier went on, 'that in the small paddock over there,' he jerked his thumb again, 'the bull is loose. So for your own sake, don't go near 'im. He's a crotchety old devil at the best of times, and is at 'is worst right now.' Another touch at his hat and the man was riding away.

Lydia stood looking after him, his words about the bull still sounding in her ears, while visions of Ryllis in the hospital bed hovered in her mind.

'What's up, Mammy?' Davie said, and Lydia came out of her dream and said to him, 'Nothing, darling. It's all right. Come on, let's carry on, shall we?'

The women, the children and the dog made their way over the grass where all around them wild flowers grew in abundance – dandelions, celandines and ragged robin, while in the lea of the brambles there were wood anemones. In the more rugged areas of the heathland the gorse flowers grew yellow and sturdy.

Over beyond the common they could see the pastureland where Whittier's sheep were grazing. They continued on, skirting the sheep field, and taking a path through the adjoining meadow, while Lydia kept a careful eye on Tinny. The dog was well trained, though, and at her command kept obediently at her heels. She was relieved and pleased at his good behaviour, for the stories were legion of the damage that a renegade dog could do to sheep and cattle.

After they had skirted a field of barley, they came to a little woodland, and here in its shade they came to a stop, sitting down in the soft grass. 'We'll rest for a while and then start back,' Lydia said, and Davie groaned and said he wasn't ready to rest yet. 'Can Hennie and I go exploring in the wood?' he asked, and Lydia said, yes, if Hennie would like to go with him.

Hennie, who was now eight years old and behaved with Davie as if she were his big sister, said yes at once, and together the two got up and, calling Tinny to them, made their way towards the woods behind.

Lydia and Evie, turning as they sat, watched them go off, and Lydia called out after them, 'Don't go too far away,' to which Evie added, 'No – and Hennie, don't pick any flowers; they'll only be dead before we're halfway home.' A few moments later the children, followed by the dog, had disappeared among the trees.

'They won't come to any harm,' Lydia said, and Evie agreed and then added, 'Davie is growing so.'

'Yes, he is,' Lydia said. 'I can't keep up with him, the way he outgrows his clothes.'

The two women took off their hats, and Lydia stretched her arms above her head and sighed. Turning to Evie she smiled. 'How are you feeling?'

Evie laid her hand on the gentle swell of her belly. 'Very well, thank you.'

'You've looked so much happier these past months.'

'Have I?'

'Yes, you have. I can see your happiness there, a contentment.'

'Well – I suppose that's what I'm feeling.'

'How does Jack feel about the new baby?'

'Oh – he's very excited, but no more than I am. I didn't think it would happen again.'

'What? Marriage? A new baby?'

'Yes. After losing Bill like that, I don't think I expected anything – but now, everything's different again.'

'It was time, Evie.'

Evie smiled. 'Yes, perhaps it was.' She paused. 'What about you? Did you ever think you might like a second child?'

Lydia considered this for a moment, then said, 'I know

it's been Alfred's wish, but it's just – never happened.'

'Are you sorry?'

'Well, for Alfred I am – but we've got Davie, and we both love him so much.'

'That's obvious to see – and the way Alfred dotes on him . . .'

'Oh, he does, he does. I see other fathers are so strict with their children, and I suppose it's the way they're brought up to be, but not Alfred. He's not like that at all. He loves the boy so much. I don't think he could love Davie more if he were his own child.'

Evie said, 'I don't know how you feel about Alfred, but you know – speaking for myself, there's something I wouldn't have believed possible, that you can love for a second time – but you can.'

Lydia looked at her, taking in her words, then said with a shake of her head, '*Twice*. Oh, heavens, with all the heartache it brings, I should think once is quite enough.'

Evie could see no gladness in Lydia's face, but Lydia smiled, as if casting the moment behind her, and said, 'Jack will miss you today, I should think.'

'Yes, I suppose he will.'

'He'll be having his dinner at his mother's, did you say?'

'Yes, that's right. So there's someone who'll be very pleased, anyway. Having her boy back for a little while, and being able to make a fuss of him.'

From the direction of the wood came Hennie's laughter ringing out. Lydia smiled at the sound and said, 'They're having fun.' Then she added, 'It's good to see Hennie looking so well, and she's such a pretty girl.'

'Thank you.'

'She gets on with Jack, does she?'

'Oh, yes, she does, and she needed a father. He helps her with her school exercises and – oh, he's so good with her.'

Lydia nodded. 'Like Alfred and Davie. Sometimes to see

them together it's – oh, it's lovely. Not the way it was with Ryllis and me and our father. We never felt close to him. It was almost as if he was afraid of it – closeness. Though I suppose he meant well.'

'No doubt.'

'I'm just so glad it's different with Alfred and Davie. I would hate it if anything should happen to – to spoil things. It wouldn't be right to allow anything to happen.'

Evie frowned. 'Of course not. What could happen, anyway?' She looked quizzically at Lydia, who, aware of her gaze, lowered her head. Then, after a moment, Lydia looked up at her and round about, taking in the woods. There was no sign or sound of the children. 'I saw him,' she said.

Evie frowned, not understanding. Then realisation came. '*Him*?' she whispered. 'You mean – Davie's father? Guy?'

Lydia swiftly put a finger to her lips and gave a nod. 'Yes.'

'How – how did that happen?'

'He came into the shop while I was there, serving. It was the greatest shock.'

'I'm sure it must have been.'

'He saw Davie too – and Alfred.'

'Did you have a chance to talk? I suppose not, being in the shop . . .'

'No – but I had to run after him with a package he left behind. We were able to have a few words then.' She paused. 'And afterwards – I met him again.'

'By accident again?'

'No. Not by accident.'

'Oh . . .'

'No, not by accident at all. I had to go to Pershall Dean, and we arranged to meet there, at the station.' Looking at Evie she could see a little flash of wonder in her eyes – and a look of doubt, as if she questioned the wisdom of such actions. 'I know,' Lydia said quickly, 'I know you think I'm mad to have done such a thing but . . .' She halted for a second, then added, 'I had to see him. He wanted me to, and he was so insistent. I had to go. I – I couldn't say no. I just couldn't.'

'Oh, Lyddy.'

'I know. Perhaps I was a fool. That's what I thought when I was there with him. We went to this little inn, but we couldn't really talk. I had to get out.'

'So – what happened?' Evie said.

'I left. I thought, *What am I doing here?* But he came after me – and we caught the train together. I got off here at Merinville and he went on to Redbury.' She sat up a little straighter now, then leaned forward and put her hands up, covering her face. When she lowered them again she said, so softly that Evie could only just hear her: 'He knows.'

'He knows what?'

'About Davie. That Davie's his – his son.' She barely mouthed the words.

'Oh.'

'I didn't tell him. I didn't need to tell him. He saw the boy and saw the likeness – and he also worked out the time. It was Davie's birthday when he came into the shop and so it was easy for him.' She sighed. 'God – I didn't know what to do. And he wants to see me again.'

'Did you agree?'

'No. I said it wasn't possible. Oh, Evie, I daren't see him again. I dare not.'

Evie sat silent, gazing at her.

'I mean,' Lydia said, 'what could come of it? Nothing but unhappiness, don't you think?'

Evie said, 'You don't sound very sure, Lyddy.'

'Of course I'm sure.'

'You almost sound as if – as if you'd like to see him again.'

Lydia gave a deep sigh and turned her head, gazing off unseeingly into the distance. 'I don't know what I want.'

'Surely,' Evie said, 'You haven't got a choice.'

'No, I don't suppose I have.'

'Of course you haven't. You said yourself, what would come of it – your seeing him again?'

'I think about him so much,' Lydia said. 'Ever since he walked into the shop he's been on my mind – even more than he usually is, for he's never that far away.'

'Oh, Lyddy,' Evie said, 'this is terrible for you.'

'There shouldn't be any questions in my mind,' Lydia said. 'I shouldn't be wondering what to do. I should know. I *do* know.'

Into the silence between them came the distant sound of Davie's voice yelling out something unintelligible, the words light on the spring air. Lydia looked towards the sound for a moment, then turned back to face Evie.

'I don't even know why he wants to see me,' she said, and then bravely she added, 'Or why I want to see him.'

Evie nodded. 'So you do want to see him.'

Lydia gave the briefest nod. 'Oh, Evie, I can't help it. I do. I do.' She shook her head. 'But I'm not going to.'

There came a burst of laughter and the sound of feet in the undergrowth, and then Davie and Hennie and the dog came running from among the trees. The time for quiet conversation was over.

A week and a half later Lydia set out once more for Pershall Dean. As before, she carried the burlap bag with the new batch of sewing to be done by Mrs Castle and her daughter. It had rained the previous day, and that Wednesday had dawned grey, but now the clouds had gone. Lydia set off from the shop just before three o'clock, stepping out smartly to get to the railway station. Her train came in on time, and a relatively short while later she was in Pershall Dean and making her way beside the green.

As she anticipated, the kettle was on in the kitchen at the Castles' little cottage when she arrived, and after the fortnightly business concerning the sewing had been dealt with, she sat and drank a cup of tea with the ladies. Afterwards, she wished them good day and took her departure.

She had only gone a few paces from the end of the lane when she heard someone call her name.

Even as she turned to the sound she knew whose voice it was, and there was Guy, coming towards her from the shade of the trees that grew on the edge of the green. She waited until he had reached her side, her face holding all the questions that were unspoken on her lips.

'I've been waiting for you,' he said. 'I got here before you and watched you walk past me into the lane.' He shook his head. 'I thought you'd never get through with your business.'

'But – how did you know that I – ?' she began, then broke off and gave a nod. 'Of course, I mentioned it, didn't I. I said I'd be here in a fortnight.'

'Yes.'

'What – what are you doing here?' she asked after a moment, though she knew the answer well.

'I had to see you. I couldn't leave it like it was. I've got to talk to you.'

'What is there to say? There's nothing to say.'

'Please. Lydia.'

She could have said no, and been adamant, but she remained standing there. He took her stillness for acquiescence, looked around and then gestured over towards the duck pond where on its bank stood an old wooden bench, half hidden behind a screen of cascading weeping willow.

'Please,' he said, 'can we sit down?'

She turned and looked over towards the bench, hesitating.

'Please,' he said.

She nodded. 'Well – just for a minute.'

In silence they walked over onto the grass and made their way to the pond. Guy saw her seated on the bench, then sat down beside her. For some moments neither spoke, then turning to her, he said:

'Lydia, if you knew how I've been waiting for this moment, looking forward to it . . . I could hardly sleep last night for thinking of it, that I would be seeing you today. My greatest fear was that your husband might come instead of you.'

'No,' she said, 'his foot's still troubling him.'

'Don't you sometimes bring Davie?'

'I have done, but the weather seemed uncertain. He's at home with his nurse.'

'He's a splendid little fellow.'

'Yes, he is.'

Silence between them. On the surface of the pond a mallard drake swam, dipping its head under the water among the reeds close to the bank. A damselfly came skimming by, its wings shimmering.

'We had no real chance to talk the last time,' Guy said. 'You went off in such a hurry – and I had so much I wanted to say.' He hesitated just for a second, then added, 'I love you, Lydia. I love you.'

'Oh, don't – please.' She raised a hand to her mouth. Already things were going too far, moving too fast. 'Don't say such things, Guy. It only makes it worse.'

'You called me by my name,' he said. 'I never thought to hear that again.'

She looked away from him, over the water, but really unseeing, only aware of the man beside her.

'I've thought about you so much,' he went on after a moment, 'and I don't mean just these past two weeks. Though God knows, you've been so much on my mind during that time. I haven't been able to sleep for thinking about you – and thinking about our son.' He sighed. 'If only I could go back and change things. I'd do it all so differently.'

'We can't,' she said.

'No, we can't.' He sighed again. 'But I find myself doing that all the time – thinking *What if? What if?* – and it does no good, of course. It's just another kind of torment.' He paused. 'Look at me, Lydia – please.'

She turned to him after a moment's hesitation and saw the pleading, the anguish in his eyes.

'Did you ever think of me over these years?' he said.

'Did I ever think of you?' Her eyes widened in surprise at his question. 'How can you ask such a thing? Every time I look at my son I see you. Oh, don't ask if I ever think of you.'

'I've grown up a little over these past years,' he said. 'When I look back at myself at that time when we met, when we were together, I was so young. I didn't know what I wanted. Though, as I said to you, I didn't want commitment. I wanted the carefree life that I'd known – and I suppose I wanted you as a part of it, that carefree life. Perhaps I wanted you without any responsibility going along with it. It's hard to think now what was going through my mind. And then of course there were my parents. They had their plans and dreams for me.' He sighed. 'I've told you all this.'

Lydia said nothing, but waited for him to go on.

He looked down at his clenched hands. 'My father had always been so good to me, and I wanted so much to do the right thing by him. Can you understand that?'

'Yes.'

'I wanted so to please him, especially when he was lying there, so ill, and perhaps I believed him when he told me that I'd get over you. What experience of life and love did I have?' He gave a little shake of his head. 'But I didn't – get over you. I never have. I don't think I ever will.'

'Guy – don't talk like that.'

'I had eventually begun to think that I would – get over you. I had tried another relationship. It hadn't worked, granted, but at least I was able to give my mind to other things – and then I saw you, in the shop, and I realised that all along I'd just been fooling myself. You and I – we'd known each other for such a little space of time – just for that one week – but it was enough. After that time you were always there, Lydia, always there.'

She said nothing. A swallow came skimming over the water and vanished beyond the trees.

'You don't know what it's like,' Guy said. 'Loving, wanting . . .'

'Don't I?' she said.

'Oh, Lydia . . .' He raised his head and looked at her. 'Is it possible that you've felt the same things?'

She could not meet his eyes now and she turned her face away. Before her the mallard still dipped among the reeds and the damselfly hovered. *Yes*, she wanted to say, and give way to the feelings, so long kept down. *Yes, it's true, I love you. I've loved you all the time. I think I've loved you since we met in the market square that day – and I've kept on loving you.* She said nothing, however. Guy's eyes dwelt on her, and then he had moved closer to her and his arms, so strong, were coming around her. And she gave herself up to the wonderful safety, feeling herself drawn against him, feeling her cheek against the rough fabric of his coat, smelling the warm scent of him, familiar after all this time. It was like coming home. She wanted the moment never to end.

'Oh, Lydia, Lydia . . .'

376

He breathed the words as he held her close, and she revelled in the sound and in his touch.

She murmured against him, weakly, 'Please, Guy – someone will see us.'

'No,' he said, his voice soothing, soft. 'There's no one about, and even if there is, no one knows me here, no one knows you – only your two ladies, and they won't come out.' His hand lay on her back, moving once or twice in gentle, soothing strokes. She could have been a child again, being comforted after a fall or a bad dream. 'Tell me,' he said. 'Tell me that you love me too.'

At his words it was all she could do not to say *Yes, yes! I love you too*, but she held back, and said instead, her voice muffled against the grey tweed of his coat, 'Whatever we say to one another now – it can't make any difference. It can't change anything.'

He drew back a little from her so that he could look down into her face. 'No! Oh, no, don't say that.'

'It's true,' she said. 'Nothing that is said between us now can make any difference.' She felt tears welling, and she fought to hold them back. 'We've got to go on as if – as if none of this has happened. We haven't any choice.'

He held her hands, both hands between his own. 'I know what I'd *like* to happen.'

'What's that?'

'I want to be with you. I want to be with you always. You and Davie. The two of you. You complete my life.'

'Guy –'

'I'd like to start a new life with you both, a new life for the three of us – and if not here then somewhere else. Somewhere far away if need be. You – and my son.'

'Yes,' she said, 'your son. Davie is your son – but he is Alfred's son also.' She looked into his eyes as she spoke. 'He is Alfred's son by dint of all the love and caring that Alfred has given him. Alfred gave him a future when he had none.

Alfred gave him a father's love when there was none. He is Alfred's as much as he is mine.' She shook her head. 'I could never leave Alfred after all he's done for me. He gave me a name. He gave your son a name. He saved me from shame and degradation – and you don't need me to tell you that those things were very real possibilities in my life. He saved me from all that, and we have a good marriage. Oh, we have our little disagreements, and on very rare occasions we say harsh things, but those things are never so harsh that they are past easy forgiveness. He loves me. He loves me, and he shows that love in a thousand ways.' She turned on the bench and drew her bag and umbrella towards her. 'I must go.'

'Not yet.'

'I have to.'

As she rose he got up beside her, but she put out her hand, staying him. 'Oh, don't come with me, Guy. Please.'

'But –'

'Please don't.'

'But we can't leave things like this.'

'We have no choice. Our time for choices is past. At least mine is.'

He shook his head. 'Whatever you say, I'm not going to let it go like this.' He reached out and caught her wrist. 'I shall be here two weeks from now, and if you don't come here then I shall go to Merinville. I must see you.'

'No – please. Please don't.' Her voice breaking, she snatched her arm from his grasp and turned and hurried away.

Chapter Twenty-One

Thursday was market day in Merinville, so the shop was expected to be busy. Alfred left the house at the usual time, going ahead of Lydia, who would follow a little later. Before she left she spent a short while with Davie, who was somewhat fractious and irritable, and giving signs of a developing cold. Eschewing breakfast – he had no appetite – he clung to her in an unaccustomed way, saying that he did not want her to go out. She had to, she said; she had to go and help Pappy in the shop. However, she promised, she would try to get back a little earlier. She left him then in the capable care of Ellen.

As expected, business at the shop was brisk. On Thursdays people came in from miles around, not only the farmers, but their wives and children too. The streets were full of people, and there were many who found their way to Canbrook's draper's. Along with Mr Federo, Miss Angel and Alfred, Lydia was kept bustling about, giving all her attention to the work at hand, and having little time to think about personal matters.

In the short period when the shop was closed for the half-hour dinner break, she and Alfred and Miss Angel sat in the back room and ate the sandwiches they had brought, and drank the mugs of tea that they had poured from the large brown teapot. Mr Federo did not join them, for he had gone out to a café a short distance away.

While Miss Angel sat on one side of the table with her corned beef sandwich, Lydia and Alfred sat on the other with their sandwiches of ham and cheese, made up for them that morning by Mrs Starling. Making full use of the time, Miss Angel's greying head and steel-rimmed spectacles were bent over a novel, while Alfred spent the time consulting one of his order books. Lydia merely ate, immersed in her thoughts.

After a while Alfred closed the ledger and pushed it aside. Taking a drink, he looked at Lydia, silent beside him. She saw his glance on the rim of her vision, but did not turn to him. He took another bite from his sandwich, but chewed without relish. When he had finished, he pushed his plate aside, brushed a crumb from his waistcoat and took up the morning paper. Miss Angel murmured an excuse me, and left the table and went out of the room into the yard. As the back door closed behind her, Alfred turned to Lydia again and said, 'Are you all right?'

'What?' Her eyes widened slightly as if she were coming out of a dream. 'What did you say?'

'I asked you if you were all right.'

'Yes, I'm fine, thank you.' She smiled at him.

'Where were you? You were miles away.'

'Oh, just – daydreams.'

She had been thinking of Guy. She had been thinking of him as he had been the day before in Pershall Dean – suddenly appearing as she had turned out of the lane, and then as he had sat beside her on the bench before the duck pond. She could see it all so clearly in her mind's eye, the damselfly skimming the water's surface, the mallard dipping its head in his search for food. She could hear Guy's voice too, feel his arms fold around her as he drew her to him. Alfred, of course, must never know that such a thing had happened. She had been a fool, she told herself; she should not have consented to sit with Guy beside the pond. She should not have been drawn into conversation. She should not have listened to him. She should have just walked on and forbidden him to talk to her. Being close to him as she had for those brief moments on the bench, she had felt all her strength and resolve draining away, and she knew that under other circumstances she would not be able to guarantee her control.

Worse, he had told her that he would wait for her again in a fortnight when she went to Pershall Dean – but she must never, never see him again. She must tell him that no further meeting could ever take place. She had built a life for herself with Alfred and Davie, and she could take no chance of jeopardising any part of it.

'Are you sure you're all right . . . ?' Alfred was speaking again. 'You didn't sleep that well last night, did you?'

'Not too well.'

'Maybe you should go home a bit earlier today. Get a bit of rest. As Davie's not so well, he'll be glad to have you home.'

'Oh, no doubt he will.' She nodded. 'Yes, I'd like to go back a bit sooner . . .' She frowned. 'But we're so busy.'

'We'll manage.'

As she turned from him he added, 'I'll pop back home meself a bit later, to have a quick cup o' tea and a break. The others'll hold the fort.'

It was like fate stepping in, Lydia thought as she walked back along beside the river: Alfred's telling her to go back home well before the shop closed. It was only three o'clock, and she would have some time to herself. Davie would be having his afternoon nap now – unless his cold had interfered with his routine. She hoped he was sleeping, for she had already made up her mind how she would use this time that she had been granted.

On entering the house she took off her cape and hat and went quietly up to the nursery where she found Davie asleep in his bed. Ellen put down her sewing and rose from her seat by the window as Lydia entered. Lydia at once put a finger to her lips. 'How is he?' she asked in a whisper, and the nurse replied, also keeping her voice low, that he was still fractious, and that he had only been asleep for a short while. Lydia nodded and went from the room.

It was twenty minutes to four. Tinny was nowhere around. He usually came to greet her on her appearing at the house, but today there was no sign of him. She went into the drawing room, to the little writing table near one of the French windows, drew out the chair and sat down. Then, she pulled pen and paper towards her, and after two or three aborted attempts, she eventually wrote:

9th May 1895

Dear Guy,

I am having to steal these moments to write this letter to you, and I must be brief as the time I have is short. I have to tell you – and there is no way of being kind – that we can never meet again, must never meet again. I beg you, therefore, do not come to Pershall Dean as you stated your intentions of doing. In any case there would be no point in your doing so, for from now on Alfred or one of his assistants will be visiting the seamstresses in the village; I shall no longer be making the journey. Also, do not think of ever coming to the shop again. My situation is such that I cannot risk any further meeting, and if you have the slightest feeling for me you will do as I ask. As you yourself mentioned, we only knew one another for a handful of days – and whatever feeling there was between us during that time is long past and cannot have any bearing upon the present.

Feelings change over the years, but even if mine had not, you and I would have no future together. For – simply put – I am not free. I have other claims upon my heart and my devotion, and I would do nothing that would put at risk these treasures and all else that I now have in my life. I have so much – and because of this, I *owe* so much. I have the love of a good man, and it is through him that I have my darling son and am able to give my son the life that he has.

Guy, my life is mapped out, but yours on the other hand is still there to be trod. I beg you, make the most of it, as I hope to make the most of mine.

You will not hear from me again, and therefore it would be better if you put me quite out of your mind. If, however, you should ever think on the past, then just remember that you always have the warm wishes of

Your friend

Lydia

She set down her pen, blotted the ink, then picked up the page and read it through. It was crude and brusque, she thought, and inelegant in its phrasing, but it would have to do. She put it in an envelope from the drawer and wrote upon it Guy's name. She had no struggle to think of his address, for she had never forgotten it. A postage stamp in the corner and it was ready.

Her cape and hat were where she had left them in the hall and she put them on. Then, taking up the letter, she left the house and walked to the nearby church where she posted it in the box that was set into the cemetery wall. Having done so she stood there for a few moments without moving, looking down at the slot in the red-painted iron post box into which it had just disappeared. It was done. There was no retrieving it. Tomorrow the letter would be in Guy's hands, and he would read the words that she had written. True or not, they would be there in his hands, before his eyes.

She turned away, and set off back the way she had come.

Ten or twelve minutes later, as she walked around the side of the house into the stable yard, Tinny came trotting towards her, his tail wagging. He would have jumped up at her in his welcome but she bade him stay. Alarmed, she saw that he had blood around his muzzle, and she said at once, 'Oh, Tinny, you've been in a fight! You poor thing. Are you hurt?' She bent to him, avoiding his licking tongue, and looked at the bloody area around his nose and behind his right ear. 'Be still, be still, and sit down,' she commanded him gently, and he sat obediently. Gently moving his ear she examined the area around it. She could see no cuts or tears. 'Well, you seem to be all right,' she said as she straightened, 'but you're a mess nevertheless, and I'm not letting you into the house looking like that. Mrs Starling'll have a fit.' She bent again and softly patted the top of his head. 'Stay there, like a good boy. Stay there.'

Inside, she quickly took off her cape and hat, then put on an old apron and went into the kitchen where Mrs Starling was at work. 'Tinny's been in a fight,' Lydia said as she took a bucket and an old rag from underneath the sink.

Mrs Starling replied, 'Yes, so I saw. I wouldn't let him in the house.'

Taking the bucket and rag, Lydia went back outside and drew water from the well. Tinny came to her as she busied herself, and then stood quietly as she dipped the rag into the water and sluiced him down. 'There – you'll look as good as new,' she said as he moved away and shook himself, 'but I wonder,' she added, 'what the other dog looks like.'

She had carried the rest of the water over to a border and was about to empty it on to the flowers when she heard the sound of horse's hooves on the cobbles. Looking across the yard, she saw Farmer Whittier riding up from the road. Tinny looked around curiously at the same moment, and stood alert, waiting as the horse and rider came on.

When Whittier drew near the back door he dismounted,

384

led his horse over to a side post and hitched up the reins. Then, turning to Lydia, he touched at his hat and said, 'You're just the one I come to see. You and another.'

Lydia was mystified. 'I and another?' she said. 'Who else would that be, Mr Whittier?'

The man turned and looked at the dog. 'That fellow there, that's who.'

'Tinny? But – but what could you want with Tinny?' Then in another moment she clapped her hands to her face. 'Oh, don't tell me he's been fighting with one of your dogs! Oh, dear! Oh, I'm sorry, Mr Whittier. He's just this minute got back with blood on him, and it was obvious to me that he'd been fighting. I've just been giving him a wash. He's not usually the kind to –'

She got no further, for Whittier stepped forward and said impatiently, cutting her off, 'Blazes, missis, 'e ain't been fightin'. No sir. He's been at my damned sheep.'

Lydia clenched her hands before her. 'Oh, God, no.'

The man nodded. 'He damn well 'as. My sheep 'ave been lambin' and I went into my field and saw the carnage there.' The flesh around his mouth was white with his passion. 'I got two dead lambs and a sheep as I'll 'ave to put down for mutton, and it's your blasted dog that's done it. I'm sorry for my language, ma'am, but that's the truth on it.'

Lydia could scarcely take in the awful news. 'But – but how can you be certain that it was our dog?' she asked. 'There are so many dogs in the area.'

'How? I seen the devil with me own eyes just last week, didn't I? And that wasn't the first time either. I knew who 'e belonged to as I've seen 'im out walkin' with you, so I knew where to come.'

'But Mr Whittier,' Lydia said, tears welling in her eyes, 'he wouldn't do such a thing. He never would.'

'You just said yourself that he come in with blood over 'im.'

'Yes, but –'

'Well, there's a certain way to find out, missis, and it won't take long. 'Ave you got some butter?'

'Butter?'

'Yeh. Be so kind as to get some butter, will you?'

She did not move, but remained there on the cobbles. How she wished that Alfred would return. She said quickly, 'Look, Mr Whittier, my husband will be back home soon. Couldn't this wait until he gets back?'

'I'd be grateful if you'd get me some butter, ma'am,' he said shortly.

Lydia could do nothing but obey. Her skirt swirled as she turned and headed for the door. She went inside and while Mrs Starling looked at her, frowning slightly, she went to the larder and took the butter in its earthenware dish and went back out.

As she stepped forward she lifted the lid and went to hold out the dish to the man. He did not wait, however, but reached out and took it from her. She watched as he dipped in his other hand and scooped out a large piece of the yellow butter. He thrust the dish back into Lydia's hand then turned and called to the dog: 'Here, boy – come here, boy,' bending slightly and patting his knee with his free hand. Tinny remained where he was, and the man turned to Lydia and said, 'What's 'is name? What d'you call 'im?'

'Tinny.'

'Tinny?'

'Yes.'

He bent and patted his knee again. 'Tinny? Come on, boy. There's a good boy.'

Tinny wagged his tail and trotted across the yard.

'Here ye go, boy.' Whittier stooped and held out his hand with the large piece of butter sitting on his forefingers. 'Here ye go, boy. Good boy.'

Tinny did not need a second bidding. At once he

stretched out his head and took the butter from the man's hand in one swallow. Then, tail wagging, he licked the remaining traces from the man's fingers.

Whittier straightened and took a handkerchief from his pocket and wiped his hand dry. 'Now we'll see,' he said.

Tinny stayed there for a moment then moved away across the yard. 'Don't let 'im wander off,' Whittier said to Lydia, and she called out to the dog, 'Don't go off, Tinny. Come here, there's a good boy.'

Tinny stopped, turned and padded over to her. As he did so, Lydia became vaguely aware of Mrs Starling's curious face at the scullery window.

'Tell 'im to stop there,' Whittier said.

Lydia nodded and stretched out her hand to the dog. 'Stay, Tinny. Sit. Sit down.'

Obediently the dog sat.

Lydia looked from Tinny to the man, but Whittier kept his eyes only on the dog. The seconds ticked by, and Tinny remained sitting on the cobbles near the back step, looking up at Lydia, as if waiting for another word from her.

Then all at once the dog gave a sort of cough, got to his feet, stretched out his head and retched. Lydia took a step forward, but Whittier put out a hand and said sharply, 'Leave 'im be.'

Tinny retched again, his sides heaving, his head jerking, and then suddenly, after one great spasm, he vomited violently onto the cobbles.

Lydia looked down at the disgusting mess and, gasping, put a hand to her mouth. Whittier ignored her and stepped forward. Bending, he put out a hand and pushed the dog to the side. Then, with the same hand, he dug into the vomit, fingers stirring, and held up a dripping gout of flesh and sheep's wool.

'There you are, missis. If you wants proof, there it is.'

Lydia said, 'What? What?' and the man held out his hand with the mess on the ends of his fingers.

'Sheep wool, for God's sake! Can't you see?'

She had no time to debate the matter, however, or even to comment upon it, for Whittier turned on the spot and moved back across the yard to his horse. Another five seconds and he had taken a shotgun from a strap on the horse's side and was striding back. Lydia's mouth opened and she gasped in horror as the man stooped and hooked two fingers under Tinny's collar, dragging the dog away.

'No!' Lydia cried. 'No! What are you doing?' She went to reach out to the man but he was too quick for her and in moments he had taken Tinny out of her sight around the end of the house. Quickly she followed.

Seeing what he was intent on doing she cried out, 'Oh, Mr Whittier, please! Whatever he's done I'll make sure it never happens again.' She was weeping, the tears streaming down her cheeks. 'I'll make sure he's never let out of the house on his own. *Please.*'

Whittier took no notice of her, but released the dog and gave it a sharp command to sit. Obediently the dog did so. They were out of sight of the scullery door now, and hidden from the windows of the house and the yard by a little screen of privet hedge. Whittier said to Lydia, 'If you don't want to watch this, missis, I suggest you go into the 'ouse.'

As he cocked the shotgun, Lydia said, 'Oh, no, wait – wait. You can't do this. Please, God, you can't.'

'I'm within my rights,' he said, and raised the weapon to his shoulder and pointed it at the back of Tinny's trusting skull.

Lydia had no further time to speak for the next second the trigger was pulled and the gun fired. The sound of the shot, deafening and exploding into the soft spring air, rang out, echoing and re-echoing, and then swiftly diminished into a stillness in which all sound was hushed. Just as the birds stopped their singing, so Lydia's own breath was stilled.

The shot had shattered the dog's head, blasting it apart and splattering blood and brains and bone over the earth and the cobbles. Tinny dropped on the spot. His legs twitched and trembled for a second and then he was still.

Lydia heard screams erupting into the quiet and realised that the sound was coming from her own lips. She stood with her mouth wide open, hands clutching at her face, and tears streaming. Whittier said to her with a little nod of his head, 'I'm sorry about this, missis, but there's nothin' else for it. It 'as to be.'

Lydia barely heard his words, and as she stood gazing down through her splayed fingers at the corpse of Tinny, the man moved back across the yard to where his horse stood waiting. In moments he had replaced his shotgun in its holster, had swung up into the saddle and was riding away.

As she stood there while the sound of the horse's hooves faded on the air, she was aware of Mrs Starling coming hurrying to her side.

'Good heavens, ma'am, what's happened?' Mrs Starling cried, and looking past Lydia's shoulder saw the body of the dog. She gave a little cry, and then there too were Alice and Ellen, their anxious faces peering around the scullery door. 'What's happened, ma'am?' Ellen said. 'There was such a loud bang, and Davie woke up.'

'Where is he?' Lydia said. 'He mustn't come down here.'

'He's still upstairs, ma'am.'

'Let him stay there,' Lydia said breathlessly. 'Make sure he stays.' She paused. 'Please, Ellen – Alice – go on now.'

As the two young women turned back into the scullery, there came the sound of hooves and carriage wheels, and the next moment the trap came up the drive and into the yard, Alfred at the reins. Lydia turned to Mrs Starling and said quickly, 'Please – will you go into the house –' and the woman at once went inside.

Lydia turned to the trap as it came to a halt, and ran to Alfred as he climbed down. 'Alfred, Alfred . . .'

'Good God,' he said, frowning at her. 'Whatever's the matter?'

'It's Tinny. It's Tinny.' She snatched at his hand and pulled at him, drawing him across the cobbles, until he came to a halt and saw the dreadful thing that lay there.

'What – what happened?' His voice was hoarse, he could barely get the words out.

'It was – Mr Whittier. He –'

'Whittier?' he broke in. 'He did this?'

'Yes. He came here. Just a few minutes ago. He said – he said Tinny had been worrying his sheep. He – he brought his gun with him.'

Heedless of his clothes, Alfred fell on his knees beside the dead animal, murmuring, 'Tinny . . . Tinny . . .' and through her own wet lashes Lydia saw the tears starting down his cheeks.

'He killed my dog!' Alfred moaned. 'He killed my dog. Tinny! Oh, Tinny!' With both hands supporting him on the ground, he struggled to his feet and turned on the spot. 'Whittier – he killed my dog.'

He turned again, full circle, as if lost, and then lurched towards the horse and trap. Lydia watched him stagger across the yard and then ran after him.

'Where are you going?'

'To see Whittier,' he said, almost choking on the words. 'He killed my dog. He *killed my dog*.'

Lydia had never seen such passion in him before. His tear-filled eyes were blazing in his pale face, his mouth stretched back over his teeth. He looked wild. She could not allow him to go to see Mr Whittier in such a state. 'Alfred, no,' she said. 'Please don't. Please don't go.'

'What are you talking about! Of course I'm going. He killed my dog.' He reached out to the cob's reins. 'You expect me to stay here when this has happened?'

Lydia opened her mouth to speak again, but no words came, for he suddenly gasped and clutched at his chest.

'Alfred,' she cried. 'Alfred, what is it?'

He could not speak. His mouth opened wider in a grimace of pain and he gave out a strangulated cry. At the same time his hands continued to scrabble at his chest, as if he would tear out his heart.

'Alfred!'

He gave no sign of hearing her, and as she reached out to him his legs gave way beneath him and he crumpled. As he fell, the horse gave a whinny and anxiously stabbed at the ground. Lydia fell to her knees and put out her arms. 'Alfred – oh, my dear!'

His face was grey, and she watched in horror as his eyes rolled up in his head. 'Help me,' he murmured through his drawn-back lips. 'Help me indoors.'

Mrs Starling joined Lydia in helping Alfred into the house and onto the sofa in the drawing room, where he lay propped up on two pillows, a tartan rug laid over him. Mr Clifford, the handyman-gardener, was then sent straight-away to Dr Norman to ask him to come as quickly as he could. He returned saying that the doctor was out on a call, but was expected back very soon; the doctor's wife would give him the message, and he would be along as soon as possible. The errand complete, Mr Clifford was asked to take care of the burial of Tinny's body.

Dr Norman arrived just twenty minutes later, and found Alfred a little improved and in far less pain, though he still seemed to find it difficult to get his breath.

Alfred's sudden illness was, as Lydia and Alfred had been sure, due to a heart condition, and the doctor confirmed it and said he was lucky to be alive. Whether the seizure had been brought on by the shock and stress connected with the dog's death, the doctor could not say. It was probable, he said, but obviously the attack could have come at any time. He stood beside the sofa, looking down at Alfred as he lay grey-faced beneath the rug, and said he must have no excitement, and no strain, physical or otherwise, and that rest was the only treatment. Further, from now on, he said, Mr Canbrook must think about making changes to his lifestyle, for another attack could be brought on with the least exertion.

When the doctor had left, saying that he would call again the following day, Alfred said to Lydia that he would like to see Davie for a minute.

'He's been wanting to see *you*,' she said. 'He's very subdued with all the comings and goings.'

'What about Tinny?' Alfred said. 'Is Mr Clifford taking care of him? We don't want Davie to see him lying there. He'd never get over it.'

'Don't worry about it,' Lydia said. 'Mrs Starling's had a word with Mr Clifford. I believe he's doing it now.'

'Where's he putting him?'

'Somewhere at the bottom of the orchard, I believe. Well out of the way.'

Alfred nodded sadly. 'You'll have to make up some story about Tinny. For Davie, I mean. You can't possibly tell him the truth.'

'No, of course not.'

A moment of silence, then Alfred said, 'I'd like to see Davie now, please.'

'I'll go and fetch him.'

Davie had been kept up in the nursery out of the way, and as soon as Lydia went into the room he ran towards her.

'Has the doctor gone, Mammy?'

Lydia could hear the sound of his cold in his voice. 'Yes, dear,' she said. 'He'll be back tomorrow.'

'Is Pappy better now?'

'Well, he's a little better than he was.'

'Can I see him? *Please*?'

'I came to fetch you. He wants you to go to him in the drawing room.'

Together they went downstairs. In the hall Lydia whispered to the boy, 'You mustn't tire him, dear. He's still very ill. Don't stay with him too long, will you?'

'All right.'

'And walk into the room, don't run.'

'All right.'

Lydia followed him and stood off to the side as the boy moved to the couch. Alfred patted the edge of the seat, and Davie, ignoring the small chair that had been placed for him, sat on the cushion close to Alfred. Alfred laid his hand on the boy's as it rested on the tartan rug that covered him. 'I'm sorry you've got to see me like this,' he said.

'Mammy said you're feeling a bit better than you were.'

'I am, dear, a little better, and let's hope I get better still.'

'Yes.' There was a restraint, a shyness about Davie. He had never seen Alfred really sick before, and he did not know how to cope with such a thing.

'But one thing,' Alfred said, 'I don't think I shall ever be as well as I was.'

Sudden alarm showed in Davie's face. 'Oh, Pappy . . .'

'I know, dear, but sadly that's the way it is, and if – if I can't always do what I want to do, I hope you'll help me, will you?'

'Yes, of course.'

'And help your mammy if she needs it, will you?'

'Yes.'

'And help look after her?'

'Yes.'

393

'There's a good boy.' He pressed Davie's warm hand. 'You *are* a good boy.'

'Am I?'

'Yes, you are. You're a credit to me. You have been since the moment you were born.'

'Have I?' Davie smiled at this.

'You have indeed, and I'm sure you'll go on being so.' A pause. 'How is your cold?'

Davie gave a tentative sniff, as if trying it out. 'It's feeling better.'

'Good. You'll soon be over it.' A little moment of silence passed, then Alfred touched the boy on the cheek and said, 'I love you, son.'

Davie looked a little taken aback. Then he said, 'I love you too, Pappy.'

Alfred grinned. 'Well, that's all we need to know, then, isn't it? Isn't it, Davie?' Then he added, making light of it, going into Mr Williams's swooping Welsh accent, 'Oh, Davie-wavie, indeed to goodness, look you, bach.' He laughed and the boy laughed along with him, and Lydia too.

'I think now,' Alfred said, 'that you'd better go on back to Miss Ellen for a while. I want to have a little word with Mammy.'

'All right.'

As Davie turned away, Alfred said quickly, 'Kiss me first.'

Davie turned back and stretched out his neck and kissed Alfred on the cheek. Alfred raised his arms and wrapped them around him, drawing the boy to him. He held him tight like that for two or three moments and then released him. 'All right. Off you go.'

Davie went out of the room and into the hall, and Alfred and Lydia watched him go. When the sound of the boy's footfalls had faded on the stairs Alfred gave a nod towards the door. 'Close it, will you, please?'

Lydia moved across the room and closed the door, then stepped back to the sofa. Alfred gestured towards the chair. 'Pull that a little closer, will you?' She did as she was asked and sat down, near enough for him to reach out and take her hands in his. Outside the open window in the cherry tree a blackbird was singing fit to burst its breast.

Alfred frowned, his mouth briefly moving as if he searched for words. Then he said, 'I want to say something. Something important . . .'

A little afraid, Lydia could feel a tightening in her chest and the pounding of her heart. She knew why he was speaking like this, why he had spoken as he had to the boy. Mistakenly she tried to make light of the moment and said smiling, 'Oh, Alfred, we've never been so serious before.'

'Well, it's a serious business,' he said, his own smile grave. The blackbird's song went on. 'Listen to me.' Alfred's words were clipped, almost brusque, as if he was controlling his voice. 'I want to tell you, Lydia,' he said, 'you've been the best wife to me.'

'Oh, Alfred –'

'You have.' He smiled again. 'I always wanted you, you know. I've told you that. Right from the time you came into the shop with your mother and there was the business with the bee. I never dreamed of course that one day I would have you, that you would be mine, but you were – and I thank heaven it happened. Thank you. For everything.'

'Alfred, please, I don't –'

'No, don't stop me,' he said. 'I've got to say these things. We know what the situation is, and if I put it off now there might not be another time. I don't need to explain things to you; you know the situation as well as I do. You do, don't you?'

She said nothing.

'Lydia . . .'

'Yes,' she said.

'Now, listen,' he went on, and flicked a glance over towards the door, as if checking that they would not be overheard. 'I know about Davie.'

'You – ? What do you mean?'

'I know whose son he is.'

She did not know what to say and she said nothing. The blackbird sang on, but sang unheard by them in the room.

'As soon as I saw them together, I knew,' Alfred said. 'Mr Anderson, in the shop. There he was, standing with Davie – and I could see the child in the man's face. Indeed in so much in him. No casual observer would have seen it – but they wouldn't have been on the lookout. I saw it at once.'

Lydia's silence gave him the confirmation of his words, and he gave a little nod. 'I knew I was right. I never doubted it.'

'I – I never asked him to come,' Lydia said. 'When he came into the shop that day I was not expecting him.'

'I never thought you were,' he said. 'No, never. Seeing you together, you and the man – I knew that, too, and I could see how awkward it was for you.'

'I'm sorry,' she said. 'I wouldn't have had it happen for anything.'

'I know that.'

'But let me say, Alfred,' she said quickly, 'he'll never come back.'

He frowned and gave a little shake of his head. 'You don't have to give me such reassurances. I'm not asking you anything about it – about the two of you, I mean – but I want you to promise me one thing . . .'

'Yes . . . ? Whatever I can.'

'If anything should happen to me I –'

She broke in, saying, 'Alfred –' but he lifted his hand from hers, palm out, and she fell silent again.

'If anything should happen to me,' he said again, laying

his hand once more on her own, 'I would want you to build a new life for yourself and our son.'

She nodded.

'You're an intelligent woman, and you've been a good wife, and you're a good mother. You would have to marry again, in time.'

'Alfred, this is no time to talk of such things –'

'No,' he said quickly, 'you're wrong; this is *exactly* the time to speak of such things, and I mean it. I'm very serious in this, and I don't want to say it again. I want you to be happy – with whoever would make you happy. I wouldn't want to think of you shutting yourself away, languishing in some everlasting period of mourning out of some mistaken sense of loyalty and propriety. You're young, and you have a long life ahead of you. You must make the most of it – and with my blessing – and I would like my boy to have a good father. A child needs a father. A good father. Do you understand?'

'Alfred –'

'Do you understand?'

'Yes.'

'Good. I'll say no more on the matter.'

Silence fell between them, and in the quiet Alfred caught the singing of the blackbird. 'Listen to that,' he said, shaking his head in wonder. 'What a sound.'

'Yes.'

Alfred lay still, for some moments just listening to the bird, then he said, 'I didn't know what was happening, you know.'

'What do you mean? When?'

'When I had that attack. It was as if I went into a – a place. Some strange place. A dark place. A tunnel, or a room, or something, but dark, very dark. Then suddenly there was – some light. Just a little light, but it opened out, and out, and then I was in the daylight again, and you were there.'

397

She felt his hands press hers.

'I don't mind saying,' he said, 'that I was relieved, so relieved – to find you there.' He smiled. 'Just as I always have been.'

A little before ten o'clock that night Alfred had another seizure. He was in his bed, and Lydia was beside him as he writhed in pain and clutched at his chest, but this time, when he went into the dark place, he did not re-emerge into the light.

Chapter Twenty-Two

It was a bright Saturday in June, and after breakfasting with Davie, Lydia had left him with Ellen, and come into the shop to work. That afternoon she planned to take him to Capinfell, there to spend the last part of the weekend with the boy's grandfather. With this intent, it was arranged that Ellen would bring Davie into town shortly before the time when they were due to set out.

The shop was already busy with customers when Lydia arrived, and she at once set to work. Following Alfred's death she had been forced to hire an additional assistant, and she had chosen a young man named Carrins, who lived nearby. A short, prematurely balding man in his early thirties, he had taken to the work with enthusiasm, and had proved to be a good choice. Miss Angel and Mr Federo were still there, and indeed it was the latter who had taken over some of Alfred's former tasks, and to whom Lydia often turned for advice in respect to the business of the shop. Further, he it was who now opened up the premises first thing in the mornings, allowing Lydia still to have breakfast with her son.

Well over a year had passed now since Alfred's death and the business had continued to prosper. Lydia worked almost every day there, and could not imagine her life now without it, and because of her commitments and responsibilities she had come to rely more heavily on those around her, not only the assistants in the shop, but also Ellen. That past April Davie had reached five years old and had started

399

school, but Lydia had decided to keep Ellen on for the time being, so that she would have her services over the long summer holidays that were to begin in July. However, when the new school term began in September new arrangements would have to be made, and would have to be thought about very soon.

For the time being, though, Lydia's immediate concern was the business in the busy shop, and she set to along with the others to serve the many customers who came and went.

The red-coated postman came calling halfway through the morning, and delivered into Lydia's hands a single envelope. This was the second delivery of the day. The first had brought a couple of bills and enquiries, but this envelope was different. It was addressed to Lydia herself.

She stood staring down at the envelope's face, thinking that perhaps there was something familiar about the handwriting, but she could not place it, and as a new customer came bustling towards her across the shop floor, she thrust the envelope into her apron pocket.

At the midday break, when the shop was shut for half an hour, Lydia went with Miss Angel into the room at the back to eat her sandwich and drink a much needed mug of tea which the girl from the teashop had brought in on a tray. At the same time Mr Carrins went to his home which was just around the corner, and Mr Federo to the small coffee shop just along the side of the square. As Lydia had her lunch, she glanced at that day's edition of *The Times*. She had just finished her sandwich when she remembered the envelope that had been delivered, and took it from her pocket. Opening it up she drew out a single piece of paper.

She had expected it to be a letter or somesuch, and was surprised to find in her hand a little picture.

While on the other side of the table Miss Angel sipped at her tea, chewed on her potted meat sandwich and read her romantic novel, Lydia looked at the picture. It had, she supposed, been roughly cut from a child's storybook. It was not large. In black and white, obviously a reproduction from an ink drawing, it showed a small boy and girl in a woodland scene. All about the pair, who walked with their arms outstretched, the tall trees were dark, shadowed and threatening. She stared at the picture for several moments, having no idea, no clue, as to its meaning, or for what purpose it had been sent to her. Then she turned it over to look at the back. There was no print on the other side, but someone had written two words in black ink: *We too?*

We too?

Lydia frowned over the inscription, and turned the paper over to look again at the illustration. Then there came into her mind the old stories of *The Babes in the Wood*, and *Hansel and Gretel*. The picture might well depict a scene from either tale, she thought, but what did it mean?

A sound came from the shop, and she realised that the dinner break was over and that Mr Federo had come back. In another minute Mr Carrins would follow, then the *Open* sign would be turned to face the door, and there would be customers waiting for attention. Lydia slid the picture back in the envelope and, drawing her bag towards her, put the envelope into it. As she did so, Miss Angel carefully put a little leather bookmark into her novel and closed the covers. 'Oh, well,' she said with a sigh and a little smile, 'No peace for the wicked. I suppose we'd better get back to work.'

Ellen brought Davie to the shop at a quarter to four that afternoon, well rested from his afternoon nap, and looking forward to the trip to Capinfell. On their arrival Ellen took him into the back room and there sat with him on the sofa, and they read together while Lydia finished serving a customer, then Mr Carrins went outside to hail a cab to take Lydia and Davie to the station. While he was gone, Lydia put on her jacket and hat and got her bag together. Mr Carrins then returned, saying that the cab was waiting, and Lydia took Davie by the hand, and with her valise in the other, said her goodbyes to Ellen and the others and went out into the square. The three assistants would continue working until eight o'clock, when Mr Federo would lock up for the weekend.

There were few people waiting for the coach and she and Davie got seats with no difficulty. Luckily, they were by a window, and Davie was able to look out on to the passing countryside.

Every other month or so, weather permitting, she took Davie to Capinfell to visit his grandfather. It was a positive exercise for both the boy and the man, and it was good too for Lydia to see her father from time to time. Occasionally still she would meet him from work when he got out in the early afternoon on a Saturday, but a visit overnight on a Saturday and Sunday was sometimes the best thing. It also allowed her to call on Evie.

The coach made good time, and by five-fifteen they were in Capinfell and in the house and Lydia was hanging up her jacket and putting on the kettle for tea. She sat down then with her father over their teacups, and they chatted of this and that. He had mellowed even more, she thought as she watched him and listened to his conversation with Davie.

A little later, they all three went out into the sunlit rear garden where her father cut half a dozen yellow roses. Then, with her bonnet on again, Lydia left her father chatting to his grandson, and made her way to the churchyard. On reaching it, and going to the grave where her mother and Ryllis lay, she stood for a moment in silence. The lilies that sat in the old pot set into the soil were wilting now, and beginning to wither, and she took them out and threw them onto the little compost heap in the corner of the yard. That done, she refilled the pot with fresh water from the pump and carefully arranged the roses in it. As she bent over them the scent of the blossoms rose up sweet under her nostrils, and for some moments she stood with closed eyes while she let the perfume drift over her. She came to the graveside every time she came back to Capinfell. Sometimes she brought Davie with her, and at other times came accompanied by her father. Today she had wanted to come alone.

Gathering up her skirts, she lowered herself to kneel in the dry grass, and the scent of the roses came up more strongly. Reaching out, she lightly brushed her fingertips against the stone, slightly warm now under the mid-summer sun.

'Hello, Mother,' she whispered. 'Hello, Ryllis.'

There was the trace of a sad little smile on her face as she took in the stone and the flowers and the neatly kept grave. 'I hope you like the roses,' she murmured softly. 'Davie and I chose them and Father cut them.' As she spoke she moved her hand to the flowers and gently touched them. 'They're very pretty.'

She leaned back on her heels, her hands lightly clasped before her. There was no one else about and no sound came but that from the birds in the nearby yew and holly trees.

'I'm well,' Lydia said softly. 'You'll be glad to know I'm well, and Davie too, of course. He's in excellent health.' Then she took a little breath, and held it for a moment, unable to say more. She wanted to cry out, passionately: *Oh, Mother, I don't know what's to become of me. I wish you were here now to talk to me, to listen to me. To help me,* but she kept silent.

As she knelt there a robin flew down and lighted on the stone. Lydia looked at the compact little form and the glowing breast and felt a little swelling of tears behind her lids. She did not move again until the bird had flown away.

Back at the house, she served Davie his supper, and an

hour after he had eaten he was tucked up in bed upstairs. Soon afterwards, when he was settled and sleeping, she came back down and began to prepare a meal for herself and her father. She had brought from Merinville some ham and she served it with potatoes and beets and salad. Her father, who was still being looked after by Mrs Harbutt – and with whom he was no better satisfied, and probably never would be – welcomed the change and ate well. Afterwards he carried two kitchen chairs outside into the yard and they sat out in the still-warm air.

A solitary blackbird was singing in one of the apple trees and Lydia listened to his song and was reminded of that day the previous year – the day when so much had changed; the day when Alfred, following Tinny's death, had suffered his fatal attack.

'What are you thinking about?' her father asked. 'You look preoccupied.'

'Oh – I was thinking of Alfred – and that last day.'

'Ah, yes.' Mr Halley gravely nodded. 'How long is it now?'

'More than a year. Over thirteen months.'

He nodded again. 'The time goes so fast. I have to say, I'm glad to see you out of mourning at last.'

'Yes, for two or three weeks now. It was time.'

'How's Davie managing. Does he still miss his father?'

'Yes, he does. As you know, he was inconsolable at first, but he's so much better now, thank goodness.'

They had brought tea out with them, and Lydia drank from her mug and then set it back down on the tray that lay on the cobbles between them.

'Davie's growing so,' Mr Halley said. 'Each time I see him I notice such a difference.'

'Oh, it's hard to keep up with him.'

'He's going to be tall.'

'Yes, he is.'

'How are things going at the shop? Are you busy?'

'I'm glad to say we are.'

'Your husband would be proud of you, the way you've managed.'

'I've not been able to do it on my own,' she protested. 'I've had help. I've needed it.'

'You mean your assistants there?'

'Yes. Thank heavens for Miss Angel and Peter Federo. Mr Federo's been a godsend. He's been absolutely wonderful. I don't know how I'd have managed without him; I've been able to put so much work in his hands. He's such a capable man – and the new man we've taken on, Mr Carrins, he's proving quite splendid. Even so –' she shook her head, 'I don't know that I want to continue with the way things are.'

'How d'you mean? In what way?'

'Well, as you know, Davie's at school now. He's been going for a few weeks.'

'So he was telling me.'

'Yes, and he loves it, and he's getting on very well, but I'll have to be there to collect him from school next term. Ellen does it now, but I can't keep her on just for little jobs like that. He's really past the age when he needs a nurse.'

'So what'll you do?'

'I'm hoping to arrange things so that I go into the shop for less time. I don't do full days as it is, but working for even less time would enable me to look after Davie without Ellen being there. I know she'll be upset to leave, but that's the way it has to be.'

Her father peered at her in the fading light. 'You seem rather unsettled right now.'

She hesitated before she answered. 'Yes, I am. I just don't know what's going to happen.'

'What d'you mean?'

Another hesitation before she said, 'With my life. Shall I go on for ever serving in the shop, until I'm a little old lady?' She shrugged her shoulders. 'Perhaps I shall. Perhaps that's the way it's all going.'

'How old are you now?' he said. 'Twenty-seven, yes?'

'Yes.'

'Well – you've still got the best part of your life ahead of you.'

'Alfred said something like that.'

'Did he now?' He paused. 'Well, he was right, and you've got to make the most of your life. For your boy's sake, too.'

'Yes, I know that,' she looked off towards the trees, their shapes fading now in the dusk, 'but that's all I can see for myself for years ahead – just going back and forth to the shop. I can't see any other life.' She shook her head. 'But there, why should I complain? Listen to me – I've got nothing to complain about. I have a comfortable life, with no financial worries. All I must think about is my boy. He's the most important thing.'

'But surely you're allowed to have some happiness of your own.'

She could hardly believe she was hearing his words. There was an understanding in him now that she had never known in earlier days. How people could change, she thought.

The blackbird had ceased his singing, and in the hush Lydia turned and looked up towards the window of the back bedroom.

'Davie's all right, is he?' her father said.

'Yes. He'll be well asleep. He was sleeping so soundly when I left him earlier. The journey made him tired, for one thing.' She yawned. 'I'm tired too. I think I'll go up. D'you mind?'

'Of course not.' He stirred, stretched. 'I don't think you'll be going to church in the morning, will you?'

'No. I want to go and see Evie before we start back.'

'Right you are.' He went on then to tell her that he would

not be needing any dinner immediately after church, as he planned to leave right away for Hurstleigh to see someone on the matter of a prayer meeting. He would eat a piece of bread and cheese on the way, he said. Lydia replied that in that case she would leave him something for his supper, for when he got back in the evening, and that she and Davie would set off early to return to Merinville.

Now, the arrangements made, Lydia got up, reached out and pressed her father's arm. 'Goodnight, Father.'

'Goodnight.'

Upstairs she changed into her nightdress – she always kept one there in the chest – and blew out the candle. As she got into bed, Davie stirred briefly and murmured something unintelligible. She stroked his hair and said, 'It's all right, my love. Go on back to sleep. Mammy's here.'

Darkness had fallen now. Lying on her back with Davie nestling warm against her, she could see the moon's light breaking between the thin curtains and filtering through the fabric. Turning her head she looked down at the shape beside her in the bed, and saw how the faint light touched the boy's crown. She wanted to reach out and stroke his hair again, but she held back for fear of waking him.

Turning her head she looked again at the sliver of moon visible through the crack in the curtains.

> *Though the heart be still as loving,*
> *And the moon be still as bright.*

Into her mind came a picture of Guy. He seemed never to be far away these days – he was on her mind more and more. She had heard nothing from him on the occasion of Alfred's death, though he must have known about it, for his own newspaper had printed a notice of the sad event. And there had been nothing from him since, but indeed, she had not expected there to be, for he would have observed the protocol of mourning and would not have been so indelicate as to intrude during such a time. In any case, at the time of Alfred's death he would have received Lydia's letter – her very final letter – telling him that they could never meet again. Clearly, then, regardless of any observation of her mourning, he had respected her words. No doubt, she now thought, he was building a new life for himself, as she had urged him to do. She must not think about him, she said to herself; he was a part of the past, and it was time for her too to think about the future.

Then into her mind came the little picture that she had received that morning at the shop. Was the handwriting Guy's? She had long since destroyed the one brief letter he had written to her, asking her to meet him all those years ago, and now she could no longer be sure. In any event, what did the picture mean, what did it signify? No, surely it could not have come from him, from Guy – but then – who had sent it?

The next morning she got breakfast for all three of them, and when her father had set off for church she and Davie left the house to go and call on Evie. Lydia had written to her early in the week, so her friend was expecting her.

On her arrival at the cottage she found that Hennie was out with her grandmother, and that Evie's young son Jonathan, nine months old now, was sleeping soundly in his crib. Jack, Evie's husband, a tall, fair, strongly-built young man, murmured to Evie that she should go off out for a stroll with Lydia, and make the most of her respite. The baby, he added, would be perfectly all right while she was gone.

So, Evie, Lydia and Davie set off along the lane and out of the village, taking the path that the two women had used so often as girls. For a few moments it seemed in some strange way to Lydia as if she had never been away, but it was only a fleeting sensation. She looked about her with nostalgia. The spring flowers had long gone, and the verges were almost totally green; just the odd spot of colour could be seen apart from the white of the cow parsley and elderflowers and the trumpets of the bindweed. Over on the hill the mustard field, once a vibrant yellow, was a pale, dull ochre. Now that the flowers of spring had gone it looked almost as if nature were taking a rest.

They walked on and ended up in the little copse in the clearing, sitting on the massive form of the fallen tree. Davie was at once eager to amuse himself and wander off and explore. 'Don't go too far,' Lydia said to him. 'Don't wander out of my sight.' He piped back, 'All right,' and scampered away, but quickly returned and contented himself with clambering over and among the branches of the tree on which they sat. Lydia kept an eye on him as she and Evie talked of this and that. As they chatted, Evie brought Lydia up to date on the local news and gossip and also on her own life. Lydia was so glad to see Evie continuing contented, and she sat there, happy to listen as Evie spoke of her husband and the baby.

Evie finished relating some anecdote concerning herself and Jack, then looked at Lydia and said, 'And what about you?'

'Me? What about me?'

'Are you happier now? It's been well over a year since Alfred's death.'

'Over thirteen months.'

'Yes, and I see now you're out of mourning.'

'That seems to be what everyone notices.' Lydia smiled. 'I must say it makes a refreshing change to be able to put on a nice dress again, and to add a colourful scarf once in a while.'

'So – what are you going to do now?'

'What *can* I do? Look after Davie and look after the shop.'

'Is that it? Just that?'

'Well – what else is there?'

'But – what do you see for the future?'

'The future. Oh, Evie, how can I think about the future?' Lydia fell silent for a moment, then said, 'I remember you saying to me – it's possible to love more than once.'

Evie nodded. 'Yes, I did say that, and it's true. Look at Jack and me.'

'Yes, and perhaps you're right where you're concerned.'

'You don't think it's true for you?'

'No, I don't think I do.'

At this point Davie's voice came to them from two or three yards away. 'Look at me! Mammy, look at me!' and Lydia turned to him where he hung half upside down from one of the branches. 'Yes, darling. Very good. Very clever.'

'Look, Mammy – I'm a monkey!'

'Yes, you *are* a monkey. A very clever little monkey.'

She continued to watch him for a moment or two in silence, then turned back to Evie.

Evie said, 'When you talk about loving someone – you're not talking about – about Alfred, are you?'

'No.' Lydia shook her head again.

'I thought not.'

'I loved Alfred,' Lydia said. 'I truly did – but in a certain way. Not in the way that I have loved – and still do love.' She put her hands to her face. She had never spoken like this before, and was amazed at her own daring, that she could voice such thoughts, such feelings.

A little silence between them was broken only by the sounds of Davie's exertions as he clambered about. Then Evie said, 'Have you heard any word from – from him? From Guy?'

'No. But I wouldn't have expected any word. After all, I've been in mourning. He wouldn't be so – improper as to intrude at such a time.'

'But it's over a year now.'

'I know that, but what does that change?'

'Well – you might – hear from him. Now that a year's gone by.'

'I – I don't think so.'

'But you're free.'

'Yes, I am.'

'And he knows that.'

Lydia shrugged. After a moment she said, 'I wrote to him. Right after he came to meet me in Pershall Dean that day, and it was just after my letter was posted that Alfred had his – his attack.'

'Oh? And what did you say in your letter?'

'I asked him never to contact me again.' Lydia found it almost painful to voice the words. 'I said that it was all over between us. I ended it. For ever. It was very final.'

Evie thought about this, then said, 'Even so – events change things. You might still hear from him.'

Lydia frowned. 'No. No.' But even as she spoke she thought of the little picture in her bag – but no, that was some foolish thing, something that could have no meaning for her. 'It's over,' she said.

'Not necessarily,' Evie replied. She gave a deep sigh and added, as if impatiently, 'Oh, why is it always up to the man to make the first move? Why does the woman have to just sit by and wait for things to happen?'

Lydia said nothing.

'Who knows,' Evie said, 'you might hear from him yet. He might write to you after a time.'

'It would be a miracle.'

'Yes, but miracles do happen. Though sometimes they need a little help.'

Lydia shook her head.

'You could write to him,' Evie said. 'Have you thought of that?'

'Oh, I couldn't. Of course I couldn't do that.'

'No, I suppose not.'

'I couldn't be so forward, and in any case, he'll be getting on with his life. I told him that that is what he must do – and a lot can happen in a year.'

'Then what will you do?'

Lydia gave a little smile, without humour. 'I don't know,' she said wearily. 'Nothing. Nothing.'

'I don't know when I ever saw you quite like this before,' Evie said. 'Quite so lost like this.'

Guy had said something about being lost. Lydia could remember his words, spoken on that day when they had met. She nodded. 'Yes,' she said. 'That's it. I suppose I am.'

Distantly, from across the village, came on the breeze the sound of the church clock. Lydia stirred. 'I must go in a minute. Father will be getting home. I want to prepare his supper for this evening, and then Davie and I must start back to Merinville. I don't like to rush.' As she spoke she had been thinking again of the little picture that had come in the post, and she drew her bag towards her, dipped into it and drew out the envelope. In the same moment Evie looked up at the sky, and said, 'You've had good weather for your little trip.'

'Oh, it's been beautiful.' Lydia glanced around at the green trees, the crops growing in the fields. 'I love the midsummer days.' She drew out the picture from the envelope. At the same time she called to the boy, 'Come on, Davie, we must think about starting back. I've got to prepare Grandpa's supper.'

'I love midsummer too,' Evie said, a little dreamily, 'and of course it's the longest day today.'

Davie had left his perch on the tree branch and now came towards his mother, brushing the dust from his hands. 'What's that you've got there, Mammy?' he said as he came to Lydia's side and saw the little picture in her hand.

Curious, Davie took the paper from her fingers as she turned to Evie. 'What did you say?' Lydia said. 'The longest day? Today is the longest day?'

'Yes, it's the twenty-first.'

'The twenty-first,' Lydia breathed. 'The longest day. Of course.'

'Oh, they're lost, look.'

The words had come from Davie as he stood beside his mother's knee, looking at the picture. Lydia turned to him at once. 'What was that?'

'The children in the picture . . .' He pointed to them.

'No – something else you said.'

'I said they're lost. It's a picture of them when they're lost. Like Hansel and Gretel.'

Lydia gave a slow nod. '*Lost*. Of course.' She breathed the words as she took the piece of paper from him. 'Of *course*.' She turned the paper over and looked at the words scrawled there: *We too?*

It was so obvious, she thought. The answer was there all the time, and it took a child to find it.

'What's the matter?' said Evie, watching as Lydia rose up from her seat on the tree trunk. 'What's up?'

Lydia looked distracted. 'This picture – and something – something someone said. Something – *he* said.'

Evie got up beside her. 'What are you talking about? I don't understand.'

'This little picture that came in the post this morning . . .' She held it out and Evie took it from her hand. 'It was a message. I see it now. You see –' she gestured to the drawing, 'they're lost.'

'Yes,' Evie said, looking at the picture. 'Yes, I see. Hansel and Gretel probably – or the Babes in the Wood.'

'Yes.' Lydia murmured the word. 'It goes along with something he said to me – when we met – and it was the same as today: the longest day.' She took a step away. 'I've

413

got to go. Now. Evie, I've got to go.' She reached out her hand and took the drawing and pushed it back into her bag. Then again she reached out, now to Davie. 'Davie, come on, we're going. We'll get Grandpa his supper and then go and get the coach.'

The two women and the child started back along the lane, Lydia stepping out smartly and setting the pace. The swift exodus had taken Evie unprepared, and she laughed and exclaimed at their hurrying. 'Why are we rushing like this, Lyddy?' she said. 'What's the hurry?'

'I told you,' Lydia said, 'we've got to get back.' Suddenly she could feel her heart beating and she felt slightly breathless. 'I'm sorry, Evie, but we've got to go.'

On returning to her father's house, Lydia found that he had just returned, and was in the kitchen cutting bread and cheese. She left him to it and quickly peeled some potatoes and prepared some greens for when he returned for his evening meal. She had also left for him a chicken pie that she had brought with her from Merinville. It was already cooked, she said, and he could eat it cold. She did all the work conscious of almost every second that passed, and wishing she could leave.

Then, at last, she and Davie were ready, and they said their goodbyes to her father, himself anxious to get off on his errand. She kissed him briefly on the cheek, and he kissed and embraced Davie, and they were on their way.

When they got off the coach outside the railway station at Merinville, Lydia led Davie by the hand into the station itself. 'Where are we going, Mammy?' Davie asked. 'Are we going on the train?'

'Yes, we are, darling.'

'Aren't we going home yet?'

'Not yet, dear. We'll catch the train. We haven't much

time, though. It's about to leave. We must hurry.' Indeed, they had hurried all the way so far, whenever it was possible, and during the journey on the coach from Capinfell Lydia had sat impatiently, willing the horses to move faster.

They were too late, however. They arrived on the platform to see the end of the train as it steamed away into the distance.

'We missed the train,' Davie observed sadly.

'Yes, we missed the train.' Lydia felt she could have wept.

'Where was the train going?'

'What? To Redbury.'

'And are we going to Redbury?'

'That – that was my intention, but now . . .' She did not know what to do. One thought that prodded at her mind was that she was a fool. She was a fool for thinking for a moment that he would remember, and yet . . . and yet he had sent the little picture . . . It *must* have been he who had sent it.

There was a guard nearby and taking Davie by the hand she went to him, and asked the time of the next train to Redbury. 'There's one in fifteen minutes, ma'am,' he replied. 'The twelve-forty-eight from Swindon.'

She thanked him. 'We'll wait,' she said to the boy, and on a positive note she added, 'and at least it'll give me a chance to buy our tickets first, instead of waiting to pay on the train.'

She went back to the booking office then and bought the tickets for a return journey, after which they went back to the platform and took a seat on a bench.

The time dragged by.

'Why are we going to Redbury, Mammy?' Davie asked, and she could not give him an answer. He enquired a second time, and she said, holding back her impatience, 'I have to, dear. That's all there is to it.'

At last the train came in and they climbed aboard. Then a minute later and the train was moving again.

Stoke Halt was the next stop, followed by Stoke Carron. After that came the junction of Redbury, where so many of the passengers were bound. When the train had pulled in, Lydia alighted and lifted Davie after her. Then, firmly holding his hand, she quickly led the way along the platform and out of the station. She had not been to Redbury in several years, but she had no time to indulge in any nostalgic reunion with the place; she must get to the town centre and the square.

The only cabs in sight as they emerged onto the street were two that were already hired. She did not know what to do – to stay in the hope of one appearing or to make their way on foot.

'Come,' she said after a moment, 'we must walk. It's not far. We can't wait around here.'

They set off, Davie's hand stretched up to grasp her own. 'Mammy,' he said, 'please, don't walk so fast. I can't keep up.' They had come out onto the street now and she quickly came to a halt and crouched before the boy, her skirts in the dust. 'I'm sorry, darling,' she said. 'I'm only thinking of myself. I'm being selfish. I'll go a little slower.' So saying, she straightened, took his hand again, and set off once more. Although she was able to force herself to slow her pace a little, it took all her concentration, for every cell of her being was urging her to run.

Then at the next corner a cab came into view and Lydia hailed it. It pulled to a halt and she gave the driver their destination. Moments later she and Davie were on board and they were starting off through the Redbury streets at a faster pace.

When they reached the square the cab driver stopped at the corner, and Lydia stepped down on to the pavement, lifted Davie down beside her and paid the fare. Her heart was beating hard in her chest, and the thought came again into her mind that she was a fool for she was merely playing in a charade.

'Where are we going now, Mammy?'

'Just across the square, dear.'

And across the square they went, and into the little garden that was set on the side, the little garden with the laburnum tree, the arch, the benches and the water fountain.

They sat down on the same bench that she had taken that summer day all those years ago, when she had come to the city for her interview and to meet Ryllis. 'Sit here, dear, beside me.' She lifted Davie up onto the seat, and put her bag next to her on the right. Looking out of the garden she saw the familiar view that she remembered from when she sat watching out for her sister when they had lost one another in the confusion. *Perhaps you don't have to be lost.* She could hear his voice. *But if you are lost, then it's as well to have a special place to run to.* And then, his words on the back of the picture of the lost children: *We too?*

She looked around her. There were people there; a couple was sitting on a bench, a youth had stopped to drink at the fountain, two young sweethearts stood facing one another, clasping each other's hands and murmuring. Strangers all, like those that moved across her vision out in the square. The clock up in the tower said fifteen minutes to four. She was forty-five minutes late. Of course there was no sign of him – but had she truly expected that he would be there? How could she have been such a fool? Here she was, a grown woman with a child, and dragging that child on a wild goose chase over the city, in pursuit of some dream that she had harboured like the most senseless schoolgirl. What an idiot she was, to have thought for one moment that he would be there, that he would have remembered – but there was the picture, she reminded herself. There was the picture.

'Are we there, Mammy?'

She turned at Davie's voice and looked down into his anxious little face, shaded by the brim of his hat. He was affected by the concern in her own expression, by the anxiety that showed in every movement of her body. She must try to be calmer, for his sake if no one else's. 'Let's take your hat off for a minute,' she said absently. 'You must be terribly warm.'

'I am,' he said. 'Terribly warm.'

She took off his hat and ran her fingers through his hair. The perspiration was damp on his smooth brow. 'There now.'

'Are we?' he said. He sounded concerned, a little worried.

'Are we? Are we what, dear? What d'you mean?'

'Are we there now? Have we got to where we're going?'

His words came through to her in the heat of the summer's day. She was damp with perspiration and saw the dust collected on her gloves and skirt. She felt the utter uselessness and pointlessness of it all. And suddenly it simply became more than she could bear and, although she closed her eyes, the tears welled up and burst between her eyelids and ran down her cheeks. She pressed her hands to her face and bent forward.

'Mammy! Oh, Mammy, no!'

Davie's cry brought a sob breaking from her lips and, angry at herself, she brushed away the tears. She must not cry in front of the child. She turned to him and wrapped her arms around him and drew him close to her. 'It's all right, my darling. I'm all right.'

There were tears, and fear too, in his own voice as he said, 'But you're crying. Oh, don't cry. Please don't cry.'

'There, there . . . I'm not really crying,' she lied. 'I'm just a little hot and bothered. All that walking in the sun, and waiting for the train. Don't be upset, my darling. I'm all right now. We'll have a little rest for a minute or two and then we'll go on back home.' She had forced the tears to stop, but she continued to sit with her arms around the boy, eyes closed, her chin resting on the top of his head, his small hand so warm in her own.

'You were late.'

The voice, soft and without censure, came to her from somewhere to her right, and she opened her eyes and saw him standing there. He wore a soft felt hat and a light jacket with a blue cravat.

'Oh,' she said. And again, 'Oh' – a little sound escaping from her throat, a little breath of wonder. He was there. After all, he was there.

He came and stood before her. 'I was here at three, just as I was all those years ago,' he said with a faint smile, 'and I waited a little while. Then I took a walk around the square, and I turned – and there you were.' He paused. 'You got the drawing. And you remembered.'

'Yes,' she said, 'I remembered.' And then: 'I could never forget.' She picked up her bag and set it down on the flags at her feet, the boy's hat on top of it, and Guy came and sat down beside her on the bench. He reached out after a moment and took her hand, then smiled at Davie who still sat held in the crook of her arm. 'How are you, Davie?' he said.

Davie, shy, and a little disorientated, pressed closer to his mother.

'Perhaps he won't always be shy of me,' Guy said.

Before she could reply, Davie, still a little distressed by the rush and his mother's tears and the strange scene, said, 'Mammy, where are we? Have we got to where we're going?'

'What, dear?' she said. And then: 'Yes, we have.'

'But – but where are we?' His anxiety sounded in his voice. 'Are we far from home?'

And now Lydia smiled, the faintest smile that just touched at the corners of her mouth. Relief. A look of relief. Her throat was tight with tears that could so easily be shed.

'No, darling,' she said, drawing him closer. She kissed the top of his head and looked at Guy over the boy's hair. 'No, my darling, we're close. We're very close.'

To find out more about Jess Foley and other
fantastic Arrow authors why not read
The Inside Story – our newsletter featuring
all of our saga authors.

To join our mailing list to receive the newsletter
and other information* write with your name and
address to:

The Inside Story
The Marketing Department
Arrow Books
20 Vauxhall Bridge Road
London
SW1V 2SA

*Your details will be held on a database so we can send you the
newsletter(s) and information on other Arrow authors that you have
indicated you wish to receive. Your details will not be passed to any
third party. If you would like to receive information on other Random
House authors please do let us know. If at any stage you wish to be
deleted from our *The Inside Story* mailing list please let us know.

If you enjoyed Wait For The Dawn, *why not try further Jess Foley titles, all available in Arrow . . .*

SO LONG AT THE FAIR

Growing up in a small Wiltshire village, Abbie Morris knows what lies ahead of her – a life of drudgery as a menial servant. But when Abbie's mother casts the family into crisis, her world is turned upside down.

Six years later, the Morrises are rebuilding their lives and when Abbie and her sister Beatie set off for the country fair, the world seems a good place. Until a chance encounter with Louis, a handsome stranger, leads to tragedy.

Abbie struggles to put that terrible evening behind her, and when Arthur Gilmore comes into her life believes she might even find happiness. But then her past catches up with her, and it seems she might never cease to pay for the night she stayed so long at the fair . . .

TOO CLOSE TO THE SUN

When Grace Harper is orphaned, her world falls apart. Life has always been hard, and now she and her little brother Billy are left homeless and alone.

But Grace must put her grief and fear aside, and think practically. Accepting a job as companion to the wealthy, lonely Mrs Spencer means that she and Billy have a roof over their heads, but just as Grace starts to find her feet disaster strikes again.

Things look desperate, and when she is offered the good life for herself and Billy, Grace is tempted. But is she, in search of safety for her little family, flying too close to the sun?

SADDLE THE WIND

In a small village in the West Country a baby girl is born into poverty. For little Blanche the future looks bleak.

Her life changes one fateful day when her mother is summoned to The Big House to nurse Marianne, daughter of a wealthy mill-owner. But although she and Marianne grow to care for one another as sisters, sisters they are not. And when Blanche meets and falls in love with Marianne's intended husband, her struggle not to betray her closest friend threatens to destroy her happiness for ever.

A powerful saga of passion and pain, *Saddle The Wind* is a thrilling, intensely moving testament to the human spirit, which builds to a spellbinding climax.

Buy *Jess Foley*

Order further *Jess Foley* titles from your local bookshop, or have them delivered direct to your door by Bookpost

☐ So Long At The Fair   0 09 941576 3   £5.99
☐ Too Close To The Sun   0 09 941577 1   £5.99
☐ Saddle The Wind   0 09 946645 7   £5.99

FREE POST AND PACKING
Overseas customers allow £2 for paperback

PHONE: 01624 677237

POST: Random House Books
c/o Bookpost, PO Box 29, Douglas,
Isle of Man, IM99 1BQ

FAX: 01624 670923

EMAIL: bookshop@enterprise.net

Cheques (payable to Bookpost) and credit cards accepted

Prices and availability subject to change without notice
Allow 28 days for delivery
When placing your order, please state if you do not wish
to receive any additional information

www.randomhouse.co.uk